MW00416488

THE MISSING:
The Andromeda Connection

Daniel Schaffer

ISBN : 978-1-7923-6678-9

Interior design by booknook.biz

Contents

Dedication

This book has been made possible only with much invaluable help from my wife, Kathleen Schaffer. I am grateful for her patience with me as she helped proof each page written, offering wisdom and valuable advice. I also dedicate this book to my mother, Marian Schaffer, who sat patiently by my side as I wrote much of the first half of the book, usually ten or fifteen minutes at a time. As she fought the losing battle to Dementia, she continued to show encouragement to me as I wrote. It was because of the legacy of faith handed down from my mom and my father Frank Schaffer, Jr. that I am a believer. Thank you, Mom and Dad. I love and miss you both.

I would also like to thank my pastor, Dr. Richard Thompson for his guidance and teaching for the past fifteen years. In a world that tries to marginalize Christ, and America's commitment to His love and doctrines you have always held fast to biblical values. Thank you for your steadfast dedication.

It is with great love that I dedicate this book to Kathleen, Marian and Frank. I also leave this legacy to my children, Jon and Kathy, and my grandchildren, Kelcey, Natalie, Frankie, and Tim. And to Troy and your two brothers who are due to be born in October of 2021, let the legacy continue. God bless you all. I love you.

— Daniel Schaffer – April 23, 2021.

INTRODUCTION

The author thanks you for your purchase of his work. Information for this book has been taken from various sources including the Bible. He wants it known that this is not a Bible study about end times prophecy. It is merely a series of "what ifs" based upon what has become, in recent years, a subject that has led to much discussion. Videos from various pastors and theologians have also been an influence.

It is not a book designed to spark arguments among believers as to whether the much talked about Rapture will be a Pre-Tribulation, Mid-Tribulation or Post-Tribulation event.

Most importantly, the author is passionate about faith in Christ as being our way to eternal salvation. You do not have to believe in the Rapture to be saved, but you do need to be a follower of Christ to experience the Rapture, if and when it comes in your natural lifetime.

Paul's letter to the Romans is rich with guidelines to Salvation with Christ. Romans 10:9-13 is a great place to start. "If you declare with your mouth, "Jesus is Lord," and believe in your heart that God raised him from the dead, you will be saved. For it is with your heart that you believe and are justified, and it is with your mouth that you profess your faith and are saved. As Scripture says, "Anyone who believes in him will never be put to shame." For there is no difference between Jew and Gentile—the same Lord is Lord of all and richly blesses all who call on him, for, "Everyone who calls on the name of the Lord will be saved."

The author's prayer is that perhaps this book will help you share your faith boldly and lovingly with those in your circle who may be seeking comfort in this world of constant turmoil. May God bless you and all your loved ones. May God bless you with strength from His Holy Spirit.

Foreword

Author Daniel Schaffer has long had a fascination with end times prophecies and thoughts about the "rapture." He has read widely on the subject and now offers a fresh and unique, yet thoughtful, story surrounding the return of Christ. Although "rapture" is not a word found in the Bible, the term identifies a set of beliefs that are biblically based. Rapture refers to the return of Christ and the gathering of believers, primarily described in 1 Thessalonians (4:13-18) and 1 Corinthians (15:50-54). The term comes from a Latin word meaning "a carrying off, a transport, or a snatching away." Many people's understanding of "the rapture" is based on popular writings like the *Left Behind* series, rather than on Scripture itself. The concept of the "carrying off," or the rapture of the church, is clearly taught in Scripture.

There are numerous different interpretations of the Bible verses concerning end times, Christ's return, and what will happen to believers at that time. Books about and reflections on end times and the rapture are considered an exercise in speculation by some Christian leaders and theologians, and therefore should not consume our time. It is true that Christians need not spend time in debate over the meaning and scope of the rapture, for this is not really God's intent. Nevertheless, the rapture should be a comforting doctrine full of hope by which God believers can encourage one another.

That is what Daniel Schaffer does in his novel *The Missing*. Current events have rekindled interest in what the Bible has to say about the end of the world and what may happen to Christian believers. Jesus said that there would be wars and rumors of wars, nation rising against nation, persecution, and hatred of believers, many turning from the faith and betraying others, wickedness growing as love for one another wanes, and finally the gospel preached to all nations. Today we are seeing tremendous shifts in power among nations and groups of people propelled by technological innovations unthinkable just a few years go. The author skillfully weaves into his story the technological advancements and media control that we know can be manipulated for diabolical ends, and whose outlines we see today in many Western countries.

Although, the topic of end times prophecies seems to be of greatest interest to evangelical Christians, mostly in N. America, it is a subject that should interest all Christians. There is no doubt that Jesus spoke of end times, most prominently in Matthew 24. Christ did predict His return and that His elect will join Him in heaven and His prediction continues to be a source of great hope for believers, especially those living in troubled times. Though we do not know when and how Christ's return may happen, for as Jesus said: *But about that day or hour no one knows, not even the angels in heaven, nor the Son, but only the Father* (Matt. 24:36), there is value in considering what Scripture tells us. Our calling is found in the Savior's admonition: *Therefore, keep watch, because you do not know on what day your Lord will come* (Matt. 24:42).

In an entertaining and realistically vivid manner, Schaffer's novel invites us to ask, "what if" and serves as an encouragement and exhortation to all believers to be prepared, as Jesus warned. *What if* the Christian expectations for Christ's return to earth are really true? *What if* His return will happen as described by the Apostle Paul in 1 Thessalonians? His novel encourages us to live with our eyes on heaven, even while we toil here on earth, living as though the Lord may return tomorrow. The discerning reader will ponder the "what if" posed by the Schaffer novel and then ask, "How then should I live?"

Dr. Richard Thompson, DMin
Bakersfield, CA

CHAPTER 1

The crowd of about thirty-five people stared into the sky from the Ahwatukee Country Club south of Phoenix, Arizona, as swift movement flashed reflections of the setting sun. It appeared that there were fifteen shiny cigar shaped flying objects in a tight formation just above South Mountain. Golden lights flashed all along the lengths of each object.

All the witnesses were expressing their surprise and awe at the way the objects crossed the sky. They flew in a triangular pattern as the entire formation went from side to side, climbed and lost altitude as one unit. They came to a stop over the crest of South Mountain, then slowly toward downtown Phoenix hovering as a group at approximately one thousand feet above the skyline. There was a low rumbling sound that echoed off the buildings on Central Avenue. Airline traffic on final approach to Sky Harbor Airport had to be suddenly diverted to the north and to the south.

Everyone's nerves were frayed at the sight. Only a year and a half ago a massive nuclear war ended after it had engulfed much of the world. Everyone currently alive lost family members. The population of the earth had been reduced by billions. Nuclear missiles had struck in virtually every industrialized country. What had begun as a stand-off between North Korea and Japan quickly expanded. Reminiscent of August 1914, national alliances which had been formed as in the previous century, had brought nation against nation such as the world had never seen before.

The formation moved to the east over Sky Harbor. They appeared to stop directly over the terminals. Suddenly, the formation shot directly up to ten thousand feet and moved directly northwest toward Luke Air Force Base, then scattered in all directions.

Reports began coming in from many major cities around the world. The flying ships were described in the same way. Shiny and cigar shaped, and they all had appeared near sunset at each location where they were witnessed. In the United States alone they were seen by large groups of people in every state. Reports also came from every continent. Earlier on the same day, many people were reported missing.

"You mean this is happening everywhere? Millions of people?"

At his desk at Central News Agency (CNA), star reporter Robert Wallace scribbled rapidly on the legal pad. He was interviewing FBI Spokesperson Nancy Logan via Skype on his laptop. Wallace was a tall man with dark hair. He was smartly dressed in an expensive light blue silk shirt. His beige slacks fit his trim body as though they were tailor made for him.

He needed to glean as much information as possible from the FBI. Nancy Logan had always been a great source for Wallace. They had worked together in Pittsburgh, before she took the job as a Public Information Officer with the FBI. Their history together had built a solid trust between them. They knew each other's families as they both came from western Pennsylvania. After honing their skills in smaller towns in both print and electronic media, they each landed at Pittsburgh's KDKA radio and television. Logan moved up the ladder in the news department, taking on tasks from Assignment Editor to Assistant News Director for Television. She then moved on to the Pittsburgh Police Department as the Public Information Officer.

Wallace knew that stories such as this can significantly advance an investigative reporter's career. He had been following up, seeking the facts behind the mass reports of missing persons.

For the past twenty-four to forty-eight hours, reports had been filed world-wide about people missing from their normal workplaces, homes and while traveling in private and public transportation. Families were frantic about children who were suddenly missing. It was impossible to explain what had happened to the millions who suddenly had "fallen off the face of the Earth." There was no sense to it at all. There were conflicting reports as to the timing of the mass disappearances. Some say that they took place earlier in the day, before the world-wide reports of unidentified flying objects began to come in. Were they related events or were they simply coincidentally close together? There were a few unsubstantiated reports of witnesses seeing people being pulled into the flying objects.

"What do the Feds know about all this?" Wallace pressed. "What possibilities are you looking into?"

Logan replied evenly, "We're checking everything we can, given our available manpower. We also lost more than our share of people."

Nancy Logan appeared preoccupied as her eyes darted around her office. As Wallace watched her on Skype, he knew that she had something on her mind other than answering his questions.

"Nancy, what's going on with you right now? I've never seen you so distracted. Your focus seems to be elsewhere."

She looked at the camera, right into Wallace's eyes, "Bobby, this has been such a surreal time. The FBI has me doing double duty in my position as PIO, plus... this is hitting close to home. My husband is among the missing."

Now it made sense, "Listen, Nancy, I'm sorry that you're hurting this way. It must be horrible to be personally touched by the biggest news story ever. I don't know what to say, really. But we need to find out what is happening here. If we can move this investigation forward, maybe we can find out what happened to Josh. Since you're the only person I know who lost someone so close to them, let me ask you this. Was there anything different about the way he was acting in the days leading up to his disappearance?"

"No, not at all. He had been to church the night before. Then early on Thursday morning, I was pouring a second cup of coffee in the kitchen and he and I were carrying on our usual morning conversation about the plans of the day. He had meetings scheduled with his agents. That's the life insurance business, you know. He was such a dedicated manager. As he walked into the bedroom to finish dressing, he was running down his schedule for the day, and we were making plans to have dinner together. Suddenly, in mid-sentence, he was silent. I asked him what he had said, and he didn't answer me. I rushed into the bedroom to see if he had had a heart attack or something. He wasn't there. He was gone. He was just gone. No sign of any kind of struggle, or anything like that. He was just gone."

"Wait a minute, you were talking one minute and the next minute he was gone?"

"No, Bobby, more like I was talking with him one second, and then in a Nano-second he was gone." Her eyes showed the strain of the past day and a half.

Wallace scribbled down this part of the conversation just as he had been doing for all the "official" information she had given him.

She continued, with Wallace still writing as fast as possible, "So, back to business here, the President will be going on the air in thirty minutes to address the situation. There are a lot of different theories on this. We don't expect the President to commit to any of them yet, but I hear that she has some strong opinions of her own."

General public opinion was that Elizabeth Blair was underqualified. She had very little experience in public office. She had been a school board member in her hometown of Lubbock, Texas. She was a member of the city council, before running for a seat in the Texas Senate. She surprised many people from Dallas, and Houston, when she handily won a seat in the Senate. After serving a year and a half in that position, United States Senator Arthur Coleman died in an automobile accident. It was then up to Governor Jane Truesdale to appoint someone to serve out the rest of Coleman's term. Truesdale chose Blair.

While in the U.S. Senate, Blair distinguished herself by being the voice of reason during one of the many shutdowns of the United States Government. Since the mid nineteen seventies government shutdowns were used by each political party to blame the others for nothing being done for the country. Presidents would veto bills passed by congress, and the Legislative branch of government would reach an impasse with the President and shut down the government.

In the long run, each successive shut down had accomplished very little. Republicans blamed Democrats, Democrats blamed Republicans, and the American public was caught in the middle. The shutdowns cause government services to be cut back for as much as ninety days. Most shutdowns were shorter, much shorter.

Senator Blair stood firm in the Senate Chamber and personally got members of both parties to compromise. That, in turn, brought the President serving at that time, to see the benefits of ending what could become a very serious problem for the nation.

Many say it was that one single incident in her public service career that launched her into the White House. She was easily nominated, and the public elected her in a close, albeit decisive, election.

Although in office for only a short time, President Elizabeth Blair had already been faced with an explosive situation when Russian President Yuri Vosolov had threatened to stop Israel from drilling for oil in the Eastern Mediterranean. Russia saw it as a threat to the artificial volatility of oil prices. Blair had deftly handled the situation like a seasoned head of state, bringing Russia and Israel together successfully to negotiate future oil prices in good faith. Even her skeptics were impressed. Being from West Texas, the President understood the oil business well. She was able to negotiate a peaceful solution that satisfied all parties involved.

But this was entirely different. People all over the globe were missing.

"Any idea how she plans to handle the situation?" Wallace probed, looking for any hint of advanced copy on what the biggest story of all time could very well be.

"None," Logan said. "However, I have a man over at State who tells me that many people who have the president's ear are actually leaning toward Alien Abduction. I mean, just look at yesterday's news. All over the world people saw the same type of flying objects. Usually, they were near major military bases or near large international airports.

"Really? Alien abductions? That's some far-fetched stuff," Wallace said.

"Not really," Logan countered. "We already know that more and more people have been buying into the idea that the government has been hiding facts about aliens as long ago as Roswell in July of 1947. Some believe the government has been in contact with aliens ever since. Then there's the fact that sightings of UFOs have jumped significantly in the last ten years. I've interviewed people who say they've seen them several times."

"And?" Wallace said, pressing for further information.

Logan obliged, "Most of the Twentieth Century, following World War II there were more and more reports of UFOs being sighted by everyone from ordinary people to airline pilots, military pilots, and law enforcement officers. Most of the sightings were near military bases that handled nuclear weapons. One of those very early stories came out of Roswell, New Mexico, which was only a short distance by air from Alamogordo, the home of the Manhattan Project during World War II. It is popular opinion by many people that space aliens are closely watching the people of Earth. These people dread the possibility that more intelligent beings fear that we will take our war-making into space and carry it to other planets. The 'True Believers' in extraterrestrial life were afraid that those alien beings will one day destroy life on Earth to prevent our war-

9

Daniel Schaffer

like ways from poisoning and endangering the rest of the Universe."

"Television shows and news stories have proffered that opinion for decades. Science fiction movies from Hollywood in the nineteen fifties did much to advance that theory with films such as 'The Day the Earth Stood Still'. Believing in extraterrestrials took on an almost religious fervor. Books like 'Chariots of the Gods' by Erich von Daniken led many people to believe that years of belief in the supreme being many have called God, was simply visitors from outer space. That 1968 best seller started many people, who considered themselves to be enlightened, to begin to pull away from traditional church and belief in God."

"Personally," Logan continued, "I'm convinced people have seen something, but I think most of the sightings are secret experimental aircraft. Our government has experimented and developed many planes that are invisible to Radar but can be seen with the naked eye."

Wallace met her explanation with a silence. Logan quickly added, "There's no official opinion for the sightings that anyone has shared with me, but I don't think you're far off on your assessment of the whole thing being far-fetched."

Wallace finished his interview with Logan, thanking her for her time and candor, "Nancy, thank you for all your help. I truly hope we can get some answers for you, and you can be at peace regarding the loss of Josh."

This whole news cycle has been one of the busiest Wallace had ever encountered. One event after the other, one rumor stacked on top of the next, were all making it hard to sort out what was truly happening.

He had to find some answers regarding the UFO angle, so he began scanning his list of phone numbers looking for NASA Director Clark Donaldson. He called, and the familiar voice of the Director's Personal Secretary, Sheryl Lopez, answered. Lopez was always ready to help Wallace whenever he called. She had many times been one of those "reliable sources" for Wallace, helping him make a deadline for airtime.

"Sheryl, Bob Wallace here. May I please speak with Clark?"

"Hello, Mr. Wallace. Mr. Donaldson is on a call with President Blair. She's asking for any information about… um… ET." That statement was more information than Sheryl Lopez would usually give on her own. And using the term 'ET' showed that her mind was on more than just being a professional assistant to a high ranking official.

"That tells me a lot," Wallace said. "Do you think you could have him call me at my mobile number as soon as he's free? I'm heading to the studio to prepare for a live cut-in as soon as President Blair finishes her remarks."

"As you can imagine, Mr. Donaldson is very busy right now," Ms. Lopez said, "but you've always been fair with us, so I'll do my best to get him to call you."

"Thanks." Wallace left his office and headed to the make-up room. It had only been an hour since his last on-air report, so he only needed a touch up. But as he sat down in his usual chair, he said what he always said, "Make me look beautiful, Hal." But this time he meant it, because he'd barely had three hours sleep in the past two days, and the dark circles were visible.

Always eager to banter, Hal laughed, "I'm afraid you'd have to go to an Earl Scheib paint booth for that much work." Hal Warner was a forty-five year old man. He was married, and one of his sons and a daughter followed him into the television and film make-up business. He had been a well-known star in the make-up business in Chicago, Hollywood, and New York before coming to CNA five years ago. Warner was deft at using the proper shading and all the right blends of pancake and liquid make-up to help an aging actor still look younger on screen. His talent was legendary.

"So, Bob," he said, "what's she going to tell us about 'the Missing'?" The frightening global phenomenon had already been shortened down to the barest of descriptions—"The Missing."

"I'm not sure, Hal," Wallace said gravely. "I can tell you she's been on an extended call with NASA. Maybe we're about to hear that little green men took everybody away."

"Well," Hal said, without surprise, "that might be true. Some religions have said for years that what some call the 'Ancient Ones' will come to earth one day to take us back to the 'Home Planet'. I can't help thinking, though, there might be some religious angle to all this. A nephew of mine has pestered me for years that his church has the answers about this kind of thing. He's a bit of a fanatic, in my opinion, always talking about something called 'The Rapture'. He's always told me that Christians would one day be taken up from earth into heaven. He said it would happen in the 'blink of an eye.' I did some of the make-up work on one of those Christian movies about something called the Rapture, and the end of the world. They weren't great cinema, but I did find them thought-provoking."

"Never saw any of those," Wallace said, "but I do remember hearing about them. I just don't like to be hit over the head with the Bible, even if it's only a movie, and I didn't want anyone seeing me there."

Wallace and Warner agreed that, even though most Christians they'd ever met were good people, there was an element of believers who were very annoying when it came to their faith. Too many Christians seemed to

13

think that they were the chosen people of God. They seemed to believe they were chosen because they were special. Both men agreed that they had never wanted to be included in a "club" that is so exclusive.

Suddenly the Presidential Seal appeared on the make-up room television screen, signaling the start of the President's address to the nation and the world. Hal Warner grabbed the remote and turned up the sound. News anchors announced the President was about to speak live from the Oval Office.

President Blair sat at her Oval Office desk facing the camera. The stress of the presidency was beginning to show on her face and in her body language. Despite wanting to appear in control, it was obvious that the President had not had very much sleep in the past few days. The sparkle that had been in her eyes when she was sworn in a year ago last January20, had been replaced by a look of grave concern.

"My Fellow Americans," she said warmly, "you all know that our nation and the entire world have suddenly been thrust into a situation of great confusion and perplexity. All of us are asking urgent questions. Thus far, none of us, has found any answers. The situation is unprecedented in human history. So, it is only natural that people are experiencing great fear and anxiety. I'm speaking to you today to assure you that my Administration and other world leaders are

Cap not necessary

doing everything in our power to find out what has happened to so many people around the world who have mysteriously disappeared. I urge you to remain calm, to restore and return to your normal routines as much as possible. Panic, fear, and rash actions will do nothing to resolve this situation. We are all in this together, and we will get through this together."

"It is understandable that many people have formed theories about what has happened. For the past four hours, I have been on conference calls with world leaders, the United Nations, and NASA to gain any information that might be helpful to sort out this series of events."

"European Commission President Karl Schwartz informs me that the nations of Europe are feeling the same baffling sense of mystery that we are dealing with here in the United States. Many ideas about what has happened are being actively explored in Europe. Herr Schwartz says Europeans have seen signs for some time of increased UFO activity. I have just had extensive conversations with NASA Director Clark Donaldson about anything our space agency might know, that would either support or discredit the main theories now coming out of the European Union."

"As you all know, many new unexplained sightings of what are called UFOs have occurred in the past decade. Just yesterday saw the largest group of sightings witnessed by thousands of people all over the world.

However, at least for now, it would be a great mistake to link the disappearance of so many people with sightings of things about which we know so little. Even so, many people believe such a linkage is possible. As your President, I assure you that this widespread theory is not in any way officially accepted or endorsed by anyone in my administration."

"Instead, I have officially given Joint Chiefs Chairman, Admiral Blanding, all the authority he requires for our military to investigate every possibility."

"The global economy, including ours, has already suffered a major setback because of the uncertainty created by the disappearances. To stem those negative effects, I am ordering a temporary shutdown of Wall Street. I am also authorizing the issuing of bi-monthly stimulus checks of two thousand dollars to every adult American. I promise you that your government, under my direction, will see to it that your basic needs are met until we can stabilize the economy. The checks will be issued exactly as your Social Security checks are issued. If you are not on Social Security, your checks will be available through your bank. All details will be fully explained later this week."

"In the meantime, my friends, let us try to remain calm and return to our normal lives as best we can. Since I have taken office and my party has gained control of both houses of Congress, we have been diligently monitoring our economy, and working on ways we can be helping everyone within our borders."

"I assure you; we will solve this mystery. Thank you, and good afternoon."

After the address, Warner turned down the television and both men sat silently for a moment, "There you are Bobby, all pretty again. Now, go in there and make some sense of everything that we just heard."

Wallace grinned, "It's my specialty, Hal. Thanks for the paint job." And off he went to the studio.

After he completed his live follow-up report on the air, Wallace hurried to his office and opened his computer. The words of Hal Warner about a possible "religious angle" compelled him to do a search of key words like the "The Rapture" and "Christian beliefs regarding people leaving earth."

"This page no longer exists" came up on one search.

"That's strange," Wallace thought. "Let's try this, then." He typed the word "Eschatology," looking for any information about "end of the world" prophecies by the world's religions. Again, nothing. "This is even stranger," he thought, "This looks like a deliberate blackout."

Every attempt to find anything online about any religious angle explaining what had happened to so many people met with the same fate. There seemed to be no sites available with any information about the subject, as it related to issues of faith. Wallace closed his laptop and walked out of his office determined to find someplace where he could find out about that kind of thing.

"I guess I'll have to do this the old-fashioned way," he thought. He went to the old Carnegie Library, just two blocks south of the CNA building, in search of a set of encyclopedias.

It had been years since he crossed the threshold of a public library. The Carnegie Public Library had been funded originally by Steel Magnate Andrew Carnegie in the late Nineteenth Century. The Scottish immigrant had made it easier for the common man to find answers to questions with a collection of books that rivaled the private libraries of wealthy men of industry. He knew that the betterment of society could only come through education. It was the internet of its day.

He eyed the Librarian, a surprisingly attractive young lady with stylish glasses, as she sat erect at her station near the desktop computers. Glancing at her nametag, Wallace said, "Excuse me, Lillian, is it?" I'm trying to do some research on Christian end of the world philosophy. Where can I find reference books or a Bible?"

She looked as though she had just taken a large bite out of a very sour lemon, and she was rather smug in her reply, "Oh, you're a year or two late, Sir."

"What?"

"We removed all the Bibles from our shelves a year ago last February."

"Why did you do that?"

"They were found to be filled with hatred and intolerance."

"Who came up with that ruling?"

"The Global Committee for Religious Tolerance and Diversity, that's who." She said defiantly. She appeared to be very proud of her tolerance.

"They presented the National Library Association with many examples of the Bible's hostile biases against women, which have been shown to be a documented source of men abusing women throughout history. It contained extreme hatred toward the LGBTQ Community. The Bible has been used to deny the right of same sex people to marry. So, all Bibles and all reference books that support the Bible have been removed.

Wallace pressed, "May I ask, where did you put them? I need them as a source for a news story I'm writing."

Lillian eyed Wallace with suspicion. "Sir, I'm afraid you're not allowed to use those books anymore. I can point you to newer books published by the new Federal Religion Office. I'm sure you'll be able to find out what

God, whoever she may be, has in store for us here on earth."

Wallace was more than a little annoyed by the fact that pertinent information he needed was no longer available, "Thank you, Lillian," he said, barely able to hide his disgust, "I'll search elsewhere."

Wallace thought twice about finding public transportation to return him the few blocks to the CNA building. Even though driverless cars and trucks had been perfected as common forms of transportation, several years ago, Wallace still didn't trust not having a human driver. He decided to walk.

CHAPTER 2

As Wallace returned to his office, he suddenly remembered hearing some stories about a co-worker who had not come to work since the mass disappearance. Not many people were very close to David Raines, the copy writer at the last desk. He was known as a quiet young man, thirty-five-years-old, who, never forced his faith on anyone. Everyone was fully aware of what he believed, however. He talked about his wife being, what he called, a Proverbs 31 wife. They had two elementary aged children. Both children were home-schooled, and Raines was so proud that they were becoming very proficient with math and English. The children spoke French as well. No one had heard from anyone in the family since the disappearance.

Wallace tried to remember the last time he had spoken with David. Their paths had crossed on occasion when he would rush any updated copy into the studio as Wallace was about to go on the air with a big story. David was very proficient in his work and an excellent writer. His style was effortless to read on the air, and his pronunciation guides were simple to follow.

When Wallace returned to the CNA building, he went to Raines' desk, looked through drawers, and found what he was looking for. It was a soft-cover New International Version of the Bible.

"Here we go. What now?"

As a boy, Wallace had gone to Sunday School for a while, but as an adult he hadn't gone to church in more than twenty years. His knowledge of the Bible's contents was very limited. He had heard people talk about various parts of the Bible, such as Revelation being the last book of the Bible with stories about the end of time.

Wallace returned to his office, Bible in hand, where he found a White House news release. He began to read it aloud as though he were reading it on the air. The more he read, the more astonished he became.

"The White House announced today that President Blair has been in consultation with NASA leaders who, for the first time, now publicly disclose that we have top-secret information about alien visitors to planet Earth from another galaxy. President Blair has met with her cabinet members to inform them that U.S. State

Department advisers have been in contact with key people in the European Union. European authorities have only now shared the results of their own investigations into the disappearance of EU citizens."

"The President today has declassified the results of these investigations. The President states that humankind has learned a great deal from these visitors. This has led to dramatic advances in our scientific achievements, including aviation and space travel."

"European authorities from the office of the Vice President of the European Commission have revealed to U.S. officials that they have been in contact with alien leaders from the Andromeda Galaxy. The alien leaders have informed a key group of officials from Earth that they are indeed the ones who have taken so many human beings. Apparently, the humans have been taken to the Andromeda Galaxy. Now and in the past, abducted humans have been part of an intergalactic exchange of cultural and scientific ideas."

Wallace sat back in his chair and with exasperation, looked at the ceiling. "Is this supposed to make everyone feel better about what's going on?"

He stood up and looked out the window. Nothing seemed out of the ordinary. The streets of Manhattan were just as busy as always. The usual heavy traffic moved slowly as pedestrians crossed the choked streets. Why would people from Andromeda Galaxy take the people they took? Why not that lady in the blue jacket? Why not that guy walking across the street right there? Why was he overlooked? There are many artists and scientists who are still walking around on Earth. It seems that those people are the kind of people who would be valuable in a "cultural" exchange.

He was thinking, "If you had just awakened from a long nap, you'd never know that anything was different."

Sensing that he had wasted enough time, Wallace turned to his desk, picked up the Bible and began to look through it.

"What was that word Hal used? Rapture, that's it Rapture. I'll look it up."

He remembered hearing about Bibles having what is called the Concordance. "This looks like an Index. 'Rapture', 'Rapture', 'Rapture'. There's nothing in this about Rapture. Now what?"

"Wait, the last book, Revelation… that's all about the end of the world, isn't it?"

Wallace leafed through the book, scanning the headings on each chapter. These things made little or no sense to him at all, completely mysterious to him. He was expecting to find the answers he sought immediately, but it wasn't to be.

As Wallace quickly turned pages, scanning the last book of the Bible, he didn't notice anything until he got to the maps at the very end. There, tucked neatly between two pages of maps titled Paul's Missionary Journeys, was a small greeting card sized envelope that said, "Please Read."

The handwriting was as neat as anything Wallace had ever seen before. He opened the envelope and took out two pages of stationery. The elegant handwriting graced the pages. As he sat in his office, Wallace began to read aloud softly, "If you are reading this, then it is apparent that you have found my Bible in my desk. Apparently, I have not come to work for a few days, and no one knows where I might be. If I'm not mistaken, that is the case in many places of employment all around the world. There are probably millions of people who were with their friends and families one day and the next day, they were nowhere to be found."

Wallace looked up at the clock and contemplated all that he had read. He felt as though he was stuck in a remarkably strange story, something that Rod Serling might have written for award winning 1960s Television series, *The Twilight Zone.*

He continued reading, "I have been a believer in Jesus Christ for more than half my life. I have also believed in what many of us call the Rapture. That is an event that, I believe, someday soon, will have all true believers in Christ taken away from this world in a mysterious way. No one will be able to explain it."

25

Wallace spoke aloud, "You're right, David, where did you all go?" And as though David Raines anticipated the question when he wrote the note, "We have been taken to be with Jesus in heaven. No one will be able to explain it. I believe that the devil will try to hide the fact that Christians have been removed from the world, and that he will have a plan. Personally, I believe that plan was set into motion many years ago by increased sightings of Unidentified Flying Objects. Flying saucers have been a topic of discussion since the middle of the twentieth century. I believe that Satan will try to convince the world that people have been abducted by space aliens. Whoever you are, I warn you, do not be fooled by anyone. You have a chance to still become a believer in Jesus Christ as your Savior. My Bible is now in your possession. You will find many passages underlined and highlighted, along with notes in the margins of nearly every page. Do not be fooled by Satan and his minions, as people have been fooled by them throughout history. I must close now and prepare. I implore you, my friend, to look up, because your redemption in Christ is near to you now. Wishing God's blessings on you, David Raines.

Wallace picked up his desk phone and called Angela Martindale, his News Director at CNA.

He spoke quickly when she answered, "Hi, Angela, I need a week or so to track down a few leads. I'll keep in touch and I'll let you know when something breaks.

Yeah, I read the EU theory about the Andromeda Galaxy. I'm not so sure that I'm buyin' into that whole thing. I have a couple other sources and some other theories to check out.

Wallace stepped out of the CNA building and onto Broadway, he hailed a cab to start the journey to his apartment. It would involve a trip across the East River on the Williamsburg Bridge and into Brooklyn. Wallace was part of the public to gentrify parts of Brooklyn, that for many years, had fallen into disrepair. The homes were generally three-story buildings, some of which were built in the early 1920s.

It was a predominantly Jewish neighborhood where, on any given Friday at sunset, families of Orthodox Jews would walk to Temple for the Sabbath. Entire families with the patriarch leading the way followed by their wives and sons and daughters. Wallace surveyed that scene as he looked out the backseat windows. It was a comforting vision, seeing families united, carrying on a tradition that had been happening for centuries in countries all over the world. That was one of the things he found so fascinating when he first moved here. Remembering some of his childhood friends such as David Solomon and Daniel Silverthorne. They were all good friends. They did theater together. David was one of the smartest people Robert knew. He went on to be a Professor of Mathematics at Penn State University.

Daniel Schaffer

[handwritten annotations: "Whole book is in 2nd person." "Can't switch 'person' should be 'Robert wondered'"]

In fact, he had worked on several of the Space Shuttle missions in the last century. I wonder if he was a part of the cultural exchange with the Andromedins.

In fact, he began to wonder (as one of America's leading journalists) why he was not taken along to cover this story?

He asked the driver to wait for him as he ran up to his apartment. He grabbed an overnight bag with a couple changes of clothes and headed out the door. He was off to JFK to catch a flight to Pittsburgh.

After what seemed an eternity of waiting for his flight to depart JFK, he arrived in Pittsburgh. He jumped into his rented Chevy at the airport and returned to Scottdale, Pennsylvania. This was the town where he grew up. Scottdale, is located approximately an hour southeast of Pittsburgh. There were always signs around town (depending on the season) for the Pirates, Steelers, and Penguins.

St. John's Lutheran Church was still on the same corner, just down the street from where Wallace grew up. It is one of the oldest buildings in Scottdale. The Church was established during the mid-seventeen-hundreds. Pastor James Hann had been the Senior Pastor at St. John's for the past ten years. Wallace was remembering he had attended Sunday School a few times when he was in grade school with his childhood friend Randy Dixon.

After establishing his temporary residence at the local Holiday Inn Express, Wallace got into his car and started northbound on Bessemer Road. He stopped by a little Pennsylvania Dutch restaurant that was frequented by his family when he was a child. His memory carried him back to a simpler time in his life. He was looking forward to the wide and thick Spaetzle Noodles. Such was the tradition of Mueller's Essen Haus.

The little diner looked just as it had before, he moved to New York ten years earlier. Frau Mueller still could be seen working in the kitchen behind the white tile counter. She could have taught master classes on German Cuisine. The secret seemed to be in the extra egg she added along with a touch more butter than the recipe called for, and those wonderous thicker noodles with Schnitzel that could be cut with a fork. The old family recipe for the Saur Kraut made Wallace's mouth water just thinking about it.

As he sat at his corner booth, he looked around the room. Not much had changed since he had sat in the same spot with his father and mother, twenty years earlier. There were post cards from all over Germany and Austria. Pictures of the Bavarian countryside had always been his favorites. He had promised that one day he'd visit the land of his mother's ancestors. So far, he had not managed to get to the Bavarian Alps. He had always imagined staying in one of those lodges with the beautiful snow-capped peaks in the background.

[handwritten margin note: were the noodles part of the secret? No. They're mentioned in prev ¶]

After ordering his meal, he pulled his laptop out and scanned his Daily Planner App. He scanned the list of questions he was going to ask one of the remaining clergymen who could still be found. 1) What is the remaining church's position on the large number of missing church members? 2) Is there any record of missing persons broken down into demographics? 3) Why is it so hard to find anything online anymore about the Christian faith?

The meal was everything that Wallace had hoped it would be. Then came the topper, he remembered that Frau Mueller's Apple Streusel as being the best in the world (at least the best in his world). The crust was so very light and flakey, that it literally melted in his mouth. There was just enough sugar on the outer crust to enhance the already sweet taste of the Apple filling.

The reminder alarm on his phone brought him back to reality. He had an appointment with Pastor James Hann at the church at 2 O'clock today. Wallace paid his bill and drove the short distance to St. John's Lutheran.

Pastor Hann was a tall man who now days could easily be found either in his office or in the Sanctuary. The sanctuary at St. Johns was one of those old classic dark places of worship. There was a large set of organ pipes at the north end of the room. They were a little dusty. Looking rather out of place beneath the pipes was a small stage area with guitar amps, and an electric KORG keyboard with an array of pedals and buttons that can mimic an entire orchestra from one unit. There was a classic Ludwig drum set on a small platform behind a Plexi-glass enclosure.

Other than the modern equipment on the stage for the band, the sanctuary almost looked as though Martin Luther himself could ascend the stairs to the large pulpit, look down upon the congregation and read aloud his 95 Theses.

Pastor Hann, wearing his clerical collar, overlay and stole was sitting in the front pew. He was looking up at the large stained-glass window. There were twelve panels depicting various scenes from the life of Christ. There was Christ in the Garden of Gethsemane. The sun shining through the panel highlighted each detailed small piece of glass. It was as though they were the brush strokes from paintings. Other panels depicted the remaining Apostles. Peter, holding the keys to the kingdom, Matthew could be seen walking away from his tax collecting table, John staring in awe at the burial cloths of Christ in the tomb.

Pastor Hann found peace each day as he watched the light shine through the windows.

He turned when he heard the large door behind him open, and he watched as Wallace entered the cavernous room, his footsteps echoing as he walked down the aisle. He watched the man stroll down the center aisle, hoping that he was not someone who would cause him trouble. Pastor Hann had been deviating from the new standard line that was becoming the norm in churches all over the United States. Instead of talking about brotherhood and service, he was preaching the "why" of brotherhood and service. He was leading this remaining flock to follow Christ as Savior. In so doing, His followers would want to live in harmony with their fellow believers and reach out to help anyone in need because they were followers. The modern church had become more and more interested in service for the sake of service. Hann had been reprimanded for his style several times. He eyed Wallace suspiciously.

Reaching his hand out to greet the pastor, Wallace said, "Reverend Hann, I'm Robert Wallace of CNA News. I'm the guy with all the questions for you regarding The Missing."

The pair exited the sanctuary through a small door, then walked into an alcove that emptied into a long hallway. Hanging on the walls were old paintings, including the painting of Luther nailing his Theses on the door at Wittenberg. They passed a small glass enclosure that at one time must have contained something important. The small brass plate confirmed it. "Guttenberg Bible circa 1455". The case was now empty.

Just to the right, beyond the empty glass case, was a heavy oak door to the office. As Wallace glanced around the office, he was impressed by the large dark walnut desk, but he noticed that the bookshelves were nearly empty. The remaining books appeared to be political and social gospel titles.

"Pastor Hann, so much has been going on the past couple of days, and I've been having trouble finding answers. I don't believe the theory about aliens from The Andromeda Galaxy. I've been thinking that there may possibly be a religious angle. Pastor, what do you think has happened to all the people who have disappeared? Is there any official comment from your church's hierarchy regarding what has happened?"

"Well, some members of our congregation are still around, but many are no longer here with us. I have checked with local Methodist, Anglican, Catholic and Baptist and many of the non-denominational churches, and this seems to be a common theme. There are a few Bishops in the western U.S. who don't want to admit that somehow God could be behind this. They are inclined to agree with many in the secular world that someone from outer space has abducted millions of people world-wide."

He reached into his lower right desk drawer and pulled out a Bible. He held it up in front of the reporter and setting it on the desk he said quietly, "These are hard to come by these days."

Hann began setting the stage for what he was about to tell the reporter. "For the past couple of hundred years, there has been a movement among Evangelical Christians. They believed very strongly that Christ was going to evacuate the church before, or even during, what the Bible calls the Great Tribulation. In fact, time and time again people tried to predict that the 'end' was near, and then nothing would happen. So, people thought less and less of those theories of the end coming soon."

Wallace, with his Tablet open and stylus in hand, was jotting down notes. "What is the 'Rapture' that I've heard about?"

The pastor was leafing through his Bible into the New Testament until he reached 1 Thessalonians.

"It comes from the Latin word, rapturo, which means, roughly, to seize upon by force or to snatch up. The Greek word is harpazo. It was found in 1 Thessalonians 4:17 'Then we who are alive, who are left, will be suddenly caught up together with them in the clouds to meet the Lord in the air. And so, we will always be with the Lord.'" Hann looked up from his Bible looking directly at Wallace and continued, "As you can tell by the first person, present tense, the Apostle Paul was expecting to be snatched up any day. So that anticipation of being taken out of this world quickly has been with the church since the beginning."

"Why did it fall out of favor among believers?" asked Wallace.

"I suppose it was because so many centuries passed without any snatching up, people just thought that maybe it wasn't ever going to happen. Personally, I believed that way for most of my pastoral career. Now, because of what has just happened, I'm reassessing my position on people being snatched up."

"When I started my ministry, I read a couple of books about Christian Eschatology and I found I was interested in the theory. I think that as I became 'more sophisticated', I felt that I needed to not be so primal in my beliefs. So, I started to deny the idea of Christians being removed from Earth without dying."

Wallace slowly looked up from his Tablet and quizzed, "So what brought you back to basics, so to speak?"

"I think that I wanted to go back in my mind and recapture that excitement of my early ministry days."

Smiling knowingly, Wallace said, "Wouldn't we all like to go back to that simpler time in our lives when we thought we knew it all?"

Villa Carmolotti was one of the oldest and most opulent summer homes for Ancient Roman Nobility, located on the Amalfi Coast just south of Naples, overlooking the bay. It's located just outside the Red Zone of Mt. Vesuvius, but still close enough to the ancient city of Pompeii to be legendary for its proximity to danger. The castle had been in the Carmolotti family for generations since it was built shortly after the fall of the Roman Empire. Shortly following World War II Giuseppe Carmolotti had to sell it to a Frenchman named Le Roux. He then bequeathed it to his son Albert Le Roux in the late 1960s when Albert was a young, world renowned playboy.

As he had grown more mature and begun to settle down, Albert Le Roux converted the Villa into a large winery. The soil in the shadows of Vesuvius is rich with volcanic ash that goes as deep as thirty-six feet. Le Roux is a Frenchman, whose family made a fortune in fashion, wine and, in Albert's case, computer technology.

Le Roux has been heavily involved in French politics for the past forty years, bribing presidents, legislators, and judges. He was known as the true power of France.

Today he was meeting with Paolino Esposito, the man he had been grooming to become the next leader of the European Union. Esposito was from Palermo, in Sicily. He was a handsome man with dark, wavy hair. Men and women had always been drawn to him. The men, because of his power and family connections, the women, for the obvious reasons. He was wealthy, handsome and was one of Italy's most fashionable men. He had that Roman Emperor look about him. His olive complexion and classic good looks harkened back to the time of the Caesars.

It had been said that his family had always had deep roots in organized crime. He was named after his grandfather, who had been a powerful leader in the Italian Parliament after the fall of Mussolini. Long after his death, the family still benefited from the leadership of his grandfather in parliament. In Rome, the people still honored his memory and respected him. The logical next step is to support his grandson, Paolino Esposito, who was from the same party and fit the profile nicely.

As Esposito entered the villa, he knew that today's meeting would include some powerful people from the Church. Not everyone from the Church was gone. Many were men who had long held positions of power in Rome.

Riding in the back seat of the Chevy Suburban, Cardinal Nunzio Assidi watched the peaceful Azure Bay of Naples outside the car's right-side window. Cardinal Assidi was in his mid-fifties and was impeccably dressed in the trappings of his high office. He had a slick handlebar mustache that ran beyond the corners of his mouth. Cardinal Nunzio Assidi had the assignment of replacing ten Bishops who are among the missing.

He had been grooming several men who led major cities' Dioceses. They were men who have shown great ambition. Each man also had amassed large sums of money which they pledged to Assidi's vision of the church. And each had a dark past that Assidi was able to hold over them as a bargaining chip. It has never been about finding candidates who were men of great spiritual conviction. He has always personally believed that God was on his side because he knew he was living out the gospel by giving his time and talent to the poor.

Soon the Villa Carmolotti came into view. It sat atop a hillside overlooking the bay. Its opulence was apparent, as the sun cast a golden glow on the building. Flanking both sides of the long driveway to the castle, mature grapevines stretched over the hillsides. It was the home of the world famous Carmolotti Wines. Assidi had been instrumental in getting the Pope to personally bless some of the vineyards from which the church would get its wine for the Holy Sacrament.

He knew what lay ahead. Albert Le Roux was putting together a team to get Paolino Esposito elected as head of the European Commission. Assidi's assignment would be to get the church to endorse the agenda that was to bring all of Europe into alignment as the top economy in the world. Russia was still a problem for most of Western Europe, but there are those who believe that Paolino Esposito could be the kind of leader to bring all of Europe, including Russia, together. Assidi wanted to get Le Roux's endorsement for his plans for the future of the church.

Pastor Hann poured Wallace another cup of coffee. They continued discussing the differing theories about what had happened to such a large portion of the population.

"What about all the radio and TV preachers who have been hammering home the gospel message and allegedly healing thousands of people for so many years? I noticed a story yesterday that Televangelist Ernest Potter had filed a lawsuit trying to get back on the air. I thought those guys would all be gone, if indeed Jesus came and snatched all the good girls and boys out of here."

Hann smiled, "Well, you yourself have done stories about some of these people. Some, though not all, were in it just for the money."

"Right. The general perception of televangelists is that they are all in it for the money. That goes back to what seems like a lifetime ago. Since the days of a massive scandal that saw a couple bring about the fall of a giant religious television empire. The leaders lived high on the hog and drastically mismanaged the money that was donated for 'God's work'. For many years, that scandal tainted all televangelists."

Pastor Hann swirled the coffee around in his mug. After a few seconds of contemplation, he spoke, "I know. I was one who spoke from the pulpit about the wrong message being put across by televangelists. In fact, when I spoke against all of them, I began to question all the fundamental beliefs. With all the talk about miraculous healing and the prosperity gospel that so many of the TV Preachers were espousing, I didn't want to be viewed as being like them, so I made it a point to not be a fundamentalist."

Wallace looked up from his tablet and raised an eyebrow, "So how do you feel about that whole idea of getting back to basics now?"

Hann rose from his chair and went to the bookshelf. There on the sparsely populated dark cherry shelves he gestured, "There used to be so many books here that would possibly hold those answers. Now, in order not to have problems with the courts, most of those books have been confiscated by the government authorities and church hierarchy. I was glad I was able to keep my personal Bible with all the Scriptures that I had underlined and highlighted. It was the Bible that I used in seminary. That was when I still was wide-eyed with a child-like faith."

"I'm afraid, Pastor, that I was born tainted. My father didn't have any use for the 'brainwashing' that my mother's parents wanted to pass down to me. He said that someday, when I got older, I could choose for myself."

Hann smiled knowingly, "The problem with that philosophy is that 'brainwashing' goes both ways. The Bible says that parents are to train up their children in the ways of the Lord."

Wallace asked, "Did you ever read any of those books about missing the Rapture?"

"Not when they were popular. I thought those people were religious fanatics. I didn't want to be painted with the broad-brush strokes of being one of them. I'd love to read them now. I did manage to read Hal Lindsey's Late Great Planet Earth, and I did find it to be fascinating. I looked up the Scripture references he quoted in that book. I found that most of them were references that I had underlined or highlighted in my personal Bible from seminary."

"So, what about now?" Wallace asked as he dug deeper into Hann's current belief system.

"Now? Now I believe that God, indeed, meant to pull the true believers out of this world."

Wallace wondered if there really was a God in heaven. If there truly was a Savior named Jesus, perhaps Robert Wallace might be in big trouble, "What are we supposed to do, then? If all the believers are in heaven, are we all going to go to Hell?"

Hann gazed out the office window onto the old St. John's Lutheran Cemetery. "So many of those people buried in that hallowed ground for the past two-hundred or so years, died with Christ on their mind. They died knowing in their heart that Jesus Christ is Lord, and that God raised him from the dead. I'd like to think that I, too, can still come to truly know Christ as Lord."

Opening his Bible, he began to read, "It says here in Romans chapter ten verse nine, 'If you confess with your mouth that Jesus Christ is Lord and you believe in your heart that God raised him from the dead, then you will be saved.' I do believe that Jesus Christ is Lord. I also believe that God did raise him from the dead. So even though I came to it late, I have come to it."

"Aren't you too late? You've already missed the Rapture."

"I believe that Jesus was talking about this sort of thing when he told the story about the landowner who hired workers at the eleventh hour and paid them the same wage as those who were hired earlier in the day."

Wallace was stumped. He had not heard that story, "I'm afraid I'm not familiar with that one."

Hann explained, "In the gospel of Matthew, Jesus tells a story that he said was like the kingdom of heaven. It is the story of a landowner, who went into the marketplace one morning to hire workers for his vineyard. He agreed to pay them denarius, a common coin made of silver or copper. So, into the vineyard they went."

"Again, at nine in the morning he returned to the marketplace and hired more workers. Again, at noon, and again at five in the afternoon he hired more workers. He had his foreman pay the last ones hired first. They received a denarius for their one hour's work. Then, when it came time for the first ones hired to receive their pay, they expected more, but they received the originally agreed upon denarius. When they complained, the owner asked if they were complaining because they received the amount they had agreed upon, or were they complaining about his generosity. Regardless of what time the workers were hired, he paid them each the same amount. I would like to think that even though I am coming to Christ this late, he will still reward me with a place in his kingdom. I believe that would work for you as well."

Wallace was bewildered, "I just can't understand how that can be, since I didn't earn it earlier in life."

Hann smiled, "Remember what the vineyard owner said, 'I want to give the one who was hired last the same as I gave you. Don't I have the right to do what I want with my own money? Or are you envious because I am generous?' I believe that goes for us too because God is a loving God who is generous."

The meeting at Villa Carmolotti was about to begin. Cardinal Assidi arrived about an hour after Paolino Esposito. Albert Le Roux was gazing out the window of his villa, overlooking his prized vineyards. He opened the ornate Spanish Cedarwood Humidor and removed a Gran Habano No 5 "El Gigante" Cigar. He placed it under his nostrils and inhaled the fine aroma of one of the most expensive and largest of the Cuban Cigars on the market, "This, gentlemen, is one of the most pleasing aromas you can imagine. That is, of course, other than the aroma of a beautiful woman."

He clipped the end and placed it between his lips and began to draw the flame of his lighter through the fine tobacco. He inhaled deeply and allowed the smoke to swirl around his head. The late afternoon sun shining through the window cast an eerie shadow on his face as it filtered through the smoke.

Offering Assidi and Esposito a Covee Jean Godet Cognac, he began their meeting, "Gentlemen, we are on the threshold of a new era. I firmly believe that total power is within our grasp. I have asked my Security Chief, Vito Lombardo, to join us for dinner later to give a progress update on where we stand with the other members of the EU Parliament. Paolino, we are about to have you elected President. Europe is rapidly becoming the leading economic power in the world."

Esposito nodded in agreement, "My sources are telling me that the United States and China are lagging far behind us. The United States has been irrelevant for several years. They never learned to take full control of their resources. Conservatives and Progressives have been fighting against each other for too long. Because of corruption by both sides, they failed to stop the erosion of their great economic power."

Le Roux drew deeply on his cigar, and then placed the tip of his finger on the end of his tongue to remove a small flake of tobacco. He eyed it and then chimed in, "I would like to think that I have been able to contribute heavily to that. I donated large amounts of cash to each side in the issues. Swirl enough mud into a political campaign and you can confuse even the most astute politico. They were never able to get anything accomplished, if they argued about the best way to attain their dreams. They had basically the same goals but disagreed on how to achieve them. Factor in the natural greed of anyone who attains power, and their country began to collapse."

Esposito nodded in agreement, "I have cousins in America who have run a successful campaign to be the true power that runs the country without anyone really being any wiser. If anyone tried to blame our family for controlling the country, it would be easy to have that person marginalized as a, how do they say it over there… a crazy person."

Cardinal Assidi added, "And the very few corrupt church leaders became the focal point in so many people's impression of the church, that the true believers had trouble getting their message across. It was, as Dickens said, 'the best of times and the worst of times.'"

The men began moving from the large living room area toward the dark hallway that led to the dining room. The large dining table had at least twenty chairs around it. Members of the service staff were putting the finishing touches on the table settings. Each setting had a large gold-trimmed charger plate surrounded by fine silverware. Forks, spoons, and knives sparkled with a shine that reflected the bright overhead lights. The butler oversaw the placement of the final setting in perfect alignment with the edge of the table. Each chair was precisely centered at each setting. It was picture perfect. The butler nodded to Le Roux and quickly made his way past the men, moving through the swinging door to the kitchen hallway.

At this point, another butler entered the room and announced the arrival of Vito Lombardo.

As Lombardo entered the room, he handed his hat and coat to the butler, who promptly left the room. Lombardo clung to a folder that he had tucked under his left arm. He was a fit looking man of about forty-five years of age. A handsome man, he was dressed in a three-piece silk pin-striped navy-blue suit. He had the look of a Hollywood leading man. On the pinky of his right hand was a small ring with a large diamond surrounded by five sparkling Rubies. There was a large diamond stickpin on the left lapel of his suit.

Le Roux crossed to Lombardo and extended his right hand, "Vito, so nice to see you. Welcome to our gathering. I trust that you have the information I requested."

Turning to the others he continued, "Gentlemen, this is Vito Lombardo, the head of my security division at Le Roux Enterprises. He is a retired Colonel from the First San Marco Marine Regiment, Special Forces. His specialty, besides his martial arts skills, includes a great talent for investigation and finding the weak spots in your enemies. Political rivals are our enemies, gentlemen. Lombardo has gathered information that should erase any obstacles to Paolino making it all the way to the top."

Lombardo took the seat just to the right of Mr. Le Roux and placed his portfolio on the table.

Le Roux put his napkin onto his lap and turned to Lombardo, "Colonel, please give us an update. Where do we stand, what incriminating information do you have on Mr. Esposito's challengers?"

Reaching for his portfolio, Lombardo began sharing the results of his investigations into Esposito's three biggest rivals for European Commission President.

"Gentlemen, Karl Schwartz, the incumbent, has so many problems with corruption that I do not believe he will be much of a threat to your election. The hatred of Jews has been a long-standing undercurrent throughout The Continent. Despite that, our polling information indicates that his lack of condemnation of the Nazis for their attempt to rid the world of Jews in the nineteen thirties and forties is a problem for him. Most people reject any glossing over of that time in history. Plus, there are issues with his new-found wealth after he was first elected to the European Parliament. Because of how he voted on certain economic issues, most people think he became wealthy because he voted in favor of certain German businessmen's pet projects."

Le Roux finished chewing his boeuf Bourguignon, took a swallow of water and chimed in, "That is true. I have believed for quite a while that it is time for Schwartz to go. That is why I have spent millions of Euros on advertising and news reports about his many shortcomings. I believe that perhaps Francois DuPont could be a viable candidate for one of the members of the Commission. Schwartz must be removed at all costs. Perhaps he might meet with an accident or sudden fatal illness."

Lombardo went on, "I do believe that we have in place the right members of the Parliament. They are the members who would elect the Commission we need, people who are friendly to the idea of a man of Mr. Esposito's talents to head the EU."

Cardinal Assidi had been silent during most of this discussion. He finished his small cup of Espresso, wiped his lips and began, "There is a great desire for Carlos Manicelli to be a member of the Council. His ideas are in line with what the church envisions over the next few years. We must make sure that the people don't begin to believe what American Evangelicals propose as the reason so many people are gone."

Lombardo gestured toward the head of the table, "Mr. Le Roux has spent quite a bit of money making sure the story is told that men from the Andromeda Galaxy have taken people on what is a cultural exchange, and that the people of Earth are sharing their ideas and learning from the men of Andromeda as well."

Cardinal Assidi agreed with this, "I believe that there is life out there, somewhere. Back in the early part of the twenty-first century, Pope Francis said he believed it is possible. He said he would invite them to receive baptism as well."

"Any way you look at it, people are open to the idea of life in other galaxies, and Andromeda is one of our nearest neighbors," Le Roux added to the discussion. "For centuries, people have believed they have actually seen some of the aliens among us. The second half of the Twentieth Century alone saw more sightings of extraterrestrials than ever before in history."

Lombardo continued that thought, "And there was the popularity of stories and television programs, as well as the cinema. There were stories about space travel that were very believable."

Le Roux turned to Esposito, "Paolino, would you be open to a high-level meeting with a leader of the Andromeda people? If we can arrange it, the media coverage might go a long way toward convincing people of the transportation of a large group of people into deep space. And it could certainly convince people that you are a natural leader, and the only choice for next President of the European Commission."

"I can begin the arrangements for the meeting. Media coverage would be a natural next step," said Lombardo. "I will make contact with them and have things ready within twenty-four hours."

Le Roux followed up with a location for the meeting, "Colonel, this is the reason I built the new base of operations at the European Space Agency on the coast near La Palue. We can have the Andromeda people there later this week. All of the facilities needed for any kind of large space craft landing and take-off are there."

Wallace received an urgent email from CNA Headquarters in New York.

To Bob Wallace;

Bob,

We have a hot story for you to cover this Friday in France. We have a reservation for you to fly out of Pittsburgh. From there you'll proceed to Paris, and finally to La Palue, France. You'll be covering a meeting of EU Commission at the European Space Agency base. Candidate Paolino Esposito and leaders from the Andromeda Galaxy will be conducting high level talks.

This story could win a Peabody for you.

Regards,

Angela Martindale

News Director

Central News Agency

Wallace was on the road, still a half hour away from Pittsburg International Airport. By this time tomorrow he should be touching down at Paris-Charles-de-Gaulle Airport.

He had less than twenty-four hours to learn all he could about Paolino Esposito. Who was this man and what was his history?

It was a hot July Friday in France. La Palue is a beach village, frequented by surfers, halfway between Brest and Quimper. Albert Le Roux bought up most of the property in that part of Brittany. It was his goal to turn the area into the center of the European Space Agency. Since he had built the center a year and a half ago, the ESA had launched five state-of-the-art communications satellites. Le Roux Enterprises had made a huge profit from each of the launches.

Traffic heading to La Palue, was very heavy and Frenchmen were in a festive mood, celebrating Bastille Day. Wallace sat in the back of the company-hired limo looking out at traffic. People were lining both sides of the road making their way toward the beach.

Wallace asked the driver where the ESA base was, and if this crowd would prevent them from getting there in a timely manner.

"No, Monsieur. We will be turning on to the access road in the next few moments, then onto a private road that is heavily guarded. The traffic is heavily regulated, and this crowd will not be in our way."

Wallace continued scanning his downloaded information about Paolino Esposito. He discovered that Esposito was the "Golden Boy" protege of French billionaire, Albert Le Roux.

As they drove on, Wallace thought, "It's interesting that Esposito is the only politician in this meeting. And he's only a candidate for high office scheduled to be in attendance. Why is it that Le Roux hasn't summoned any current members of the Parliament to this meeting?"

As he read on, he discovered that Esposito was the recipient of Le Roux's unlimited resources backing his candidacy. Trying to make sense of the whole thing, Wallace dug deeper into Esposito's life.

Knowing that what he was reading could very well have been put together by a public relations firm, he started checking with sources in law enforcement. For the past five years, Wallace was in an on again off again relationship with Manhattan Assistant District Attorney Olivia Meyer. She had worked for the FBI, prior to taking her current post. She had also cultivated professional relationships within the offices of Interpol. Wallace had called her just before he left Paris for La Palue and was waiting for a return call from her with information that he had requested.

Wallace was formulating his story. He was going to give background information on the candidate who had the full backing of the most powerful man in Europe.

Opening the word processor on his laptop he began typing. "Paolino Esposito, who is a leading candidate for the office of European Commission President, has been an unknown to most of the world. Esposito was born and raised in Palermo, Sicily. Though he is the son of a purported Sicilian crime boss, there is no indication that young Esposito has ever participated in any criminal activity himself.

Esposito is backed by powerful forces within the EU. Albert Le Roux, the man who has helped bring about successful missions in the European space program, is supporting the political neophyte. Some are wondering why this rookie is the beneficiary of the blessing of such a powerful man."

Wallace's phone rang. Seeing the caller I.D., he noticed Olivia Meyer's name, "Hi Olivia, thanks for getting back with me. What have you found out?"

"Hi Bobby. How have you been?"

"Fine. What's going on?"

"Yeah, nice to hear from you too," there was a slight irritation in her voice. "Well, Bobby, all my contacts in the Italian police agencies, as well as Interpol, tell me that outside of some youthful indiscretions such as running numbers in lotto scams when he was a teen, he has a clean record. There are no records of any crime committed by Paolino Esposito."

"Liv, I am sorry about the way we left things the last time we were together. I would like to see you..." his phone went dead. "Liv, Liv, hey, what happened here?"

The limo driver answered, "Sorry Monsieur, we have turned on to the ESA access road and security blocks all cell phone and radio traffic."

"Well, that's just great, now she's going to think that I hung up on her."

"I wouldn't worry about that too much, Monsieur. If she is a woman who loves you, she will wait to hear from you again and be ready to forgive. My wife and I were like that. She loved me and forgave me often."

"You say you were like that. What happened? Did she pass away?"

"That, I could not tell you sir. She just disappeared one day. I hope that what they are saying is true. I would like to think that she was one of those who was taken into space to create better understanding between humans and those from some other world. And it is my desire that I will one day be taken, and we can be together again."

Wallace smiled, "Was she in some high-powered job or a scientist or something like that?"

"No, she was a music teacher."

Wallace paused in thought then asked, "Let me ask you this: did she belong to some church somewhere? And did she ever talk to you about heavenly things or the end of the world?

The driver looked into the rear-view mirror and solemnly answered, "Oui. It is true. She told me that someday people who were followers of Jesus would one day, perhaps not in our lifetime, but someday, be taken suddenly to heaven. She always wanted me to go to church with her to hear some preacher talk about that subject. I always had better things to do so I never went."

"That sounds a lot like the stories I've heard. Even I knew people who talked about that kind of thing, but I never gave it much thought."

The driver pointed forward and to the right, "There you are, Monsieur, those buildings are the main offices of the La Palue headquarters of the European Space Agency. It is still about five more minutes before we arrive at the launch area. That's where Hangar 39 is located."

"I remember," said Wallace, "Launch Complex 39 was where the Apollo 11 departed for the Moon in 1969 from Cape Canaveral, Florida. I like the symbolism of this hangar number and the Apollo 11 launch site."

The Peugeot 607 moved down the road past the office complex, and there, just beyond the display of European Space Agency rockets was the largest building at the seaside complex. The building had an eerie presence as it loomed in the distance. As the car stopped in front of the Gargantuan building, Wallace stepped out of the car.

As he stretched to his full six-foot one height, he looked up toward the roofline. Other media members were arriving at the same time. Each person had basically the same reaction. Some stared with mouth wide-open, some just stopped in their tracks and looked at the largest aviation hangar they had ever seen.

Camera crews and correspondents made their way toward the large hangar door. As Wallace and the rest stepped through the small door in the lower right corner of the giant hangar, they stepped into an arena sized room that looked like Wimbledon Stadium without the seats. It was a huge area that housed what appeared to be an enormous shiny cigar shaped craft. It looked like something out of a nineteen seventies sci-fi movie. The ship looked like it could easily be a part of the fictional "Battlestar Galactica fleet."

Wallace walked underneath the starboard side landing gear. He looked up into the well that would hold the retracted gear. It was immense, almost the size of a Boeing 747 fuselage. There were at least twenty lights in the opening.

Just as everyone was getting acclimated to the size and the grandeur of this entire spectacle, the VIP entourage entered, with Albert Le Roux leading the way. He was flanked by security personnel, including security head Vito Lombardo.

The entourage also included Cardinal Assidi, Paolino Esposito and several support people. Le Roux stepped forward and stood at the base of a ramp that had just been lowered from the craft.

A tall slender man moved gracefully down the ramp toward Le Roux. He was the Ambassador for the Andromedins. His suit was shiny, almost a gun-metal gray. There were two silver stripes down the outside leg of his trousers. He was a handsome man, in an odd sort of way-very exotic looking. He was introduced as Ambassador Baalazaar. He exchanged pleasantries with Le Roux, and they spoke for a moment or two. The two stood there, the Andromeda man towering over Le Roux, as he stood at the base of the ramp. Baalazaar's long arm reached out and touched Le Roux on his right shoulder. That move was then repeated on the left shoulder. As each touch occurred, there was a slight glow. It was as though there was a soft night light being turned on at each shoulder.

It was then that Le Roux returned to his group of colleagues and spoke, "Ladies and gentlemen, we are going to proceed aboard the ship. The media will accompany us."

Wallace and representatives from all major European news networks, as well as all the news services and members of the waning print media, followed the Le Roux party up the ramp.

There were three sections inside the craft. The front section was obviously a control area. Through the wrap-around plexiglass walls one could see large computer screens with what appeared to be navigational aids.

There were also ten arrays of blinking lights and what appeared to be digital countdown clocks, but they didn't have standard Arabic numbers. Instead, each unit scrolled through several series of Hieroglyphic type symbols.

The middle section appeared to be a first-class seating section. The wide seats each had a large desk-type tray with the fifteen different types of outlets, compatible with all U.S., European and Asian power sources. The press corps took their assigned seats. Wallace's seat was five rows back on the port side. He thought to himself that he was glad to have a window seat. He always liked to sit by the window whenever he traveled by any mode.

The rear third of the cabin appeared to have a large conference room with enough seating for at least thirty people. The correspondents each stood facing the rear as they took their seats. In the forward part of the passenger compartment, just outside the control-room, there was a podium with a microphone. An officer of the crew came along the center aisle and passed out a program, printed in the five different languages which were spoken by the reporters.

As everyone looked over the schedule of events, Le Roux, Esposito, Assidi and Lombardo made their way to the rear, along with Ambassador Baalazaar and another Alien man who appeared to carry some sort of recording device and a tablet with a writing stylus. Lombardo and another of the uniformed Andromedins stood flanking either side of the door. They were studying all the correspondents as though looking for conspirators who might strike at any moment.

An Andromedin Officer came from the bridge and stood at the podium to speak. Wallace picked up the earphone hanging on the back of the seat in front of him and placed it on his ear. The voice in his ear spoke flawless English, with a slight Chicago accent. As he was listening to the translation, he could also hear the speaker's actual voice which sounded like a series of clicks, groans, and grunts.

There was something about each of these tall, slender Andromedins that gave Wallace pause. Each of them was built exactly alike. And their faces were emotionless. Perhaps he had been tainted by humans and their myriad of emotions. It was probably better to not let emotions cloud one's point of view. Emotions have, historically, caused people to make rash decisions from marrying the wrong person, to fighting at the drop of a hat, to crying at the least important things.

They were being told, by one of the officers, that they were about to take a ride into Earth's orbit, "Do not worry when we break the pull of Earth's gravity because we have mastered artificial gravity equal to that on Earth. Soon the meeting in the conference room will reach a conclusion and all the parties involved will hold a news briefing. At the briefing, you will learn about the people of Earth who have come to our galaxy to share cultural ideas, and what we have learned from each other about creating a long and prosperous relationship between our peoples.

CHAPTER 3

Each passenger felt a tingling sensation as the seats began to vibrate, almost imperceptibly at first, but with increased intensity until a low, dull forceful shaking could be felt. The craft seemed to rise about six inches in the hangar, and the view showed slight movement.

Wallace watched out his window as the sides of the hangar appeared to move slowly. He looked forward into the control room area. It was a beehive of activity as the tall Andromedins went about their business with a smooth, choreographed efficiency. The symbols on the large monitors appeared to be counting down at a steady pace. Wallace glanced, once again, out his window as the huge hangar doorway slid closely by. He looked across the aisle at Suzanne Coppin who was here representing BSN (British Satellite News). She was rapidly typing her story as she took in the sights and sounds of what promised to be a ride like no one here had ever experienced before.

Wallace returned to his laptop as he began to put down in words what he was feeling, "After boarding this strange vehicle less than half an hour ago, we have begun to depart the European Space Agency Hangar 39. This reporter has flown on virtually every kind of aircraft known to man, from hot air balloon rides in Albuquerque, to being launched off the deck of a U.S. Navy Super Carrier, to luxurious first-class airline flights or private business jets, but the excitement of this particular ride will leave all those other experiences behind."

The sense of movement outside the windows stopped, and the vibrations in the seats ceased momentarily. He paused his writing to look around him. Outside he could see ground crew members waving hands in a circular upward motion. The vibration started to increase, and the accompanying sound added to the sensory experience of someone about to be launched into flight.

The cabin was filled with the sounds of excitement as nearly every one of these jaded news correspondents vocalized with various degrees of ecstatic "oohs" and "ahs". From a few rows behind Wallace someone uttered a child-like squeal of delight Wallace, himself was feeling the tickle of butterflies in his stomach and pins and needles tickling his legs as the front rose, pushing him into his seat back.

Everyone felt a sensation of movement as the ship began to rise, and suddenly the sound of whistling air passing across the outside of the ship matched the vision of the space port quickly falling out of sight below them. The aspect outside changed as well from a bright, sunny day in southern France, to a view of the Atlantic Ocean and the Mediterranean Sea slipping past below. The sensation of rapid movement was also starting to lessen. The sky turned from sunny daylight to the darkness of the void of space. It was like nothing Wallace had ever experienced before.

One of the Andromedins came down the center aisle asking each person if they would like something to drink. Everything was being offered, from water, coffee, or tea to soft drinks to beer or hard liquor. Wallace had always had a fondness for twelve-year-old Glenfiddich. However, he knew that to give this story the proper coverage he had better keep a clear head. "I'll just have a black coffee, please."

Many of his colleagues opted for the stronger spirits and he could see glasses of Scotch, Bourbon, and Tequila being served to the reporters. Wallace smiled to himself as he accepted his coffee, as everyone else was drinking their booze. Perhaps it was a little bit of smugness, or perhaps he was just proud of his own personal self-control.

Laughter could be heard from the conference room as the doors slowly opened and two of the participants stepped out. They were each carrying a tablet and writing stylus. They went into the control room at the front and placed the tablets into a slot. They closed the cover and pushed a series of buttons. Lights began to glow and the Andromedins, who showed no expressions on their faces, looked toward each other, and gave a slight nod. As the lights changed from flashing red to a steady blue light, they removed the tablets from their slots.

With tablets in hand, they proceeded back down the aisle of the main cabin and returned to the conference room. The noise from the room continued, though not as raucous as it had been when the doors first opened. The men disappeared into the room and closed the doors behind them.

The Andromedins' lead officer once again came out of the control room and moved to the podium. Each member of the press corps pulled their earphone up to their ear and listened intently, "Ladies and gentlemen of Earth. Our mission is approximately half-way finished. We hope that you have enjoyed our hospitality. We honor you, and your skills to impart important information to your people. In a short while, we will hold an official news conference. After a few statements about today's mission, we will allow a few questions from among your group. Please feel free to have more refreshments and continue your writing and preparations for your reports."

He quickly slipped back into the control room as everyone began typing frantically again. There were a few old school type print reporters who still liked to use a Paper Mate and a "Reporter's Notebook". The narrow spiral bound paper notebooks looked like something you'd see in a museum collection of journalism tools at Northwestern University.

The photojournalists each had their hand-held cameras at the ready and were rehearsing in their minds the questions they would ask about what today's meeting had accomplished.

Wallace was fascinated as he quietly watched the behind-the-scenes technical aspects of what was happening. He had been watching the crew members of the ship as they went about their business in the control room. He marveled at how accurate the Star Wars ride at Disneyland had been. He was comparing it to this real flight. He was familiar with hydraulic assisted flight simulators and virtual reality video games and how realistic those things were. He began to type those observations into his laptop. He smiled as he added these thoughts to his rough draft story. In a way, the "what if" of the whole thing was funny.

He was just finishing off his final sip or two of cold coffee when the Steward returned with a carafe of hot coffee for him. (How very observant they were).

Returning to his typing, he continued, "For so many years, you and I have been able to play realistic Virtual Reality games that would transport us to different worlds. When we could couple the visual with physical sensory activity, it seemed so very realistic. I must applaud the makers of those games for their skills at creating such marvels of reality. As we took our trip today, I was struck by how accurate our creations are compared to what we've experienced here today orbiting the earth. As we passed over the Northern Pacific Ocean, I looked down and thought of how our many friends and family members must have felt as they were taken aboard a ship such as this. The fleet of ships must have been enormous"

"As we anticipate the outcome of this high-level meeting, many are wondering why a candidate for the European Commission Presidency would be involved. Paolino Esposito holds no position of power currently in European government. Apparently, even the Andromedins see it as a foregone conclusion that Esposito will be the one to head up the Commission."

The door to the conference room opened and the entourage re-entered the passenger compartment. Word began to circulate among the correspondents.

One of them had questioned the Steward and found out that the tall thin man was Ambassador Baalazaar from the Andromeda Galaxy. He moved forward and stepped to the podium.

As he did so, one of the Andromedin security personnel approached Lombardo and handed him a Tablet. Lombardo scanned the document and swiftly moved toward Le Roux, who leaned into him to listen intently.

He passed along the information, "Sir, the one in Row 5, Port side window seat, I don't like what he has been saying in his story. I'm afraid he could cause trouble for us."

Le Roux looked at the tablet and responded, "We must keep a close eye on this one. If he is trouble, find out what is dear to him and perhaps we will need to intervene. Being able to read what is written by each of these people with each key stroke is very good asset."

"You're most likely correct, but I'm not totally convinced he has any idea about what really is happening here," Lombardo scanned the tablet once again. He was looking for clues. Was Wallace suspicious about this ride into space? What does he think he has figured out?

Ambassador Baalazaar stepped forward to the podium. Everyone reached for their earpiece to listen to the translation of what was about to be said.

"Ladies and gentlemen of Earth, I trust that you have had an enjoyable trip with us today. We have been spending our time together orbiting your home planet. Our cruise today has allowed leaders of Earth and citizens of the Andromeda Galaxy to reach decisions, regarding the people who have left Earth. We selected people who could communicate the needs of Earth and return someday to you, having learned new technologies that will make your lives better on your home planet. We have agreed to send communications from your loved ones within the next year."

It had only been a moment since Baalazaar had passed by. Wallace scrunched up his nose. He wiped his eyes and commented silently, "Did someone strike a match in here? What is that smell?"

Each of the reporters was typing rapidly or recording either audio, or audio and video. Wallace looked across the aisle at Suzanne Coppin of British Satellite News, who had a look of intensity in her eyes. She was rapidly typing on her Notebook. She looked over at Wallace and said, "Robert, did you lose anyone in this migration of people to the Andromeda Galaxy?"

"I knew a few folks who are no longer around. They disappeared right around the same time. I didn't lose family members, so I doubt I'll be hearing from anyone."

She paused a moment as she stared wistfully out the window, "I lost my grandmother. She was a retired teacher who had taught English Literature for forty years. I suppose the Andromedins needed to learn about our society through our stories and poems. That might be the reason that they took her away because she labored quietly those forty years. I'm sure she's not the only English Literature teacher they took with them, but I wonder why they chose her?"

Wallace responded, "I wonder why many of the missing people were taken. There are so many reports that children from infancy to about age ten or so were among them. What would the Andromedins want with them?"

"That's one question I'd like to ask as well."

"Not if I ask it first," Wallace continued typing, adding to his list of questions. "I'll make a deal with you, you ask why they took the old, retired English Lit teachers. I want to know what value a child would be to a 'cultural exchange' between our peoples and theirs."

Ambassador Baalazaar paused for a moment as he looked at his notes, "I know that there are still many unanswered questions and your readers, viewers and listeners want to know what has happened. As we continue in this process of learning from each other, those questions will be answered, I'm sure. I'd like to ask the man who organized this meeting to step up here for a statement or two and then we will open the session to questions from you. Ladies and gentlemen, I present Monsieur Albert Le Roux."

Le Roux stepped to the podium, "Thank you, Mr. Ambassador. Ladies and gentlemen, thank you for coming today to share this historic event. Signor Paolino Esposito is one of the leading candidates for becoming the next President of the European Commission. I thought it would be important for him to meet with the distinguished people of Andromeda Galaxy. Signor Esposito has many great ideas for moving forward in this relationship between our planet, and the people of Andromeda. We have learned so much because of our friendship with the people from our neighboring galaxy: The leaps and bounds in computer technology and aviation; the advances in communication satellites in the past few decades have grown by leaps and bounds. I have personally benefitted because of the success of much of this technology. A long time ago someone from Andromeda, shared knowledge with someone from Earth. and our lives have changed completely. Communications technology has allowed us to save lives with rapid deployment of First Responders to emergency situations of every type. Now, I would like to introduce to you, Signor Paolino Esposito, a top candidate to lead The European Commission. He and the Ambassador have just agreed to some exciting research that will make our economy become the number one economy in the world."

Esposito stepped forward to the podium. He smiled and nodded toward the cameras as they zoomed in from a three shot to a single shot on him, "Thank you Monsieur Le Roux. I am honored to be here today and to be a part of this historic event which will have tremendous benefits for the entire human race."

"For decades, the technology has existed to miniaturize massive amounts of information. As you know, for several years, Le Roux Industries has been a leader in the development of this technology. It is exciting to know that not only can we store medical and financial information on a piece of media smaller than a grain of rice, but I have just struck an agreement with our hosts that will expand our technological horizons even more. With the help of the Andromedins, we will soon be able to upload information from each unit in real time. That information can then be stored in one of more than a dozen data centers. That is not necessarily a new idea. However, it is the best news about what is coming in the next generation of implanted devices. What is being developed is a device that can collect information imported directly from the host's brain. A device with continual updates can literally become a part of the person with the implanted device."

Wallace began to fidget slightly as he remembered some of the things that Pastor Hann had shared with him. For many years, some companies have been implanting chips into the hands of employees for security purposes. Hann had mentioned that in the Bible it mentions that someday, people would be able to do business only if they accept what is known as the "Mark of the Beast." It would be something placed on the right hand or the forehead. The Bible says that people who took that "mark" would be swearing allegiance to a world leader that people used to call the Anti-Christ. He typed into his laptop, "Mark of the Beast?"

Esposito continued speaking, "As you can see, this new technology will afford us the opportunity to do things that have never before been possible for humans. Some researchers believe that someday, we will be able to communicate with each other without speaking. When those devices can 'download' our thoughts, we will be able to communicate with each other without the person speaking. It also would allow us to detect illnesses incredibly early and be able to cure some diseases before they even get started. As you recall, just last year, medical science was able to eradicate practically every kind of cancer. Imagine if our parents' generation had access to this kind of technology, cancer could have been wiped out in the Twentieth Century."

Esposito looked toward Le Roux, who nodded slightly to him. Esposito continued, "So ladies and gentlemen, at this time you may ask questions of Monsieur Le Roux, our hosts from Andromeda or myself regarding anything you have seen here today."

Le Roux stepped forward and took over, "We'll begin with a question from Oscar Walters, Science Editor of the New York Times."

Oscar Walters was representing the print media at this conference. He rose and addressed those standing at the podium, "Mr. Ambassador, as we understand it, you are able to travel from your galaxy to ours in a relatively short period of time as we measure it on Earth. How are you able to do so, and will we soon have that technology in our space programs?"

Ambassador Baalazaar began to speak. For those in the electronic media, the direct feed to the translators fed into a central device which translated what was said into virtually every language on earth, "That is a very good question. As you may or may not know, we measure 'time' as you call it a little differently than you do on earth. For example, what you would call a minute, or an hour are broken down into one hundred units instead of sixty, as you have on Earth. We can cover great distances through deep space by manipulating what your scientists have for a century or two called Black Holes, or Worm Holes. Those are channels that can take us great distances through space in a very rapid amount of time. Therefore, we can travel what you would call one hundred Light Years in about ten or fifteen minutes of your Earth time."

Suzanne Coppin of BSN raised her hand and was acknowledged, "Mr. Ambassador, regarding the people of Earth who were taken to your home planet, how were those people chosen?"

There was no reaction on his face, and the Andromedin spoke in a flat tone, "They were chosen randomly at times, but also, people who were highly educated were chosen. Our desire was people who could learn from us, as well as those who have much to share with us."

Coppin continued, "That answers one question for me personally, why would my grandmother be one of those chosen for a cultural exchange? She was a highly educated woman and teacher." She glanced toward Wallace and smiled a wry smile and then continued, "Many of our viewers would like to know why you would take children."

Le Roux looked toward the Andromedin and smiled slightly as the Ambassador spoke, "The simple fact is, Ms. Coppin, children offer great hope for the future. Children of all ages can absorb so much new information.

Wallace raised his hand and spoke urgently. He didn't wait to be called upon, "Signor Esposito, Robert

Wallace of the Central News Agency USA. Is there any research about the safety of the implanted microchips?"

Esposito smiled with the practiced smile of a true politician, and began dancing around the issue, "Thank you, Mr. Wallace. For approximately the past forty years, these microchips have been used to store information in dogs, cats, and other animals. Physiologically, animals have had no problems after the first few years. And those early problems had more to do with unsanitary injections of the chips, which caused infections. The chips themselves seemed to work well and helped many people be reunited with their precious animal companions. In the past decade or so, microchips have been in use in humans. When various companies began using the chips for their employees, some of those same problems happened with unsanitary injections causing infections. However, people learned from their mistakes, and those problems have been overcome. As with the animal companions, the information stored on the chips was very handy for the companies involved. Personnel records could be stored and updated quickly. Also, there was the security factor in the microchips. With the identification information stored on the chips, someone whose security clearance is not high enough could immediately be prevented from entering a secure area."

Wallace followed-up immediately, "Don't you think that there could be privacy issues? People may not want the chip implanted. Also, is there any way that a person could opt out and have the chip removed? And what about hacking and stealing of personal information."

Smirking slightly, Esposito replied, "I do not believe, Mr. Wallace, that anyone will opt out of the program. We have been moving slowly toward a cashless society for many years. This will make it easier to conduct business and it enhances security. The security protocols are beyond anything we have seen. The Ambassador tells me that the best hackers in any galaxy have been unsuccessful at trying to steal information from any of the chips, once implanted. Reprogramming anything in these chips is virtually impossible."

Wallace quickly countered with, "The old adage in America has always been, 'The minute you make something idiot proof, they'll come up with a better idiot.'"

"I assure you, Mr. Wallace, we are not dealing with idiots of any kind." It was obvious by his expression that Esposito was tiring of this line of questions.

Le Roux summoned Lombardo to follow him to the conference room. Inside the spacious room Le Roux spoke harshly to Lombardo, "I do not like that American's questions. He is accusing me of misconduct."

Lombardo replied, "American journalists have always thought that all leaders are corrupt liars, so they suspect the worst. They influence their viewers to be suspicious of what their leaders are doing."

"That is true, but we cannot afford to have people suspect us of doing anything that would harm them. Remember, it is our goal currently to guide a lost world in the right direction. People are worried. They worry that such a large portion of our population has just disappeared. They worry that another world war is on the near horizon. It is up to us to quell any kind of talk that would add to public fears."

Lombardo knew what his task would be. It was up to him to make sure that Wallace or anyone else could not impede the progress being made by Le Roux. This man has great plans to bring peace and prosperity to this world.

He stepped to the rear, checked over his shoulder at the conference room entrance, then opened the rear door to the compartment. Convinced that no one inside the vehicle saw him exit, he stepped down two steps. He looked around the large hangar filled with people, and handed a paper to a man in coveralls, "Read this note and then shred it."

The man glanced down and read the note, "To: William Davidson, V.P. and CEO, Lombardo Security, USA. Check into the background of CNA journalist

Robert Wallace. Make his life miserable. Put your best people on this to stop him from reporting any story that would negatively reflect upon Le Roux Industries and the current meeting with representatives of the Andromeda Galaxy. He must be stopped. Also, you may use anyone close to him for persuasion." The man nodded and stepped out of sight as Lombardo closed the door.

CHAPTER 4

Olivia Meyer stood in front of the building that housed the Manhattan District Attorney's offices. She searched the streets for a taxi. Dozens sped past her. She stepped into the street and managed to get a Yellow Cab to pull over. As she climbed into the back seat, there he was again lurking on the sidewalk just outside the main door of her office building. The man had a dark, foreboding presence about him. He looked like an ex-military special forces man who was in top physical condition. He had what appeared to be a scar on his right cheek from a bullet that had grazed him in a close quarter combat situation. For the past few hours, she had seen him several times. The man seemed to have been following her for the past few hours. As she had made her way between her office and the courts, the man with the slicked-back black hair and an expensive Italian suit was lingering and watching her, as she would pass by his location. The first time she noticed him he was in the Criminal Courts Building just around the corner from her office on Hogan Place.

As she climbed into the cab and told the driver her destination, she investigated her compact mirror and saw the man jump into the next available cab. As her cab pulled away, she told the driver her destination. As they headed for Dominic's Fine Dining, she noticed that the cab behind hers stayed close.

At Dominic's, she exited her cab and walked quickly to the front door. She turned and saw the man get out of his cab two doors away.

Olivia made her way to the rear of the restaurant and found a seat in the corner booth near the kitchen. Holding the large leather-bound menu in front of her face, she felt safely hidden from her stalker. Who was this man and what did he want?

As an Assistant District Attorney, she was used to seeing unsavory characters within proximity. Usually, it was nothing. After all, they were near the Criminal Courts building. She decided on the corned beef on rye and slowly lowered the menu. There he was, two booths down, across the aisle. He was facing her, slowly stirring his rum and Coke. He nodded to her, raised his glass, and smiled a half smile.

He rose from his booth and walked to hers. He placed his drink on her table and sat down, "Do you mind if I join you, Miss Meyer?"

"Do I actually have a choice? I'm afraid I don't know you. I just came in here for a quick lunch."

"My name is Andrew Benetti. I work for the American branch of a European security agency."

Olivia eyed him as she took a sip of her water. "Mr. Benetti, why have you been following me? And what does a European security agency want with me?"

Benetti took a drink and fiddled with his cuff links. He broke the silence, "Miss Meyer, you are familiar with the journalist Robert Wallace, correct?"

Olivia was still feeling upset with Robert because the last time they spoke, he was rather curt with her and hung up without saying good-bye. "Yes, I knew him. But I haven't seen him for more than a year. Why do you want to know?"

"We happen to know that at one time you and Wallace were very close."

A look of melancholy crossed Olivia's face, "Yes, there was a time that Bobby and I were *very* close. I thought we'd get married and have a life together. But that just wasn't in the cards for us."

Then Benetti spoke the words that stung deeply, "You had a child with Mr. Wallace, didn't you?"

Olivia was seething, "I don't know where you got this kind of information, but it is none of your business."

Benetti rose from the booth and started to leave. "Miss Meyer, we have made it our business. He won't be around much longer. There are people who want to silence him. And he will be silenced."

With that, Benetti turned and walked out of the restaurant.

Olivia sat in total disbelief.

The countryside in east-central Ohio was cool and damp following a July rain. Even though it had cooled the temperature, the humidity was increasing. Pastor Hann, from Scottdale, Pennsylvania, was entering an area just northeast of Dresden, Ohio. There were small cabins scattered around. At one end of the site was a large shelter with about two dozen picnic tables jammed against the north wall. It was musty and rather dreary. Not far away was the Muskingum River. It was a peaceful setting that at one time had been a vibrant Boy Scout camp known as Camp Dickerson. The Dickerson family had donated a portion of their farmland to the Scouts for a camp. Adjacent to the camp, the Dickerson farm still was used to grow corn and there were at least thirty acres of peach orchards. The peaches had a reputation in that portion of Muskingum and Coshocton Counties as being sweet, succulent treats.

Hann was with a small group of people from his church. They each carried note pads and back packs with sleeping bags attached. The trip here had taken them nearly seven hours. They had taken many back roads to avoid detection. Hann felt that the long trip was worth it to find some like-minded individuals.

Correspondence with other pastors in western Pennsylvania, and eastern Ohio, had brought them together. People who were not taken in the Rapture found themselves now becoming strong believers. They joined Hann on this pilgrimage.

Reverend Hann walked toward the man in the clerical collar, the man he had been seeking. Hann extended his right hand, and with a warm smile he said, "Father Reilly, James Hann from Scottdale, Pennsylvania. I have with me five members of my congregation who have made a new commitment to Christ, the commitment we should have all made years ago."

Reilly was a Roman Catholic Priest who, like Hann, had changed from a life of religion to a life of following Christ. He was dressed in a traditional black suit with a black shirt and white clerical collar. The shirt was dirty after being worn while doing some hard labor, converting the old Boy Scout campground into a new camp for refugees of faith. After shaking hands with Hann, he apologized, "Pastor Hann, please pardon my dirty hands, welcome to New Zion. We have been busy cleaning up this old campground. It has been here since the late 1940s. I am honored that you and your friends came here from Pennsylvania. We hope that this will be a place where we can gather and worship the Lord without any interference from the authorities, or anyone in the hierarchy of any church organization."

"I'm hoping that as well. It is our belief that we can help each other and at the same time spread out into the countryside and help others who missed the Rapture. They still must find the grace that our loving God wants us to share with the entire world." Hann stepped over to one of the picnic tables, put down the large briefcase, which was jammed full of books, including his precious Bible. He had been carrying this Bible since he left United Lutheran Seminary in Gettysburg. He loved his time at seminary. Besides his major in Divinity, he had always been a student of United States History. From the school at 61 Seminary Ridge, he could survey the entire battlefield upon which so many young American boys had shed their blood, those dreadful first three days of July 1863.

This new location was a beautiful spot for gathering the new flock to do the hard work that lay ahead. Around the perimeter of the campground was a lush forest of Beech, Tulip Poplar and of course, Buckeye trees. The Buckeye trees were the tallest in the surrounding woods. They stood as much as sixty to seventy feet high and were close to two feet in diameter. It was, to Hann, reminiscent of much of his beloved Western Pennsylvania.

He was only going to be here for a few days, and then he would return to Scottdale, for his next Sunday service. The congregants were few, but he knew he had to be there for them.

The journey into space was coming to an end. Wallace, Coppin and all the others were preparing for the landing by finishing their initial rough drafts of their stories. They compared notes and impressions of the journey.

Wallace noticed that he had come under the harsh gaze of Lombardo and Baalazaar. It made him a little bit nervous, but then, as an investigative reporter, it was just the sort of thing that he lived for. He sat silently as he packed his laptop back into its carrying case and stared out the window. The sky was beginning to get lighter, and then suddenly there was a loud roar followed by a dazzling red, yellow and blue light show of flames outside the windows. Many people let out fearful gasps. Others were used to the many stories of space craft re-entering Earth's atmosphere, and the friction that caused a great deal of fire.

As the flames began to lessen, there was a shaking of the entire cabin and the sound of deceleration. The Earth below began to get larger as south western France came into view. It was beautiful. The space port at La Palue came into sight, and before they knew it, they were hovering just a few feet off the ground outside the massive hangar from which they had departed. They began to slowly back into the hangar just as they had left it only eight hours earlier.

Wallace was closely observing the personnel and the positions they took as the craft backed into the hangar. "That guy had a long shift. He was in that same place when we left. What a boring job," he said to Suzanne Coppin. They both agreed that it looked so very similar. The lighting was very strange. It was almost as though it were filtered light, giving off an artificial glow. Even though everyone looked as though they had not moved from their previous positions.

Again, Wallace noticed the piercing stare of Lombardo, "I wonder what that guy wants with me. I'm not sure that I like him at all."

Coppin smiled and said, "Be careful, Mate. He looks like the kind who used to take your lunch money and then stuff you into a locker."

They both laughed, but there was an air of truth to the light-hearted comment. Lombardo did not look like the kind of man who would put up with any trouble from anyone, least of all a television reporter.

The ship came to a halt inside the hangar and the stewards came to each row, dismissing people to the exit. Being in row five, Wallace was one of the early departures. There, just outside the hangar, was the company hired limo.

The driver waved to Wallace and beckoned him over, "Welcome back, Monsieur. Did you have a good meeting?"

"Yes, very informative. It's amazing what they can do these days."

"Oui, Monsieur. Right after you went into the hangar, the security personnel came and gathered up all of us who were waiting for you. They took us into a very nice lounge near the main offices. We were fed a very good lunch, and we had plenty of coffee and soft drinks. And the pastries were magnifique. The time passed by so quickly we didn't even notice you had left."

Wallace climbed into the back seat and began to think about all he had seen and heard today. They began their long drive back to Charles-de-Gaulle-Paris Airport. He passed the time away reading his notes in the laptop. He looked at the brochure that had been handed out. It was very professional. A top-notch PR firm had put together a fine presentation. He remembered the physical sensations of all aspects of the flight. Then there were the visual effects. He began thinking of how many virtual reality games he had played when he was younger, and how completely realistic the CGI effects had become. Then he wondered if he was reading too much into this whole situation.

Another thing was bothering him. What was all the talk about those microchips being inserted under the skin? Downloading information from your brain into the chips seemed fantastic.

Taking out his laptop, he began typing some random thoughts about the day's activities. "A trip into space that was as smooth as sitting in your own living room. Visually, it was so very real. Some of the Andromedins appeared to perhaps be robotic. Something about Ambassador Baalazaar was so very disquieting. I can't put my finger on it, but I just didn't really trust him. Paolino Esposito was the kind of man who could persuade anyone to do whatever he wanted them to do. Even though he has only held lower-level political positions, he was as polished as any politician I've ever seen. All the talk about implanted microchips was a little hard to swallow. What about privacy? Maybe Europeans don't care about that, but in the States, we cherish our privacy. What's next?"

As his limo pulled up to the terminal building for Trans-Atlantic Airlines, Wallace exited the car. The driver handed him the small bag in which Wallace had packed only a few things. Perhaps he wouldn't have to check the bag and could just carry it on board with him.

Just thirty feet away from Wallace, a man was watching him closely as he passed through security. The mystery man had not been noticed by Wallace. The man was dressed in coveralls and an orange vest, as though he worked at the airport. As Wallace placed his bags on the conveyer at the security checkpoint and as he was cleared, the two men made brief eye contact. Wallace felt that there was something wrong. A chill shot down his spine. He started toward his gate, but there was baggage cart in the way. He moved it aside and continued.

The man went to the side of the security area, showed his ID badge, and was ushered through. He went out the tarmac access door next to Gate 27 A and down the stairs to the baggage handling area. He stepped up to the baggage access door. He took the place of the worker who was already there. Once inside the baggage hold, he reached into his vest pocket and pulled out a small device that appeared to be a timer attached to an explosive device. He placed it directly under the part of the cabin where Wallace's seat, 14C, would be. The timer was set to go off in four hours, just south of Iceland, somewhere over the North Atlantic.

In the waiting area at Gate 27A, Wallace sat reading reports filed by other reporters who had made the trip with him. They were all glowing reports of a smooth trip around the world at least sixteen times. The main emphasis of each of these online reports was the excitement for the soon-to-come new technology that would supposedly enhance world banking and security.

Still, something in Wallace's mind was making him very uncomfortable. He thought about the man who was watching him so closely. He turned to look out the window at his plane, and noticed the man crawling into the baggage hatch. Who was this guy? Wallace stood up to stretch his legs. The foreboding that he felt made him pick up his bag and laptop carrier and exit the concourse. Had he heard an audible command to "Go" or was it just his imagination?

With his head moving as if on a swivel he made his way to the exit and caught a cab. He told the driver to take him to Saint-Lazare Rail Station at 3, Rue d'Amsterdam. He was formulating his plan as they drove through the streets of Paris. So much history here. The Eiffel Tower, the small bistros where American writers and artists had spent much of the Jazz age between the two World Wars of the Twentieth Century. Such romance was passing by him so quickly, as they sped along. In the distance he could see the outline to Notre Dame. He remembered looking through old video reports of the massive fire that had nearly destroyed the famous structure in 2019. It was amazing how quickly it had been restored to its historic glory.

At the station, after paying the driver, he entered the cavernous terminal. Inside, he studied the trains and their departure times. His plan was to get to Calais and make his way across the Channel and then fly home from London. Which was the earliest train? He chose one that would depart in fifteen minutes.

CHAPTER 5

What was it that had made Wallace so paranoid? Why was this time different than all the times he was uncovering some vast conspiracy by business leaders or politicians during his career? He had been threatened many times in his professional life, but now he was truly nervous. He was still watching the faces of everyone who looked like they could be a spy. It was such a "cloak and dagger" feeling. No one seemed to be paying any attention to him this time. Perhaps he was just paranoid, but he was sure that he wasn't supposed to take that Trans-Atlantic Air flight. He made his way to the platform and quickly boarded the train that would take him out of France.

The Departure of the Calais-bound train was right on time. He was on the next leg of his trip home. He had so many questions. Why was he being watched?

On his laptop he opened the file with his notes from the trip into space. He read those thoughts he had put down digitally. He turned off the Wi-Fi connection to prevent anyone finding him on his trip out of France. Someone must have been reading everything that he had written. His questions about the reality of what he had experienced. He quickly shut down his laptop. It was a precaution that he probably didn't need to worry about, but he'd rather be safe about it. At least, he had backed everything up on a Flash Drive. That way, he can find another laptop and then upload from Drive D.

The French countryside was peacefully flowing by at a quick pace. The sun had gone down at about the same time Wallace boarded the train. He would be ready to board the cross-Channel Ferry at about Sunrise. Sitting in his tiny compartment, he decided to try and get some sleep.

The passengers were settling in for their flight from Paris to New York's JFK. Seat 14C was unoccupied, so Johnny Thompson, the young man in 14D, moved his laptop onto the empty seat. He leaned forward to look out the window next to his new bride. The two of them first met in Paris, two years ago. After returning home to Harvard Law, they decided to return to Paris, for their wedding. He watched as the coastline swiftly moved beneath them.

He smiled at her and said, "Well, Mrs. Thompson, what do you say we agree to come back every year for our anniversary?"

"Ms. Steinhardt-Thompson if you don't mind. And yes, I think that's a great idea." This was something they had been eagerly awaiting, for the past ten months. With all that had been happening in the world, they kept putting off the trip until things settled down. Now that there was an explanation as to where their friends had gone, they felt comfortable moving on with their lives.

The voice came on the intercom, "Ladies and gentlemen, from the flight deck, this is Captain Miller speaking. We are approaching our cruising altitude of thirty thousand feet. We anticipate smooth cruising as the weather ahead is clear all the way to JFK. We should arrive there on time unless otherwise notified. Despite the delay leaving de-Gualle, we are easily making up time.

The flight was close to forty-five minutes late leaving Paris and now people worried that they might miss their connections at JFK.

As the plane came near Icelandic airspace it shuddered with the muffled sound of an explosion in the baggage compartment below the cabin. In the Cockpit, the captain and first officer looked at each other with terror in their eyes. From the cabin they could hear screams of fear. The cabin lost pressure and began a rapid descent from nearly thirty-thousand feet toward the icy-cold North Atlantic below.

In the cabin there was a large hole in the floor below row 14. The people in that row were gone. Flight attendants reacted with the quick reflexes for which all their training had prepared them. Smoke was billowing up through the hole in the floor. Fire extinguishers were put into action immediately. People were starting to be overcome by the lack of pressure in the cabin. The roar rivaled that of a close passing freight train. Seats near row 14 were beginning to sag terribly sliding into the hole.

The plane had fallen twenty thousand feet in only a minute or so. There was fear from the crew that the plane would disintegrate. The pilots were fighting to regain control. They performed a forward slip to drop with more control. They were calling out to Iceland seeking emergency landing instructions. The situation was becoming more and more desperate. The plane was shaking severely. Just as they were approaching Iceland the captain warned the cabin crew to prepare for a hard landing.

"This is going to be a rough one, Tom. I'm going to try to make it to that glacier over there. It's not perfectly flat, but maybe some people will survive this. They continued to lose altitude fast, and it was becoming clear that they wouldn't make it to the smoothest part of the glacier.

The plane clipped the extreme south end of the glacier and began to break apart. The fuselage broke into four pieces. People and seats went in all directions. Luggage and cargo were scattered everywhere. The wings broke off the big jet splashing fuel over a wide area. Sparks set off the fuel that trailed behind the spinning, forward section of the fuselage. Fuel that remained in the small-still intact wing sections caught fire and exploded, sending shrapnel flying into the air. Any survivors in the cabin were in danger of being impaled by shards of metal and composite material. When all the turmoil had died down a few people managed to make their way out onto the glacier. They were struggling to move with broken legs and torn muscle. It was a devastating sight. Miraculously, there were at least fifteen survivors. Some others were beginning to make their way out of the rear portion of the jet.

Now, the only sounds came from the whimpering injured people, all walking around in a daze. The fires had burned out quickly. Soon more survivors made their way out of the twisted wreckage. It appeared that the total was now thirty survivors.

Wallace arrived in Calais, France. He didn't want to check his laptop to see what was happening in the world. He needed to see how close he could come to going off-grid. He paid cash for a ticket on the Ferry to get across the Channel for the ninety-minute journey to England and boarded right away. He was ecstatic that he had arrived in time for the next departure.

The Spirit of Britain departed right on time, and Wallace was finally off the Continent. Dover was just ninety minutes away. He had thrown away his phone, so his first stop in Dover would be to buy a new disposable phone. *The Spirit of Britain* was a good, stable boat. There were only about one hundred passengers on board. Wallace leaned on the rail near the Forecastle and watched as the White Cliffs of Dover drew closer. He left the railing and headed for the lounge. It was early in the day, so he just ordered a coffee. The strong, black brew was just what he needed, as he looked around at the twenty people in the lounge at the time.

Wallace began to hear conversations among some of the passengers about an airliner that was missing near Iceland. There was no information regarding what flight it was, but apparently it had departed Paris just a few hours ago. He checked his watch and thought back on his time waiting in the terminal. He thought again about the strange man who seemed so interested in him, and why he had suddenly crawled into the plane Wallace was scheduled to board. It couldn't be the same plane, could it? He shuddered to think that someone may be after him for reasons unknown. If someone were after him, how could any civilized person try to bring down an airliner just to kill one man? It couldn't be the same plane. His flight must be almost to JFK by now. Until he would find out anything different, he was content to deny that it could happen.

The crossing of the Channel was relatively uneventful. At this, the narrowest part, the English Channel can be very rough at certain times of the year. This July day, however, the crossing was as calm as anyone could imagine, a quick ninety minutes, and Wallace was ready to be on dry land once again. Even with the morning breeze cooling things a bit, the temperature was heading for a nice seventy-five degrees this afternoon. Wallace didn't have plans to spend the afternoon in Dover, however.

Leaving the harbor, Wallace made his way to the business district. He soon saw a business that had just what he was looking for. "Mobiles to rent." The Brits call cell phones, "mobiles". It was a phone store. He would not have to buy it. A temporary phone with a temporary number. He checked his wallet and found that he still had enough cash. He would not have to leave a paper trail.

He paid cash for the phone. As he hailed a cab to take him to the railway station, be called Suzanne Coppin at BSN. It took several minutes for her to answer.

"Suzanne Coppin."

"Hi Suzanne, Bob Wallace here, I'm on my way to London" there was a silence on the line for a moment and he thought that perhaps he had been disconnected.

Coppin responded with some suspicion in her voice, "Bobby? You… how did… Bobby, is it really you?"

"Yes, it is. What do you mean, 'is it really you?'"

"I thought you were on that flight that went down! I mean, the news out of New York is that CNA reporter Robert Wallace was listed on the manifest for Trans-Atlantic Air flight 225. It went down somewhere near Iceland. It disappeared from Radar just south of Iceland."

"Oh, my dear God… I changed my mind and skipped out on that flight. I took the ferry. I can't really explain why I did that. I mean I had already passed through security, and then…"

"Bobby, we need to stop right here. Where are you now… no wait, don't say anything… the number you are using looks like a local phone. When you get to London, page me at Charing-Cross Station. When can you be there?"

"I'll see you in exactly two and a half hours."

"Be careful, Bobby. Watch your back. I mean it. Be careful."

He hung up and was shaking as the reality hit him someone wanted him dead. Why would someone want to kill him? Or perhaps he wasn't really a target, and it was just coincidence that the plane he was supposed to be on crashed in the North Atlantic.

Reports were just beginning to come in with more frequency to the CNA newsroom. There were reports that the plane Robert Wallace was booked on made its way to land and crashed on a glacier. There were unconfirmed reports that there had been some survivors. News Director, Angela Martindale, was ordering everyone to check with all their contacts to find out if Wallace was still among the living.

The reports were not encouraging. Icelandic officials were saying almost all on board perished. The injured were seriously hurt and many of them might not make it. They had to know. There were next-of-kin protocols, and even though Robert was a public figure, no one wanted his mother to find out about his death on television. Other outlets were being discreet by stating that an American journalist may have been on the flight, but nothing had been confirmed.

Daniel Schaffer

Albert Le Roux's phone rang on the private line. He reached across his desk, cleared his throat, and picked it up. The voice on the other end was that of his head of security, Colonel Vito Lombardo. His words were right to the point, "It has been accomplished."

Le Roux thanked him and hung up. He smiled, thinking of himself as the power broker controlling his hand-picked man, who would make Europe into the world's most powerful "nation".

All his plans have been falling into place. Up to this point he had been behind the creation of some of the most elaborate space craft simulation equipment on Earth. He had courted a brilliant young politician who was as eager as he to rule over Europe as one nation. He then contacted his life-long friend Baalazaar and his "alien civilization", or so it appeared, and used this to enhance his plans.

It was true, millions of people were missing. His elaborate planning, and the quick thinking of his staff of leadership-minded people, seem to have found the answer to the mystery.

They had given the world's leading correspondents a news story that they disseminated to their audiences a new set of facts.

The one potential stumbling block in his plan was now no longer a problem, and the way forward would now be unencumbered.

Feeling very good about all this, he clicked the intercom button and told his secretary to summon Paolino Esposito and Cardinal Assidi to his office.

The train ride from Dover to London had been just a little more than an hour. Wallace picked up a paging phone at Charing-Cross Station. He paged BSN knowing that Suzanne would understand it was he who was paging her.

Within short order, the phone rang, and he answered it, "Yankee Stadium, visitors' dugout. How may I direct your call?"

Wallace could hear the smile in Coppin's voice as she said, "You are so cryptic. I'm at baggage claim."

Wallace started to cross the massive lobby of the facility. There was such a clamor as the sound of thousands of heels on the hard floor was almost overwhelming. There had to have been two-thousand people moving along in a finely choreographed dance. He wove his way in and out of the crowd as though he was the lead dancer.

Coppin saw him approaching her. People were arriving or preparing to depart in all different directions. The cacophony of so many voices speaking many different languages besides English and Fre filled the room. London was truly an international city. She raised her right arm so he could see, and he responded in kind.

As they closed the distance, she was the first to speak, "Bobby, I am not sure if you are aware of the magnitude of what has happened. A few hours after you were to depart Paris, an airliner went missing in the North Atlantic, just south of Iceland. Apparently, the pilot was able to make it to land and managed a crash landing on the Vatmajokull Glacier. There were thirty survivors, initially, but since then, five of them have died. They say there had been a small bomb in the baggage compartment that blew a hole in the deck, taking out a whole row of seats, and blowing a hole in the fuselage. As the pilots fought to bring it in for a landing, the skin around the hole began to peel away. Control became harder, making a safe landing impossible."

Wallace stood there, stunned as he took in all that she was saying, "I may be able to describe the man who placed the device."

They began walking out of the station to Coppin's Mini Cooper. He tossed his bags into the back seat. Out of habit he started to enter the right front door, "Oh, steering wheel over here. It's been a ...een to England. I forgot myself."

CHAPTER 6

"What do you mean, he wasn't on the flight?" Albert Le Roux was livid as he paced back and forth between his large oak desk and Colonel Vito Lombardo.

Lombardo had faced some of the most hardened criminals and enemy special forces for most of his professional life, but he was just a little tentative as he searched for answers for his employer. "Monsieur Le Roux, I put our best man on this. He placed a bomb that was just large enough to eliminate Wallace and should have allowed the crew to safely land in Iceland. Something went wrong. Perhaps the charge was too large for the intended job. At any rate, had he been on the flight, he would have been among the dead."

"Why didn't we have someone else watching Wallace leave the terminal? There is no excuse for this man to still be alive. I fear that he is one who could potentially be a major thorn in our side and interfere with our plans. I don't care what you have to do, but you must find him and eliminate him," Le Roux said as he turned his back to Lombardo and walked toward the bookshelves lined with books on international law.

It was as though Lombardo had just had a sudden genius thought, "I am sure that we can find a few 'witnesses' who saw Wallace place the bomb himself, and then leave the airport in a hurry. We just don't know where he went from there."

Le Roux smiled a crooked smile as he rubbed his fingers on the edge of his glass. He reached for one of the books, a book on international laws that governed air travel. He turned to Lombardo and said, "We will see to it that his life is ruined and that he is executed for murder. I can see to it that we bring back the Guillotine, a just punishment since the plane was filled with French citizens departing from France. It is only right that he be returned to France. We will find a jury that will convict him easily."

Even though the first part of their plan failed to kill Wallace, both men were satisfied with the second part of their plan.

Lombardo made a promise, "I will utilize every resource at my command and make sure that we find him. We will reach out to the United States, Britain and in France. We will find him."

In the Manhattan District Attorney's office, Olivia Meyer was online looking at the latest notices sent to the DA. She let out an audible scream when she read the announcement that Robert Wallace, news reporter for CNA, had been seen planting an unknown package on the airliner that crashed in Iceland.

It was beyond Olivia's comprehension that the man she had loved at one time and, truth be told, still did love dearly would be capable of such a heinous act. The Bobby Wallace that she knew so well, surely could not be capable of killing people on an international airline flight. She had spent her entire professional life, almost fifteen years, prosecuting hardened criminals. Robert Wallace has absolutely nothing in common with anyone she had ever brought to trial in the past.

She picked up the phone and called Glenn Allen, her contact at the FBI. His private cell phone went straight to voicemail, "Hello, Glenn, Olivia Meyer here. I am totally surprised to hear that Robert Wallace has been accused of murder in the bombing of the Trans-Atlantic Air flight yesterday. I need to know what is going on. What have your team members been hearing? Where is he? How on Earth could he have planted a bomb in a secure area and, more importantly, why? Please call me when you can."

After hanging up, she summoned her investigator, Alan Bricker. She went back to her computer searching for anything else she could find. It appeared that the charges were going to be brought by Interpol. If he was caught in the U.S., he was to be extradited to Paris to be charged in a French court. That only meant one thing. The French had brought back executions by the Guillotine, after many years with no capital punishment.

Alan Bricker entered her office. Bricker was a former NYPD Detective First Grade who had been working with Olivia for the past five years. Their professional relationship was very successful. Bricker's skills as a detective helped assure that all potential defendants were truly guilty, and that all the proper procedures had been followed in preparing to bring them to trial. Bricker was fifty-five years old; his face was handsome with lines and creases revealing years of grueling police work.

Olivia's cell phone rang. It was FBI Special Agent Glenn Allen, "Olivia, Glenn. What can I do for you?"

She quickly grabbed the printout and sat down, "Glenn, thanks for getting back to me. I have a report here that Bob Wallace of CNA is wanted by the government of France for murder. What do you know about that?"

"Olivia, the bad news is, Wallace was booked to be on an airliner from Paris to JFK, and there is a witness who claims that he was seen placing an unknown package in a bag that was later placed onto a baggage cart headed for that plane."

Olivia paused a moment, "How reliable is the witness? I mean, is it possible that the witness could have been mistaken? Or is there any chance that the witness had been paid by someone in order to throw off finding the real killer?"

"I suppose those are possibilities, yes. But there is no reason that it could have happened that way. Investigators were able to find Wallace's fingerprints on the edge of one of the baggage carts that would have delivered bags that were gate-checked in Paris."

After meeting at Charing-Cross Station, Wallace and BSN correspondent Suzanne Coppin were driving across London. They were going to her apartment. She had a proposition for him, "Bobby, you need to get back to the States, but travel on commercial airliners could be dangerous for you. We may have a way to avoid commercial air. I have just been assigned to report for BSN from the White House. It is an exciting opportunity for me professionally. And it is an opportunity to get you there on our corporate jet with me. We're scheduled to depart Heathrow in about an hour and a half."

Coppin was driving as though she were chasing someone through the streets of London. Wallace was leaning hard from left to right like he was helping her by leaning into the turns. He finally broke the tension by asking her, "Whew, is our next stop Le Mans? I think you have a chance at winning there." They shared a light laugh. "When were you assigned the Washington, D.C. post?"

"I found out this morning when I reported to the network. When you called, I had just stepped out of my office. I was going home to grab my 'Go Bag' and leave for Heathrow. We'll depart from the corporate terminal. That beats crowding in with passengers on commercial flights."

Still struggling to hang on, he gritted his teeth and spoke, "Amen to that. I probably don't need to tell you this, but I'm a little leery of commercial flights."

. The Mini-Cooper slid up to the curb, in front of her flat and she spoke as she climbed out, "Just sit tight, Bobby, I will only be a moment to get my bag and we can be on our way. I should only be a few moments."

She trotted across the sidewalk and up the front steps to the lobby. Standing at the elevator, her phone buzzed with an email notification. Her email box was jammed with information from the top stories of the past four days. The latest notification made her gasp as she read the words, "Central News Agency reporter

Robert Wallace is being sought in connection with the murders of passengers on board Trans-Atlantic Air Flight 225."

She was now at a crossroads. She knew where the suspect was right now. However, she had known Wallace for the past three years and was totally convinced that there was no way he could possibly have done anything like that.

She paused, then picked up her bags and headed back to the car. At that moment, she decided to trust Wallace. She could have trouble for harboring a fugitive, but she decided she'd first wait for him to be proven guilty.

Pastor James Hann sat in his office gazing out at the traffic passing by. So much was on his mind. He had, within the past week, taken a group of his parishioners to a small campground in Ohio. He had returned to Scottdale, Pennsylvania to continue shepherding his flock. His desire was to possibly inspire them all to live a closer walk with Christ as Savior.

Hann's sermons for so many years been little more than feel-good messages about Jesus who was a "best buddy". The talks were without calls to individual accountability for our actions. Going to church more a social activity. It was like being a member of a club. This club involved being decent, moral people, who met once a week to discuss how good they had been in the past week. This group of people always felt that they were respectable people, therefore Jesus would be pleased with them, and allow entry to heaven when they died.

Hann felt that now it was time to turn things around. It was different now. Too many people were downplaying the importance of following Jesus.

He was checking news on the internet when he saw the story of Trans-Atlantic Air Flight 225. As he read about the few survivors, he took a moment to pray for them.

Hann continued to read and was shocked when he read about Robert Wallace being suspected of planting the bomb that brought down the airliner. This man could not be the same man that Hann had come to know. Wallace was so very eager to learn about the Rapture. He seemed to think that the theory of space aliens doing a mass abduction of millions of people was not the answer to the question of what had happened to all those people.

He read on and saw that there was evidence against Wallace. Apparently, his fingerprints were found on a baggage cart. That seemed like damning evidence, but Hann still was not convinced.

Coppin sat down in her car, started the engine, but instead of putting it in gear and pulling away from the curb, she turned to Wallace and said, "I don't know if you're aware of this, but you are wanted for murder. Reports say that someone saw you putting a bomb on Flight 225.

"Wait… wait… wait… what are you talking about?"

"Apparently someone saw you plant a bomb on that plane as it sat on the Tarmac."

"But there is no way I could have gotten to that plane to do something like that!" Wallace was stumped. Why would someone say that? He thought back again on the man who bypassed security and went to the baggage loading area before disappearing into the baggage hold. He didn't appear to be a killer, but then again, many hit men don't look like murderers.

Coppin handed her phone to him. It was open to the email with the news report. He read the message. There was the line about his fingerprints being on a baggage cart. He thought back to right after he passed through security. For some reason, unknown to him at the time, there was a baggage cart in his way as he walked toward his gate. Wallace remembered how he reached out and grabbed the cart. He couldn't figure out why that cart was there. Perhaps, someone saw him do that. After it was revealed that he wasn't on the flight, someone figured a way to blame him.

His mind was swirling frantically as he remembered as much as he could about the entire day, beginning with his arrival at the European Space Center. Some people on the ride heard him as he wondered aloud if they were on a ride at Disney World. It's possible that the organizers of the gathering might have been offended by his reaction.

If someone were offended by his perceived indifference, why would they want him dead? If that is the case, why didn't they simply kill him when he was alone, instead of planning on taking so many other people with him?

He looked at his colleague and said, "I am struggling trying to figure out why someone would want me dead."

Coppin shook her head in wonderment. She too had been remembering everything she could about the aftermath of the news conference that followed the ride into space. She was convinced, along with almost every other correspondent there for the trip. It appeared Wallace was the only one there who was not totally impressed with the ride into space, and the news of upcoming technology that would change how the world would do business for the rest of time. He had expressed his concerns about privacy issues. He had also spoken about his fears that hackers could be able to easily steal information. He worried that everyone could lose all their personal information. Everything in a person's life, from banking to healthcare and personal history, being in one location makes it too easy to lose.

He had also spoken about his fears that uploading information from the implanted chip directly into the brain could that allow a central entity to control your thoughts. Paolino Esposito had assured everyone that there was no chance of that happening.

Coppin checked the rear-view mirrors and as she pulled away from the curb she spoke, "I'm beginning to think that perhaps you asked the wrong questions of the wrong people."

"Or maybe, the wrong questions of the right people. Maybe these people stand to gain millions of dollars with this technology. Any disparaging words from national media could end a financial empire before it even got started," he was looking out the window watching the traffic as he pondered what a monster he may have created.

They were on their way to Heathrow for a private jet ride to the United States.

Olivia Meyer's workday had started with the devastating news that the man she had loved for the past five years was a prime suspect in the mass murder of passengers on Trans-Atlantic Airlines flight 225 from

Paris. It had not made it to JFK. She opened the file folder that had each notice about the horrible news of the day. There was a warrant on file with Interpol. French prosecutors wanted him arrested and brought to Paris to face trial.

Never in her professional life had Olivia even considered ignoring a warrant for someone's arrest. She was so convinced that Robert Wallace was not guilty of this heinous crime that she considered ignoring the warrant.

Glenn Allen had been scheduled to meet with her this morning just before she was due in court. Pacing around her office, she could not get Wallace off her mind. She had no idea where Wallace was. Looking outside, it was obvious that the last night's weather forecast was correct. Although the forecast was for rain, it was supposed to hold off until mid-afternoon. The streets below her office had a shiny glow. Rapidly flowing water filled the gutters, dragging leaves and a large amount of trash on its rush to the sewage system. The grating over the opening of the sewer was beginning to be clogged with soda cups, straws, and hamburger wrappers. People are so very sloppy with how they dispose of their personal trash. It really is sad to think that humanity hasn't improved how it cares for the environment. The city produces more than ten thousand tons of trash every day. That trash is gathered by a small army of workers dedicated to moving the waste from Manhattan to trucks exporting it to landfills in Pennsylvania, Virginia, New Jersey, and Upstate New York. Why do people to just throw their trash into the streets?

She was pulled away from her thoughts of careless humans by the arrival of Glenn Allen. Allen stands about five feet ten inches tall. Ruggedly handsome, African-American, with a no-nonsense air about him. As he moved to the front of her desk, she gestured for him to have a seat, "What can you tell me about Robert Wallace, Glenn?"

Allen placed his wet umbrella on the floor next to him, "I'm not totally sure that Wallace is responsible for this crime. He was seen at the airport in Paris, that is true, but he had absolutely no motive for planting an explosive device. And in checking his background, he has zero experience with explosives at all. His military experience was strictly administrative. He was a Third-Class Petty Officer, Personnel Specialist in the Navy. He worked in an office and would not have handled weapons of any kind. He was also a part of Armed Forces Radio and Television Services."

Olivia sat quietly, taking all this in. As she processed the information, she knew that her trust in Wallace was well founded. Once again, she picked up the latest dispatch from Interpol regarding the crime, "I know that people in Europe want him to be arrested and extradited back to France. Do you have anyone there investigating the eyewitness reports? Do they have him on video surveillance planting the device, or at least getting into position to place it on the luggage carrier?"

"No, the footage that I have seen of him getting his fingerprints on the baggage cart simply shows him putting his hand on the cart to move it aside as he moved to his departure gate. Then he sat in the waiting area for about fifteen minutes before getting up and, for reasons unknown, quickly departing the airport."

"Is there anything that the FBI can do to clear his name on this?"

It was obvious in his tone that there wasn't much that could be done by the U.S., "We don't have any authority to investigate in France beyond looking at what Interpol will share with us. What they have shared with us, in my humble opinion, gives us enough to create reasonable doubt. I don't really think, though, that would stand up to scrutiny in an international court."

Olivia was tapping a pencil on her desktop, "Please see what you can do, Glenn, to muddy the waters for us. We need enough time to mount a good defense for him."

"Olivia, I will do whatever I can to keep him from being sent back to France, but I have very limited powers for this."

Allen then picked up his umbrella and raincoat and left her office. She turned back to the window, "Oh, Bobby, wherever you are right now, be careful."

At Heathrow Airport in London, Coppin parked her Mini-Cooper in the private parking area of Gold Eagle Flight Services. Gold Eagle was the service that was often used by BSN to shuttle personnel back and forth from England to the U.S. The office lobby looked like any corporate flight company's waiting area. There were tables with reading lamps next to comfortable over-stuffed leather chairs gathered in small clusters. A small table sat in the middle of each group of chairs. Each table had electrical charging stations with both British and U.S. compatible outlets.

Wallace entered a few steps behind Coppin. His eyes were searching the room, looking for anyone who might know that he was wanted for murder. Coppin told him to have a seat, pointing to the chairs nearest the South doors. He sat down and pulled his cap lower over his eyes. His aviator sunglasses with the mirrored lenses reflected her as she walked to the counter and showed her credentials. She then gestured toward Wallace. This made him squirm slightly in his seat. Was she endangering him by pointing out who he was? The fashionable lady behind the counter smiled and nodded in his direction. She handed two folders to Coppin who then turned and walked over and sat on the chair to Wallace's right.

"It's all set, Bobby. We'll be boarding in about fifteen minutes."

Wallace was somewhat confused as he whispered to her, "What did you tell the lady at the counter? Does she suspect anything about me?"

"Don't worry, Bobby. We do this all the time. We have an arrangement with Gold Eagle. There have been many times in the past that we have shuttled secret passengers internationally. I have personally escorted members of the British Royal family when they needed to go to the States without arousing any undo interest."

"I feel almost like a gangster, or James Bond sneaking around in His Majesty's Service."

She smiled, "Okay, you enjoy those feelings. If you're with me, you will be safe and arrive home unnoticed."

She kept an eye on the Canadian built Bombardier Challenger 350 sitting just about twenty-five yards outside the doors. The flight attendant came walking toward the building, and Coppin rose from her seat. She walked toward the door as the attendant entered the lobby, "Good afternoon, Miss Coppin. It's wonderful to be flying with you again. It has been a while since you last made this trip with us, hasn't it?"

"That's right, Caroline. It is good to see you again, as well." Gesturing to Wallace, "Caroline McNeice, this is my special friend Wally Dobbs. He's going to be my guide as I settle in to my first week in New York before going to Washington next week."

Wallace nodded and exchanged pleasantries with Miss McNeice. Then he and Suzanne entered the cabin and found their way to their seats. There was seating for eight on the Challenger 350, and Wallace felt like a little boy as he plopped down in one of the soft leather seats. It was obvious to him that he needed to act like he was used to flying on a fine business jet, even though it was his first ride in one.

Suzanne smiled at his look of excitement, "Don't worry, my friend, I felt the same way when I took my first ride on one of these. Gold Eagle offers us a great discount for the reviews we give to our biggest corporate sponsors. The company has been able to expand their fleet because of the business we have sent them over the past few years."

Still, it was hard to hide his boyish excitement. He sat, looking out the window. Suzanne reached in front of him and closed the blind, "We don't want anyone on the outside looking in and… shall we say, getting jealous of our good fortune, now do we?"

"I guess I need to be cool, don't I?" He sat back and put a neck pillow behind his head, "I should have been a billionaire. This is the way I was meant to travel."

"As an internationally wanted man? I don't think so. We have a long flight ahead of us."

The engines began to whine slowly as they warmed up and in just a moment or two the jet began to move. Soon they were airborne, and on their way across the Atlantic.

Without warning Ambassador Baalazaar had mysteriously appeared in Le Roux's office. The Ambassador stood, arms crossed, as Le Roux did his best to explain what had happened to Robert Wallace, "I know that we have lost track of him, but I have sources all over the world who can locate him."

Baalazaar was totally in control of the conversation, "Albert, we have known each other for most of your life. In fact, I have known you since the day you were born."

"What do you mean, since the day I was born, Mr. Ambassador?"

"Albert, you have always wanted to be a king, and you have proven that you will do anything to get what you want. There is nothing new about that kind of desire, Albert. I knew you in the garden. Because of what happened there, I have owned you since then."

stared blankly at Baalazaar. There was a ace that Le Roux had never seen before.

Baalazaar smiled a crooked smile and said, "It doesn't matter that you don't know what I mean. Because in the Garden, you... all of you were so easy to entice therefore, I knew you. I knew your father, I've known every father... you're all the same, you want to be little gods in your own world."

Even though Le Roux wasn't totally sure, he thought he knew what Baalazaar was talking about. Human nature. He had gone to Catholic school when he was a boy. He had heard Bible stories, but as far as he was concerned, none of them made any sense. He had been a young man who would someday own and rule the world. Le Roux had certainly achieved some of his goal of owning and ruling so much in this world. Even before his twenty-first birthday, Le Roux had become one of the richest men in France. His wealth afforded him a lifestyle that most Frenchmen could never even hope to attain. He had earned his wealth by using his knowledge of computer science to copyright multiple software programs. He had become a prideful man. Many of the political leaders of Paris had been elected because of the support of the young computer mogul. His family's wine business had also come under his control by the time he turned thirty. With both the wine and computer software businesses, Le Roux was now in line one of the richest men in the v

He had mainly used his wealth to imple agendas in government and business ac

Now he was on the threshold of truly controlling Europe, and making sure that Europe, under his guidance, would be the world's leading economic power. He had the backing of the very powerful Andromedin Ambassador named Baalazaar. This man from another galaxy had frequently cleared the way for him all his life. On many occasions, Baalazaar had shown Le Roux what he needed to do to increase his scientific successes. Now, Le Roux wanted even more. He was on the right course for achieving his personal goals. He didn't necessarily want to be the king, he wanted to be the power behind the king. Now that day was in sight.

Reverend James Hann was surprised to see Julian Lewis waiting at his door as he approached his office. Lewis was a wealthy Scottdale businessman. He was a sharp dresser whose clothes were expertly tailored. They were made of the finest materials. He also liked to flaunt his wealth to anyone who would listen to him. He kept four luxury SUVs in his garage for use by out-of-town guests of the church. Many times, in the past few years, Lewis had personally provided the funds needed to bring the church through various financial crises. He had inherited automobile dealerships all over southwestern Pennsylvania from his father and grandfather before him. One of the earliest Mercedes

Benz dealerships in the United States was owned by the Lewis family.

In a calm voice, Hann welcomed the surprise visitor, "Julian, good morning. To what do I owe this pleasant surprise?"

"We'll see how pleasant the surprise is, Jim. I'm expecting Kathryn Armstrong to join us at any moment. We need to talk."

Kathryn Armstrong was the widow of real estate king Daniel Armstrong. She was in her late seventies, with shiny silver hair that was cropped short in a nineteen fifties style. Her face was wrinkled with deep lines at the edges of her eyes. She had a severe look on her face. There was a deep line between her eyebrows where a frown took up permanent residence. She was devoid of any joy. Her vast real estate holdings in Scottdale made her a natural leader on church committees and boards. She could be counted upon for advice on matters of church property.

"What do we need to talk about, Julian?" Hann was now beginning to feel uncomfortable.

As Kathryn Armstrong joined them, the three entered Hann's office. Hann gestured for them to sit on the sofa and chairs in his office. The seating area was a more informal way of having conversations with people, giving a more peaceful atmosphere in these situations.

Lewis immediately took the chair. Mrs. Armstrong, however, did not sit. As Hann sat on the sofa nearest Lewis's seat, she hovered between the two. She then spoke from this lofty position, "Jim, it is becoming more and more obvious that your sermons are starting to make people uncomfortable."

Hann knew she was uncomfortable because he was preaching directly from the gospels and the letters of Paul. Hann asked her, "How do you mean, Kathryn? I've only been teaching from the Bible."

Lewis took up the conversation, "Jim, you've been saying that the reason so many people are missing from this world is that they were taken up in something called The Rapture, and that they were the true believers in Jesus Christ. Jim, don't you understand if they were 'the true believers in Jesus Christ' what does that make the rest of us?"

Hann was ready for this, "Julian and Kathryn, that's just it I'm telling you, my friends, we had never truly committed our lives to Christ before. It is time that we see we need to come to Him and recognize him truly as the Son of God, our Savior."

Kathryn rejoined the conversation, "Jim, because of your accusation that we are not true believers, most of the people in our congregation have agreed that you are no longer needed as our pastor. In fact, we are voting this Sunday afternoon that we no longer wish to be categorized as Lutherans. There was too much violence in our history to be called Lutherans, or Catholics or Methodists. Many members of those churches have also voted to join us in the United Church of God's Truth. We will become one body with them and follow the new guidelines set forth by The Global Committee for Religious Tolerance and Diversity. No more will church be pitted against church. Our Priests and Pastors will all agree with each other. We will be joined by the leaders of other religions, and finally bring peace and unity among all the people of God and the other gods who rule from the hereafter. We believe that God wants us to all be of one mind in our beliefs."

Lewis interjected loudly, "That's right, Jim. We feel that with your insistence on becoming 'true believers in Christ' you are standing in the way of true religious unity."

Pastor Hann paused before speaking, "So, you're saying that my services are no longer needed. I believe you are wrong, but because of my extensive studies in Revelation and Daniel, I understand why you are saying what you are saying."

Lewis rose to stand beside Armstrong in a show of unity. He nodded as she spoke, "Jim, we want to thank you for your years of service to our congregation, but under the circumstances, you are being terminated immediately. There is a nice severance package that includes continued medical and dental insurance for the next six months, and you will also continue to be paid for the next six months. Please understand that this is nothing personal against you. We just want to become unified with likeminded believers."

"Kathryn, Julian, I am not offended. As I think about it, I am relieved. I am ready to move on with my life. Thank you, and you will be in my every prayer."

He stopped one last time in his office where he quickly jotted a note to Wallace telling him where to contact him in Ohio. He gave directions to the Dickerson Camp, put it in an envelope and left it with the receptionist with instructions to give it to Wallace if he comes in searching for Hann.

As a single man, Hann didn't have a large number of possessions. He went to his apartment and gathered a few things together, a suitcase full of clothes, a laptop computer, and an iPad. He packed his car and headed westward to Ohio.

Wallace and Coppin had been in deep conversation. A few short hours ago they had passed over the airspace where, they conjectured, the bomb had gone off and ultimately brought down flight 225. Their flight seemed to pass by quickly and before he knew it, they were beginning their descent to prepare for landing in Newark, New Jersey.

"I almost hate to see this flight come to an end. I may never again get a ride on a private business jet. Who knows what is waiting for me when we get back to the States?"

"That's where we come in. You have a new passport in the compartment on the arm of that seat. We will be able to avoid the authorities, but your professional life is probably finished."

That was a harsh reality that was just beginning to sink in. He opened the compartment and found a brand-new British Passport. There was his picture, but the name read Walter Dobbs. It showed that he had passed through Calais, and Dover and then departed England from London.

Route 16 south of Coshocton was not busy this afternoon. As the sun was about to go down, Hann was only about ten minutes away from Camp Dickerson. His mind went back to early this morning. He wasn't happy that those who were left in his congregation weren't willing to listen to the good news of Christ. Why can't they see that what has happened here was the culmination of all the stories, prophesies, and guidelines in the Bible? The Prophets Daniel. Isaiah and John, in Revelation, spoke of "The Last Days" or "The Day of the Lord", all meaning the coming of the Messiah. These prophesies meant the end of the world.

Jesus struggled to get his message across to most of the religious leaders of his day. Quite frequently, religious people don't quite grasp the concept of a savior offering up himself in place of the sinner. Hann thought about how even he thought he knew all the answers until so many went missing. Then his heart opened to the knowledge, with faith, the Bible had more answers than he could fathom.

God offered the gift of salvation through Jesus' sacrifice on the cross. John the Baptist called him the "Lamb of God and Jesus fulfilled this sacrifice by being the perfect lamb." It seemed too simple. God offered this gift to His creation. As he drew near the camp, Hann was happy in the thought that he was now ready to take the next step in reaching out to a lost world far beyond the walls of St. John Lutheran Church.

There it was. Nestled against a hillside, twelve barracks type cabins and one community building. The Fireflies were just beginning to sparkle, as the area grew darker in the shadow of the wooded hillside. The thought came to him that God was showing him that the people in this little camp were like those Fireflies, little, tiny lights, sparkling in the darkness. He smiled as he pulled up to the community building, and Father George Reilly rushed to meet his car.

Father Reilly and Pastor Hann met in a warm embrace. There was laughter coming from the community building as people were clapping and singing. Reilly spoke exuberantly, "Welcome back, Jim. We've been having a great time together while you were gone. Your call didn't really surprise me that much. It is understandable that there are people resisting your attempts to bring them to the saving grace of Christ."

"I know, in some ways I was expecting it. It's hard for people to surrender to the fact that they can't earn what God offers. The gift of salvation takes faith. I was a believer in Jesus, the man, for most of my life. I don't hold it against them, but I'll keep praying for them to learn the Way."

Father Reilly told his story of dismissal from Our Lady of Sorrows Roman Catholic Church in New Philadelphia, "I was told by our new Bishop that I was no longer needed. The church didn't need some 'religious fanatic' going against what the church was teaching. Individual accountability instead of what the church was returning to just didn't fit their plans. The church was going back to what your Martin Luther fought so hard to change. Indulgences. Rome has set up a new guideline of prices for people to make sure they get to heaven or get their loved ones to see Paradise. The prices are becoming set in stone."

133

Hann reached into the back seat, and grabbing his bags, followed Reilly to the source of all the joyful noises floating into the night air. Inside the brightly lit room there were now about seventy-five people. Reilly explained, "We have representatives of nearly every mainline denomination of Christian churches. We have Methodists, some more Lutherans, Church of Christ, and believe it or not, even a few Baptists who missed the Rapture."

Hann smiled, "I thought they'd all be gone."

Pastor Philip Langley, who was standing nearby joined them, "Sorry, gentlemen, I didn't mean to eavesdrop, but I couldn't help but hear your conversation. Yes, I'm afraid there were perhaps as many Baptists as any other group who thought they were saved but had never really followed through with the commitment. It's one thing to believe in God, but another thing altogether to be a follower of Christ. I knew my Bible forward and backwards, but I thought that's really all I needed. Only a few of us missed the train."

"I was just telling myself the same thing on my drive over here," said Hann, "I was one who believed in God, but I hadn't really made the commitment to be a Christ follower."

The men all exchanged handshakes and hugs and then made their way to the buffet table. Every kind of casserole you could imagine was on the table.

There were hamburger casseroles of all varieties of all variations with corn, green beans and some that were laden with onions. Langley called upon Hann to follow him to the next table. There were all kinds of Mexican dishes with a wonderful aroma wafting up as the men approached it.

Pastor Freddie Jose Batista came forward and pointed out the many choices, "Gentlemen, welcome to heaven's favorite dishes." All the men chuckled, "Here are Flautas, Enchiladas, Albondigas Soup, Chicken Tortilla Soup, and of course, everyone's favorites... Tacos."

Batista went on to explain that there were several folks there from his church in Chicago. La Puerta del Norte Iglesia lost almost all their members in The Rapture. Batista said he was a lay pastor who only filled in as a Sunday School teacher when needed but was only a part time attender to the church. His wife and three children were taken up, but he was one who had been left. He had found a new home among new believers.

CHAPTER 7

The beautiful Bombardier Challenger 320 business jet taxied to a stop in front of Gold Eagle Flight Service's Newark, New Jersey offices. Caroline McNeice pulled the lever and opened the cabin door and lowered the stairs. She smiled at Wallace and Coppin as they gathered their belongings and moved to the front to exit the craft, "Good to see you again, Suzanne. I look forward to our next trip together. And Mr. Dobbs, I enjoyed meeting you. I do hope you will choose Gold Eagle again sometime."

All three exchanged final pleasantries as they parted ways. After they had cleared Customs, a limousine awaited the new arrivals just outside the main doors.

"Where do you want me to drop you... 'Wally'?"

Wallace, or Wally (as he was now going to be known) thought about it and looked at his watch. It was about 7:30pm, so it was an easy choice for him. He told the driver the address of Olivia's Apartment on the Upper West Side of Manhattan. He knew that she wasn't expecting him. He could possibly find himself in jail before the night was over if she carried out her duty and called Interpol. His new Passport would work on most people, but Olivia was the woman he had left to go cover a big news story more than a year and a half ago. She may very well be angry with him and not forgive.

Despite that possibility, he wanted to see her again. There had hardly been a day that she hadn't at least crossed his mind. She was a beautiful lady, as far as he was concerned. She didn't fit the fashion model ideal, but he had never been excited by women who looked like waifs. His ideal woman left no doubt that she was a woman. Olivia Meyer was definitely a woman.

The trip across the George Washington Bridge was quite a sight to behold. The diamond-like shimmer of the Manhattan skyline had always fascinated him since the time he first saw it on television. The lights in the buildings called out to those who wanted the excitement of the Big Apple. For decades, Manhattan's skyline had welcomed people from all over Europe, as they made the Atlantic crossing to start their new life in a new world.

Wallace's cab dropped him in front of Olivia's building. The long, red entry canopy was as crisp looking as the last time he had seen it. "The New Amsterdam" was emblazoned on the front of the canopy. He hoped that she was home from work. Sometimes she had to work late and would not return home until past nine. He rang up her apartment. What he heard next was such a welcome sound, "Who is it?"

"Liv, it's me, Bobby. I'm hoping I can see you for a few minutes."

"You... I don't..." without another word the door buzzed open. He took a breath and entered. It was such a familiar trip. He always took the stairs to the second floor rather than wait for the elevator. Her door was two doors down from the stairway. He raised his hand and with a slight hesitation he timidly knocked.

Olivia opened the door and the two stood there facing each other, silent for a moment, "Bobby, come in. The last time we spoke, you got the information you needed from me and hung up on me." She turned her back to him and walked into the living room.

He followed close behind while speaking and what he so desperately wanted to say came pouring out, "Liv, I'm sorry, we pulled into a cell phone dead zone just as I was beginning to thank you. I wanted to try to apologize for not staying in touch. I truly have missed you. I need to tell you that the news story that took me away from you was an important event, but I have since come to understand that people we love are so much more important than anything else. Maybe you'll never be able to forgive me because I said that I loved you and then promptly took that assignment overseas. We shared so much that last night I was here. I cherish those moments. I told you then, and I'd love to be able to try and make amends so I can say 'I love you' once again and not leave this time." He searched her face for the reaction he could only hope for.

"Bobby, so much has happened since that night. I know what you said then, and as I waited for you to come back, there have been so many things happening. I'm not sure if we can just take up where we left off. Bobby, you're a wanted man! Interpol has issued a warrant for your arrest and I am duty-bound to have you taken into custody."

"I understand. I expect nothing less from you. You're an honorable person and a dedicated officer of the court. I had to take this chance just to see you and tell you all that has been happening in the past few months."

She rose from her chair and strolled to the kitchenette, opened the refrigerator, and pulled out the pitcher of iced tea. Looking back to him she smiled a half smile and said, "If I remember correctly, you love Arnold Palmer Iced Tea?" Without waiting for an answer, she proceeded to pour the tea over ice.

"Bobby, I know all about those who are missing. I lost someone so very special to me. I am happy to hear that people from Andromeda Galaxy have taken people so that we can learn from each other and prepare for a much better world. All that I have read and heard about that ride into space the other day, with all the reporters from Europe and the United States, has given me hope that I will see her again. I am terribly alone right now and so very sad."

"This is one of the things I wanted to tell you. I was one of the reporters on that ride. I had expressed some thoughts on my observations, and I have suddenly come under intense scrutiny by someone. There was something about the entire thing that made me suspicious."

She held up her hand to stop his talking, "Wait, don't tell me your suspicions about the whole thing being fake, that news conference has given me some hope that I haven't had in months."

He thought about all he wanted to tell her about his suspicions. He chose rather to share his heart, "Liv I didn't tell you this enough before. I've loved you for a long time. I was excited to take the overseas assignment, but I missed you the whole time I was there."

The sound of her Black Forest Coocoo clock struck the nine O'clock hour, "Bobby, I truly missed you the entire time you were gone. I've withheld a secret from you, and I need to tell you, even though it's difficult. That night, we shared ourselves completely, and it was the most wonderful feeling to share that deeply."

"Well, there's more to that night than just a good time that we had together."

He glanced down at his iced tea and said, "There was much more in the intimacy we shared. I meant it when I said 'I love you' that night. I had come to love you dearly."

"I know, Bobby. I felt the same way. But Bobby... I got pregnant that night."

"What? What? Why didn't you tell me before?"

"I couldn't take the chance that you would come to me and stay with me out of obligation instead of love."

Wallace was dumbfounded. He looked at the floor before softly speaking, "Pregnant... you were pregnant? Why didn't you tell me? You shouldn't have had to go through that by yourself."

"I wanted you to want me, not because you had to, but because you wanted to be with me."

Wallace got up from the sofa and started pacing back and forth slowly, "Pregnant... I can't believe that you kept that from me... pregnant. I can't believe that I'm... a father."

"I named her Roberta. I was looking forward to her learning about her about her father."

"Her father? Her father was too busy running away to play news reporter in another part of the world. If I had known I had a child I would have been here with both of you. I would not have let her out of my sight."

Tears began rolling down Olivia's cheeks, "That's what I mean. I didn't want you staying with us because you were trapped into staying with us. And... I... I... never let her out of my sight. Then suddenly she was gone."

He quickly embraced her. Squeezing her tightly, not wanting to let go, "What was that like? What did you see? Were you with her when it happened? I can't imagine what that must have been like."

"Neither can I. It's been a nightmare. And then that European guy and those spacemen explained how they wanted so many children so they can share their knowledge of space travel and science and make this world a better place. I can't not believe that's where she went."

Wallace mulled the thought of telling her his theories after looking into the space connection, and the possibility of a Christian angle to the missing people. The only choice he had was to tell the truth, "Liv, I have been looking into this whole thing. I have investigated several different possibilities of what happened. I don't believe that any spacemen from Andromeda Galaxy gathered up millions of people and took them away."

Olivia was wiping away more tears, "Then what other explanation could there be?"

"What do you know about Christianity, Liv?"

This was almost too much for her, "What on Earth are you talking about?"

"I'm talking about an event called The Rapture. Somewhere in the Bible they talk about God taking all the Christians out of this world and up to heaven."

"But she had never been to church in her little life. I didn't have her baptized or christened, or whatever they call that. How could she have gone to heaven?"

"My actual knowledge on the subject is extremely limited, but what I have heard from others, is that when someone is old enough, they can either accept or reject the invitation to come to Jesus. Somewhere in the Bible, Jesus said once that he wanted the little children to come to him, or something like that. Apparently, little children haven't had the chance on their own to accept or reject Jesus. I don't understand it, myself, but it's as good an explanation as anything I could ever come up with. I've met some people I'd like you to talk to. They have studied more than I have and can explain it for us."

Olivia turned back to their original conversation. She let him know in no uncertain terms that even though she trusted that he couldn't have murdered all those people on the airliner she was obligated to take him into custody.

"I understand, Liv. I know that you must do this. I won't resist, but I'd like it if you could stall the proceedings a bit. I did not place the bomb that brought down that plane."

"I know that, Bobby. But once the word gets out that you're here in the States, we'll need to act and prepare for your extradition. I will hire the best defense lawyer possible, and we'll fight it together."

It was midnight when they were too exhausted to talk anymore. Olivia left the room, returning quickly with a pillow, two sheets and a blanket.

"This is actually a comfortable sofa. Your condo is probably under surveillance." As she handed him the bedding, their hands lingered as they touched.

"I should probably go somewhere else. The temptation to be close to you is too great."

"You're okay. We both know that we can't be too close right now. You get a good night's sleep, what's left of it. I'll wake you at seven and we can go to my office together. We'll plan our strategy as we go tomorrow."

Wallace smiled, blew her a kiss, and laid out the sheets and blanket. After a long day, he was asleep quickly.

His sleep was interrupted several times with visions of the Trans-Atlantic Airlines plane going down. He was seeing the passengers in panic. The terrible images haunted him. Each time he awoke in the night, the radiance from the lights outside cast an eerie shadow on the ceiling above the sofa. He was seeing what appeared to be scaly, winged creatures that would fly menacingly toward his face, screeching. The dreams also were filled with bare limbs that were black shadows against a dark sky. He awoke, covered in sweat, shivering from a severe chill. He walked to the kitchen. He stood by the sink, and in a moment of reverie his mind was going through all that had happened in the past week. After looking into the possibility that so many people had been taken from this world, he had been seeking answers. Governments and business leaders were saying that the people had been taken to another galaxy. He had possibly been into space aboard an alien spacecraft. He avoided being on board that ill-fated airliner because he thought he heard a voice telling him to "GO". After he had arrived in England, he learned that he had been accused of planting a bomb on the plane. With the help of his friend Suzanne Coppin, he made it to the United States. Now, he was on the verge of turning himself in to face those murder charges.

He had never been much of a praying person, and this might just be another one of those times when he called out to the ceiling as he was facing trouble. He raised his head upward and prayed for strength and wisdom in his upcoming battle, "God, if you are there, and if you hear me, please help me. I am in the biggest trouble of my life.

In Europe, the political mood was moving forward at break-neck speed. Paolino Esposito was about to step into power as the President of the European Commission, the governing body over the Parliament.

Albert Le Roux was smiling broadly as he handed a crystal flute of Dom Perignon to Esposito, "Here, my boy, I told you when we first started down this road that you would one day rule Europe. Now we can bring peace to the world and achieve what we want, a total one-world economic system. Since the Euro was the universal currency for the EU, we will continue with that for a short while. The U.S. Dollar has steadily lost its clout beginning in the early 2000s."

Anyone other than Esposito would have trouble trying not to appear giddy. He grew up around power, and he knew how to stay cool in situations such as this. Even so, he was very excited to be the new President of Europe. His hope was to become the most powerful man in the world.

He spoke to Le Roux with appreciation, "Monsieur Le Roux, I am thrilled. Thank you for mentoring me through this process. I have learned so much from you and your staff."

Cardinal Assidi joined the two of them as they continued their celebration of the good news. Assidi had just returned from a meeting with other Cardinals as they decided who would replace the Catholic Bishops who were taken, along with so many other people world-wide. He was in a very positive mood, "Gentlemen, I believe congratulations are in order. The future looks prosperous for us."

Le Roux corrected him, "The future looks very prosperous for the entire world, Nunzio. We soon will be bringing peace and prosperity to everyone. Yes, the future looks prosperous for us, but that is merely because we are making the world that way for everyone else. They win, and we win as well. We are ready to move forward with some of the greatest plans to ever be set into motion."

Olivia's alarm clock went off at 5:30 am. She quickly sat up in her bed and forced herself awake rubbing her eyes lightly. It had been well past midnight when she was finally able to get to sleep and she was very tired. As she got out of the bed, her thoughts went to Wallace on the sofa in the other room.

She walked into the living room and found Wallace sitting on the edge of the sofa with the sheets and blanket neatly folded and stacked with the pillow on the opposite end. He jumped up in a hurry, "Good morning, Liv. Did you sleep well?"

"It was a short night. I like to get to the office by 7 am. We can get a good start on planning your defense. I'll show you the list of the best defense lawyers in New York. We need to make sure that everyone knows that you did not kill all those people on that airliner."

They both hurriedly ate an English muffin and downed a cup of coffee and headed out the door. It was a quick walk down one flight of stairs and out the front door to the sidewalk.

They had not gotten more than twenty feet down the sidewalk when two large men came out of nowhere and quickly put hoods over their heads and dragged them into a waiting van.

Le Roux was enjoying the view of the bay as he talked to Vito Lombardo, "Where did your men find him?"

A sinister, satisfied smile came across Lombardo's face. His pride was excruciatingly saccharine, "I told you that we'd be able to locate him. He must be one of the most stupid fools on the planet. My men found him coming out of the apartment building of that prosecutor girlfriend of his. It looks like they took up where they left off before he got her pregnant a year and a half ago."

Le Roux said, "Really?"

"I can only assume they resumed their affair. He spent the night there. Draw your own conclusions if you like. I believe that we should just kill him there and not worry about Interpol. Let them think that he simply escaped their dragnet. Of course, we can't leave Meyer alive to challenge our plans."

Le Roux gave the order, "Let's make sure that he does not have a chance to cast any doubts about the Andromedin connection. He was saying things on our trip that could make people believe it was all just a big special effects show. I have too much invested in this project to have some fool from the American news media ruin everything. He can't be allowed to see the light of day again."

The van cut in and out of traffic as they made their way across the George Washington Bridge and headed for New Jersey. Wallace could tell that they were making a sharp right turn. He could not see for himself, but he and Olivia were being taken to a warehouse complex on the Hudson River.

Max Giovanni was the driver, and the man in charge. He spoke to his partner, "We'll be there in a minute. The boss wants us to find out what this guy knows and then take care of them both."

Lou Pintano was showing genuine concern for his own future if they were caught, "But she's a Manhattan Assistant District Attorney. They'll be doing everything they can to find her and then we'll be in Ossining before we know it."

"Don't worry about it. We have it all figured out. It looks like she took up with an international fugitive. We took pictures of the two of them in her apartment. Those will be published, and her reputation will be thoroughly ruined."

A sly sneer crossed Pintano's face, "Yeah, people need to close their curtains if they don't want people watching them. I'll email them to Mr. Lombardo, and he'll see to it that she gets smeared completely. Then, dead, or alive, she'll never be prosecuting a case here again."

The van pulled to a stop in front of unit G-5. Pintano jumped out and opened the giant overhead door. Giovanni pulled into the warehouse and brought the van to a sudden halt. Both Wallace and Meyer rocked violently, and Olivia's head smacked the side of the van putting a small gash just at the crown of her head.

As she groaned Wallace immediately inquired, "Was that your head hitting the wall?"

"Yes, but I'll live."

Each of them had their hands duck taped together, but he tried to reach out to her to comfort her as best he could. The sliding door made its distinctive grinding sound as it was hurriedly flung open. They could hear the voices of the two men. Each had distinctive Brooklyn accents as they barked orders to the captives to get up.

Wallace leaned forward to get to his knees before rising into a crouching position. He then stood just a little too tall and hit his head on the top of the door.

Giovanni was showing no sympathy for his detainees. Then he turned to his junior partner, "Charlie, pull her out here and put her in the chair. I'll get this loser over there too."

On command, as if he too were afraid of Giovanni, he pulled Olivia out of the van and roughly stood her up on the garage floor before walking her to one of two chairs that were in the middle of the large room. He made a major mistake as he spoke, "Should we leave the hoods on them, Max?"

"SHUT UP, you idiot!"

"Oh, yeah… Joey… sorry." He sat Olivia down hard on the old heavy oak dining chair.

Both men pulled ski masks out of their jacket pockets and pulled them down over their faces. Giovanni told Pintano to remove Robert and Olivia's hoods. The bright morning sun shining through the east facing window made them both to squint as their eyes adjusted to light again. It had been about an hour since they were taken.

Giovanni turned aside to Pintano and said, "The boss will be here in about ten minutes. Watch what you say, idiot."

CHAPTER 8

It was a beautiful sunrise at Camp Dickerson. The campers were beginning to stir. The kitchen crew had been working for the past hour preparing the breakfast. Pastor James Hann and Father George Reilly met outside the dining hall. As they sat at the picnic table just outside the kitchen door the pleasant aromas of bacon, eggs, fresh-baked biscuits, and gravy wafted through the screen door.

They each opened their Bibles and began to read from Matthew chapter 24. Beginning at verse 4 from the New International Version, Hann began to read, "Jesus answered: 'Watch out that no one deceives you. [5] For many will come in my name, claiming, 'I am the Messiah,' and will deceive many. [6] You will hear of wars and rumors of wars but see to it that you are not alarmed. Such things must happen, but the end is still to come.

Reilly interjected, "Jesus called those 'birth pangs.' We've lived through the most violent century in history. The Twentieth Century saw more world wars and death was dealt to humans in wholesale lots. I believe the birth pangs were in the early stages in those days."

Hann continued to read, "Then you will be handed over to be persecuted and put to death, and you will be hated by all nations because of me. At that time many will turn away from the faith and will betray and hate each other, and many false prophets will appear and deceive many people. Because of the increase of wickedness, the love of most will grow cold, but the one who stands firm to the end will be saved. And this gospel of the kingdom will be preached in the whole world as a testimony to all nations, and then the end will come."

Hann added his opinion, "I think that those who were taken in the Rapture were the ones who stood firm. People like I was, were too busy doing what we thought what Jesus would do. I did a lot of the things that Jesus commanded us to do, but I had a belief that we're all going to heaven, just taking different trains. So many different religions from so many parts of the world. I didn't want to offend anyone by telling them that Jesus is the only way to get to the Father."

Hann continued, "But the only thing you would have been doing was saying what Jesus said about himself. He said, 'I am the way, the truth and the life. No one comes to the Father except through me.'"

"You wouldn't have been arrogant, you would have merely stating what Jesus said," Reilly insisted.

"Jesus then warned that when we see what Daniel called the abomination that causes desolation, standing in the holy place, that there would be great distress like nothing ever seen since the beginning of the world. He also said that no one should collect their belongings, but they should head for the mountains."

Hann looked up at Reilly and said, "I believe that the one who will cause that 'desolation' is standing by to take control of this world."

Reilly agreed, "You are correct, my friend. We have our work cut out for us. Those of us who missed that first call, still have a chance to bring more souls to Christ before he returns."

Hann continued to read, "Listen to this, skipping ahead a couple of verses, 'So if anyone tells you, 'There he is, out in the wilderness,' do not go out; or, 'Here he is, in the inner rooms,' do not believe it. For as lightning that comes from the east is visible even in the west, so will be the coming of the Son of Man. Wherever there is a carcass, there the vultures will gather."

"Then he warns that the sun will grow dark, and the moon won't shine either. The stars will fall from the heavens and soon people will see the Son of Man coming in the clouds."

As Hann placed his hand lovingly on the pages of the book, he and Reilly held hands and they began to pray. They prayed that they would begin to see others come to Christ as Savior before the end came. They finished their prayer time as others from the cabins made their way to the dining hall.

Joshua Dickerson, owner of the adjacent farm and a member of the community, pointed to the gateway entrance to the camp, "Who's that?"

Everyone looked and saw a lone man wearing a Shalwar Kameez (the baggy pants and long top shirt) the traditional clothing of an Afghani man looked somewhat out of place in this part of Ohio.

The man looked as though he had been walking for days on end. He raised his right hand in a sign of peaceful hello. Hann and Reilly walked out to meet him. They were cautious, as he appeared to be a Muslim man. It was understandable that there would be some distrust. Considering the many killings of Christians by Muslims and even the murders of so many Muslims in the past few years by non-Muslims.

He spoke as he drew closer to the pair, "Peace be with you. I have been led here by a vision."

Father Reilly answered his salutation, "Good morning. Welcome to Camp Dickerson. What kind of vision led you to us?"

Hann was aware of accounts of Muslims seeing visions of Christ. He remembered the words from Acts 2:17 that in the last days, God would pour out His spirit on all people, that sons and daughters will prophesy, and young men will see visions and old men will dream dreams. This could very well be this Scripture playing out right before their eyes.

"My name is Mohammed Zacharius. I had a dream last week. In that dream I saw many blossoms blooming on Peach Trees. Each blossom had the face of Jesus at the center of it. Thousands of blossoms with the face of Jesus staring back at me from an orchard that looked just like that one over there. Then all the blossoms began to swirl around and came together into one single face. Then Jesus spoke to me. He told me that he was the true Messiah and that I am to accept him as my Savior. I have had visions before, but this was the first time that Jesus came to me and told me so many things. Then He told me to begin walking west from where I was in Western Pennsylvania."

"I was so ashamed that Christ had seen me there. It is horrible, as I look back on it now. I had been there to kill people in a Christian church. The dream came to me last Saturday night, the night before I was to enter a church and begin firing my weapon. I had hand grenades to throw as well."

A buzz of conversation quickly went through the crowd before Reilly asked the man to continue.

"Instead of finding a church filled with people to kill, I started walking westward on Sunday morning. Each night as I stopped to rest, Jesus came to me again and told me to keep going west. Two nights ago, I was near Cambridge, and Jesus told me that someone in a pickup truck would stop at a rest area and give me a ride. I was told to ride with the man to Dresden, Ohio. When I got there, I was supposed to walk north until I saw peach trees."

"I know that you gentlemen will be able to help me make sense of all this. It has been about three years since I began to question my own faith in Islam. I continued to do the daily prayers and go through the motions, but something was missing. I didn't know what it was until all this began."

Le Roux was awakened from a sound sleep. It was two in the morning as he sat bolt upright in his bed. The full moon outside shone brightly into his room. The sheer drapes allowed the beautiful, filtered glow to cast wavy shadows on his wall at the head of his bed. Normally, if he awakened at this hour with a full moon, he enjoyed looking out the window at the bay below him. This time, though, there was something that made the hair stand up on the back of his neck. He was sure that he could hear breathing in the room with him, but he was certain that he was alone.

He went to bed alone at midnight. His security detail was outside his room which gave him a sense of safety. Yet the breathing had a pronounced rattle. It sounded as though someone with Pneumonia were lurking behind the wall in his master bath.

"It's no use, Albert, I am here. I have been here since you moved into this house. I was the one who provided it for you. Since you first started in the business world."

Baalazaar came from the shadows and into the master bedroom. The rattle in his voice was more pronounced right now as he chuckled slightly, "By not giving credit to God for anything in your life, you are giving me credit for everything without naming me. The more I gave you, the easier it was to keep you away from God. I kept giving to you so you cannot go to God now. You are doomed to be mine now forever."

Le Roux stood by his bed, dumbfounded at what he had just heard. He had no idea how Baalazaar had gotten into his room without being detected. And what was he talking about when he said that he had provided all that Le Roux possessed?

"Am I confusing you? That's what I do well. People don't understand who I truly am. I was around from the beginning of time. I was there when all this was created. I am your god. You worship me by all you are doing. I have put into your head every idea you have had that has given you so much success. All your money and power come directly from me. I have provided it all for you. I know that you are grateful for it because you have been doing all my bidding, often before you planned out your moves. You are a child of mine."

Baalazaar left the room just as suddenly as he had entered. Le Roux stepped into the master bath. No sign of Baalazaar was left behind, only a slight aroma of a match that had been recently struck.

Le Roux returned to bed. He surveyed the room. He loved the furnishings that were so richly appointed. The finest furniture money could buy filled the room. The full Moon shining through the sheer drapes cast a beautiful blue glow on everything.

He thought about what he had just heard from Baalazaar. What did he mean that he had provided everything that Le Roux had? Looking out the window from his opulent canopy bed, he could see the Moon glow on the bay below his room. It was beautiful to behold. He spoke aloud in the darkness, "Everything I survey is mine. I got it all by my own hard work. No one has given it to me. No god of any kind has given it to me. I got it myself. I am proud of all that I have accomplished."

Wallace and Olivia Meyer were in a large warehouse sitting on two solid oak chairs. Their eyes were finally adjusted to the harsh sunlight that was shining through window to the east. The sounds of river traffic could be heard coming from the nearby Hudson River.

Giovanni told Pintano to wait with the captives, "I'll go outside to meet the boss and when he gets here, we'll clear up this whole thing."

Giovanni picked up another ski mask from the front seat of the van and made his way to the door. Outside he paced nervously. He was about to see Andrew Benetti, the Chief Security Adviser for Albert Le Roux's American business branch.

Giovanni squinted as he looked at the Manhattan skyline. He had always loved that view because it reminded him of what his great-grandfather had seen as he arrived from Sicily in 1946.

His reverie was broken as Benetti's car arrived. The long black Cadillac pulled up in front of Giovanni. The driver exited and ran around to the rear passenger door, flung it open and gave a nod to Benetti as he emerged.

Benetti gave a cold stare towards Giovanni, who bowed slightly revealing fear and respect for the boss.

Benetti scowled as he nodded, "So you were able to grab them both? It is a good thing. Signor Lombardo was running out of patience with me. When he loses patience with me, he and I both lose patience with the two of you."

"Yes, boss. We waited out front of her apartment last night for him to come outside, he spent the night, so we had no choice but to take her too."

"That is unfortunate that he stayed. It means that her death warrant is assured. It also means that we need to be extra careful. You don't kidnap a Manhattan Assistant District Attorney without some potential blow-back. If she totally disappears at sea, that could throw the dogs off the scent for a bit longer."

Giovanni handed the ski mask to Benetti, who refused it, "We won't be needing these. They won't be around to identify us in court."

Mohammed Zacharius had been seated at one of the dining tables with Hann and Reilly. He sniffed the air and said, "You know, I have never had bacon in my life. I have always wondered what you 'infidels' found so good about that vile meat. However, perhaps I'll try just a taste of it this morning. Maybe just one piece with my oatmeal. Perhaps one piece won't kill me."

Dickerson laughed out loud and replied, "No, one piece shouldn't kill you. I certainly hope not, because I have more than my share of 'just one piece' of bacon in my life."

Reilly grinned, "I'm sure that we all have. But don't overdo it on your first bacon feast. One piece maybe should be your limit. Or, no more than two."

The dining hall was filled with chatter as each cabin at the camp was now represented. Some people stared at the new member of their group, not having seen the arrival of the strangely dressed man. Some people stared with distrust at this man. They had heard the stories over the years of the vicious mind of Muslims, and they weren't sure if this one might not be up to no good as well.

Pastor Hann rose from his seat and strolled up to the front of the dining hall. He spoke into the microphone, "Good morning brothers and sisters. We have a visitor with us this morning who has a tremendous story to tell of how he came to be with us. Perhaps he can share with us later. First, though, let us give thanks for our blessings."

They all rose and joined hands and gave thanks in unison. Zacharias reached out and held hands with those on either side. It felt good to feel a sense of belonging. For several years, he had grown uncomfortable with the faith of his fathers. He didn't feel as though he belonged. This morning, however, these complete strangers seemed to welcome him as though he were one of them.

As Hann sat down with his group he said to Mohammed, "It is God's desire that no one will be lost. It is up to us to come to the grace that He offered us through Christ.

Mohammed answered quietly, "It is so hard to do for a Muslim. We have been taught for centuries that Christians were the enemy of Islam. They murdered and raped so many of our ancestors during the Crusades. For that reason, many Muslims still to this day refer to Christians as Crusaders. Christians were not living the commands of Jesus and showing what you have called God's love. It was a bloody time for all our ancestors. Mine fought with Saladin against the Infidel invaders of our land."

Father Reilly interjected, "Yes, it was a horrible time. There were promises made that winning back the Holy Land would result in special places in heaven for those who fought hard. It was, I suppose, our version of Jihad. People do so many things at times in history to assure themselves a place in the glory of God. The different gods of history have brought about holy wars for their glory. Usually, some leader of that faith urged the faithful to use brutality in the name of their deity."

Mohammed said, "I always hoped that someday, we can all get along and you will all come to know the peace of Islam."

Hann brought the whole conversation back to the original point of the visit of Mohammed, "Gentlemen, we can't fix the present and the future by dwelling on the past. The future, now for us, is to bring more people to know Christ."

"I believe that is why Jesus led me here. I need to know why he would come to me in a dream and bring me here. I never heard of Dresden, Ohio before this visit."

As they sat at the table, Hann and Reilly began to lead Mohammed through the process of confessing sins and accepting the grace that God gives through the sacrifice of Christ. They showed him in the Bible Romans 10:9 that if you declare with your mouth that Jesus is Lord and believe in your heart that God raised him from the dead, you will be saved.

Andrew Benetti confidently strolled into the waterfront warehouse and stood facing Wallace, "Mr. Wallace, you have caused some concern with important people in Europe. We know, your television people think you can create the news, but not this time."

Giovanni gestured to Pintano to take off his ski mask. Pintano showed a little confusion, "Don't worry, they won't be able to identify us."

At that, a shot of terror went down Wallace's spine. Olivia looked at him with concern. She knew that this was probably going to be a final ride for them. She tried not to think about something like that. She thought of how many times she had prosecuted cases of kidnapping and how the odds are slim of finding the victim alive after the first forty-eight hours.

Benetti picked up a push-broom and unscrewed the handle. Walking around behind Wallace, he cracked the handle against the back of the oak chair. It made a loud crack and Wallace and Olivia both jumped. Benetti laughed out loud and spoke with some glee, "Just think, I could have waited to hit you in the arm. That cracking sound would have been your upper arm or shoulder. You're not going to need to use your arm after today."

He then thumped the stick against the back of Olivia's chair causing the captives to jump again. Giovanni asked Benetti, "How do you want us to handle this, Boss?"

As the captives listened in horror, Giovanni and Benetti discussed wrapping them in weighted canvas and throwing them into the Hudson just outside this warehouse. They decided against that, because of the possibility of the bodies coming ashore before being washed out to sea. They settled on a similar plan, but that involved taking them further downstream in a boat, going a few miles out to sea and dropping them overboard. With that plan, the odds were slim that they'd be washed up on a beach somewhere. Obviously, the goal was to make sure that the bodies would never be found.

As he climbed into his own car and pulled away, Benetti ordered Giovanni and Pintano to put Wallace and Olivia into the van "We'll drive them down to Edgewater. Our company has a boat there. Once we get them past Sandy Hook, we'll spend about an hour on the water. The currents there most likely will not bring them back upriver."

Wallace and Olivia were pushed roughly into the van. They each had their hands duck taped behind them. The smell inside the van was repugnant since it was used most of the time to transport people to and from construction jobs. The smells of paint, turpentine, and sweat comingled in their nostrils. Wallace was sniffing and trying to turn his head to his shoulder to wipe his watery eyes and nose. In his position it was a near impossibility. The van was moving southward from the warehouse when they stopped to get gas. Giovanni and Pintano got out of the van going opposite directions to the restroom and store. Benetti's car had pulled up to the curb a half block away.

Wallace was inspecting every square inch of the floor of the van. He noticed that the sliding door had not completely closed. That would explain the rattling that took place on the trip so far. He nodded to Olivia and motioned toward the door. They turned back-to-back and began to help each other loosen the tape. It was surprisingly easy to undo the tape on Olivia's wrists. After helping her free her wrists, Wallace also had begun to pull the tape from his own wrists.

Wallace swiftly reached for the handle on the slider. Flinging it he almost collided with the gas station attendant to who let out a cry. As the attendant backed away from the van, Wallace and Olivia made a run toward the street. Giovanni came out of the restroom stunned, shouting as he saw his captives running away. He started running after them. Pintano ran out of the attached bodega with his can of Coke and a large bag of potato chips. The attendant threw down the windshield washing squeegee and ran back into the station.

Wallace and Olivia made their way to the side of the bodega and ran down the alley with Giovanni in hot pursuit. Pintano dropped his chips and Coke and gave chase as well. Wallace grabbed a dumpster and pushed it into the alley to slow their pursuers. Olivia cut through a nearby yard with dogs giving chase as she ran across the lawn, ducking around a swing set. Wallace jumped the short chain link fence and was hot on her heels. One of the dogs caught up with him and took a bite at his leg and managed to tear away a portion of the leg on his trousers. Giovanni and Pintano were closing the gap on their prey. Pintano pointed out the slowly swinging child's swing and the dogs barking at the front portion of the fence. As he grabbed the top pipe on the fence he shouted, "This way!"

They ran through another yard and into the street. Looking each way trying to plot their escape path, Wallace glanced to the right and saw Benetti's car bearing down on them. He called out to Olivia, "Go through that yard, no fence in front."

Squeezing between the shrubs and one of the houses they heard the crack and echo coming from a Glock Nine Millimeter. Wallace was familiar with the sound as he had covered some news stories with active gunfire in battle situations. This was, however, the first time either of them had ever been the target of someone firing shots in anger. The piece of wood siding next to his head splintered sending chips of old lead paint flying. As they were about to go into the back yard, he noticed an opening to the crawl space under the house next door. Hoping the shrubs would cover them, he grabbed the back of Olivia's jacket and pulled her toward the opening, "In here, quickly!"

Inside the crawl space they both tried to suppress their heavy breathing. A moment elapsed when they saw the feet of the three men run past them.

They could hear the trio cursing at their bad luck at losing their captives. Benetti called out, "Maybe they went down that alley. Go check both directions for them, I'll get back in my car and go to the next street."

With that the two hunted prey hugged each other close and tried not to make a sound.

"Rats!" Wallace whispered almost too loudly. Two beady little eyes seemed to be staring at them from the studs under the floor above them. "Man, rats creep me out."

Despite their roommate in that cramped little space, they managed to get control of their breathing and settle down.

CHAPTER 9

The celebration was going strong, even after five hours. The European Parliament building in Brussels, Belgium was a joyous place. Paolino Esposito had taken office as the President of the European Commission earlier that same morning. The reception line ran outside the building down Chaussee de Wavre to Rue Wiertz and around the grounds of the Parliament complex making a complete circuit two abreast. Esposito proudly shook hands with and spoke a few words to each person who came to congratulate him.

Approaching the main entrance to the building was Maurice Andrieu. The man was sweating profusely. Andrieu was a man who stood just under five feet eight inches tall. His skin tone was swarthy as the perspiration beaded on his forehead and under each of his eyes. His large brown Fedora was pulled down low putting a shadow over his eyes. Those eyes shifted from side to side taking in all the sights. His mood did not seem to fit in with the large festive crowd.

The security was very tight. There were dogs sniffing for explosives and a ring of five metal detectors allowing for quicker access to the man of the hour. Andrieu was walking briskly toward the first metal detector on the left. He passed through quickly without a problem. His place in line gave him a special view of the floor of the Parliament chamber.

Esposito was laughing and in a very jovial mood. It had been a long road arriving at this day. He had worked his way up through local offices to regional political positions. The past ten years had passed by so quickly as he learned the ins and outs of being a power broker. It had been about five years ago when Albert Le Roux took him under his wing. He had recognized the young Esposito's potential as a leader who could be led by a powerful man such as Le Roux.

Andrieu shuffled forward, and person by person he worked his way to next in line to see the new President of the European Union's Commission. As he stepped forward, he extended his right hand, "Congratulations Signor Esposito. I am so happy to tell you that you hold a special place in the hearts of so many people from Europe."

His words did not sound sincere. But Esposito smiled and thanked him for his support. Looking around, Andrieu grabbed a trophy off the desk of one of the MPs. The trophy was topped with a statue of a Spanish Conquistador with a drawn sword. Andrieu hefted the heavy trophy above his head. To the absolute surprise of everyone within the five-foot radius of that desk, he swung it hard at least four times. The cracking of Esposito's skull echoed with each blow above the din of voices in the room. Blood spattered onto the floor and the hands and faces of everyone gathered around them. The loud shrieks and curses from everyone nearly overcame the loud voices of the security personnel as they wrestled Andrieu to the floor, his face smashed against the hard floor at the foot of one of the desks.

Esposito lay crumpled on the floor as the blood gushed from his head. A look of shock was on his face as he appeared to stare at the ceiling in the large Parliament Chamber. The vacant look in his eyes seemed to get more distant as life was slowly ebbing from him.

The security staff quickly moved around Esposito and Emergency Medical personnel gathered around him, trying to keep him alive. It was possible they were too late. Heart monitors were attached and were getting very low readings. The heart monitor began to send a shrill steady high pitch signal that his heart had stopped. The doctor had arrived. He looked up at Le Roux and slowly shook his head.

Le Roux turned to Cardinal Assidi and said, "Can't you do something? This can't be happening."

As the security people beat Andrieu into a near coma, a chill came over the room. Standing behind Cardinal Assidi, unseen by anyone else in the building, was the dark presence of Baalazaar. The long, boney fingers of his left hand clamped down on Assidi's shoulder. Baalazaar's hand reached out, took Assidi's and guided it to cover the broken face of Esposito. The bleeding miraculously stopped.

Le Roux was shocked. Esposito was a dead man just a few moments ago. The doctor had indicated that it was hopeless. Le Roux had seen Assidi put his hand on the face of the new President. The heart monitor slowly started beeping again but the blood flow stopped. There was a gurgling sound emitting from Esposito's throat. He choked twice, and then his eyes opened. There was fear in his eyes. What had happened? Why was he on the floor?

Cardinal Assidi looked astonished himself as Le Roux asked him, "Nunzio, what did you do? He was dead, he had flatlined right before their eyes. A man can't just wake up like that when he has died."

Assidi answered in disbelief, "I felt a strange power come over me, Sir, and at its leading I put my hand on his face. I felt a surge go through me and then you saw what I saw. I feel that perhaps, Signor Esposito is more than just a man. Perhaps he has been sent directly from God."

Everyone in the remaining group at the scene began to whisper. They felt they had witnessed a miracle that could only have come from God himself. After seeing Esposito sit up, Le Roux immediately turned and walked up the aisle to a bank of reporters who were standing in the foyer. They had witnessed much of what had just happened. Le Roux wanted to control the story.

The reporters began shouting over each other, "What has happened, Monsieur Le Roux? Why all the security and medical personnel? Is Signor Esposito alright?"

Le Roux put his hands up in a "keep calm" motion, "Ladies and gentlemen, please, one at a time. There was an attack upon Signor Esposito. He was severely wounded by a blow to the front of his head. After heroic efforts by emergency medical personnel, the doctor had pronounced him dead. Momentarily, Cardinal Nunzio Assidi, the Spiritual Advisor for The President, placed his hands on him and within a few seconds Signor Esposito came back to life."

The reporters were in a feeding frenzy, "Back to life? How is that possible? That is some kind of miracle!" They had just witnessed an impossibility. No one can perform a miracle like that.

This was the opportunity that Le Roux needed to take his plans further than even he had imagined. He shouted above the voices of the media, "Please, please, listen to me. Cardinal Assidi told me that Signor Esposito came to life after being dead for about three minutes. The Cardinal confirmed the fact that this kind of thing could have only happened to someone who is divine. Listen to me carefully, now. Signor Esposito is the Son of God, returned to life. He has come back to us and will divinely lead us into a paradise here on earth. There was complete silence in the room.

At least four hours had passed since Wallace and Olivia took refuge in a random crawl space. They had gotten used to the musty aromas, and the rat soon ignored them. One could say the rat had gotten used to them as well.

"I don't know about you, but I'm ready to get out of here." Wallace reached out and patted Olivia on the knee. They both slowly rose and made their way back to the opening. Wallace looked out into the connecting yards. It appeared that none of their pursuers were still in the area.

Olivia followed him into the yard. They both began walking, staying close to the buildings in the alley. In a few more hours, it would be dark, and neither of them knew exactly where they were. Without their cell phones, it was impossible to check for their GPS location.

"At least they didn't take my wallet," Wallace whispered, "I still have a good bit of cash."

Olivia was making plans to leave the New York area behind, "I need to get a burner phone. I have a brother in New Jersey. I can call him, and we can borrow one of his cars and get as far away from here as possible."

They had been walking for forty-five minutes. They approached another bodega and Wallace went inside while Olivia hovered just inside the door, watching the street. He bought the phone and a pre-paid phone card, she activated it and called her brother, "Philip… how are you doing? Yes, I know. I didn't go into work today. I got tied up in a case that I can't mention right now. I wonder if I could borrow your Mazda. I'll need it for a few days. You know how it is… I don't usually need a car living in Manhattan… but I need to follow up on a couple of leads out of town. Great… I'll catch a cab and come to you."

Someone had tried to kill the new leader of Europe. The would-be murderer was in custody. Now came the major task of finding out who had hired him.

It didn't take long for the conspiracy theories to come together. Who would want to kill Paolino

Esposito? He had the support of nearly everyone in Rome. He also had the support of anyone who had ever made money from one of the many Le Roux enterprises whether wine or electronics.

The deepest basement of the 453 Avenue Louise in Brussels had at one time been used by the Gestapo, when Belgium was occupied by the Nazis in World War II. Two months ago, the building had been purchased by Albert Le Roux. He knew when he had purchased the eleven-story building that he would use it to help persuade people to fall into line with his ideas.

It had been three days since the attempt on Esposito's life. The arresting officers had beaten Andrieu severely. He lay in a heap on the damp, cold floor. Andrieu looked up through swollen eyes at the dirty, dingy tile walls. It looked as though a thousand years' worth of dirt and tar-filled cigarette smoke clung to these walls. He knew the history of this building. Everyone in Brussels had heard the horror stories of what took place there when the Gestapo used it as a place to extract information from unwilling witnesses. How many times had the sound of breaking bones had echoed off these walls?

He looked up and saw a man coming toward him, holding a pitcher of water and a towel. He lay on a reclined bench that was tilted upward at the feet. His head was between two one-inch-thick bare dowel pins that dug into his shoulders and collar bones. He whimpered softly as the man in a black, skin-tight T-shirt came to him.

The man smiled, showing teeth that were stained by tobacco and decay. The smile oozed with evil pleasure, "Monsieur Andrieu, welcome to my office. I will be asking you a few questions after I help you cool your head a little. Just try to relax. The pain will not last forever. And you needed to wash your dirty face before the interview begins."

With that, the man tightened a belt across Andrieu's chest and then he strapped his wrists to the bench. He laid the towel on Andrieu's face and began to pour the water right in the center of his face causing Andrieu to choke and sputter. The cold water poured through the towel and into his nostrils. The glint in the smiling man's eyes confirmed years of experience in the art of torture.

As the pitcher was emptied Andrieu let out a loud cry. The Smiling Man asked, "What's that, Monsieur? You still feel dirty? Well, let me help you get completely clean." He then reached on the shelf to his right and picked up another pitcher of water. As he poured, he continued to breathe heavily as Andrieu struggled for breath.

This process went on for about ten minutes before the towel was removed. "There you are Monsieur Andrieu, all clean. Now we can begin our interview."

Andrieu lay there shivering from the cold and from the fear of the unknown. He had expected to be arrested, but this torture was never in his thoughts.

The evil, smiling man picked up a pair of jumper cables, attached one to Andrieu's left index finger, strapped in tightly against his side. The other, he waved around in plain view of Andrieu.

The man's breath reeked of cigarettes and bourbon, "Monsieur Andrieu, this shouldn't take long. The sooner you answer, the fewer times you'll need to have your battery charged. When did you plan to kill President Esposito? Who put you up to it?"

He touched the other end of the jumper cables to the index finger of Andrieu's right hand. Andrieu did not answer the questions. The man turned to a rheostat switch attached to a car battery. He slowly turned it up, and Andrieu's groans began to increase in intensity as the rheostat turned up.

Andrieu spoke through clinched teeth, "I was not sent to do this by anyone. I did not want Esposito to be the most powerful man in Europe. He is the son and grandson of murderers. They killed members of my family. We cannot have him leading us. He must... he mus... t... die."

The power from the battery increased as Andrieu screamed louder. Suddenly the screaming stopped and Andrieu's body shook violently. He groaned. A raspy rattling came from his throat. His heart had stopped. He was dead.

Ferdinand Martinez, a Member of Parliament from Spain, had witnessed the attack. It was in fact his trophy presented to him by his constituents calling him the greatest MP ever to represent Madrid that was used in the attack. Martinez had been one of the most vocal supporters of Esposito's chief rival for the EU presidency, Jorge Cortez from Costa del Sol, Spain.

Because of this association, Martinez was suspected of being a part of a plot to kill Esposito. He was taken into custody for investigation by Interpol, and he was taken to the old building at 453 Avenue Louise in Brussels. It was there that he faced harsh interrogation from Interpol Agents who were hand selected by Albert Le Roux and Colonel Vito Lombardo. For three days he faced waterboarding, and electroshock trying to establish a connection between Martinez and the Belgian madman Maurice Andrieu. Word on the streets was that Andrieu had died in custody while trying to "escape".

Agents increased the pressure on Martinez. He had to have been involved in the assassination plot, but he didn't show any sign of being connected with Andrieu in any way.

During the three days that Andrieu faced his deadly interrogation he admitted that he hated Esposito. He had originally planned to attack Esposito and to choke him with his bare hands. But as he came face to face with him, Andrieu noticed the trophy on Martinez's desk. Andrieu picked up the trophy and repeatedly struck with great force. As the interrogation of Martinez continued, it was beginning to look like he had nothing to do with the attack. There was merely the coincidence that the trophy was nearby simply offering Andrieu an opportunity.

Since Andrieu was dead, Le Roux explained that they needed to show people that anyone who attacks a "god" such as Esposito, must be punished. Plans were put into motion to have a sham trial. Those plans included at least three "eyewitnesses" who would testify that Martinez had deliberately placed the trophy nearby so that Andrieu could find the weapon of opportunity.

The witnesses were told to say that they had heard Martinez speak against President Esposito. They each had a slightly different story of events where they had heard Martinez speaking against Esposito. They also said he spoke against anyone who voted for him rather than Jorge Cortez. It sounded believable and the arrest moved forward. The announcement was made that Martinez was to face a quick trial. Le Roux appointed an attorney for him who was fresh out of law school.

This young, inept barrister would be snowballed by the prosecutors on the payroll of Le Roux.

The cab ride to Olivia's brother, Julian Meyer's, home took more than an hour. As the cab pulled up in front of a modest two-story home in Hoboken, she reached over and paid the cabbie. She and Wallace stood in front of the house for a moment or two gathering their thoughts. There were so many memories there for Olivia. This was the house where she grew up. The blood-red shingle siding looked much as it had the day, she started Kindergarten. On the screened-in front porch, she had her first kiss from Danny Klein after Senior Prom. Olivia' mother, Sylvia Meyer had been relatively young when she had a stroke and passed away. Olivia remembered that the last time she visited, the inside of the house had changed very little.

"I certainly hope Julian has taken care of Mother's old Mazda. It's more than twenty years old, but it has always been a reliable car. I don't know exactly how far we need to go to get away from these people, but it should get us there."

"I know people in Scottdale, Pennsylvania, who have answers to questions that we have," Wallace then looked down at the sidewalk and apologetically said, "Liv, I am so sorry that I dragged you into this. I'm sorry that I left you alone with our child. I have been trying to sort out so many thoughts in the past six months. We are living in times that are more troubling than we have ever faced before."

Olivia thought about it a moment, "I have also felt like the times have been troubled since I became an Assistant D.A. I have been in the court room with some of the most abhorrent people anyone could ever imagine. But since you got home, I'm inclined to think the trouble that has followed you may very well be the worst I've ever seen."

Julian Meyer opened the front door and ushered the pair into the living room. "Man, you two look like you've been playing at the landfill, and you both smell like you rolled around in the worst smelling part!"

He looked at Wallace with a sneer, "And you... what kind of problems are you causing for my sister now? The last time I saw you was before you abandoned her, just before she let us know she was pregnant. You have a lot of nerve showing your face around here again."

It was a half-hearted sounding defense, but Olivia stepped up for Wallace, "Julian, when he left, he didn't know yet. And so much has happened since then. Listen, we need to borrow your Mazda."

"I'm not sure that's such a good idea. This guy is wanted by cops all over the world. Did you hear the news about that new leader in Europe? Some idiot tried to kill that Esposito guy."

Wallace was totally taken by surprise, "What? When? How did it happen? Did they shoot him in the head?"

"No, some guy tried to beat him to death with a trophy of some kind. The first reports said that he had died. But then, some Cardinal healed him, and he appeared to be unhurt. Personally, I think it was all faked. They want that guy to look like some kind of Superman." Julian had strong opinions. "I suppose that if you weren't wanted all over the world, this would be the kind of news story you'd be in the front row drooling at the opportunity."

Olivia quickly interrupted, again coming to Wallace's defense, "Bobby is not guilty. He was framed, and I'm doing my best to see that he gets cleared of the charges."

"Sis, you are a great lawyer, but you're blind to this guy's true personality. He's selfish and doesn't care if he drags you down just to save his own hide."

Wallace spoke up for himself, "Look Julian, I know that I have had a single-minded focus on my career at times, but your sister is right about this situation. I did not do what they say I did. What I did do was express doubts about those missing people being taken to the

Andromeda Galaxy as part of a cultural exchange of ideas and knowledge. I think some people in Europe are trying to take control of the situation and make the world think that they have all the answers. They want to control people and if you look closely, I'm sure you'll see that the whole thing is a power trip for someone. Follow the money. I think that rich, control freak Le Roux is behind the whole thing."

Julian was beginning to show more interest in what Wallace was saying, "Why do you think that? I mean, I've always believed that powerful men have ruled over us all since the beginning of this country."

Wallace couldn't wait to express his theory on the rich people, "It's a fact of history in general. It's sociological. There have always been the rich, and there have always been the poor as well as those in between. Being rich, or poor doesn't make a person evil. It's what's in their heart. There have been great kings and queens, presidents, prime ministers who have been benevolent leaders. And there have also been evil leaders. In the 20th Century, Communism ruled Eastern Europe and much of Asia. People flocked to the idea of Socialism and Communism because it was supposed to do away with the rich ruling class. When the State owned everything and shared it equally among all people, it was supposed to be a perfect world. But the leaders of those governments were just as evil as any despot king or dictator. The ruling class had all the privileges and best food, housing, and could travel freely anywhere they wanted to go. The workers, who were supposed to benefit from the Utopian government had nothing. They were ruled with an iron fist. They were worse off than the workers in a factory run by some rich family."

Julian contributed his opinion to this conversation, "Our American politicians have always been corrupt too."

"Poverty has always contributed to crime," said Olivia.

"But not all poor people are criminals. Historically, many poor people of all races were hard working honest people. A moral society will always have a lower crime rate. Our morals have all but gone from us. That's why we've had so much crime," Wallace was trying to show both sides of the coin.

Olivia agreed, "It's what kept me working long hours for many years. I have prosecuted rich guys and poor guys. The one thing they did have in common was a lack of caring for their fellow human beings."

The conversation came to an end when Olivia went into the kitchen for a glass of water. As she returned, she said, "Now that we've solved all the problems of the world, what's our next step, Bobby?"

"We need to get out of the Metropolitan area."

Julian gave Olivia the keys to the Mazda, and turned to Wallace, "If you hurt my sister again, I'll come looking for you. And then you'll wish you were in jail instead of facing me."

"Don't worry about it, I will never hurt her again."

Wallace took the car for a fill-up of gasoline, while Olivia took a shower and changed into clean clothes that had belonged to her mother. She felt fresh and clean for the first time in what seemed to be an eternity.

When he returned, it was his turn in the shower. Hopefully, Julian would part with some of his older jeans and shirts. The dirt and grime slid off his body and his hair felt clean for the first time since he left France. He thought about what lay ahead. He must get to Scottsdale and see if Pastor Hann could help him stay out of sight.

In Brussels, the word was spreading through the population like a wildfire. The only thing anyone could talk about was the miraculous recovery of the new President of the Europe. Many people heard that Cardinal Assidi had healed him after some deranged person picked up a trophy off a Parliament Member's desk and bludgeoned President Esposito to death. But he was only dead for about three minutes when

Cardinal Assidi put his hands on the president's face and healed him.

Everyone was hearing eyewitness reports of how Esposito sat up and, to everyone's amazement, appeared unhurt. There was blood on the floor, but there were no wounds on his head. Those who were waiting in line in the foyer heard all the noise of the cracking bone and the shrieks of those who stood near the deadly attack. They didn't know what was happening, but they were quickly ushered out of the foyer and into a chamber just to the side of the European Parliament Hemi-circle. The story grew more and more spectacular with each passing hour.

People were saying that the attacker had died while trying to escape from police custody. And he apparently had an accomplice from Spain, who had provided the weapon.

CHAPTER 10

The Pennsylvania Turnpike on Interstate 70 through western Pennsylvania has tunnel after tunnel. Wallace remembered back to when he was a child and his father would honk the horn inside the tunnels bringing glee to the children in the car, but probably irritating to all the vehicles around them. Wallace smiled as he thought about it and it became too great a temptation for him. The horn echoed inside the long tube, bringing a snoozing Olivia back to consciousness, "Why did you do that? Nobody honks their horn in tunnels anymore."

"This boy does. If I can relive my childhood on the Pennsylvania Turnpike, I'll do that every time we go into the tunnels."

They both laughed and talked about all that has been going on in Europe. It was an amazing story coming from Brussels. Apparently, this Esposito had really been murdered. The doctor on the scene verified that Esposito had suffered a severe, fatal head injury.

They sat silently for a few moments as they contemplated the stories of the miraculous healing. The scenery along the Pennsylvania Turnpike was beautiful. Wallace imagined the old growth forests looked how they must have looked when the Native Delaware people inhabited this land. The lush green Elm, Poplar and Maple trees stand in beautiful contrast to the white bark of the Birch trees.

As they entered another tunnel, they both commented on the dark feeling that seemed to be hovering nearby. Well into the passageway Wallace and Olivia each jumped at the same time as they thought they had seen a dark presence pass by.

Olivia's voice was quivering when she asked, "What was that? I thought I saw something swoop low over the roof of the car."

Wallace was astounded by what he thought he had seen, "I don't know exactly, but I saw it as well. It was dark, and it was flying low, in and around the traffic ahead of us."

A bright flash of sparks flew just ahead of the line of traffic. Wallace hit the brakes and swerved quickly to the right, coming precariously close to the wall of the tunnel. About one hundred feet ahead of the Mazda, a semi-truck spun around as the tractor separated from the trailer. With NASCAR driver-like reflexes, Wallace quickly guided the car between the separated parts of the tractor-trailer. The sparks intensified as the fuel tanks on the truck caught fire. At least five cars around the Mazda crashed together violently.

Wallace and Olivia's car had already made it through the crash site and quickly came out the west end of the tunnel. A Pennsylvania State Trooper was approaching the tunnel from the west. Wallace pulled the car onto the right shoulder as the trooper hit the lights.

Baalazaar was waiting in Le Roux's office as he entered. His voice was low, and it rumbled quietly as he informed Le Roux that his agents had located Wallace and had set into motion a chain-reaction traffic collision that would have surely killed him.

"As long as he's truly dead, I don't care if it's by traffic accident or under the sharp blade of the Guillotine," Le Roux sounded very relieved that the American troublemaker was dead.

Paolino Esposito was high on the energy that goes with having just survived a death experience. He had just taken office as the President of the European Union's

Commission. He was ready to truly take power as a leader.

It was well past midnight the day after the assassination attempt, in a rare moment of solitude he paced the floor of his office. He could hear the light echo of his leather shoes on the hard floor. Though he was alone, there was a sense that someone else was in the room with him.

His name was spoken in a whisper. It sounded as though the whisper were coming through large speakers on the ceiling of the room, "Paolino … you are mine… you have been chosen."

He turned around to see who was speaking but saw no one. The voice echoed again, "You are mine… I saved your life, and you are mine from this day forward. I will give you everything you've ever wanted in this world. You will be the envy of people all over the world. You will one day soon rule the world."

"Who are you? Where are you… I can hear you, but I can't see you."

"You don't need to see me right now. I am your light. I started you on the road to leadership when you were a very young man. I will guide your every step as, you become the leader of the world."

The presence in the room was a heavy one, as it lingered but Esposito was not uncomfortable with it. To him, the voice was soothing. He felt as though he knew the voice. He had heard it before guiding him through his early political career.

He thought back on his career in politics. Local politics were very corrupt in Palermo when he started in the family business. Esposito's first opponent, Michael Lazzarone, was not available for interviews two weeks prior to the elections. He had disappeared. He had been leading, according to all the pre-election polling data. Esposito mysteriously won the election in a close race that required a recount that lasted for thirty days. There were accusations that Esposito's family had eliminated the competition. There was no evidence to implicate anyone in the Esposito crime family. There was no evidence to implicate anyone, for that matter. If he had been murdered, his body was never found. It was as though Lazzarone had dropped off the face of the earth.

The west end of the tunnel on the Pennsylvania Turnpike was a very busy place. Ambulances were arriving and departing. Wallace pulled out his passport and driver's license with the name Walter Dobbs on them.

He told Olivia, "In case anyone asks, my name is Walter Dobbs. That's what my passport and driver's license say.

"Walter? Where did you get that name?"

"My friend Susanne Coppin with BSN set me up with a counterfeit passport and driver's license to help me get back into the States."

"I knew that she helped you get back into the country, but you didn't tell me about the counterfeit passport. Wow, if I was planning to prosecute you, I'd have another charge. Please don't tell me that there are more potential broken laws."

The seriousness of the situation brought them back to reality. The state trooper approached to talk to them about the accident. There were seven cars in the crash with at least three fatalities. The semi truck's saddle tanks had burst into flames the second Wallace and Olivia had driven past the scene. The truck driver didn't have a chance of survival. The drivers of the two cars on either side of the truck were also killed instantly.

The trooper grimly approached them and asked for identification. The questioning was routine. What did you see? Where were you in proximity to the accident? Where are you going? There was nothing in the questions that concerned Wallace. After answering the questions and giving false contact information to the trooper Wallace and Olivia were dismissed.

Back on the road, the reality was starting to settle in for Wallace. This is the second time in the past three days that he had barely escaped death.

Baalazaar was livid! Inside a cave just outside Naples, Baalazaar was screaming at the demon that had just told him of the failed mission to kill Wallace.

"We cannot have this happen again. An airplane crash, a multi-vehicle pile-up in the United States. These failures must stop. I don't care that you had it planned out perfectly. YOU FAILED!"

As the screaming intensified, the cave filled with more demons. There were four others floating near the ceiling. Baalazaar snapped his fingers and pointed to the demon cowering on the floor. The other four quickly descended on him. He flattened and seemed to gain a liquid-like consistency and flowed down through a crack in a corner of the cave.

Baalazaar raised both hands, doubled his fists and clapped them together. Lightning flashed from the pinnacle toward the corner of the cave, sending a fireball blazing down the crack behind the demon.

As they were coming closer to Scottdale, Wallace called the church looking for Pastor Hann, "Hello, may I please speak with Pastor Hann?"

The receptionist informed Wallace that Hann was no longer at the church, Wallace decided to take a chance and identify himself, "Oh, Mr. Wallace, Pastor

Hann left instructions that if you called, I was to give you his new phone number."

He called the new number, and Hann told him everything that had happened since they last spoke. He gave instructions on how to find Camp Dickerson. Hann talked about all the things God seemed to be doing for them at the camp, including the Muslim man who had found them because of a vision given to him by Jesus. It was a very exciting time for everyone there. Many people who had only been church attenders had become followers of Christ with a deep faith, the likes of which they had only heard others speak of in the past. Hann encouraged him to come quickly.

Wallace turned to Olivia, "There's been a change of plans. We're going to stay out of sight in Ohio for a while. Hann is with a group of people in a camp compound near a little town called Dresden."

"Why is this a good idea?" Olivia wondered why this place was so important. "I'm not sure I can get away from my office for much longer."

"I'm not sure that you can go back there again. If you'll recall, there are people who saw you with me. It's true, they were trying to kill both of us. If you go back, it's possible that they may turn you in. We can't take that kind of chance."

Olivia sighed, "I suppose you're right. So where is Dresden, Ohio?"

"All I know is that it is about a half hour north of I-70 at Zanesville. I'm not too sure how much further that is from here."

In short order, they were back on 70 headed westbound. In about another hour they crossed into West Virginia. Wheeling was on the Ohio River. Now they were less than an hour and a half from Zanesville.

Baalazaar raised his hands once again and conjured up the demon he had sent back into the pit. The fellow came back through the slit in the corner of the cave. He was still smoldering from head to toe. His thin, leather-like wings stretched out to their full eight-foot span, and as he flapped them, and the smoke dissipated.

Baalazaar's eyes were narrowed to tiny slits as he spat his next commands at the demon, "You now have one more chance to redeem yourself in my eyes. Go back to wherever you lost track of Wallace, get back on his trail and find him."

With that, the demon left the cave, closely followed by the four who had helped Baalazaar dispatch him into the pit.

In no time at all they were at the scene of the crash in the tunnel. They went into the State Highway Patrol office, as they tuned into computer language and flowed into the internet searching for Wallace. they examined the records for information on the crash and found that Wallace and Olivia were headed to Scottdale. In a heartbeat the group was hovering above the town seeking where Wallace might be.

Shortly after passing through New Concord, Wallace and Olivia crossed into Zanesville. They exited at Maple Avenue Route 60 and followed the directions Hann had given Wallace. It was only about forty minutes until sunset.

It was a rather quick drive north through Zanesville, and within about twenty minutes they had passed through Dresden and found the location of Camp Dickerson. It was just as Hann had described it. There were Peach Trees filling the ten acres adjacent to the campground.

As it started getting dark, the same dark presence that Wallace and Olivia had noticed in the Pennsylvania Turnpike tunnel seemed to descend upon them. As they approached the gate to the camp, the shadowy entities swooped down to the road.

Suddenly, the dark feeling of evil lifted. Something had cleared it away.

The demons were on the road in front of Wallace and Olivia, well prepared to run them off the road and into the culvert at the side of the road. Before they could carry out their task they were set upon by a host of heavenly beings. Bolts of light flashed from their fingertips, sending the demons shattering like glass, that quickly blew away from the area, leaving no trace of them.

The five demons were lined up in front of Baalazaar as his voice boomed, "What do you mean, you found him, but you could not get to him?"

"As we were ready to cause them to crash into a cement culvert, we were interrupted by a host of heavenly beings. Whatever is in that camp is under heavy guard by hosts of heaven ready to do battle. I know that I have faced at least one of them when we held people in our grip at **Buchenwald**. Simon Wiesenthal was protected by this same angel. After the war, Wiesenthal hunted down so many of those that we had put into power. Because we never killed Wiesenthal along with so many of God's chosen race, he struck back and made the world remember what had happened there. Now that same angel is back, protecting a different camp."

It was true. God had taken the horror of the concentration camps of World War II and turned them to the good, bringing his people together, once again in His chosen place, the Promised Land, Israel. Without that horror of the Holocaust, the re-birth of Israel might never have happened. God's people needed to get away from Europe and into a land where they could protect themselves from governments that would want to eliminate them.

Baalazaar exploded with anger, "We have faced them so many times in the past, but always there have been those who have chosen to follow us, despite the hosts of heaven showing them the way to God. This world has always been mine since the day Adam and Eve fell under my spell! I managed to take their churches and turn them into places where people followed my lead instead of the leadership of God. I will win in the end! This small enclave of people in Ohio will not overcome what I have in store for this world!"

The warm July nights in Ohio were about to turn into warmer August nights. The Fireflies turned the surrounding fields and orchards into a sea of sparkling diamonds. There were chirping crickets and croaking frogs in a nearby pond. The cacophony of sound was comforting to a city boy like Wallace.

After they had dinner, Pastor Hann and Father Reilly sat with Wallace and Olivia in the cafeteria sharing with each other what had been happening.

Hann directed is gaze to Wallace, "I heard about the airline crash in Iceland, and how you were accused of being responsible. But I thought it made no sense that you'd cause a plane crash. It wasn't logical. Things are happening in Europe right now that are so much in line with Bible prophecy that it can only be looked at as setting the stage for the last seven years of life on this planet as. We believe that Jesus is very close to returning. Those of us here at this camp are ready for his return."

Wallace was eager to share about the last few days, "I don't fully understand what's going on. After I heard a voice telling me to "GO" at the airport in Paris, I took the ferry from Calais to Dover and then went to London. My friend with BSN picked me up and through some covert action set me up with a new identity and passport and driver's license. Then she brought me to the States on a private charter."

"When I got to New York, I went to see Olivia. We talked all night and early the next morning we were abducted by someone who had plans to kill us."

"Kill you? Why on earth would they want to kill you?" Hann was bewildered by this story.

Olivia added her recollection of the tale, "That's just it. They questioned both of us and roughed us up a bit. Then we heard them planning to take us out to sea and kill us."

"We managed to escape, borrow her brother's car and head to Scottdale. When I called the church, that's when I found out that you were no longer there."

"Yes," said Hann, "the powers that be decided that I was becoming too much of a religious fanatic and they no longer wanted to hear the truth of the Bible. It says in second Timothy four – three, there would come a day when people wouldn't want to listen to sound doctrine but instead follow their own desires. They would gather teachers around them to tickle their ears with what they wanted to hear, instead of the truth."

He went on the explain how he had contacted Father Reilly and a few other like-minded searchers, who wanted to draw closer to Christ, instead of just asking what would Jesus do?

They all continued talking into the night and sharing what the Bible said regarding the very days they were now witnessing. There were moments of laughter and moments of prayer. Before they knew it was nearly midnight. Even though they were exhausted in mind and body, their time of sharing and praying calmed them and they were able welcome a peaceful sleep.

CHAPTER 11

Esposito was conducting his first high level business meeting in a conference room. His excitement was apparent as he was ready to fully take charge. He knew that he had enemies who were not happy that he was the leader of the European Council. He had made it his mission to go after all his opponents and make sure that they don't stop his plans. *didn't*

was The Spanish Member of Parliament, Ferdinand Martinez *is* in custody. The word coming to Esposito has been that Martinez *~~will~~ would* be put on trial for his involvement in the assassination attempt. Even though he may not have been involved, his trial *was* is ready to begin tomorrow.

After he is found guilty, he will face the Guillotine, and that will dissuade others from trying to get in his way.

"Ladies and gentlemen, today we will begin the process of getting the world banking system in line. We need to do away with the different forms of cash from each country including the Euro. Banking information will be available for everyone at one location. When an employee receives a payment for services rendered, it will be automatically deposited in their central bank. In exchange for security, people will pledge their allegiance to us."

As Esposito finished his speech, a courier arrived with a note from Albert Le Roux a note said "Ferdinand Martinez will go on trial tomorrow. The witnesses are lined up to level their accusations that he had conspired with Maurice Andrieu to kill Paolino Esposito."

Esposito smiled slightly and nodded to Cardinal Assidi, who asked if he could address the gathering of legislators. He was granted permission, "Ladies and gentlemen of the Council. I am honored to have been invited to this prestigious gathering today. I have been in prayer constantly since I felt the life return to our glorious leader, Signor Esposito. It is a fact that he was truly dead, and I was able to bring him back to us. I felt that God himself had passed through my hands and into the once dead man giving him life once again. I feel that I have been given the authority to speak for God. He has told me that Signor Esposito is truly chosen to be our leader. We are to worship him because God has entered him. When we look at Signor Esposito, we are truly seeing God on earth with us. God wants us to grant him the power that He has granted by raising him from the dead. We have seen His son return to us. I propose that we worship him and encourage the world to worship him as well."

Esposito feigned modesty and took the baton of anointed leadership, "Thank you, Cardinal Assidi. And once again I thank you for being in position to follow the guidance of God, my father. If we could have everyone seriously consider your proposal, I would like to see a vote to grant me unilateral power and leadership within the hour. Please, my brothers and sisters, make this vote unanimous. Any resistance could cost many lives as I seek to bring about peace to the lives of all people."

The courtroom was filled to the choking point. News media people from all over the world were clamoring from the gallery, and those who could not get into the room were milling around on the benches in the overflow area in the hallway. So many trials have been called "The Trial of the Century." This trial was taking on the same circus like atmosphere.

Ferdinand Martinez, the Member of Parliament from Spain, was led into the room in shackles. His eyes vividly showed his fears. The crowd created quite a stir.

Martinez had been accused of being a co-conspirator in the assassination attempt on Paolino Esposito. It was a trophy on his desk in the Parliament Chamber that was used to bludgeon Esposito to death.

Of course, the judge was hand selected by Albert Le Roux, and he entered the court grim-faced, knowing full well the task he had in front of him. The leader of Europe had just taken office when someone assassinated him. Were it not for the miraculous intervention of Cardinal Nunzio Assidi, everyone would be looking for a new leader. Such a tragedy, considering the man in power is a god on earth.

There were angry rumblings from the crowded gallery. After the judge took his seat on the bench and all the observers settled into their places. The rumbling of voices stopped, and the trial got underway.

The prosecution's case was laid out in orderly fashion. The defense attorney had attempted to stop the steamroller that was about to run over his client. He knew that there was not any real solid evidence linking Martinez to Andrieu and therefore, there is no real suggestion of conspiracy to commit murder.

Witnesses came forward, swearing that they had seen Martinez and Andrieu meeting in dark corners of cafes. It was becoming apparent that Martinez was doomed and there was not anything that could be done to stop it. Every objection raised by the defense was quashed by the judge. It was apparent that the magistrate was under the influence of Albert Le Roux. The trial lasted one day with very little deliberation assessing the guilt or innocence of Martinez. Very early on the second morning of the trial the verdict of guilty was passed down. With that announcement, Pilar Martinez let out a scream of horror for her husband's fate.

The judge immediately pronounced the sentence of death by the Guillotine. It was to be the first public execution in more than twenty years. The crowd let out with a roar of approval. The members of the media rushed out of the courtroom to file their stories in the adjacent press room. TV reporters took up their positions in the front of the court building, and the media feeding frenzy was on. Would there be any appeals? Would Martinez finally admit to his part in the plot, and would he perhaps get a lighter sentence if he named other co-conspirators?

In the Parliament Chamber, Esposito stood in front of the lawmakers, calling for a vote which would give him unprecedented power. He had ideas that would truly bring peace to this world, as only a singular leader could do.

Cardinal Assidi entered the chamber from the side with a look of urgency on his face. Esposito had been following the story of the trial before this legislative session began but had not yet heard the announcement of the verdict. Assidi came to Esposito's side and whispered in his ear. Esposito smiled broadly and stepped up to the podium, "Ladies and gentlemen, the man who was involved in the attempt on my life has been found guilty. He will be executed by Guillotine next Sunday morning." Without pause, Esposito continued, "Now we have very important matters at hand. I am asking you to grant me unlimited powers to rule Europe. I vow to bring peace and prosperity to all the world."

The secretary called for the vote. Even though some of the members weren't totally on board with the idea of granting Esposito full power, they felt compelled to grant it because the promise of peace was too enticing.

Almost immediately, Esposito began to work on his plan to centralize the banking system. What the world did not know, is that Le Roux Industries had been manufacturing a microchip. A microchip that can store every person's complete personal information. *could*

Pilar Martinez was allowed into the visiting area with her husband. They were able to make contact, and the tears flowed freely, realizing how little time they had left together.

Pilar held her husband's hands across the table, "Mi amor, I do not want to live without you. I know that you did not do what they say you did. Please, let us seek a reprieve for you."

The attorney who presented such a lack-luster defense entered the room carrying a file folder. His body language showed that he was not going to be the bearer of good news. He stood by the table and shuffled his feet. Not making eye contact he mumbled, "President Esposito turned down my request for a reprieve. I thought that since he is the son of God, he must be ready to forgive. But he not only refused to forgive, he also refused to discuss it. His representative told me that because the crime was so heinous, it was not a forgivable offense."

Pilar stood and pounded on the attorney's chest, "You must go back and try again! We support Signor Esposito as President of the commission, and we would have supported giving him power if he had asked. Por favor, go back again and help save mi marido! Por favor, por favor!"

"I cannot go back. I have exhausted every avenue to overturn the verdict or to re-try the case. They will never allow you to walk away from all this."

Le Roux sat at his desk, rubbing his hands gleefully and smiling as if he was the winner of a castle on the Rhine.

He had just heard the news that the EU's new leader had been granted unilateral powers to make decisions, without needing the approval of political rivals. Paolino Esposito had recently survived an assassination attempt, having literally been brought back to life. He was now able to institute laws allowing him to take control of the European banking systems.

The wealthy, powerful families that had ruled the financial world for centuries would now come under the control of Esposito, and the de Facto control of Albert Le Roux.

He called his contacts in China to step up production of the silicon chips that would soon be implanted under the skin of everyone in Europe, perhaps even the world. As he hung up the phone, he was startled to see Baalazaar standing in front of Le Roux's desk, "Happy today, aren't we? It is only beginning, my friend. Your wealth will bloom far beyond anything that you currently can imagine. I have given you the world. But there is one thing that you need to remember. I am your god. You will follow my leading and I will lay the world at your doorstep. Take my hand, I want to show you something."

With that, Le Roux joined hands with Baalazaar, and in a heartbeat they were standing in the chamber of the Parliament Building in Brussels. Le Roux and Baalazaar were invisible to the people in the chamber.

They stood beside Esposito. Baalazaar placed his hand on Esposito's shoulder and in the blink of an eye they stood atop a mountain in the Alps. Below they could see all of Italy, Austria, and France. Behind them on the other side of the range was Switzerland. Baalazaar directed his gaze toward Esposito. With eyes piercing those of Europe's supreme leader the strong request was made, "Look around you. All that you see, I will give to you if you bow down and worship me."

Le Roux answered with Esposito, "I will, My Master. I am yours and I will worship you as my god."

Just as quickly as the promise was made, Le Roux was back in his office at his desk, rubbing his hands with glee and smiling ever so broadly.

At the same moment, Esposito stood before the European legislature. He had a new sense of empowerment.

Early on Sunday morning, Ferdinand Martinez was awakened by two prison guards and Cardinal Nunzio Assidi. He stood petrified in his cell. He was quaking with fear, as tears streamed down his face. The guards stripped him naked and pulled a clean, white gown over his head. They had trouble getting his hands steady enough to pull them through the white linen sleeves.

The front of the gown was open, exposing his chest, covered with thick wiry hair.

The four of them began the long walk to the courtyard of the prison. There in the center was a tall platform with thirteen steps leading up to a tall structure that housed the Guillotine.

There was a crowd of nearly three hundred people, spitting angry words at Martinez the moment he came into view. Across from the Guillotine platform was a scaffolding that contained television cameras from major networks around the world. Martinez and his escorts descended the stairway from the prison hallway to the courtyard. The shackles chafed his ankles and the chain rattled with each step. The jeering crowd overpowered the quiet sobs of Pilar Martinez as she stood by the pathway. She reached out and touched the long gown on her husband. He looked longingly at her, pursed his lips, and mouthed, "I love you, mi amor."

The twenty meters walk to the bottom step to the platform seemed to take an eternity. Slowly taking each step one at a time, Martinez looked at the surrounding crowd calling for his death. Tears streaked his dirty cheeks. As he stepped onto the platform, he looked down at the at the base of a trough that would guide his head into the large wicker basket placed there. Such a strange thought came to his as he wondered if he would see anything as his head rolled into the wicker basket.

The two guards forcibly laid him face down with his head going through the lunette which was to hold his neck in place.

Assidi raised his hands to silence the angry crowd, "Ladies and gentlemen, I know you are thirsty for the blood of one of the people responsible for attempting to kill our lord, Signor Esposito. In a few moments it will be over, and we can move on to more important matters of saving this lost world."

He then turned to Martinez, "I pray that Signor will have mercy on your soul. As you lie here, call out to him and he will take you to paradise, when he finishes his work here."

With that, the executioner raised the weighted blade to its full height. No one was sure what they heard Martinez cry out as the blade made its rapid fall, separating his head from his body. To some, it sounded as though he cried out the name, "Jesus."

CHAPTER 12

It had been nearly twenty-four hours since Martinez was executed. News media programs were playing video of the execution at least once per half hour on every channel. The official government statements stated that they were showing it as a deterrent to anyone who would even consider going against official policy.

The other top news story was an update on the progress of implementing the wide distribution of microchips. The Le Roux factory in China had stepped up production. Millions of the chips had already been manufactured and shipped to Italy and France. The plan was that within six months there would be microchips available for every European citizen in every city within the EU.

In the Parliament building in Brussels, Paolino Esposito walked briskly down the hall from his office to the legislative chamber. His Chief of Staff walked beside him, taking notes as Esposito gave the orders that would soon become law. These were the orders to begin implanting microchips into the citizens of the EU.

Another order put the wheels in motion that would begin centralizing all banking. Soon there would be no more need for Francs, Deutsche Marks, the Pound Sterling or even the Euro. All banking and exchange of money would be conducted electronically.

At their next session, Parliament would unanimously endorse these laws.

Le Roux had a full day's schedule of meetings ahead of him. People plan so many things without knowing what the day will hold. He sat at his desk, proudly viewing his full calendar. Meeting after meeting was planned. He was to sign papers that would open a new data storage facility in Paris. His plan was that Paris would become the new Capitol of Europe.

"Good morning, Albert," the now familiar voice of Baalazaar softly came from the darkened corner of Le Roux's massive office. The office had all the trappings of a powerful man, including pictures of Le Roux with world leaders and celebrities. Le Roux had always led an exciting life. He had one of the largest yachts in the harbor at Monaco, where he owned two of the largest hotels and casinos. His star had been rising all his life.

Le Roux responded, "Good morning, my lord. You would be very proud of me. We are about to take further steps toward ruling the entire world."

"Yes, Albert, you are correct. And thanks to your obedience, my plans are now unstoppable. I thank you for being a good and faithful servant throughout your life. You have been mine since childhood. Now it is time for you to collect your true reward."

Le Roux looked puzzled. He wondered how it could get even better. He possessed more than any other human being alive today. He controlled all of Europe's economy, and now Baalazaar was telling him he was about to collect a true reward.

"My lord, you have given me so much already, what could be my true reward beyond everything that I have today?"

Baalazaar explained to him, "Albert, everything that you have done for me has laid the groundwork for all that is to come. Your factories churn out the microchips that are needed to bring more people under my control. Now, your work for me is done. The material things of this life are nothing - they don't last. It is time for me to bring you home to me."

At that moment, Le Roux clutched his chest and fell forward, hitting his head on the edge of his desk. He slumped to the floor, sighed, and breathed his last breath.

"Sleep well, Albert. I have planned for this moment since you toyed with your first computer as a nine-year-old. Thank you for your service to me."

It was only a matter of moments before the word of Le Roux's death flashed around the world. The financial capitols of the world saw fluctuations in the markets, as people wondered what would become of their investments in the vast empire of Le Roux Industries.

Esposito made the announcement in the newest session of the Parliament. He asked for a thirty-day period of mourning, in honor of the visionary man who had given so much of his life for the unification of Europe, someday bringing the world together. Very few people in history had ever worked so tirelessly to develop products and bring together the people who could make the necessary personal sacrifices for the good of the world.

The thirty-day mourning period began officially in Brussels and spread to the other capitols of Europe. In Paris, Berlin, Vienna, all the way to Rome, people closed shops.

Everyone working for Le Roux Industries went home for the rest of the week. Because of the importance of bringing the microchip distribution to the entire continent, they would be required to return to work and be at full capacity beginning the following Monday.

Colonel Vito Lombardo had spent the morning on the phone with Cardinal Assidi. They were formulating plans for a security force for Lord Esposito, as they had started calling him. It had been decided that the rather significant security force previously assigned to protect Albert Le Roux would be the basis of a large, uniformed security detail. In addition, they would have an elite group of secret police to serve Esposito.

Cardinal Assidi, for his part, was making plans to significantly change much of the plans for worship within the church. He was asserting his position as the de facto head of the church, after his heroic action bringing Lord Esposito back to life. Camera crews had recorded the attack with the trophy. The sword on the statue was quite solid, and the head wounds were deep. It had been noted by attending physicians that his brain had been exposed, and only a true godly miracle could have saved him.

In Washington, D.C. President Elizabeth Blair was conducting a high-level meeting. The Oval Office was filled with leaders from both parties in each of the legislative bodies along with the Secretary of the Treasury, Lexi Anthony.

At precisely thirteen hundred hours, President Blair called the meeting to order, "Thank you all for being here. The Europeans are beginning to streamline their banking process. We here in the United States have been working with a near cashless society. Direct deposit of pay checks has been happening since the nineteen eighties on a wide scale. Most people use charge cards or debit cards for all their financial transactions. The Europeans are beginning to implant microchips into people that will contain all their financial information. Secretary Anthony will now fill us in on what we currently know about the chips."

"Thank you, Madam President. This is true. Le Roux Industries Microchips have been in use for nearly twenty years on a small-scale basis. Various companies have used them to keep personnel information instead of punching a time clock. I believe, along with members of the House Finance Committee, that we should offer this opportunity to Americans who would like to better organize their banking and financial transactions."

People around the room all nodded in agreement. The Republican members were a little concerned over security and the possibility of it becoming mandatory. They didn't want to appear to take away freedom of choice from American citizens.

President Blair allayed the concerns by assuring those present that because we are not Europe, our leaders uphold freedoms here.

The noon break for the Congress and Senate Members would come to an end in short order and each legislative body would propose a bill that would allow banks to offer microchips as an option for interested customers.

August was passing quickly. It had been nearly a month since Wallace and Olivia had traveled north of Dresden, Ohio, to Camp Dickerson. Pastor Hann and Father Reilley along with the twelve other leaders, had formed a tight-knit community, into which everyone fit perfectly. They were sharing their time and talents with each other. The growing season was at its peak and tomatoes and other vegetables were being harvested from the gardens at the camp. The lost art of canning tomatoes and green beans was being practiced as the inhabitants were preparing for the coming winter. Activity in the kitchen was led by a few of the older ladies, women who had learned the art of canning from their mothers and grandmothers.

The men had also learned knitting and sewing, skills that most young men didn't learn. Many young women had not learned how to do this either. Someone had found an antique spinning wheel in a nearby barn and figured out how to spin yarn. Some even took up the art of storytelling as they made the spinning wheel whirl, turning wool into yarn. It became apparent to most that the old fashion phrase of "spinning a yarn" must have had its origin just like this. Some ancient mother somewhere would tell stories to her young as she made yarn that would be turned into clothes and blankets.

At the morning worship, talk was turning to news coming out of Europe that Albert Le Roux had died of a heart attack. He had amassed one of the largest fortunes in the world from wine business, electronics and well-connected political influence. Now he was dead. Europe was on the verge of going to a totally cashless society, by implanting microchips from Le Roux Industries under the skin of every man and woman in Europe.

Pastor Hann mentioned how the Bible tells us that in the last days, no one would be able to do business without receiving "the Mark of the Beast."

Father Reilly added his theory, "This very well could be the beginning of those last days. If it becomes law that everyone needs the chip to do business, Bible prophecy states that you have to give your allegiance to the leader."

CHAPTER 13

L ord Esposito is our Divine One!" The members of the European Parliament were shouting with great gusto. Paolino Esposito had just finished telling the governing body his plans for centralizing the European economy. He was making plans for a larger public gathering. Cardinal Assidi had already lined up the fifty-thousand seat King Baudouin football stadium in north west Brussels. People from all over north-western Europe were beginning to arrive in Brussels for the coming weekend gathering, which had been in the planning stages for a few weeks.

The excitement had been building as the Cardinal was circulating stories about the divinity of Paolino Esposito. The young man who had been the grandson and son of purported crime figures from Sicily, had risen to heights he could have never dreamed of when he was a college student. When he was serving on the University Student Council he had been bitten by the political bug. He always took charge in every situation, and those with whom he had worked always looked up to him. Now, thanks to Cardinal Assidi, he ~~will~~ be revered even more than he could have imagined. He ~~is~~ being hailed as a god.

In addition to ordaining Esposito's deity, Cardinal Assidi had been writing a new set of devotional prayers and a new Missal that would be put into the churches and the church schools. It was time to begin acknowledging the holiness of Lord Esposito. Every morning the Creed was to be recited in the schools, "We believe, on this earth, in Lord Esposito alone! We believe in the central church leadership which is our sole source of grace!"

Cardinal Assidi ordered special posters depicting a heroic Paolino Esposito standing before a large crowd with their hands raised in praise toward him. The aura around his head appeared to be a halo. Assidi imagined a day when families all over the world would pray to Lord Esposito and place shrines with his picture in their living rooms.

Traffic bringing those who were coming into Brussels for the weekend choked the roadways more than usual. Under normal circumstances this much traffic would be leaving Brussels for the weekend. Each car carried at least four people, as festive songs echoed throughout the countryside. There were families with people in their thirties and older folks in their sixties, seventies, and eighties. One centenarian who made the trip from Paris told her children and grandchildren that the mood almost matched the excitement when Allied Liberators joined the Free French fighters and marched into Paris, as the Nazis escaped just ahead of them.

There were very few hotel rooms remaining in the capitol city and many people took to camping in the city parks. Tents were springing up in the parks and vacant lots on the outskirts of Brussels. Soccer balls were kicked about, and laughter filled the air. People were so excited about the coming peace. In their hearts and minds, Lord Esposito was going to bring peace to all of Europe. No more fights over territory, or money. Jobs were going to become abundant. For the first time since medieval Europe was under the heaviness of serfdom, the rich aristocracy would hold no more power over the people.

Lord Esposito was in total control. People who had never been inside a church in their entire lives now looked forward to hearing the wise words of the son of God.

Cardinal Assidi looked out over the gathering of nearly one thousand bishops and Cardinals brought together to hear him speak. Over the centuries since the Middle

Ages, this ancient basilica had been the scene of so many great gatherings. As the church had held control of Europe prior to and throughout the time of the Crusades, this august body was gathering now to bring Europe back under control of the Church.

"Gentlemen," Assidi began, "the time has come for us to bring our continent forward into a new faith. We have seen with our own eyes that God has given us His son again, living here among us, a son of Rome. The ancient Holy Roman Empire is emerging once again as a new force to be reckoned with." Assidi spoke with such strong confidence.

The group rose as one with thunderous applause. Could it be that they had lived to see the day that has been promised for so long? He continued, "Brothers, it is time to send missionaries to the whole world, and that includes the United States of America. For at least the past two centuries, we have seen Americans sending missionaries to all parts of the world, including here, the birthplace of Christianity. We now have the assurance that we are once again the one true church. No more will Americans pull people away from our followers for their own brand of faith. We will send those of you who have come here from America back home with a renewed fervor to bring people back into the fold and tell them about our Lord Esposito. We have seen with our own eyes how he was raised from death, completely healed of a fatal head-wound. We will make it our goal that world-wide, there will be no more Catholics, nor more Methodists, nor Lutherans, Anglicans, or any other denomination of churches. When they hear our message of truth, they will have no choice but to become followers of Lord Esposito with the same fervor that has overtaken us."

The body of men shouted, "The Lord Esposito is our Lord. He alone is great among the earth. We will give him praise and glory. He comes in the name of all that is holy. He is our Lord and leader!"

One bishop from Los Angeles, California called out, "Cardinal Assidi, we believe that it's time for you to become our new Pope. It is time once again to have a Roman leading the Roman church. You, after all, are wholly responsible for healing Lord Esposito and restoring his life. That is a miracle of miracles. Therefore, you must be our leader, our Pope."

Once again, those in the crowded room rose and exploded in thunderous applause. Assidi nodded with affected humility. It was his dream to be elected Pope and head the church. Now was the time to rise to the occasion. For too many years, the Pope was a man from outside Rome. They have come from Poland, Germany, South America, and Africa. The time was now to restore leadership to a true Roman for the church of Rome.

Lay people gathered in fellowship halls in church buildings across the United States, Including the dining hall at Camp Dickerson. They were watching the satellite feed from Rome, as the church there was taking on a new challenge. It was apparent that there was a big plan to unite the entire world with one church, and one church only. The early goal of the Church, to bring the world to the saving grace of Christ, was now being replaced by a goal to unite all churches under one umbrella, under the leadership of a mortal man.

Father Reilley shook his head as he slowly walked to the coffee pot to refill his heavily stained mug, "This is sad for me, my friends. I had always thought that the church was following Christ and not following an individual man who was in Rome. I always respected the Pope, whoever he was, but the Pope was not the center of the Church. He was the leader ordained by God to lead us and that is all."

"Any man is just a human being, and that is all," said Pastor Hann, "Christ was the only human being who was fully human and fully God."

Those gathered in the dining hall pondered these thoughts. Many of those here had little or no history of church attendance in their lives. Those who had considered themselves to be Christians, only did so because they weren't affiliated with any religion. Wallace was among those. He knew so very little about the faith.

Since gaining some knowledge of the Bible's description of the Rapture, he was now interested in learning more. As the others sat around the tables talking, he stepped outside onto the patio at the entrance to the hall, and sat in one of the Adirondack chairs, staring out at the surrounding woods. The soft whisper of the light breeze blew through the branches. Behind him, the sound of the fountain was soothing, as the water fell into the pool below. Nearby he heard the soothing evening cry of the Mourning Dove, "Cu-da-cu, cu, cu."

Wallace then began to have a conversation with God. He spoke of how he had not been a believer, but now he wanted to follow Christ. "Lord, I don't know what to say to you. I'm sorry that I haven't been interested in learning about you in the past. I always felt unaccepted by church people who made me feel I wasn't good enough to be a part of their group. I want to be a Christian now, if it's not too late. I am begging you to please help me become a true follower of Jesus."

He felt a comforting warmness come over him as he finished speaking. It was almost as though God was telling him, "It's okay. I love you. I will help you believe. Just have faith."

He looked up and saw Olivia coming from her cabin at the opposite end of the camp. There was something different about her. Her beauty seemed more radiant now than he had ever seen it. In his heart he realized he had always loved her. As she walked toward him, the setting sun behind her cast an angelic glow. In his mind she was a work of art. Even though he had never known about it, this lovely lady had given birth to his child.

As she sat in the Adirondack chair next to him, he was overwhelmed with the need to ask for her forgiveness, "Liv, I am so truly sorry that I wasn't there for you to be a father to our baby. I was selfish and I am ashamed. Please forgive me."

"I'm sorry, too. Much of the fault is mine. Instead of telling you, I selfishly wanted to show how strong I was. I wanted to be an independent woman who didn't need a man around."

"I've always believed you were a strong woman. That's what attracted me to you. I love your strength, not just as a woman, but as a human being. You're not afraid of anything."

He searched her eyes and touched her cheek, "I'd love to marry you, if you'll have me, after all I put you through. I do love you."

Colonel Vito Lombardo who gruffly answered his private line as his assistant, Andrew Benetti called. Benetti tried to calm his boss, "Colonel, I believe that I have information on where Robert Wallace has been hiding."

Benetti was pacing back and forth in his office overlooking the East River in Lower Manhattan. It had been several weeks since he has been able to convey good news to the Colonel. Usually when things don't go the Colonel's way, it's dangerous to be on the receiving end of his wrath. Benetti had called in a few favors from acquaintances he had made in U.S Law enforcement.

"Colonel, Wallace came back into the country with the help of a journalist from England. He traveled with a false passport. When our men found him with his girlfriend he had just returned to the States. After they escaped our people, they went to a town called Scottdale, Pennsylvania. He knows some preacher there who was fired by his church. Apparently, that preacher moved to a little town in Ohio."

"A few days later, Wallace called the church looking for him, and he was given a phone number to call. We have traced the phone to a little farm outside Dresden, Ohio. We believe that Wallace and Meyer are there now. We'll try to get someone on the inside. If we find him, I'll get back to you right away."

The sign above Camp Dickerson did not indicate that anything had changed from its days as a Boy Scout camp through the 1990s. The people who now occupied the cabins were on fire for Christ. They would go out into the surrounding towns and share the gospel to with anyone who would listen, even though it was difficult. Occasionally, someone who had heard the message from these new disciples of Christ would come to the camp wanting to hear more.

It was just a little after noon on a late Friday in August, as the filthy man came through the gate and slowly walked toward the main assembly hall. He had the look of a homeless man who had been sleeping wherever he could find a spot in a field or a store-front doorway. He smelled like the garbage dumpsters that he had been searching through for his next meal.

Pastor Hann and Father Reilly had been joined by Wallace as they were cleaning the patio outside the kitchen. Reilly thought back to the time when their friend Mohammed Zacharius walked through that same gate. The Muslim convert had found Christ because of a very vivid dream where he saw the face of Jesus on peach blossoms. He had known more about Jesus now that he had spent the past month or so with the new believers at the camp.

Mohammed had become one of the most prolific evangelists. His discipline during his time in Islam was transferred to his newfound faith in Christ. Even though he now knew that it was by grace he was saved, he still loved to adhere to a disciplined prayer life. He studied the Bible day and night. He was becoming one of the camp's leaders. Some there had begun calling him the Apostle Paul for his radical turnaround in his faith.

Hann, Reilly, and Wallace walked toward the stranger as he lifted his head and sniffed the aroma of the evening meal being prepared by the camp's kitchen staff. A large turkey had been in the oven for most of the afternoon. The man raised his right hand in a friendly wave, "Hello. Pardon me, but whatever is cooking here smells so good, and I haven't had a decent meal in almost a week. I'm sorry, I probably stink. I'd be willing to help wash dishes and take out the trash, if you'd let me eat a good solid meal."

"You're welcome here, Brother. We are a small community of followers of Jesus Christ. It is our desire that you eat not only the food we offer from our kitchen, but that you will feast on the solid food from the heart of God. It's been called The Bread of Life by many people." Father Reilly extended his hand to the man who had introduced himself as Danny Lloyd.

Lloyd told them that he had been in the Navy during the last Middle East conflict and when he got out, his training had been in the security business. He had been hooked on pain killers because of a back injury that kept flaring up. He was stationed on an aircraft carrier off the coast of Israel and Lebanon. He was injured fighting with a drunk sailor as he was serving on Shore Patrol duty. After that, he couldn't hold a job. He explained that it had been two weeks since he had gotten high, and he was trying extremely hard to stay clean.

Suddenly he turned and stared at Wallace and asked, "Haven't I seen you someplace before?"

There was a moment of awkward silence before anyone chimed in with an answer. Father Reilly briefly answered for Wallace, "Bobby, this is Danny, Danny this is Bobby. We can have Bobby show you around the camp later. He'll get you some clean clothes."

Wallace gestured toward the men's shower, "Come with me. We can stop by the men's barracks and I'll get you a clean change of clothes."

The two walked away from the rest of the group to the far corner of the camp. Once inside the barracks, Lloyd gladly took the hygiene kit and clean set of dungarees. They were like the ones he wore in the Navy. He smiled at Wallace and thanked him.

There was something in Lloyd's smile that bothered Wallace. He did not quite trust this stranger.

Paolino Esposito was holding an audience with a group of business leaders. His large office had high ceilings, ornate walnut trim and large windows that faced east. The men and women in attendance were gathered from nearly every major manufacturing company in Europe.

They were making plans to increase production of automobiles, general aviation and commercial airliners, and long-haul semi-trucks. Europe, in just the first two months of Esposito's leadership had vaulted to number one in manufacturing of these goods.

"Ladies and Gentlemen, thank you for taking the initiative and moving forward with cutbacks in labor costs and increasing quality, while increasing value. Our products are some of the best in the world. Our work forces are among the best anywhere. We are now ready to step up to the next level with electronic monetary exchange. We will do without cash, streamlining business practices making it easier for everyone to purchase our products."

Esposito was giving details on the next major change that was now being implemented throughout the Continent. It was a great experiment with electronic microchips being inserted under the skin of every employee of all these companies. All money was now being handled electronically. Paychecks were automatically deposited in much the same fashion as they had been since as long ago as the nineteen seventies and eighties. The main difference now was that these people carried neither cash, nor credit/debit cards. It was a very efficient manner of doing personal business. To have the chips inserted under the skin of the right hand an individual had to sign a very lengthy agreement that gave the state, total control over their lives. All their medical, financial, and personal information was stored on each chip. The newer, more advanced chips also were able to download information from a person's brain, including appointments, phone numbers, passwords, and anything else that people previously guarded closely.

In addition to the individual chips storing information, there were hundreds of data storage centers all over Europe. Switzerland was a major repository for stored information. Just outside Bern, there was a facility that could hold the information from every person with the chip. Whenever anyone came within range of a Wi-Fi hot spot, their stored information would automatically upload to the network. At the same time, any updates to the system were automatically downloaded to the individual's microchip. It seemed to be very efficient and after only a few bugs that needed to be worked out, officials were extremely pleased with the entire system.

Reilly, Hann, and Mohammed Zacharius had been walking the perimeters of the grounds at Camp Dickerson searching for someone. Mohammed, for the third time, had checked the men's shower room when he came back into the sunlight and called out to his brothers, "He is still not in there. It is a complete mystery."

It was late afternoon and it had been nearly five hours since anyone had seen Robert Wallace and Danny Lloyd. Wallace had taken Lloyd for a clean set of clothes and a shower. Neither man could now be found. Olivia had been checking each of the barracks buildings with no luck.

They all came back together at the kitchen doors and Olivia spoke first, "I am becoming more concerned. It's not like Bobby to miss saying 'good morning' to me."

"The last we saw of him was last evening when he showed Danny Lloyd where the showers were and finding him a fresh change of clothing. I could tell that he thought there may be something suspicious about our new arrival." Hann was thinking back on how Wallace had first looked at Lloyd when he first arrived. "I think that maybe Wallace thought the guy didn't look like a seasoned street person."

Olivia shared her impression of Lloyd, "I've seen many homeless men in the criminal justice system, and he looked 'seasoned' enough to me."

It had become obvious to everyone that Lloyd and Wallace had both left the camp. But where were they?

Wallace slowly came awake. He could hear the rumble of a car's engine. He was surrounded in a darkness that reminded him of the times he played hide and seek with his cousins, and he'd hide with one of the older kids in the closet of his parents' bedroom. There was no smell of mothballs emanating from big plastic garment bags. In here he could sense the aroma of car exhaust, though it was a faint smell.

Thinking back, Wallace remembered gathering a clean change of clothing for Lloyd, and then showing him to the showers. He was next to his bunk when Lloyd re-entered the barracks and while chatting with Wallace, he gave himself away. As he reached into the old, tattered olive drab army coat, he had worn into the camp, Lloyd pulled out a taser. Arrogantly, he admitted he worked for Le Roux Enterprise's American security office, "I'm here to take you back to Paris. This time you won't get away."

It was as though a bright light flashed in Wallace's brain and he fell to the floor with a spasm. Though the pain in his knees was great, the over-all seizure caused by the jolt of electricity coursing through his body made him forget hitting the concrete floor hard with both knees. He faintly remembered a second man entering the room and hearing the two men talking. Wallace thinks he heard them say they had a car parked just outside the perimeter of the camp.

The question now was not so much how he got there, but how was he going to get out of this mess? The road they took had quite a bump, and there was a distinct double thud as they crossed what could have been a railroad track. They stopped quickly and then pulled out onto a smoother road. The sensation of traveling faster told Wallace they must be on a highway. But where were they going? The low hum of the engine lulled him back into a sleepy state. He tried to keep his eyes open.

The dull throbbing in his knees kept him from falling completely asleep. He began reciting Bible verses that he had memorized over the past few months, since he first met Pastor Hann and had decided to follow Christ. He was determined to stay awake and figure out a way to escape. He knew that there was a trunk release in many vehicles. He felt around the inside of the trunk lid for the little "T" shaped trunk release tab. If he would find it, he'd have to be discreet.

He listened intently to see if he could hear any conversation coming from inside the car. The only thing he could hear was news-talk radio. The host was touting what was going on in Europe right now. Apparently, they were now becoming the number one economy in the world and were slowly inching toward a cashless society. Wallace remembers reading in Scripture that there would be a new way of doing business in the "Last Days." The host was challenging his listeners to contact their representatives in Washington and let them know that the United States needs to step up and go cashless as well. All healthcare would be paid for through a central payment plan. For the first time in history, people are literally getting good healthcare in Europe, without having to pay anything for it at any of their doctor's visits. At least, that's how it was being reported.

"Here it is," Wallace whispered to himself. He had found the trunk release handle. Now it was a matter of waiting for the right opportunity. There was a slight gap in the trunk liner that allowed him to see the taillights. They had just come on. He surmised that it must be getting dark. His chance could be coming sooner than he thought. Just wait for it. Just wait.

The tarmac at the municipal airport east of Zanesville was bustling with security personnel. They were busily readying the Canadair Regional jet for take-off when its passengers arrived. The plan was to hustle Wallace out of the country to the Bahamas. It was a secret mission. They didn't want to involve U.S. law enforcement and go through the long and drawn-out process of requesting extradition, to allow them to take him to Europe.

The car carrying the trio was eastbound on Interstate 70. They took the Sonora Road exit, speeding through the intersection of the East Pike, headed onto Airport Road. It was their misfortune that Muskingum County Sheriff's Deputy Lonny Miles was ready to pull out of the Denney's parking lot, witnessed their infraction and hit his flashing lights to pull them over. They sped further south on Airport Road causing Deputy Miles to turn on his siren. He radioed in for back-up. The rental car was not responding to his request to pull to the side of the road. He was immediately joined by a second Deputy Sheriff, Tom Baker. Deputy Baker was able to pass the speeder, and immediately began to run a traffic break to slow him down. Between the two deputy cruisers they managed to get the car, driven by Danny Lloyd, to stop.

This was Wallace's chance to be rescued. He pulled the yellow trunk tab and popped the trunk. He was suddenly face to face with Deputy Miles, who was in a semi crouched position with his gun drawn. "Don't make a move! Put your hands up and lie down on the ground! Face down, NOW!"

Wallace quickly complied to the command without saying a word, but with a sigh of relief.

Lloyd tried to explain that they were working as Bounty Hunters to take Wallace back to Europe. Deputy Miles immediately took charge of the situation, demanding that Lloyd and his partner sit down along the side of the road. They both submitted to the request. They had been in the security business long enough to know that even if it is small town law enforcement, it is best not to argue. Deputy Baker had been on his radio talking with County Dispatch. He was told that he and Miles were to bring all three men into county lock-up on North 4th Street. The County DA would be waiting to help with booking the three men. Since one was an international fugitive, this could bring even more scrutiny.

After booking Wallace into the Muskingum County Jail, the two men from Le Roux Industries U.S.A., were fined for speeding. They had told the deputies that as Bounty Hunters they were taking Wallace who was a runaway fugitive. They said that putting him in the trunk was their way of guaranteeing he would not escape. Since they had not harmed him, they were released. They then telephoned the main office in New York.

Colonel Vito Lombardo spoke angrily into his phone to his U.S. office, "You know what you need to do." His anger began to seethe, and it was obvious to the crew on the other end of the line in the U.S., "I don't care what you may or may not think. Zanesville, Ohio is just a bump on the map compared to the centers we are now operating in. We need Wallace to either stand trial for murder in France and executed or just simply be executed. If we can't get him extradited quickly, then he must die there in that little town. Yes, Mr. Benetti, you have the resources and weaponry to take on a regiment of Royal Marines. A small-town Sheriff's office in Ohio should be no problem at all. The American government is powerless to complain too much to us. They have been neutered for many years and they'll never have the nerve to challenge us. Just get it done. If you can't extract him cleanly, kill him quickly."

Lombardo's men were slowly filtering into Zanesville and checking into the hotels in or near downtown. They each took time to either walk past the county jail or drive past it. They were gathering intelligence. Danny Lloyd, having already been there, was able to tell his fellow Lombardo men what he remembered about entrances and exits, as well as the number of Sheriff's personnel he was able to remember.

Andrew Benetti himself had come to Ohio to participate in this operation. His experience in the military afforded him skills in military operations. What was being planned for later this afternoon, was truly a military operation. The Muskingum County Sheriff's deputies were also trained in military operations. There was a meeting scheduled in Benetti's room at ten thirty this morning. Most of the plans had already been made.

Benetti detailed the plans with each of the five leaders of the operation. An electronics specialist was available to each unit of team members.

On this early Saturday morning nobody seemed to notice the two, rather utilitarian looking RVs cruising the downtown streets. Every RV looked like any other Class A recreational vehicle except they did not have a fashionable exterior paint scheme. Each RV was plain beige. Each one had what appeared to be a satellite dish on the roof. Unseen by anyone on the outside, each vehicle contained ten heavily armed men, ready for action.

A few men were on foot, in plain clothes walking around the beautiful Muskingum County Courthouse. The land just to the east of the courthouse was hallowed ground, honoring those from Muskingum County who gave their lives in the Korean War and World War II. The pair of RVs with twenty men men inside were each making the rounds from Main Street to 4th Street to Market and back along 5th Street. No one seemed to notice or find this cruising of RVs suspicious.

Vehicle number one contained Squad A under the direct command of Andrew Benetti. Looking at his watch, with satellite phone in hand, he was ready to send a group text to the leader of each vehicle. "It's time to jump into the pool."

At that text message, the microwave dish on the roof of each vehicle emitted a steady pulse that shut down all cell phone service in downtown Zanesville. The land lines were affected by a loud buzzing sound that made it impossible to communicate. All two-way radio service was eliminated within the Courthouse and jail. The men in each RV jumped out and took up positions inside and outside the jail. Adding to the confusion a few Flash-Bang grenades were set off wherever any potential challengers to their plan were gathered. The early morning crew members inside the jail were taken completely by surprise. Deputy Sargent Philip Howard grabbed his walkie-talkie and shouted for back-up. There was no squawk back from the device. No one seemed to have heard his call.

The masked leader of the invaders sternly shouted at Sargent Howard, "Drop the radio and put your hands, palms down, on the desk. Don't even think about doing anything stupid. Do as I say, and you'll get to go home tonight."

Howard complied as men rushed around him, crashing through the doors toward the jail cells. Having heard the Flash-Bang grenade from the floor below, Deputy Tom Baker, who had been filing paperwork ran up the steps and looked at the lobby. It was there that he saw Danny Lloyd. He turned immediately and ran back downstairs toward the holding cell containing Robert Wallace. Having seen Lloyd with the invaders it was Baker's gut that told him that this was related to the traffic stop and arrest he and Deputy Miles had made the day before. Running down the hall, he shouted to the deputy at the entry to the cell block, "Grab a shotgun, put on a vest and take cover!"

A few more deputies took up positions together in the gateway area as Baker ran to get Wallace. He unlocked the cell and cuffed Wallace's hands in front of him. "Come with me. I don't know what's going on with you, Mr., but someone apparently is trying to break you out of here and that just ain't gonna happen. You're comin' with me to a safer place."

Wallace didn't ask any questions as he jumped to his feet and followed Deputy Baker deeper into the labyrinth of jail cells. Gunfire could be heard as they turned the corner and headed toward a door that led to the parking area between the jail and the court facilities. Baker crouched behind a sheriff's van and ducking down he looked under the vehicle to see if anyone was nearby. After scanning as much of the lot as he could see, he motioned for Wallace to follow him. The pair ran around the corner where Baker had parked his personal vehicle. In short order they were quickly on their way out of the downtown area. As they crossed the Y Bridge, they flew along Linden Avenue up the river toward Adair Avenue making their getaway clean. Baker then tried his cell phone; it was still not working. They stopped quickly at a small market and he ran inside shouting to the clerk, "Call the Highway Patrol. Tell them there's been an invasion of the downtown jail facility. About fifty heavily armed men have taken over the jail. There is no communication in or out of downtown. They'll need SWAT and other tac units forthwith. Zanesville PD should also be notified."

With that, Baker ran back to his vehicle and got back on the road. He headed north on Maple Avenue and turned into a neighborhood of two-story homes that were built in the nineteen thirties. He pulled into the driveway of his home and the garage door opened as he slid the car quickly into its lair.

The two men sat in the silence of the garage for a moment before Baker spoke, "I don't know what it is about you, but those guys must think you're the worst guy on the face of the Earth to design such an elaborately planned attack. That guy that was driving when you were in his trunk yesterday was one of them. That's why I came and got you."

"They say that I set off a bomb in an airliner and killed a bunch of people."

"Yeah, that's what I gathered from the paper-work they filed yesterday, you're apparently a pretty dangerous fella. I don't see it in you, but we had to go through the motions and get you ready for extradition to France. But as far as I'm concerned, nobody comes into my town and tries to steal one of my prisoners," Baker guided Wallace down to the basement. At the base of the steps and slightly to the left there was a mid-nineteen-sixties fallout shelter. "You can hide out here and we'll see what happens."

Paolino Esposito stood quietly in his office looking out into the night-time city skyline. Esposito proudly smiled to himself as he thought of how he ruled not only this view, but almost all of Europe. The constant advisory voice in his head from Baalazaar continued to inflate his pride. He poured himself two fingers of Glenfiddich, took a sip, "I am now going to create peace in this world."

Suddenly, Baalazaar appeared from the shadows and put out his boney-fingered left hand, "Reach out and take my hand, Paolino. I will show you everything you need to know to rule not only Europe, but all the world."

The countryside sped past at a dizzying speed, and soon Esposito was standing in the huge hangar at the European Space Agency's space port. They stood in the shadow of the giant spacecraft. This was the craft that gave the world's media a trip that was described as a trip into space by reporters from all over the world. The purpose of the trip was to explain what had happened to so many people who had disappeared from all over the world.

Baalazaar showed Esposito around the craft. He led him up the stair, "This is a very good piece of work. Monsieur Le Roux spared no expense in following my requirements for this craft. It looks so very realistic. Computer screens with all the latest navigational software and deep space telescope video on the big screen monitors, coupled with hydraulic legs, and a Gimble table in the floor to give realistic feelings of movement."

Esposito smiled as he patted one of the landing Struts, "So, the entire trip was merely a ruse?"

"Signor Esposito, I have been proud of you since you were a child. You have grasped the entire issue here. I am sure the world's missing people were taken by another race of people from another galaxy. It was my idea to sell the world on that theory."

He explained the elaborate plan that had been in the works for nearly thirty-five years, "Albert Le Roux was given so much power in business and finance because he had good ideas that would revolutionize the electronics business. Major developments in computer technology came, not only from the United States, but from our good friend Albert Le Roux. Albert found you, and he knew that you would be the one we needed who would become the leader of the world."

Esposito thought about that last statement, "What do you mean Albert found me?"

"My son, it has been in the planning since ages past that I would one day give you the reins to lead people. You are a god and with my help, you will rule the world. People everywhere will come to know you and bow down and worship you."

Esposito still bore the scar from the attack that, was supposed to put an end to the plans of Le Roux and Baalazaar. The left side of his forehead had a slight mark. Baalazaar had brought him back from the dead but left a slight mark as proof of the terrible wound that Esposito had received. This mark was to be a constant reminder to the world that this man was truly a god and that because of his miraculous resurrection from the dead, people would be willing to follow him blindly. Baalazaar reached out his hand to touch the scar, and once again Esposito was standing in his office looking out at the city lights. He instinctively touched his scar once again. He was feeling the power that was given to him. He knew that he was indeed the chosen one.

Camp Dickerson was abuzz with the quickly spreading word that Wallace had been jailed in Zanesville. WHIZ

Radio was now reporting that a massive gun battle had broken out at the County Jail. The first accounts were very sparse on information. It had been a very well-organized attack on the facility. But no one knew why it had taken place.

Olivia suspected that the people who had been after Wallace and her were behind the attack. She took Pastor Hann aside to tell him more about what had happened to the two of them in New Jersey. Hann knew some of the details, but the zeal with which these people were trying to pursue Wallace needed to be understood.

"I'm afraid that Bobby is in grave trouble, more trouble than he's ever been in. The men who kidnapped us in New Jersey were only the beginning. Because he had expressed doubts about the news media's trip into space, I'm afraid that he'll never be able to get away. I'm afraid that this time they'll kill him, rather than let him escape."

Hann took her hand, and the two of them dropped to their knees right there in that corner of the pantry. They prayed earnestly for Wallace's safety, he would not be extradited to France. Failing that, they prayed that someone would be able to rescue him.

The fallout shelter in Baker's basement was directly under the front porch of his St. Louis Avenue home.

It was about fifteen feet long and eight feet wide. The entryway had an outer door made of a single sheet of steel a half inch thick. There was a three-foot entry hall, and on the left, a slight turn, and another steel-plate door into the shelter. At the west end of the room was a gun safe. There was also a small refrigerator at that end of the shelter. Otherwise, the shelter was unfinished, just a hollow-sounding room with a small table and chair at the east end.

Wallace sat down, exhausted. "I have to check in with the jail," Baker told him. "I wasn't officially on duty at the time of that attack. There will be video footage of me being there, but I hope that you and I were able to get out of there without you being caught on camera." He hadn't known that the electronic disabling had also knocked out the cameras and recording equipment.

"You stay here, there's bottled water and some food in that 'fridge there. I don't know how long I'll be gone. You may be alone for a day or two. That radio over there is battery powered and there are extra batteries on top of the gun safe. You shouldn't come out for at least forty-eight hours, and then be very cautious about going outside."

As he left, he pulled the steel door closed behind him, pulled his car out of the garage, and left the house.

After heroic efforts of the Muskingum County Sheriff's Department, Zanesville Police Department and units from the Ohio Highway Patrol, the smoke had cleared downtown, and an accounting was taken of the damage and casualties. There were fifteen of the invaders lying dead inside and outside the jail and courthouse area. One RV was destroyed but the other had gotten away as far as Greenwood Avenue and was abandoned at the cemetery. Eyewitness accounts say that five vans collected those who were in the RV and they headed out the East Pike.

Deputy Baker arrived at the jail and quickly entered the building. There were four wounded deputies and officers being attended to by EMTs. Several yellow blankets covered the bodies of the invaders.

He checked in with Sargent Philip Howard whose upper left arm was bandaged and, in a sling, "That guy you brought in yesterday is missing. We think that these scumbags hustled him out of here in the RV that got away."

Taking a chance, Baker lied, "I left just before all this went down. I was at home when I heard what was going on. What does the security video show us?"

Howard frowned, "Somehow, the video surveillance was disabled. The RV we found up at Greenwood had what appears to be all kinds of sophisticated electronic jamming equipment inside. You weren't on duty this morning, so why did you come in and when did you leave?"

Baker, feeling the need to come up with a good explanation, said, "I wanted to make sure my paperwork was properly filed, it looked to me like everything was in order, so I bailed out before nine."

"It got pretty hairy here at about nine-thirty. About thirty of those guys rushed in here with Flash-Bangs. My ears just quit ringing a few minutes ago. The morning watch had just finished with roll call and they were about to hit the streets when the attack started. They had body armor and their weapons close at hand. We had that bit of luck on our side. The over-nighters in the drunk tank got a big surprise, and maybe this will help them take the pledge."

Inside van number one was Andrew Benetti and five other men from his unit. People were making excuses regarding what had gone wrong and Benetti was trying to find out what had happened to Wallace, "I don't care what you say, that guy has some real good protection. I don't know who he knows, but we've got to bring it to an end as soon as possible.

The five vans poured up and down the rolling hills of southeastern Ohio on the East Pike as they spread eastward getting away from the authorities as quickly as possible. They got to the Sonora Road entrance to I-70 and quickly made the transition toward the Ohio West Virginia border. Wheeling was a little more than an hour away.

Benetti turned to Lloyd who was sitting directly behind the driver, "The Andromeda Council is not pleased that we keep failing to capture or kill Robert Wallace. We found him once recently in Dresden, Ohio. Let's stake out the place and see if he returns. Then we'll grab him."

As four of the vans continued toward Wheeling, Benetti's van left the interstate in Cambridge and circled back toward New Concord. They exited there taking back roads to avoid detection. Within an hour they were approaching Dresden.

Four of the men left the van and made their way on foot to Camp Dickerson. The late afternoon saw a drastic drop in the temperatures as the men topped the hill overlooking the camp.

Lloyd shared information about the layout of the camp with his small squad, "These people should be an easy target. There is nobody there with any martial training in firearms or hand to hand fighting. We'll have no trouble taking them down and getting him out of there."

Colonel Vito Lombardo had just finished his dinner with Cardinal Assidi. They had been discussing plans for the church in Rome. Lombardo told Assidi that the pieces of the puzzle were falling into place and there were fewer and fewer challengers to his ascension to the Papacy.

"Nunzio, I have eliminated nearly every obstacle to you taking over completely. You will be able to run the bank, the history archives and everything about the church. Nothing will be able to prevent us from achieving one hundred per cent dominance bringing more and more people to worship Signor Esposito. It won't be long before the people of the United States will also fall into line behind our leadership. They have a history of independence, but they truly respect strength and leadership."

Assidi was feeling comfortable with the future of the church under his leadership, "My family has come a long way from the first converts into the faith during the Spanish Inquisition. One of my ancestors was a Spanish Jew who married into the Assidi family after the conversion. Some people would consider me as being of Jewish heritage. It was so long ago that the Jew in me has been totally washed away."

"I believe that we should be able to discredit Wallace, no matter what he says on television."

Benetti and his men waited until dark came upon Camp Dickerson. They were planning to locate Wallace. As the late afternoon light began to fade, the pale luminescence gave way to pitch black. The stars began to twinkle on this moonless night while a light show performed by the fireflies played out to the rhythm of the sounds of crickets and frogs. Thousands of tiny yellow-green blinking lights seemed to say, "we can light the way for the world."

After having studied the layout of the camp from afar, the men were ready to move in and seek their prey. The last of the kitchen workers closed and locked up the kitchen and made their way to the barracks. Benetti's men took up positions near where Wallace had been last seen when he was at the camp.

Leading the group was Danny Lloyd who knew the entire layout. They decided to spend the night and observe who was still there in the morning.

Benetti called the group together and they discussed their plan of attack, "I'm not sure that he would even come back here. After the damage we inflicted downtown I think that Wallace is going to go deep underground to avoid us from now on."

The few hours Wallace waited seemed an eternity. He left the shelter, climbed the steps to the living room.

Continuing to the second floor, he scanned the street, looking for any sign of trouble. Seeing none, he found the keys to the second car Baker said he could use and left the house.

It was only about five minutes before sunrise when Benetti's men stormed the camp. They shouted for everyone to come out of the barracks with their hands in the air and gather in the yard by the dining hall.

The frightened campers obeyed. Pastor Hann spoke for the group, "What's going on here? What do you want from us?"

Danny Lloyd clapped back, "Shut your mouth! We don't need to hear from you."

Benetti walked up to Hann. With a cursing voice that was dripping with anger, "Where is Wallace? He is a criminal and we need to take him back to France."

Hann's voice was surprisingly calm, "We haven't seen him since someone snatched him away yesterday. I thought that your people probably already had him in Rome, or Paris, or somewhere else by this time."

"He got away from our group and now we need to find him again." Looking around at the group, Benetti's eyes came to rest on Olivia. "You're the one we saw him with back in New York, aren't you?"

There was no answer, but by the terror in Olivia's eyes, Benetti knew that he now had a bargaining chip, the perfect bait to attract Wallace to come out of hiding.

"Take the girl. He'll come to us, so we won't need to keep searching for him."

Benetti turned to Hann, "When your boy shows up, tell him we have his girl and if he values her life at all, to call this number."

He handed Hann a card with contact information on it and he and the group left the camp and were back on the road headed east.

Word reached Rome that Olivia Meyer was in custody, and that it would not be long before Robert Wallace would be captured and brought to justice by a European court. Lombardo smugly sat back and propped his feet up on his desk. The stub of his cigar had long gone cold. He picked up the desk-top lighter, pushed the button and inhaled deeply. Smoke swirled around his head as he watched the yachts softly bobbing in the Bay of Naples.

Even though Albert Le Roux was dead his legacy had lived on. His laboratories churned out updates almost hourly regarding his computer chips. It would not be long before the chips injected under the skin could upload information directly to the brain.

A central power would be able to control behavior of large groups of people.

Lombardo called the private number of Paolino Esposito to let him know that Olivia Meyer was in custody. Meyer's capture was good news to Esposito, but he was beginning to tire of all the drama regarding Robert Wallace and his girlfriend. Ignoring the advice of Lombardo, he suggested they begin to devote fewer resources to hunting Wallace down, "Look, Vito, I am aware that Wallace has doubts about the Andromedins being the reason for so many missing people. Because of his doubts, you fear that he can damage our program. We only need to remind the public that he's suspected of mass murder for planting a bomb on an airliner."

Lombardo disagreed, "Sir, we cannot take any chances that he could make people doubt our story about Andromeda being connected to the missing people. He has had a large following on American news programming for the past seven years."

Esposito quickly changed the subject, "My dear Vito, it is time for me to change my priorities. Palestinians keep launching missiles from Gaza into Israel and the Israelis have been retaliating. I have sent an ambassador to each capitol.

As North Maple Avenue gave way to Frazeysburg Road Wallace watched the landscape turn into rolling farmland. Last fall's bales of hay were stored in the large barns of the smaller family farms. Tall silos held fodder for the Jerseys, Guernsey and Holsteins that dot the pastures. In less than thirty minutes, Wallace had made his way back to Camp Dickerson.

Approaching the encampment, Wallace slowed the car and looked at each vehicle in the parking lot. There weren't any unfamiliar cars. Each one could be attributed to someone who was at the camp when he was last there. It appeared that it was safe for him to continue through the gate and go inside.

His plan was to get Olivia and leave the area. He thought that perhaps they could go to Arizona or California, somewhere far away from the people who were after him.

As he climbed out of the parked car near the dining hall, Pastor Hann came running toward him. Hann's expression was not the same calm and controlled look Wallace had come to expect over the past week or so.

"She's gone, Robert. They've taken her away."

"What are you talking about? Who's taken her away?"

Hann put a reassuring hand on Wallace's shoulder and said, "Remember Danny Lloyd? He and some other men in paramilitary uniforms left about a half hour ago with Olivia in their vehicle. We were told to tell you they are taking her back to New Jersey, and that if you ever wanted to see her alive again, you should get to the Eagle Flight Services corporate jet hangar in Newark, New Jersey."

The memory of the last time Wallace had seen that facility came flooding back to him. It was there he had entered the United States fleeing these same people who now had Olivia. Even though she was an officer of the court in New York City, Olivia knew him well enough to know that he could not have done what European authorities were saying he had done.

Olivia made the choice to throw away her career and help Wallace evade capture. Even if she wanted to make sure that he stood trial of that for which he was accused, her career was effectively finished. Now she was being taken back to where she had first made that fateful decision.

It was now up to Wallace to make a sacrifice for her. Would they let her go if he offered himself as a trade? His thoughts were interrupted by the sound of footsteps on the gravel. Deputy Baker spoke, "I'm glad I have a tracker on my car. That's how I knew where you were. So, they took her to New Jersey? That's convenient. I don't know if you noticed, but I don't talk like everyone else around here. I'm told I have an accent. I grew up on the Jersey Shore, and still have family there."

Wallace wasn't sure where this conversation was going, but he was ready to hear where Baker was going with this. "I'm still peeved at these people ruining my weekend plans. I might as well see what I can do to ruin their plans."

Wallace smiled, "I think you want to seek a little revenge."

At this Mohammed Zacharius, who had been listening intently to the conversation, chimed in, "Gentlemen… Brothers… if you'll recall, I was sent here on a mission to become a Martyr. I have had extensive training in martial arts and firearms. Perhaps I could be of some assistance to you."

It was obvious that a rescue operation was in the initial planning stages. Baker, Zacharius and Wallace made their way into the dining hall.

Baker poured himself a cup of coffee and took a seat at the table nearest to the coffee maker. "I have some vacation time coming, so I can get away from my job for a week or so."

He took a long chug from his coffee cup and made a face of disgust. "Whew! That's strong enough to kill tree stumps. Does anyone want me to cut off a stick of coffee for them?"

Zacharius, who was raised on strong Arabian coffees, made a face and shook his head, "No. I know good coffee, and you can't use the words good and coffee in the same sentence when referring to this sludge. I think that was first brewed when the Shah of Iran was overthrown, and it has been sitting around being heated and re-heated ever since then. I'm not sure I'd even give that to someone I was wanting to make sick."

"It would do the trick though," said Wallace. "I'm not totally sure what we can do to get Olivia released by these pigs. I think that our best bet is for me to turn myself in and let them take me back to France, or Rome, or wherever they want me."

Zacharius shook his head, "These men have no intention of letting her go, even if you pay your own way back to their prison in Europe. We need to find a way of getting her away from them safely."

Baker then added the trump card, "Remember, I'm from Jersey. My brother is a Lieutenant with the Newark Police S.W.A.T. He served as a Navy Seal for twenty years and has no love for outsiders coming into this country and taking the law into their own hands. He and I have already spoken about the anger we both feel about what they did in Zanesville. I think I could get some help from him and my other Brothers in Blue from Newark."

Pastor Hann had been hovering around the edge of this conversation and he spoke up, "Gentlemen, you're talking about making a bad situation worse. Also, if Wallace goes back to New Jersey, even if the Europeans don't take him back to Rome or Paris, the FBI in New

York will likely want to take him into custody to hold for an extradition hearing before likely turning him over to the European authorities. Either way, Wallace is in grave danger."

It was then that Wallace reasoned, "It doesn't matter to me who sends me back to stand trial in Europe, as long as those guys let Olivia go. I can keep her from being arrested by the Feds by telling them that I took her with me against her will. That should keep her from being charged as an accessory or aiding and abetting, or whatever trouble she could be in."

Baker continued, "For that matter we could all be up the creek for hanging around you, but as I told you earlier, I don't believe you did what they said you did. Frankly, I don't like the way those guys in Europe are trying to bully their way into our business in America."

Zacharius asked, "So what should we do with him?"

Deputy Baker shed further light on the plan that was hatching in his mind, "I say we keep you out of sight when we get back there. We can claim that, as law enforcement officers, we have you in custody and will let them take you back after the proper papers are filed. We can't do that until they release Ms. Meyer. Once I get together with my brother, he and I can set up a tactical plan to take them out. Maybe we can get them extradited back here to face the music for what happened in Zanesville. We may live in a small town compared to the big population centers of Europe, but there's a lot of pride in our community, and we don't intend to let them get away with what they did."

CHAPTER 14

Benetti continued to show his authority to everyone who was in the van. He had given orders that his phone was not to be answered unless it was from headquarters in Paris, or from Rome. He didn't want to talk to Wallace until he was sure that he would be on his way to New Jersey. Then, before it was too late to back out of the situation, the Europeans would have complete control over Wallace and Olivia Meyer.

"Ms. Meyer, I don't know if you realize how much trouble you find yourself in. You aided a known killer to escape our pursuit. Whether or not you like it, Mr. Wallace will be joining you in Europe, as the two of you stand trial in international court for terrorism and mass murder. You will be charged as an accessory after the fact. I'm sure that, as a prosecutor, you know how much trouble you are facing. Perhaps, if you help us convict Mr. Wallace, we might find mercy on you and give you a short sentence in prison in Rome."

"Don't get too sure of yourself, Mr. Benetti. You aren't out of the United States yet, and Bobby will have to face an extradition hearing before he can be released to you. And as for my complicity in this alleged crime, once again, it will be up to the United States government to decide my fate. I'm afraid that you can't just enter my country and arrest people who are not currently in your jurisdiction."

"Be that as it may, Ms. Meyer, your federal agencies are not aware of our activities at this time. So, you shouldn't get too sure of yourself. As a duly sworn agent of the European Union, with full diplomatic status, once we get you on board the airplane, for all intents and purposes, you will be in Europe. Your government won't be able to stop us. And the day is coming when there will be no more United States in North America. You see, events happening in Rome right now are taking us toward a true new world order. It will be simple to accomplish because people have been seeking peace and stability for centuries. What centuries ago, was called Pax Romanus, is returning. This time it will be for good."

Muskingum County Sheriff's Deputy Tom Baker, along with Arab Christian, Mohammed Zacharius and Central News Agency investigative reporter Robert Wallace, were driving east on Interstate 70 approaching Wheeling, West Virginia. They were making exceptionally good time on their hurried, and largely improvised rescue operation to Newark, New Jersey.

Baker had been on his phone for most of the trip talking with his brother, Lieutenant Gary Baker, a Veteran Navy Seal, who was now in command of a SWAT unit with the Newark Police Department. They knew they were in pursuit of at least three men who had kidnapped a Manhattan Assistant District Attorney, after entering the Muskingum County Jail, in downtown Zanesville, Ohio. Deputy Baker explained to his brother about the carnage that had been left behind. Included in the aftermath of that melee were at least seven dead perpetrators and several wounded county deputies.

Lieutenant Gary Baker sat ramrod straight in the command seat of the SWAT Lenco BearCat G3 vehicle. Each time his unit was called into action, he was thankful for his years of experience as a U.S. Navy SEAL. His training put him in a great position to command police officers who are ready to go into the midst of some of the most dangerous operations a metropolitan police department can face.

His current team was made up of two women and five men. Each one of them was blessed with taut muscles, and their senses were razor sharp. As they rode toward the Newark International Airport, each team member sat silently, mentally preparing for the coming confrontation with an unknown number of soldiers. It was an army from Europe they were facing. The last time Americans faced a European enemy on our home shores it was Great Britain in the War of 1812. Who were these people, ignoring all convention and invading this once great nation?

The plan was simple enough. The NPD SWAT was to surround the offices of Gold Eagle Flight Service at Newark Liberty International Airport. They were then to make sure that a Manhattan Assistant District Attorney was released.

Lieutenant Baker had been on the phone with Newark flight services explaining the situation. An official request had been made that these men were not allowed to depart with their hostage. As a result of that conversation, flight services had been in contact with Gold Eagle to inform them that their flight would not be allowed to take off until the situation could be resolved.

By taking turns driving, Deputy Baker, Robert Wallace and Mohammed Zacharius made record time as they closed in on the home stretch, going northbound on I-95 toward Newark, New Jersey. Baker was behind the wheel now as they closed in on Newark Liberty International. He was in constant communication with his brother and the SWAT members who had closed off the area around Gold Eagle.

They continued to travel northbound. Passing by the main entrance to the Newark's Liberty International Airport, one would never suspect that at that very moment, a drama was unfolding just off Brewster Road at the recently completed Gold Eagle Business offices.

Luxuriously appointed, Gold Eagle's business had been ferrying executives to and from major European hubs for the past year and a half. Many times, customs inspections had been thought to be too lax. It was said that quite often, members of major crime families and known drug lords had managed to enter the United States without much scrutiny.

Often, private jets from points unknown would taxi up to the hangar at Gold Eagle's facility. As the plane would enter the hangar, the large doors would close behind it, hiding who or what was on board.

Some people conjectured that there was a secret tunnel under the hangar. If, indeed, someone could smuggle people in and out of the country this way,

Gold Eagle Flight Services could well be used by any group of unsavory people to further their own agendas. This alone made it a perfect cover.

The ease with which Robert Wallace re-entered the United States when he was an internationally wanted man is a perfect example of how easy it could be, if one had the right connections.

Andrew Benetti was showing some strain as he paced the room in front of Olivia Meyer. He was concentrating as he measured each word, he carefully uttered, "Yes Sir. I am aware that this could become a situation of extreme negative publicity for us. Yes Sir, I'm sure that we can still prevent Wallace from sharing his suspicions to the public. Yes Sir. The woman will be released immediately. I will contact the officer in charge of the SWAT operation… Oh, yes Sir. Then will we be allowed to depart as soon as the paperwork has been filed? Yes Sir, I look forward to being on home soil, breathing the air of Italy once again."

CHAPTER 15

Paolino Esposito set the phone down on the ornate desk. He was in the Papal Quarters of the Vatican. The Supreme Leader was having one of his frequent audiences with the head of the church. He winced slightly as he touched his forehead, "Il Papa, I know that you healed me completely of my wound and you restored my life, but I still feel slight twinges of pain where that man buried the trophy in my head. Please take away the pain if you will. I'll see to it that I nominate you for sainthood. You are well on your way there, as far as I am concerned. My followers are also thankful for all you have done for me and for all of the world."

As he tried to show strong leadership, Esposito continued, "Tell me, Excellency, will the American police officers keep their word and let our people come home? Remind me to send some complimentary wine to their headquarters." Satisfied that he was showing a great talent for his negotiating skills, he instantly sent a memo to his secretary. The finest Italian wine was soon on its way to New Jersey.

It had been only a week since Cardinal Nunzio Assidi was elevated to the Papacy. The Roman Catholic Church had a long history. Since it was managed by men, there were dark places in its past. Despite the great good that had come from the church, many people were at times led astray by the harshness of men and their selfish, lustful desires. This man who currently held the highest position in the church was one whose influence and leadership promised to leave a blemish on the long-arching story.

Esposito's phone rang. The caller ID showed that the head of security, Colonel Vito Lombardo was attempting to call the supreme leader of Europe. Esposito swiped the red icon to send the call to voicemail.

No longer stroking his forehead, Esposito turned to Assidi, "Nunzio, we need to find a way to silence the American journalist, Wallace. We have already tried to besmirch his name and take away any credibility he had. And as far as his whore is concerned, her reputation has already been compromised because of her association with Wallace."

"Yes, My Lord. You are correct in your assessment of Wallace and Ms. Meyer. But I truly believe that what will happen in the next few months will remove his influence on the general public. You have set into motion a new loyalty to you and to your Office. Neither Robert Wallace nor anyone will be able to stop you and your plan to bring peace to this turbulent world."

The vote in the Bundestag ended with a near unanimous resolution to throw the entire government of Germany behind the leader in Rome. Germany was soon to be an independent nation no more. It looked as though most of the former European Union was falling in line with the suggestions of the newly formed Roman Parliament. Old rivalries were falling by the wayside, and new alliances were being formed.

Even Great Britain, that one-time world dominator, was debating the formation of at least a provisional alliance with the Roman government.

Not since the time of the Caesars has there been such unity on the continent of Europe. Even in the days of the EU, there had been rivalries that prevented total unity.

Now, this Sicilian was uniting Europe, appearing to bring back a form of Pax Romanus. There were some who compared what was happening to the tactics of the Mafia. Whenever any politician wanted to balk at following the Roman leadership that promised economic stability and peace in a turbulent world, mysterious deaths and sickness happened.

History reveals to us that in the middle of the twentieth century, the U.S. Dollar was the main world currency. Since the latter part of the century, the U.S. Dollar began to lose its status as the most desired monetary unit. Since the Oil Embargo of the early nineteen seventies, the Dollar's status was put into questions by the members of the Middle Eastern Organization of Petroleum and Exporting Countries.

For most of the mid twentieth century the United States was the world's leading supporter of Israel. At the same time, the U.S. was selling weapons and other military hardware to Saudi Arabia in exchange for stability in oil prices. For the most part, the U.S. and Saudi Arabia were allied in keeping the Soviet Union out of the middle east. After the fall of the Soviet Union, it seemed as though there would be no more trouble from Russia. However, that began to change in the early twenty-first century as Russia began to attempt a return to international prominence as a world leader.

Now, under the leadership of Signor Paolino Esposito, the U.S. Dollar was losing value. The Yen, Pound Sterling, Ruble, Franc, and Deutsche Mark were all about to drop by the wayside in favor of a one world monetary system that would be completely electronic.

Electronic monetary exchanges had begun in the twentieth century, when banks began wiring "money" to each other without any actual currency changing hands. The leap today into a cashless society would be only a giant step.

Karl Schwartz, the now former Chancellor of the former nation of Germany stood before the Bundestag to announce that in less than two weeks, all the former nations of Europe would be a part of this new Roman Empire. The United States of Europe had been a dream of many people for much of the past century.

Schwartz began, "Mein Damen und Herren, we have now joined the rest of the states of Europe to unite behind the government in Rome. I have it on good authority that many of the nations of the western hemisphere are soon to vote on becoming members or associates of Rome as well. The only places where people are having trouble seeing the light of unity are the Arab nations and the Jews of Israel. They, rather than see the advantages of unity, continue to mistreat one another. Signor Esposito has promised that he has plans to bring about peace in that region for the first time in history. That is something that we look forward to seeing in our lifetime. Peace, peace… truly, peace in our time."

The capacity crowd rose to their feet in the large room, and the cheering filled the room, echoing from the domed ceiling. Some estimated that nearly nine hundred representatives of the people, along with guests, crowded the seats and aisles. The cacophony of sound was like the raging wind of a hurricane, punctuated by whistles and shouts. It must have sounded this way when Adolph Hitler stood at the head of the old Reichstag in the nineteen thirties and laid out his plans for the new Germany. That was before he led his country into the abyss of destruction at the hands of a world united against him.

Herr Schwartz stood at the podium, raised both arms, and pushed downward with his hands to silent the exuberant crowd.

"Next, we must do our part to bring the Jews and the Arabs into line with a world united in peace, just as we are at peace with Rome and the rest of Europe."

Signor Paolino, the soon to be supreme leader of all Europe, and nearly half the world, sat in the large leather chair in his office as he watched the proceedings in Berlin. He smiled with the satisfied look of a beast that had just devoured a most satisfying meal. His former political rival for the leadership role of the European Union had fallen into line and become a staunch ally.

Almost all Esposito's former rivals had become people who were willing to try achieving the same goal. They wanted to see a unified and politically strong Europe.

Esposito had always been a fan of history and was fascinated by the Roman Empire. His grandfather used to say their family had been powerful members of the ancient Roman government who had been favored by the Caesars from Augustus, and even into the reign of Constantine.

His father and grandfather were also powerful men in Sicily for most of the twentieth century. They had controlled exports of Esposito Tomatoes, Olives, Olive Oil, and the finest Semolina Wheat Flour. Following the fall of Mussolini in 1945, the family took control of not only food production, but also local and regional politics. It was often said that that if a person of power disagreed with what the Esposito family wanted, that person's health would take a serious turn for the worst.

Paolino Esposito had become a local Politian in Sicily moving up to the highest peak of leadership in Sicily, Italy and ultimately Europe. He now stood on the brink of ruling most of the western world, but Russia and the middle east had not completely succumbed to his charm and leadership. Many pundits around the world were saying that it was only a matter of time before the whole world would see that this man was exactly what a wounded world needed.

In recent years, the world had come through a major war, an apparent alien invasion from outer space, more than one widespread pandemic and an economic downturn that threatened even the financial well-being of some of the world's wealthiest families. It was a fact that the rich were getting exponentially richer, and the poor were becoming worse off than at any time in recent history. The middle class had all but disappeared from Europe, Japan, and the Americas. The world was crying out for a supreme leader, a savior who could turn things around and restore a good life to all who desired it.

Paolino had the ideas, and technology was about to make it easier to control the wealth behind the world's economy.

CHAPTER 16

Olivia Meyer sat gazing out the window of Gold Eagle Flight Services. She was watching intently as Lieutenant Gary Baker of the Newark Police Department SWAT escorted Andrew Benetti and his men across the tarmac toward the waiting Canadair jet. The plane had been sent from France as the culmination of a deal between the government based in Rome and the local police departments of Newark, New Jersey, and New York City.

Lieutenant Baker glared at the men he was escorting. In his mind he was formulating a chastisement he wanted to deliver but would not because of orders from above. He had been instructed to merely see to it that the men boarded the airplane alone without taking more than the clothes on their backs. Baker rested his hand on the Ruger Super Red Hawk handgun holstered on his hip. He wanted it known that regardless of who came into his city, if they meant harm to anyone in his care, he would not hesitate to use deadly force. It did not matter to him if they were the most dangerous criminal element or revered diplomats.

Benetti knew from the look he was receiving from Baker and his team of officers that he was lucky to be leaving without a major incident. He was an outsider. The number of forces he would have faced would far outnumber anything he could muster while here. He did think, however, that the day would come when this humiliation would be avenged.

Without any further incident, he and his charges boarded the airplane and the door closed behind them. As he took his seat, he looked out the window and flipped off Lieutenant Baker and the other officers. Adding insult to injury he could see Robert Wallace standing just behind Olivia Meyer as they looked out the window of the Gold Eagle terminal. He vowed to himself that this disgrace would also be set right one day soon.

Headlines blared harshly across all major online news services. From tabloid sources to the legitimate, historically trusted news sites. Immediately following the newest session of Congress, the United States seemed to be on the verge of ending centuries of sovereignty. The proposal before the legislators was to join with other nations that had thrown in with the rapidly expanding government taking Europe by storm.

Following the lead of Great Britain, the governments of Canada and Australia voted to form a provisional alliance with the rest of Europe. U.S. President Elizabeth Blair had begun pushing for the U.S. to come along side with Paolino Esposito's government. She had won over most of the opponents to such a move. She proposed that it would be universally advantageous to follow Esposito's lead in finding a long-sought solution to the problems that had plagued Israel and her neighbors, since the inception of the Zionist movement in the late nineteenth century.

No one had heard any of the ideas Esposito was promising as a solution. All anyone knew was that he said he will "bring peace". The economy of so many of the Arab nations was based upon the West's insatiable thirst for Crude Oil. The past thirty years or so had brought a collapse of those economies. Royal families had benefitted from high prices of oil for so long. The sheiks, princes, kings, and dictators had long enriched themselves with the profits, when all the while their subjects continued to wallow in the depths of poverty.

More people in the developed countries were now using alternative sources of energy in their homes, businesses, and modes of transportation. They were using everything from Solar Power, wind turbines and even waterpower. One could now drive a car that used hydrogen power which produced water as its "exhaust". After so many years of fighting about the inefficiency of those methods of powering the world, it was finally economically sound to produce power without the use of petroleum products or coal.

Israel had become the world leader in wind powered generators, and methods to recharge electric vehicle batteries. Instead of plugging into wall outlets, the vehicle's motion kept a full charge in the batteries. It had only served to increase the tensions between Israel and the surrounding Muslim nations.

It had been almost a year since the death of the French businessman Albert Le Roux. However, in that time, his business continued to prosper and churn out the latest in microchip technology. The newest chips were showing great promise for storing a person's complete personal, medical, and financial history. The greatest leap in the technology had a built-in search engine. The person who had the LR-XV microchip implanted in their brain would be now have all the knowledge known to mankind available upon request. Amazingly that information could then be uploaded to the person's brain.

Early experiments had been conducted on prisoners. Many of the test subjects experienced severe headaches. The initial models, the LR-X through LR-XII models saw some of the prisoners died of brain infections and cerebral hemorrhages. But the LR-XIV and LR-XV had overcome the problem rather well.

In the chambers of Paolino Esposito representatives from Le Roux's microchip division were buzzing with measured excitement as they presented the latest findings on the LR-XV.

"Excellency, we are even on the verge of being able to remotely control a person's thinking and reasoning process." Jacques Surrat was the chief engineer of Le Roux's microchip research and development division. "We just need to find a common frequency to control groups of people. The only problem we haven't solved yet is finding individual frequencies so no individual could fight the urges that would be given to them."

Finally, after what seemed an interminable and uncomfortable length of time, Esposito broke the silence, "Thank you Surrat, you and your people have been doing a marvelous job keeping things moving forward. Just leave the paperwork and reports for me to look over. I'll get back to you soon."

The men departed the chambers and headed outside into the warm Roman night. Back in his chambers Esposito re-lit his Habano No 5 "El Gigante" Cigar, took a deep draw and sat in the haze of the aromatic smoke. It was a habit he had begun as a young man in his late teens and early twenties, but his mentor, Albert Le Roux had introduced him to this fine cigar.

As Esposito cleared his throat and gazed out the window at the Roman skyline, he was struck by the contrast in architecture that still honored the ancient, as it blended with some of the ruins left over from the Empire of the Caesars.

There was a slight stirring of the air, and a chilling presence seemed to enter the warm room. He turned to look behind him. There, standing in the darkest corner was an apparition that he had not seen for weeks. The man who had become known as Baalazaar, the Ambassador from the Andromeda Galaxy, stood where there had been no one before. His eyes glowed with an eerie cat-like radiance.

His voice seemed to drip with a sweetness of sound, yet at the same time it had a slight buzz like, a split reed on a woodwind instrument, "Paolino, my son. I have been watching you for so many years. I chose you on the morning of your birth. From that moment on, you were the chosen one."

Esposito stood slowly and turned toward the sound of the voice. He squinted, trying to make out the silhouette. "Paolino, I have set you aside for a great work. My servant, Albert Le Roux has done a wonderful job of preparing you for the position that you now hold. You have started with great strength and now it is plain to see that you and I will rule this entire world together."

Taken aback slightly, Esposito responded, "Together?"

"Of course, together. I have set you into this position. I have kept you there by healing you and bringing you back from death. Albert Le Roux was a faithful follower of mine. I gave him great riches, all with one important goal in mind. Your position today is the culmination of that goal which I set forth in the life of Albert so many years ago. His one purpose in life was to invent original ideas or improve upon existing ideas for great electronic equipment that everyone in the world would need one day. You hold in your hands now the technology to rule the world. Your subjects will need the LR-XV microchips to do business, stay healthy, or hold a well-paying job. All this technology was set into motion when I chose Albert Le Roux more than seventy years ago, even before he was born."

"Mr. Ambassador, what is my role in all of this? I am the supreme leader of Europe, working to bring the rest of the world under my leadership. What else do you want me to do?"

Baalazaar held up his left hand and swept it across the head of Esposito, "I brought you back to this life to serve me. I want you to have people believe in and worship you, but I will be the one they are following and worshiping."

Esposito turned again toward the window and looked out upon the city of Rome. So much history was there. As he had been told by his grandfather, the blood of the Caesars flowed through his veins. He stood there proudly as he took another deep puff from his cigar. The smoke billowed around his head leaving an intoxicatingly beautiful shine in the moonlight.

He turned back to Baalazaar and smugly said, "And if I want to continue on without the help of the Andromedins, who's going to stop me?"

"My son, you need to know that you are going down a dangerous path if you choose to defy me. I do not come from Andromeda Galaxy. I am not an ambassador; I am a Prince. I have been called many things throughout history. I've been ruling this world almost since the beginning. I was there when Adam and Eve fell from grace. I was there with the Centurions when they crucified Christ. I was there with the Cavalry at Wounded Knee. I was there with Hitler, Stalin, Pol Pot and I was in Selma and Birmingham and Atlanta with the Ku Klux Klan."

"I have powers greater than anything you have ever seen. My power flowed into you when I brought you back from the dead. The world thinks that Assidi healed you, and therefore they have such respect and reverence for him. It was my hand that controlled Assidi. He has never been a man of God, as so many people think. He has always been a corruptible man. He was weak in so many ways. He loved wielding power over people whenever he preached or conducted music. He loved being the center of attention and he built a massive bank account which allowed him to travel and do whatever he wanted. He had certain desires that I, and only I could satisfy for him. I chose him at an early age as well. As he grew up, he looked at his church leaders with envy. Instead of listening to their words he looked at their position in life. He wanted to be a celebrity loved by so many people."

"We have a problem, Paolino. I want you to double your efforts to find the American Journalist, Robert Wallace. Right now, as I am speaking to you, he is trying to convince people that you are leading them to utter destruction. You are to find him and stop him, by any means!"

Just as suddenly as he had appeared, the room warmed again, and Esposito saw that Baalazaar was gone.

CHAPTER 17

Robert Wallace felt right at home sitting in front of a video camera. This was not the studio of Central News Agency, but rather a hidden basement in New Jersey. He was embarking on a whole new kind of reporting. He was secretly recording and uploading to social media news reports that he was gathering from many sources all over the world. He was also utilizing what he had learned from his biblical studies as well as the writings of those who had studied and written about eschatology since the beginning of the twentieth century. His almost ceaseless source of study had been the works of those who had been warning people about the potential future of a one world government that controlled every aspect of a person's life.

Remembering his job skills as though he had only been off work for the weekend, Robert Wallace was doing what he was meant to do. He was a consummate journalist. He was a professional who would report news impartially. In the past, he had never let his personal opinion color his news reporting. However, he was now on a whole new mission. He was now a News Commentator.

Since he began studying with Pastor James Hann and the other members of the group of believers in the compound at Camp Dickerson in Dresden, Ohio, Wallace had made the commitment to follow Jesus as his personal savior. He then began studying the meaning of so many Bible stories, and what prophecy meant. He studied the works of at least ten expositors of Bible Prophecy written over the past one hundred years. Those writings have become harder and harder to find because of the stringent laws that had been passed deeming Christianity to be hateful.

The more he learned, the more he wondered how anyone could think that Christianity could be hateful. There were a few Christians who did not act like they were new creatures in Christ. They would gossip and marginalize people whom they were supposed to love. Some of them acted like it was their duty to see who would or would not make it to heaven. Some saw their sin and turned away from it. Others did not.

Now his goal in life was to let people know that the stories about Jesus, and the second coming, were much more than just a collection of nice little stories. He also felt it his duty to warn those who were left in this world of the coming evil of the Anti-Christ. He felt certain that Paolino Esposito was that man.

To continue his reports, he had to make sure that the authorities could not find him. He made his telecasts from a different location every day. He posted them on the Dark Web, going through servers all over the country.

His new partner in the stories was Mohammed Zacharius, the young man who had found the believers at Camp Dickerson. He had come to America to become a Muslim Martyr. But he was visited in a dream by someone who explained to him about the grace that could be found in Christ, he embraced that salvation and gave his life to Jesus, that "Someone" in his vision.

Zacharius had been a computer programmer in his native Iran. His skills helped Wallace keep a few steps ahead of the authorities. They were also unable to block any of his reports. Thanks to Zacharius, people were becoming increasingly aware of the dangers that lay ahead. Wallace and Zacharius would record the reports and then put them on the network within an hour of recording them. The report would go through at least five servers before appearing available to the public.

"Good evening, this is Robert Wallace reporting the results of my studies. I am passing along to you my eyewitness reports, and things which I have come to know by faith.

One more nation in this big world has decided to make it a much smaller world by pledging allegiance with European leader, Paolino Esposito. Argentina became the newest state, if you will, of the… I like to call it the New Roman Empire."

Wallace tapped his foot switch to advance his teleprompter. At the same time a picture of the U.S. Capitol was displayed over his right shoulder.

"Meanwhile, this afternoon, President Blair made another plea for the United States end our independent nation status and join as well.

Opposition leaders vow to fight the move with their last breath. Indiana Senator William George announced that the holdouts have been invited on a fact-finding tour to Europe to meet with President Esposito. The feeling in Europe, and in President Blair's party here at home, is that if they could only see for themselves what is happening in Europe, they'd change their minds."

"It is the opinion of this reporter that uniting our nation to Europe, at the loss of our great nation's heritage, will culminate in our having sided with the wrong people. The United States has a long history of doing many things right. We have many stains on our record, but by and large, the USA has done the right thing many times."

Wallace then made a strong, passionate point that the U.S. was instrumental in bringing an end to World War I and kept Hitler from winning World War II.

After cautioning the House and the Senate against throwing away the U.S. sovereignty, he went on to explain the significance of implanted microchips in the human brain.

"This reporter was on board the now infamous space flight where reporters from around the world were taken into orbit. While on that flight, I noticed that there were a few things that didn't make sense to me. I was making notes in my computer. These were just short thoughts for me to revisit after the *flight* was over." Wallace slowly emphasized the world *flight* each time he said it.

"I mentioned in my personal notes, that the *flight* was very comparable to the Star Tours ride at Disney World and Disneyland. Later in the… *flight* one of the creatures who had been introduced to us as beings from the Andromeda Galaxy spoke to us. We were told the missing people of earth were taken to Andromeda as part of an exchange program.

One of the newest scientific inventions we were getting from them was the implantable microchip upon which your entire medical history, financial history and current financial status could be stored. We were told that soon the world would be conducting all its business with these microchips. I typed the thought "Mark of the Beast?" in my laptop. I wanted to be able to do more research on something that I had been able to do in the two days prior to the *space flight*."

"The only thing I can surmise," said Wallace, "is that they had a tracking device to read each keystroke of my computer. My personal study notes were a possible threat to their plans. I believe that the final straw to them came when we landed. I noticed as we returned to the hangar the ground crew members were in nearly the same position as when we took off."

Wallace then explained how he had seen a mysterious man shadowing him at the airport in Paris for his return flight to New York. He told the incredible story of how he heard an audible voice tell him to not get on that airplane.

"I left De Gaul and went to the train station to go to Calais for a short Channel crossing to Dover. It was there that I met a journalist friend from Britain who helped me enter the country, and then secured papers for me to travel to the United States. I had become a wanted man, accused of murder in the bombing of the airliner over the North Atlantic. I am still wanted by European authorities and must stay out of sight."

He then went into a new realm with his reports. Instead of simply telling of the dangers of a one world government and a one world leader, "The Germans thought they had the great leader in the nineteen thirties and nineteen forties. It is no different this time around. Ladies and gentlemen, I urge you to listen to what I have to say. If you can find a copy of a Bible, start reading in the New Testament. In those pages, if you look around you, you will see that what is going on today in Rome is part of what many Bible teachers have tried to warn us about. Now, I must admit, I too was very skeptical of such notions. But when I read First Thessalonians 4:17, I saw the references to believers in Christ being 'snatched up' and taken into heaven. In Revelation, there is so much written about (though the Bible never uses the term) the 'Anti-Christ'. We are also warned not to take what is called 'the mark of the beast', that will be needed to do business in the Last Days."

"I need to sign off now and move on to another location. I know that you need this message just as much as I needed it years ago. I resisted for too many years. We have entered what the Bible Prophecy teachers have called the Great Tribulation. If you can believe what is being taught about that time, we will have three and a half years of peace and prosperity before everything begins to fall apart. Watch and pray. Do not give up the faith. God be with you. Lord willing, I'll try to be back here tomorrow at the same start time. Remember that you can watch these reports and share them with your friends, unless the authorities remove them. If that does happen, try to read your Bible, there are many of them lying around in the homes of the people who were taken from this world last year. God bless you, and please continue to pray for me and this ministry."

Wallace then stood and walked toward Zacharius, "Thank you Brother. Any word on whether or not they are closing in on us?"

Zacharius only smiled. His pure white teeth stood in stark contrast to his deep olive skin. There was a slight pride in the fact that he had been able to avoid detection thus far, "I am going through a different server in Chicago, tonight. When you use the same servers time and again, you run the risk of being found. I wouldn't want to have that happen."

Wallace patted him on the shoulder and smiled, "Neither would I." He then turned to Olivia who was sitting on a stool near the exit. He said, "Are you ready, Pretty Lady? Let's get out of here."

CHAPTER 18

At the urging of President Blair, the ten Congressmen and Senators who were opposed to joining with the European government were at Andrews Air Force Base, boarding the Military Air Transport Service Lockheed C-130 Hercules, for their flight to Europe. It was not going to be a luxurious flight, but instead of jump seats lining the outer walls of the plane, airline seats had been installed. The nine-and-a-half-hour flight would be filled with much discussion about the issue at hand. Most of these legislators were sternly against being absorbed by Europe. At least three of them were beginning to warm to the idea. It was hoped by POTUS that these few would be able to persuade the others to make the vote unanimous.

The United States began losing its influence on the world stage as early as the late nineteen fifties and into the sixties, when the Vietnam War became such a watershed moment tearing the country apart.

The sky was turning a deep gray in the east as the afternoon shadows grew longer. The mighty Hercules taxied toward the Runway Two-Five, for a takeoff into a light westerly wind. The weather forecast over the Atlantic promised a relatively smooth flight. The Lockheed C-130 Hercules was not known for its lavish amenities, but its ruggedness made it ideal for hurricane hunting, and as a cargo-carrier, as a troop carrier dropping special forces soldiers and sailors behind enemy lines, and as a solid gun platform hovering over a target, rapid firing 20 Millimeter cannon.

Robert Wallace and Olivia Meyer left the make-shift secret basement studio. Evening was beginning to take the reins from late afternoon. Soon it would be dark, and the lights of the Manhattan skyline would shimmer with a sight to rival the stars in the heavens. Perhaps this is what draws so many people to the Big Apple. Though Wallace had always been a small-town boy, he had always found great excitement and beauty in that view. It was there, only two weeks after beginning his job with CNA, that he met and fell in love with Olivia. Their professional lives, especially his, took them in different directions.

When they reconnected last year, for him it was love all over again. He deeply regretted that he had ever left her behind to chase all over the world for news stories. Then there were the harrowing events in New Jersey when agents from Albert Le Roux's company tried to kill them. After they managed to get back to Ohio, and with the group of believers at Camp Dickerson, he let her know of his deep love for her.

In the sight of the happy witnesses at the camp, Pastor Hann joined them in marriage, and for the most part, they have been inseparable. Now, being apart for even a day seemed like an eternity.

Zacharius pulled around the corner in the late model SUV. The look on his face showed a bit of concern. "Get in. We may have been located."

Wallace and Olivia wasted no time and quickly jumped into the back seat just barely closing the door before Zacharius screamed away from the curb. As they sped away a black SUV came around the corner at a high rate of speed, almost hitting the cars that were parked nearby.

Wallace quickly turned to watch behind them. There it was, a black SUV with dark tinted windows all around. Was it a government vehicle? How many people were in it, who were they, and how did they find him?

Zacharius said, "I got into the car and as I pulled away, I noticed the SUV tailing me about three vehicles behind. I started to take different side streets to see if my suspicion was accurate. After two turns my mind was made up. I got a look at one of the men. He was with the group who had Olivia with them and were demanding that you go with them to Europe to face charges."

"I saw all of them get on the airplane in Newark." Olivia said as she continued to twist and turn to look over her shoulder. "If indeed one of them is back, could it mean that all of them returned to the U.S. to come after us?"

Wallace reached out and took Olivia's hand. We are in God's hands. They can't have us."

The red-carpet reception at Rome's Ciampino International Airport was as elaborate as any seen in recent years. The Congressional delegation from the United States was arriving for high level meetings with Paolino Esposito and his ministers.

Led by Indiana Senator William George, this group of ten legislators were in Italy at the behest of President Elizabeth Blair. The effort by President Blair and Paolino Esposito was to convince these men and women to get into lockstep with Blair and Esposito. Their desire was for the United States to become a part of what many have begun to call the New Roman Empire.

Senator George and Congresswoman Carrie Ellsworth, from the San Joaquin Valley in California, were the two leaders of the dissenting factor fighting to keep the U.S. independent and not become a part of a one world government. It was becoming more and more difficult to keep the U.S. Dollar intact. That has been a hard task for nearly thirty years. The World Bank had dropped the U.S. Dollar ten years ago as the benchmark standard for monetary value.

The ten legislators tentatively made their way down the stairs to greet the reception committee. Paolino Esposito was at the head of the reception line. In his mind he was thinking that these American legislators currently stand in the way of bringing all the former might and industrial power of the United States into his coalition of industrialized states.

Germany had always been a powerful and innovative nation that now is standing alongside Esposito. Esposito thought that if Germany, with her long history of pride and scientific imagination could be joined by the United States, his empire would be able to do anything. The great future that this world has longed for over the centuries was finally coming to pass.

Paolino Esposito had always considered himself a great leader among his peers. As a teenager his group of friends set up small businesses that included everything from shaking down pushcart owners for protection from the other gangs to selling drugs to the children of wealthy businessmen. Some of his friends from his youth followed him into the world of local politics in Sicily.

Another of his friends went on to work for one of Europe's richest men. Colonel Vito Lombardo went from being a local policeman in Palermo, to head of security for Le Roux Enterprises. The two had followed each other's careers, so it was natural for Albert Le Roux to have an interest in the political fortunes of Paolino Esposito.

Esposito needed to convince some Americans who stood in the way of his creating a one world government that they should fall in line with the rest of the willing world. His purpose was to make them toe the line, or there would be consequences.

Baalazaar had convinced him that everything would come together. The man the world knew as the Andromedin Ambassador had revealed much about the future to his protégé.

Storm clouds began gathering in the western sky. The Mediterranean had been roiling for the past eighteen hours, sending an ominous charge through the air. Just as Senator William George reached his hand out to Esposito's, a sharp bolt of lightning surged across the sky creating a jagged, evil looking frown, shooting from west to east. It changed from orange to amber to a shockingly bright white that contrasted against the slate grey sky.

A light, distant thunder rolled about twenty seconds later. The storm was getting closer, but it was still far enough away to allow time for all the dignitaries to seek shelter.

Mohammed Zacharius deftly drove the dark blue SUV carrying Robert Wallace and his wife Olivia. They were heading toward The Hudson River on the way to Manhattan.

Wallace made sure Olivia was hidden from view on the seat next to him as he turned to watch behind them. It had been a few moments since they had seen the black Chevy Suburban a few car lengths back. "I haven't seen them for a few minutes. Do you think we lost 'em?"

Zacharius had been watching his rear-view mirrors as he urged the car forward, "I haven't seen them since we made that shortcut down two side streets. Let's take a chance and hide here before we continue."

They found a large parking space under some trees on a quiet residential street. Everyone ducked down to stay out of sight. It was hard to notice, but the soft sound of the Chevy Suburban slowly drove past. A beam of light shone into the interior. It was a blessing for Mohammed, Robert, and Olivia that they, too, were in a tall SUV. Otherwise, the occupants would have been able to see down onto the seats as they passed. The Suburban passed by, and in a moment, sped up and turned at the next intersection.

Mohammed asked, "When do you think it'll be safe to move on?"

Wallace wanted to be overly cautious if need be, "I think we should give it some time. They might just be up around the corner waiting for us to make a move."

Mohammed agreed, "I can wait here all night if I have to. I surely dislike those men."

"I don't think they're very fond of us either," joked Olivia. The three of them laughed and relieved the tension a bit.

In Rome, the pomp and circumstance of a state visit continued. Idaho Senator Samuel Hassler smiled politely as he shook hands with Paolino Esposito. One by one, the entourage went along the reception line shaking hands with Europe's most influential people. Ten legislators from the United States, who were not willing to fall into step with the world that was marching toward a one world government, were each polite as they kept up appearances for the media cameras.

It was a well-known fact that the United States was no longer the world power it had been in the first half of the twentieth century. Crime had risen tremendously, and much of the public was willing to look the other way. Crimes that included murder and extortion were looked upon as no longer such heinous offenses. The public had come to accept excuses that ranged from a hard scrabble life, to passion, to lack of understanding between right and wrong.

It was easy to see why so many Americans were willing to join a central government and allow one man to be a strong leader. When times of trouble arise, people will give up much of their individualism. History records that the promise of Communism seemed like a good idea to so many people. The future looked so bright to them when Lenin and Trotsky and the first generation of Communist leaders in Russia took charge of the country. The people had gone from a monarchy with a family ruling them for centuries to a ruling party that took the place of the ruling family. The monarchy was not a benevolent figurehead. The royal family became more obsessed with advancing their own lifestyle and the largely agrarian society suffered. People longed to have more power in their lives. Then came Karl Marx, and the promise of a Utopian society in which the common working class would be able to control their own destinies.

In a short while, for the "common good" the leadership started to suppress people who were dissenters. People were executed for disagreeing with the leadership. Millions of the common people died at the hands of the Communist Party. The leaders and high-ranking officers of the Party enriched themselves with the luxuries that the royals had enjoyed, while the Proletariat suffered more and more.

Then entered the ultra-right-wing Fascism of Benito Mussolini, followed closely by Adolf Hitler. Both men came to power with a promise of strong leadership. The Nazis of Germany were the National Socialists. They were basically the same as the Communists in the sense that they too were Socialists. The strong central government promised to take care of the people. The people again suffered, especially those who were deemed by the Party to be undesirables. Germans called Jews, Gypsies, Slavs and the mentally deficient to be Untermenschen, sub-humans, who were not worth caring for. In fact, the Untermenschen were to be eliminated from society, murdered, so they could not reproduce.

As had always been the case, as the world slipped more and more into chaos with many issues affecting daily life, people wanted someone to save them. The environment, the rich becoming richer on the backs of the poor, and the high cost of just getting by were enough to make people take a long look at their lives.

There had been such devastating wars in the twentieth century, and diseases seemed to increase in intensity. The global FLU Pandemic at the end of World War I killed millions of people around the world. In the early twenty-first century came the Corona Virus that killed millions worldwide, as well. Disease and war played heavily on the hearts of every man, woman, and child. The time was right for someone to take control.

This was the time for that one leader to form a powerful central government that would be able to lead all people. This benevolent society would assure that the poor were taken care of and supported by the rich – a promise that many had only dreamed of before.

Outside the gates of Camp Dickerson (also known by many as "New Zion") a crowd had gathered; the crowd was chanting accusations at the people inside the compound.

A familiar face was at the head of the small, yet noisy crowd. Former guest at the compound, Danny Lloyd, held a powerful bullhorn to his mouth, "You people are a part of the most hateful group in history.

You call yourselves Christians, yet anyone with a sense of justice knows that you belong to a group that has only caused more pain and trouble in the world."

At this, others in the group raised their placards and in unison chanted, "You are blind followers of a blind religion." They held signs proclaiming that they were a group called "Antrelige". They were anti religion, believing that religion has killed more innocent people in the world than any plague or disease.

Danny Lloyd called out once again, "Jesus Christ was only a teacher. He was not the Son of God. He did not rise from the dead. He was only a man, who, with his band of brainwashed followers succeeded in brainwashing thousands. You must give up your studies of the Bible and accept the fact that you are not welcome in today's world."

Pastor Hann looked at his fellow believers, "It looks as though we are about to head into a new phase of persecution. So far, it's just been words, but the day will come when we will be threatened with bodily harm if we don't recant our pledge of faith in Christ."

Lloyd was only a few feet from where Hann had spoken and he called out, "That day is today, Pastor. We cannot allow you to poison anyone's minds with your lies about some perceived savior from a couple thousand years ago. You and your people will have twenty-four hours to make your peace with us and join our ranks, or we will come for you. We, the people of Antirelige must put a stop to this Christianity here and now. You cannot go into the world and lie to people spreading your hateful message."

Lloyd strutted back and forth in front of the gate. He was feeling power as he had never felt before. Danny Lloyd was one of the minor soldiers behind Colonel Vito Lombardo when he worked for Le Roux enterprises. Now that Lombardo was a high-ranking officer in the security forces of Paolino Esposito, Lloyd fantasized becoming one of the trusted higher-ranking officers within the security forces. That put him in line to be an important man in the newly formed one world government of Lord Esposito. He pictured himself surrounded by beautiful women, driving fast cars, and being appointed to a governorship of one of the vast territories, perhaps even the United States. He envisioned being drunk with power and glory.

Vito Lombardo and Paolino Esposito were in an intense discussion regarding what a few Christians were beginning to talk about, world-wide. Esposito was filled with emotion as he spoke, "People are trying to stop what we are striving to accomplish. They are saying that I am not to be trusted. They say that I am what they call 'the Antichrist'. I don't even know what they mean by that."

Lombardo tried to set his leader's mind at ease, "Lord Paolino, when I was a young man, I wanted to go into the priesthood. The Christ is the 'Christened' or 'anointed' one. You, Sir are anointed to be our leader. Therefore, you are The Christ."

"I feel that way, Vito. When I was brought back from death, I came into a whole new understanding and enlightenment of what I was to do. I have been christened to bring true peace to this world."

"That is true, my lord. You know so many things that we mere mortals can only imagine. You have vision to guide us into a whole new world. People have lived with war for so long that they don't know how to have peace."

Esposito smiled a slight smile. He was a proud man, having lived a life where things came easily to him. He grew up with the attitude that because he was the son of a powerful man, it stood to reason that he too, would one day become a powerful leader of people. That was the whole reason he went into politics. Even though Benito Mussolini was such a reviled character in history, many people in Italy still revered the man. He was seen as having been a powerful leader in a highly patriarchal society in the 1920s, until the day he was captured and killed.

Esposito wanted to be that kind of a powerful man. He had never married, but there were plenty of beautiful women who were ready and willing to give themselves to him and to bear his children. To be the mother of a future leader of the world was a powerful aphrodisiac.

A chilling breeze entered the room. Suddenly, from the darkest corner of the room, came a voice with which Esposito had become remarkably familiar. "Gentlemen, good evening. I could not help but hear the concern in your voices about people trying to paint my young leader with a broad brush, staining his reputation. Those Christians have tried to stop my work for centuries. I have been able to convince many of them that it is in their best interest not to take everything they read in their scriptures as truth. Many of them have seen my light and followed it. Some of those have gone back to their old beliefs. However, I have a plan that will get them to bring new believers to me."

Vito and Esposito exchanged glances before Paolino said, "Don't fear, Vito. Baalazaar always knows what to do and what to say. He is the reason that I live. He's the reason that you and I are going to be very well off."

Through a smile dripping with the confidence of a man who was totally in control, Baalazaar said, "True, Vito. When you follow me, you will have the desires of your heart.

Baalazaar took both men's hands and mysteriously transported them to the top of the tallest building in

Rome. It was still under construction, to someday house the governing body with representatives from every corner of the globe.

From their lofty perch, they were amazed to see airplanes coming and going from every airport in the entire Province of Lazio.

He then showed them visions and spoke to them as though narrating a film, "Gentlemen, the representatives from the United States are continuing to cause us problems. I cannot allow that to continue. Even though some of them are beginning to see the future that we envision, they are still holding out. I am afraid that they will not have the opportunity to change their votes when they return home. I have made sure that their lofty ideals will soon fall back to earth."

Taken aback, Colonel Lombardo spoke, "What do you mean, Mr. Ambassador, 'seeing to it that they will not get home?'"

"Do not concern yourself, dear one. You do not need to do anything. Just put your trust in me, and in your Lord Esposito. Those people will not get home to vote against our plans."

Esposito, somewhat entranced, answered, "I understand, Baalazaar."

Captain Cheryl Bloom was a fifteen-year veteran of the Air Force. She had risen quickly through the ranks and upon her next promotion, it had been suggested by those in the know, that she was in line to become the first female pilot on Air Force One. She was an aviation expert. With Captain Bloom's experience and skills, it was only natural for her to be entrusted with the U.S. Congressional delegation on such an important mission.

The congressional delegation had been in talks with leaders of the Esposito government. These legislators have been strongly against voting for the United States becoming one of the many provinces in the new one world government. It was possible that one or two of them had changed their minds. A majority vote would assure dissolving the United States as a sovereign nation. If that were to happen, the United States would become a part of very progressive government. Paolino Esposito, for all intents and purposes had done away with national rivalries.

Even though two members of Congress had affirmed to the media that they would vote in favor of the move, it would not be enough to overcome the negative votes of the remaining holdouts. With this, the United States would remain an independent nation.

The four engines of the C-130 were humming with the beautifully tuned sound of a fine orchestra. There was a slight tear beginning to show on the leading edge of the wing just to the outboard side of the number one engine. There was a slight vibration that increased as the tear in the wing began to slowly open bigger.

In the cockpit, Captain Bloom turned to her co-pilot and spoke, "Lieutenant, did you feel that?"

Lt. Gerald Davidson replied, "Yes Ma'am. That was strange. It sounds like something is coming apart. Could we have lost a wing panel?" They each looked out their respective sides of the plane but could see nothing out of the ordinary.

"Or perhaps something inside the wing? Either way, Gerry, I don't like it." Captain Bloom checked the gauges and did not see anything amiss. However, she did notice that the controls were a little bit sluggish, compared to usual.

During the pre-flight inspection no one had noticed a hairline cracks on the leading edge of the left wing. The top of the wing changed its shape which made the plane harder to steer. As the panels were near the outside of the number one engine making it invisible from the cockpit or anywhere on the plane what was wrong.

Suddenly, Captain Bloom felt a heavy surge to the left, and in her peripheral vision she saw a large piece of metal fly up and away from the wing. It tumbled into the slipstream and crashed against the horizontal stabilizer. She was fighting to keep control, but the mighty Hercules was moving in a large wide arc to the left. As Captain Bloom fought to keep control it was becoming more apparent that she was losing control of her airplane.

"Lieutenant! Get on the radio to Andrews. Give them our position and let them know that we may be going down. I'm going to try and slip to lose altitude." With that, she gave heavy right rudder and struggled with the yoke to perhaps, at least, make a controlled crash landing in the Atlantic south of Great Britain.

"Captain, I'll ask if there are any Navy ships near us. I hope there are, but if we can't gain control, here, they're only going to find airplane parts and bodies."

Captain Bloom valiantly fought the controls, but it was becoming lost cause. In the passenger compartment, the members of the congressional delegation and the four members of the media were in panic mode. The electronic media members turned on their cameras to record what was happening. At least, this would provide possible evidence for investigators. The cacophony of voices made it hard to concentrate on what was happening to the airplane.

The Hercules began a pancake spin. The wings no longer provided any control. Captain Bloom realized that she could not save her airplane and that all on board would either die in a few minutes, or be severely injured, fighting to survive in the cold Atlantic. Ocean. Her mind was racing wondering how this could have happened. She was always very thorough when she did a walk-around pre-flight inspection of her airplane. It had to be something that was deliberately done. How could the panels have stayed intact over the Mediterranean and across France and into the air over the Atlantic? The dizzying effect of the spin was beginning to take its toll on her and the passengers.

Lieutenant Davidson had now lost consciousness, and Captain Bloom was beginning to black out. She struggled to write information on the pad attached to her right knee. It was no use; she was blacking out. Her last words, hastily scribbled on the pad were, "I love you daddy."

The C-130 disintegrated as it drew closer to the surface of the Atlantic. Just coming to within sight of the crashing airplane were two U.S. Navy F-10 AB fighter jets from the U.S.S. Nimitz. They were streaking towards the doomed airplane. The crew watched in horror, as first one wing came off completely, and then the entire tail section of the cargo plane broke away. From then it was just a matter of short seconds before the second wing came off and the remainder of the fuselage nosed downward and cork-screwed its way into the cold, blue sea below.

Before losing consciousness, Lieutenant Gerald Davidson had managed to tell Andrews Air Force Base what had happened. News spread quickly through the military that one of its airplanes had gone down in sight of two fighter jets. The pilots had given a very thorough description of what they saw. The tough Hercules airplane came apart completely before plunging into the ocean south of England and west of France.

Outside the gates of Camp Dickerson, Danny Lloyd led the ever-growing crowd in chanting "Hey, Ho, your religion must go! Hey, Ho, Religion must go!"

Pastor James Hann turned to his friends, who were standing together just inside the dining hall and commented on what was happening outside the gates, "What those poor fools don't understand is, they are participating in a religion all its own. They are following 'lord' Esposito. They will be following him to their own death. He has hijacked faith in Christ by allowing himself to be compared to the true Messiah. Too many people in this world are falling into that same trap. It is our job to try and put a stop to it by sharing the truth with a lost world."

These days, Father Charles Reilly kept his clerical collar as loose as he could. In his days as a Roman Catholic Priest, he proudly wore it and reveled in the power and glory it brought him. He was a middle-aged man with ginger-red hair. His complexion was pale and freckled. He looked every bit the Irish Catholic priest. Instead of totally giving his life to Christ when he was ordained, he felt a desire to someday be looked up to as a holy man. It was only after so many people world-wide were suddenly missing that he remembered what he had heard about the Rapture. He was now a man on a mission. He wanted to make sure that those who are still in this world hear the true message of salvation.

Speaking to Hann, Fr. Reilly said, "We need to be prepared for the worst. Though, that would absolutely be one of the best things, I live by Philippians 1:21, 'to live is Christ, to die is gain'. But if I die for Christ, I will gain."

Hann replied, "If we can go on living for Christ, we could help show the way to Him for many others. Even those poor souls out there could share in that salvation if they'd only listen." He looked at his fellow campers and began to formulate a plan. They needed to see that at least some would be able to get away from the compound, so they could be the nucleus of a new group of believers. Pastor Hann and Father Reilly had begun an intense teaching program that would lead to some members becoming preachers and teachers. A group of twelve new leaders were being prepared to become the next band of pastors. Deacons had laid hands on them as they were charged with bringing more believers into the fold. There were four of them who were talented at memorization. Each one of them had begun to memorize the entire Bible. Two of them were already into the books of first and second Chronicles of the old Testament, while the other two were committed to memorizing the entire New Testament. Having easily memorizing the gospels, they were now into the epistles of Romans and first and second Corinthians.

If the day ever comes that there will be no Bible available, these four people will be able to relay and teach the message. Someone will be able to transcribe the Word in a new way.

It had been at least a half an hour since Mohammed, Robert and Olivia had parked under the large trees on the side street. They had been pursued by a group of men in a black Chevy Suburban. It was obvious that they were not U.S. Government authorities. They were the men who had held Olivia prisoner at the Gold Eagle terminal at Newark's Liberty Field.

Robert and Olivia held hands as they slouched in the back seat of their SUV. The excitement of the earlier chase had given way to a new calm feeling since no vehicles had passed by the area for at least these past thirty minutes.

Breaking the silence, Mohammed spoke first, "I think I'll take a short stroll and check if I can see any sign of that SUV.

He reached up and turned off the dome light so that it would not turn on when he opened the door. As he departed, he cautioned, "You are the two who are being targeted by these people. Stay here until I return. If I don't return, you'll know there was trouble. Get out of the car and go the opposite direction. Hopefully, they don't have both ends of the street under surveillance."

When he was gone, Olivia looked at Wallace with a slight smile and said, "Alone, at last. Although, I do wish he would come back soon and tell us that it's safe to move along."

"Mohammed is a great driver and a very observant man. He has always been aware of his surroundings. I wish there were more like him in our corner for this fight." Wallace checked his watch. It had only been about five minutes since Mohammed left. "I think he'll be returning any moment now. We saw them turn right at the end of the block. If they continued back to the main thoroughfares, perhaps they think we were far enough ahead, and we got away."

His assessment of the timing was correct. Mohammed came back around the corner, and as he walked back to the car, he kept going past them.

Wallace turned around as his gaze followed his friend back down the street. Under the streetlamp at the other end of the street, Mohammed stopped and slowly eyed all four corners and the parked vehicles up as well as down each side of the street. He then turned and quickly made his way back to Robert and Olivia.

"I didn't see any sign of their car within a four-block radius. I think, we should go back in the direction we came from and make our way out of town another way."

It was a tight fit, but their SUV managed to turn around and head back to where the whole chase started. Cities were trying to save money in so many ways that they had all begun cutting back on the number of streetlamps. So many streets had dark places that made it easy to stay hidden on side streets. Even the main streets were darker than they had been before all the talk of space aliens living among us.

The car radio was tuned to WCBS News Radio, "...the Air Force plane crash was witnessed by pilots of two Navy fighter jets in the area. The congressional delegation was on a fact-finding tour for the past week in Rome, with the Paolino Esposito European government. The doomed delegation on board the C-130 Air Force plane were planning to vote against the U.S. joining the European government. They had been sent on the mission by President Elizabeth Blair."

Wallace forcefully spoke, "I don't like it. Those people were murdered. I don't know how it was done, but they were standing in the way of Esposito having his way here in the United States.

Mohammed spoke up, "There is a lot of distrust of America in the Mediterranean region. I was taught from the time I was a child that America is the great Satan. Israel is the Little Satan to the people of my country. Islam teaches that America and Israel are the reason for all our troubles."

Olivia added, "I know that our history has not been perfect, but there has been a lot of good done by this country, especially in the middle of the twentieth century fighting Hitler, Mussolini and Communism during the Cold War."

Mohammed didn't disagree with her, "Yes, but you have to realize that what people in that region have been taught for so long makes it difficult for them to sympathize with the Americans in this situation. They are believing that the only way for our region to find peace is through what Mr. Esposito is offering. Since becoming a follower of Jesus, I now look upon you as my brother and sister and not as my enemy. I am so sorry for the loss that has just occurred. All those years ago when the World Trade Center and Pentagon were attacked, I understand what the people of my country were thinking. Now, however, I appreciate the anger and tears your country's people felt at that same time."

CHAPTER 19

A t Camp Dickerson the situation was starting to turn very ugly. The people outside the gates had been throwing rocks and bricks for about thirty minutes, and now the first of a barrage of Molotov Cocktails flew over the main gate. The believers inside began to scatter. Pastor Hann led those who had the assignment of memorizing the Bible into the dining hall.

He was met there by Josh Dickerson, a man whose family had owned this property since the late seventeen-hundreds. He quickly ushered all five into a cold storage cellar that had been used for more than two hundred years to help keep peaches, apples, and melons fresh. He led them to a back corner where a shelving unit hid a doorway, "Follow me."

As the door slid open, he flipped a switch that, turning on a string of low wattage light bulbs that dimly lit the passageway. As the party hurried down the tunnel, he urgently gave some directions, "This will take you into the spring house on the hillside. It is hidden from the view of the main gate. When you come out of the building, make a left turn, and follow the path. You'll go through a small wood. On the other side you'll find an old van. The keys are under the sun visor. I know, real secure, right? Follow the gravel road and you'll come out at the edge of my farm. Out the driveway, turn north and you'll be headed toward State Route Sixteen. That'll take you all the way to Coshocton."

Hann wondered aloud, "What's there? How do I know there aren't more of these people there?"

He received his answer when Dickerson handed him a card hastily pulled from his billfold, "When you get there, Go up Main, to East Main to that address. When you meet the owner, you'll be pleasantly surprised to see my brother Paul. He's my twin, and he too, is a new believer in Christ."

With that, Dickerson stopped, turned around and headed back into the cellar where he pulled the shelving unit back into place, hiding the door to the passage. Next to the shelves was a wall phone he quickly used to call his brother to tell him about Pastor Hann and the other believers who would be coming to see him shortly.

Returning to the dining hall he could see flames flickering as fire spread all along the driveway. The dry grass was easily lit, and the fire was spreading toward the dining hall, the small barracks buildings, and shower house. Feeling helpless as he watched the flames spreading, Dickerson cried out to God for help.

Mohammed Zacharius drove into a basement parking garage in The Bronx, New York. The dimly lit corner parking space in the southwest corner was open, just as he had anticipated it would be.

"Where are we now, Mohammed?" Bob Wallace was curious. The last time they had spoken about where their next stop would be, Mohammed told him that he had friends who were curious about Christ who would be willing to help him get out of New York.

"Is this the place you told me about? Are you sure these people won't be upset with you for leaving your Muslim faith?" Wallace had heard all the stories about strict followers of Islam who were sworn to kill anyone who would fall away from or even question the words of the Prophet.

Mohammed turned to Wallace and Olivia, "Last night, I had one of the most vivid dreams I have ever had, as intense as the dream that brought me to faith in Christ. Someone, maybe an angel, visited me, hovering over my bed, and told me to come to this place. My friend from childhood lives in this building. I saw in the dream this parking space in this corner. I know that it was God speaking to me through an angel."

Until now, Olivia had remained silent, "I trust you, Mohammed. I know that anyone who comes to the faith the way you did has to have been visited by angels or even heard God's voice speaking to you."

Mohammed Zacharius had come to America with the sole task of becoming a martyr for Islam. However, he had been visited in a dream by someone explaining to him that what he was planning was wrong. He then heard the story of Jesus and His love for all people, even someone who was intending on taking lives, including his own. He learned through that dream, and then he saw the face of Christ looking at him from the faces of everyone he was preparing to kill. There were men, women and children with sad eyes looking at him with the face of Christ. Their voices softly spoke to him saying, "Mohammed, I love you. I want you to believe in me and follow me."

It was then that he received directions to Camp Dickerson. He was told to listen to believers in Jesus. The people in that camp would take him into their family of believers and welcome him with open arms.

"I received the message last night that my friend Ibrahim had also heard an angel speak to him about helping me. I am bringing us here, strictly on faith, that Ibrahim will do as my dream told me. I have confidence that we will be safe. However, I want you to stay here while I go and make sure Ibrahim followed the same instructions I was given."

Mohammed stepped out of the car, but before closing the door he leaned in and said, "My brother and sister, if I am not back in fifteen minutes, leave the neighborhood quickly." And with that he was gone.

Pastor James Hann and four of his fellow believers came out of the Spring House on the Camp Dickerson property. Hann scanned the area, and just as Josh Dickerson had told him, there was the small path that led directly to the wooded area at the edge of the camp. Hurrying along the path, into and out of the woods, they found the 2015 Chrysler Pacifica Van. The finish had seen better days and the oxidized red paint almost seemed powdery.

The door opened with a tightness that made Hann think that perhaps it would not open at all. There was a low-pitched squeak of metal rubbing metal as the door opened. The keys were under the visor, where Dickerson had said they would be. Hann smiled as he remembered the sardonic way Dickerson had said, "I know, real secure, right?"

The group hoped that the engine would not be prone to seize up. Sure enough, even though the battery was a little low, the van started on the second try. All on board the let out with a "Praise Jesus" as Hann put the van in drive and started down the driveway toward the road. Turning left, he headed out toward the state highway that would take them to their next stop.

Mohammed Zacharius made his way up the steps of the old apartment building to the fourth floor. This was the apartment he had shared with his old friend, Ibrahim Soliman. He approached apartment three and knocked. He could hear footsteps on the old bare wood floor, and then the series of deadbolts and chain locks were released. The door opened slowly and there, staring back at him were the eyes of the young man with whom Mohammed had spent his childhood. They had spent Fridays at worship and were together throughout all their martial training. The red rimmed, swollen eyes showed that Ibrahim had obviously been weeping.

"Mohammed, my brother. Then my dream was true. I have not made a mistake. I am to welcome you in." Ibrahim quickly embraced Mohammed and they both stood for a moment shaking with emotion.

"Yes, my brother," Mohammed spoke, "I too, was told in a dream to come here."

Ibrahim implored his friend, "Are these Christians really our enemy? Aren't they really followers of the God who had spoken to our father Abraham?"

As they walked into the apartment Ibrahim said, "And if I am not mistaken in interpreting my dream, you have two people with you who are running from soldiers of Paolino Esposito."

"That is true, my brother. We must get out of New York and find our way back to other brothers and sisters in Christ. We must all carry on this fight to alert people about the evil that this man Esposito is attempting to bring upon this world."

"I have viewed many of this man Wallace's webcasts. He makes a great deal of sense. I found a Bible that was written in Arabic in a nearby apartment. People who came here from Lebanon had lived there. They were believers in Jesus, but suddenly they were gone."

Josh Dickerson grabbed the garden hose near the dining hall and aimed it at the base of the intense flames. It had been a long dry summer in this part of Ohio, and the grass was extremely dry. The hose sputtered before allowing a steady stream of water out. The dirt beneath the dried grasses did not absorb the water as one would think.

The angry crowd had to part quickly as a pickup truck barreled down on the main gate. The gate crashed to the ground as the Toyota Tundra plowed through it.

Dickerson was taken by a temporary fury. He picked up a large rock from the base of the fountain just outside the dining room door, and with the deft skill of a center fielder, he hurled the rock toward the truck smashing the driver's side of the windshield. The truck swerved violently and nearly hit Josh as he jumped to safety.

The crowd of raging people had charged in, following the truck. They grabbed Josh and dragged him to the front of the dining hall. Suddenly one of the leaders grabbed a stone and threw it toward Josh, striking him in the right side of his head. The cracking sound could be heard all over that end of the camp. The others then began to pick up rocks and throw them at the now limp body of the man for whose family the camp had been named.

Danny Lloyd was the leader of this group of fanatical warriors for Paolino Esposito. It was Col. Vito Lombardo who had personally put Lloyd in charge of this. Lloyd had taken to his task with great zeal, rounding up the new followers of Christ and, for the most part, imprisoning them. Many had been put to death.

Every person who died had been offered the option of leaving behind the false religion of Christianity. As Dickerson lay dying, the angry mob fanned out across the compound seeking anyone who was there.

Lloyd had come to Dresden and Camp Dickerson at the urging of the Andromedin Ambassador, Baalazaar. This made Lloyd feel even more important. It was Col. Lombardo who had assigned him his post of rooting out Christians. At the same time Baalazaar had directed him to this place. It was common knowledge that Baalazaar has spoken to and guided Paolino Esposito. That means that Lloyd is being guided by the same person who has influenced and empowered the leader of the world. Lloyd wished if only his mother had been here to see how successful, her son had become. He resented Christians because they had had such an undue influence on his mother. She had been a World History professor at a small Bible college in New Jersey. He was only glad that she had been taken to the Andromeda Galaxy to learn what they could teach her, and she could share her knowledge with them.

The search in the Atlantic continued. The snowy white caps on top of the blue waves at this location only hid its secrets at the deepest depths. The search craft could see parts of the airplane, the seats and pieces of luggage were near, or at the surface. The airplane had fallen from an altitude of nearly nineteen thousand feet. It was obvious that there were no survivors. The U.S. Navy pilots had watched as the left wing ripped apart, and then tore off. It had appeared to them that as the left wing came off, the pilot struggled to use the yoke and rudder to maintain control. She then went into a flat spin, pancaking until the right wing tore off.

Investigators from the National Transportation and Safety Board were rushed to the scene from the south of England. There would not be much to tell from this cursory aerial investigation. They would only be able to do a thorough investigation when ships picked up the pieces and returned them to Washington.

Recovery would continue for the week. The search for survivors had already been called off.

Olivia and Robert Wallace were still sitting in the SUV in the corner parking space. There were only a few low wattage light bulbs, and they were spaced so far away from each other that their purpose of providing security in the dank basement garage was easily defeated. The wall just ahead of the car was growing a black shiny moss, as a light flow of water cascaded down that side of the garage.

Olivia looked all around, scanning for any sign of Mohammed's return. They were here because

Mohammed had dreamed that his childhood friend wanted to learn about Jesus. Did his friend have the same dream?

Wallace commented, "Mohammed has the deepest faith of anyone I have ever known. The story of how he came to know Christ through a dream is phenomenal. That's a dream one only reads about in the Bible. He is the only person I know who has had God talk to him through dreams."

Wallace quieted himself quickly when he heard the stairway door close. Mohammed and another man came walking toward Robert and Oliva. Both men were smiling as they approached the SUV.

Mohammed eagerly opened the door and provided introductions. There was a great deal of joyous, yet subdued laughter as Mohammed told Robert and Olivia all about his best childhood friend, "Ibrahim and I met in school after my family moved from Iran to the Palestinian Authority. We used to sneak out of Friday prayers and run to the edge of our district. It was there that we would pick up rocks and throw them at the Jewish boys walking to Yeshiva. Remembering the fear that Mohammed and Ibrahim inflicted on these youngsters going to their school, brought laughter to the two young Palestinians. It had been good practice for one day in the future when they would join the army of Martyrs of Islam. Then they would be using more than small stones.

Mohammed and Ibrahim joined Olivia and Robert in the car, and they pulled out of the garage. Mohammed explained that he and Ibrahim had prayed to the Father of Jesus, and that now they were all one family.

Ibrahim told them that he had heard word on the street about security forces chasing an American journalist who was spreading lies about Paolino Esposito. When he had the dream about Mohammed becoming a follower of Jesus, he knew that he too must become a disciple as well.

Ibrahim spoke, "I have always trusted my brother Mohammed. When, in my dream, I found out that he had decided to follow Jesus, I knew that it was the right thing to do. I had the warmest feeling inside my heart that God was speaking to me as well. I knew that I had to find out more. In the dream, I was told that Mohammed would be coming to my apartment. I woke up this morning and went to a suitcase I have in my closet. In that suitcase was a large amount of cash I had been given to fund an attack on America."

Mohammed joined the story telling, "Go ahead, my brother, tell them how much cash you have with you right now."

Ibrahim smiled slyly, "I am carrying close to three hundred and seventy-five thousand dollars in this suitcase. Cash money will not leave a paper-trail."

"It's ironic that the money given to me by people who wanted to ruin America's economy will be used to save the world. I shall use it to bring Jesus to the world. Mr. Wallace, you shout warnings from God and the Bible readings, telling people about Rome's desire for all the world to follow Esposito. I heard you say last night that Esposito is trying to bring us one world government under his leadership."

Wallace spoke up, "Chapter thirteen of Revelation is filled with references of one world government and one leader. The groundwork has already been established to create a one world monetary system. Revelation even reveals the religious leader who healed the political leader when he was dead."

He went on to explain that the microchips being inserted into people all over the world, especially in Europe, are in line with the biblical talk of the "mark" that people will need to conduct business.

"One of the little-known facts about those chips is this," Wallace continued, "Le Roux microchips went through six hundred and sixty-five experimental versions before settling on the current one. The six hundred sixty sixth one can communicate with the brain. It has its version number imbedded in each individual serial number. The number is six hundred and sixty-six. So, when Revelation chapter thirteen verse eighteen uses the number six-six-six in referring to the man who will require the mark for doing any business, it was looking down through the centuries to this day, and this microchip."

Olivia added her insight, "Something that isn't mentioned in that verse is that the mark they talk about is only for doing business. It doesn't mention anything about how this, the latest incarnation of the chip, allows a central computer to input information into a person's brain, and keep track of the person by accessing the chip. So, I guess modern man has added his own 'improvements' to the ancient evil."

CHAPTER 20

C ol. Vito Lombardo entered the office of Paolino Esposito. Under his left arm he held a long tube containing plans and blueprints.

Esposito motioned to the long conference table near the large window, "Colonel, what do you have there?"

Lombardo opened the tube and unrolled the paper, "My Lord, I have the plans and blueprints for the Jewish Temple in Jerusalem. I know that you have promised representatives of Israel that you planned to rebuild the Temple for them. I also know that the Dome of the Rock currently occupies the site, and it would be impossible to put the Temple there."

Esposito corrected Lombardo, "My dear Colonel, I have done much research on this matter. In fact, the Dome of the Rock is not located exactly upon the site of the Jewish Temple originally built by Solomon. Much research by scholars over the past few centuries has put the location just north of the Dome of the Rock. In fact, many believe that the Dome of the Tablets marks the location of the Holy of Holies in the ancient Temple of Solomon. So, if we were to build my new temple on that location, people would have no choice but to realize my greatness and bow down to me. But I'm also hearing that other researchers put the ancient Temple site is further in the City of David."

Lombardo went on to explain that more and more ammunition left under the Temple Mount from the 1967 Six Day War is being found daily. Lombardo's idea was that if there was a need to utilize the same site as the Dome of the Rock, there could be an accidental explosion of the old, unstable ordinance.

"That would not be necessary Colonel. If we put the new Temple on the site of the original, there would be no need to get rid of the Dome of the Rock. You may forego the plans you were making." Esposito smiled at the Colonel as he looked closer at the plans laid out before him. "Here is the current location of the Dome of the Rock, and over here is the current location of the Dome of the Tablets. If the scholars are right, that is the location of the Holy of Holies. I believe we can rebuild the Temple and keep the Muslim leaders pleased with the deal for sharing the Temple Mount for Peace."

Col. Lombardo rolled the paper and returned the plans to the protective tube, "I will begin the process of procuring all the materials for this project. My Lord, I know that soon, everyone will rejoice that you have found a way to bring about peace in the Middle East. No one else has been able to accomplish this. You truly are the Messiah, not only to the Jews, but to all the world." With a bow toward Esposito, he left the room.

Within the House and Senate chambers there was an overpowering sense of mourning. Everyone, regardless of party affiliation, spoke little as they walked through the Capitol building. Advisors for the President were in conference with the leaders of the House of Representatives and Senate. They were seeking a fast-track vote to join the many nations that have allied their governments in submission to a one world government, seated in Rome and led by Paolino Esposito. Many of the ideas included absorption of all national debt as now there would be a whole new monetary system.

The biggest obstacles to approval of the plan to join the rest of the world under the leadership of Rome had been gone for thirty days. The plane crash over the Atlantic had removed all opposition to bringing the United States under the control of Esposito.

The flags had been raised back to full staff. It was time to get back to the basics of running the country. President Elizabeth Blair had given a very convincing plea to the House and Senate that joining Paolino Esposito would be good for our country. Peace had been elusive for so long, and here was a strong leader who was bringing peace to the world.

Members of the House of Representatives found their seats. The usual long-winded speeches in favor of or opposing an act of Congress did not take place. The few who did speak kept their discourses short. The six opposition Representatives were no longer involved in the debate. Most members of the House had already desired to wipe out America's debt and then, perhaps, represent America in the central government of Rome.

The Speaker of the House called for a moment of silence to remember the six Members of the House who died a little more than a month ago. Then, with no further discussion, the voting began. The Bill passed swiftly with only two dissenting votes. Those came from members who were symbolically voting to honor the memory of their friends who had opposed the legislation.

CHAPTER 21

L ive television coverage of the action within the U.S. Capitol building was on every news channel in the world. Paolino Esposito had been watching with great interest. As usually happens, without warning Ambassador Baalazaar appeared in the room. There was a smile on his face as he spoke, "Paolino, my son, by now you have heard that the Americans are only a few short steps away from joining our coalition. Soon the final roadblock keeping you from achieving complete leadership of the world will be gone. I am pleased with the name many are calling this government. New Roman Empire fits so aptly. My friend Benito Mussolini had dreams to have this happen, and many thought he would be the one to revive the government of the Caesars. However, that was not time. The time was not right, yet. The current technology was not available.

Before we could properly control the masses, I had to wait until science and technology caught up. Now I will be able to realize what I needed to accomplish. Germany was well on its way to achieving world domination, but Hitler rebelled against my influence. Had he only stayed out of the way and let his generals lead the army, they might have achieved complete domination. His attack on the Jews was just as I wanted him to do, however, he started too late to achieve the elimination of the descendants of Shem. This time, with you my son, if you continue to obey my leadership, my goals will be accomplished. And you will become the greatest leader in history."

Baalazaar patted Esposito on the head and suddenly, Baalazaar was gone. Within two hours, word came to Esposito that the American Senate had quickly followed the lead of the House of Representatives and passed the Bill HBSB 1776 10. America would be represented in the Roman Senate by fifty legislators, one for each of their states. After President Blair signed the Bill, within thirty days, the Empire would officially expand into the Western Hemisphere.

Robert Wallace was listening intently to the news on the car radio as they made their way out of New York. He jotted notes on his notebook computer chronicling all he was hearing. The long and storied history was coming to an end. Wallace was a descendent of Continental Army soldiers who had fought for the independence of this country. He was also fiercely patriotic and had always been a champion of America's leadership role in the world.

Now all this seemed to be coming to an end. Olivia sensed his melancholy mood, "It's been coming for a lot longer than just these last few months, you know."

"I know. I have covered news stories all over the world and have seen the lack of respect of America for a long time. Countries that had been our allies more than two centuries, now felt compelled to shun the United States' leadership in everything from manufacturing to money. Too many people for so long had stopped trying to make this world a better place. For the past few decades, this country had slipped back onto the edge of the abyss of civil war that promised to tear the country apart, even more than our original Civil War did in the mid nineteenth century. Some of the issues remained the same. There had been a great divide among the people of this country. Whites and people of color resented each other. My profession, journalism, had slipped into the trap of sensationalizing every rift between groups of people. It sold newspapers, as the old phrase went, but it was driving a deeper wedge between groups of people in this country. It is true that many of those divisions existed for centuries, but the twenty-four-hour news cycle and unbridled social media platforms in the hands of hate groups only exacerbated the discord. Even among groups of people where unity should rule, sports teams, police forces, military units and, yes, even within the Church there were divisions.

Wallace continued, "One of the problems Christ's Church has had over the centuries is that they didn't practice what Jesus commanded in John 13:35 'By this everyone will know that you are my disciples, if you love one another.' In fact, that was always one of the reasons I didn't see any need in my life for Christianity. I saw how they treated each other, race against race and denomination against denomination. Why should I want to follow a religion that didn't practice what it preached?"

Ibrahim Soliman had been quietly listening, "That was always one of the reasons that Christians were not to be trusted," he said, "They could not even get along within their own faith. As I got older, I started to notice that same pattern among followers of Islam. We fought amongst ourselves because of which sect of the faith we practiced, and we even held certain nationalities of Muslims in lower regard than those who were born in the home of Mecca and Medina. We were horrible to each other, just as your Christian brothers and sisters were."

Olivia shook her head, "Human nature. It is just human nature. That is something that's been around since the beginning of time. As I study my Bible, I am seeing that people seem to stick with their own families or groups, to the exclusion of those who are from a different clan."

Wallace continued the thought, "But, as believers, we who follow Christ need to love one another and respect each other. Even if we don't hang out constantly as friends, we still are called upon to love one another. Many of us have different interests and that means we also would want to be with people who have like interests. But we still should respect all others. Especially those who have chosen to follow Christ." Wallace seemed to be preaching a sermon on brotherhood. "Ephesians 4:29, says it all, 'Do not let any unwholesome talk come out of your mouths, but only what is helpful for building others up according to their needs, that it may benefit those who listen.' I want to be a good example of the faith to anyone else who observes me in action."

Reflective after their discussion, Wallace, Olivia, Mohammed, and Ibrahim all sat silently for the next thirty minutes as they made their way to their next stop. It was almost time for Wallace to set up for his next Podcast. He needed to state his views about the United States coming to an end and joining a one world government.

At the White House, the TV cameras were all set to record this moment in history. President Elizabeth Blair was about to sign into law the dissolution of the United States of America. She entered the Oval Office. Cameras flashed. Dignitaries gathered around her. She sat at the signing table before the Bill and the array of pens laid out side by side for the ceremony.

President Blair spoke, "This is a very solemn occasion. It is with very mixed emotions that I am about to sign HBSB – 1776 - 10. I am aware that the numbering is a little different than the major legislation that has come before Presidents in years past, but this bill is vastly different. It was a joint proposal from House and Senate, hence the HBSB prefix designation, and, we are paying homage to the year of our nation's founding, 1776. Finally, we honor the ten members of the House and Senate who tragically lost their lives while researching the effects of this legislation. It is only fitting that we honor Senators William George, Samuel Hassler, Hanford Danson, and Clifford Davidson. We also honor Representatives Maxwell Burrows, Rebecca Sewell, Norman Dodge, and Diana Charles, Carrie Ellsworth, and Antonio Tortelli. Each of these hard-working servants of the people had a long and distinguished career representing their states and districts. They will be sorely missed. Now, let us proceed."

The cameras recorded the strokes of each pen used. President Blair distributed the pens after she used them to write her name. It was understood that one of the pens would be saved and presented to Paolino Esposito as a token of the newly formed friendship and oath of loyalty to his government.

Someone shouted from the hallway outside the Oval Office, "This is an abomination, Madam President. America needs to stay close to God and not the Anti-Christ Esposito. Robert Wallace is right! America is now doomed. Stand up, Americans, fight this terrib…"

It was a surprise that it took so long for the Secret Service agents to pounce upon this man. He was deep within a cluster of at least twenty observers who were in the hallway. In the confusion, the man emerged from the melee bloodied and shaking. His nose appeared to be broken and agents had his hands cuffed behind him. He winced as he was taken to the floor. One of the biggest agents pulled the man's arms up until his cuffed wrists were nearly directly between his shoulder blades. There was a loud crack and the man screamed again, "Please stop this abomination… you people are dupes of the Anti-Chri…" with that a fist hit the man hard, stopping his tirade.

He was picked up and carried out of the hallway and through a paneled door. It led to one of the many passageways through which officials and Secret Service agents traversed through the White House. The man was out of sight and silenced. All those who had stood with him were also taken into one of the passageways for further questioning. It was not known if this was part of an organized group protest, but it was widely known that in recent weeks, a few members of the White House staff had become followers of Christ. Though they remained loyal employees of the executive mansion, they were still viewed with suspicion. Many people on staff considered themselves too enlightened to become followers of some ancient religion. Faith in Christ no longer held any mystique among the educated masses.

Those who were truly enlightened were excited to see what was coming for the world. It looked as though there would finally be peace and harmony among nations. Perhaps the United States of America would no longer be a nation but would still be a proud "state" among the many former nations of the world that had also become states in the new government.

Paolino Esposito was seething as he paced back and forth in the office of his security chief, Col. Vito Lombardo. "We must find this Robert Wallace. He should have been captured and put to death a long time ago. The man has been doing a podcast calling me 'The

Anti-Christ'. I suppose in a way he is partially correct. I am not in any way a follower of that man who died so many centuries ago. He was weak. I am a strong leader. My followers will reach out to each other and bring about an end to his 'regime'. He will become a footnote on the ash heap of history. People will forget him. I know they say their Bible is filled with precautions about someone taking power and leading a one world government. There is no reason to fear. I will bring peace and I deserve to be given all the praise and honor that is due me for removing all the obstacles of peace and prosperity. There will be no more poverty and no more wars once I get complete control of people all over the world. Find Wallace. I want him put to death."

"We have come close too many times without success Lombardo responded, "I know that he travels with his wife and two Muslim converts to Christianity. They are always just a few steps ahead of us. I have all confidence, My Lord, that they all will be caught."

Lombardo left the room and suddenly there was a quick chill in the air. Without looking up, Esposito responded, "Good evening, Baalazaar. I have grown accustomed to the way you enter a room. To what do I owe this pleasure? Do you know where Wallace and his minions are right now? We must find them. His podcasts are becoming too popular. In fact, I have heard of people who are refusing to accept the microchip to do business. They will not be able to conduct any business and they will starve to death."

Baalazaar exhaled an icy breath, "My dear Mr. Esposito. In years past, the men I chose to further my kingdom here on earth failed me miserably. They did not stop people who interfered with my plans to defeat Yahweh. Hitler and Stalin were supposed to bring me glory, but they fought each other. I could not stop them. They were my disciples, but they thought they knew better than I what I wanted. I wanted an end to the Hebrews. I wanted to destroy any vestige of Christianity or Judaism. They each put themselves up as great leaders and each had a very loyal following. They were able to lead people who killed and maimed Jews and Christians. They were cut from the same cloth, ordering the deaths of millions of people who tried to get in their way. They each thought they knew better than I how to win their wars. They failed miserably. My caution to you, my son, is to listen and follow my instructions closely.

This time I will win. You are my representative in this world, my son. I cannot have any mistakes by my anointed followers anymore."

CHAPTER 22

Pastor James Hann and the other refugees from Camp Dickerson or New Zion, as it was also known, arrived at the address on East Main Street in Coshocton, Ohio. Coshocton was a pleasant little city with a rich history going all the way back to the founding of the Ohio Territory.

The name Coshocton is taken from the Lenape Delaware Indian name for a river crossing Koshaxkink. The Walhonding and Tuscarawas Rivers meet there to form the Muskingum River which flows through Zanesville on its way to the Ohio, at Marietta.

Many homes in Coshocton had been important stops on the Underground Railroad. It seems as if the spirit of those days had been reborn. The town had become a hiding place for today's Christians who were fleeing from those who would do them harm for their beliefs.

Paul Dickerson, the twin brother of Josh Dickerson of Dresden, had sheltered many people who were fleeing the authorities for their beliefs. His brother had called him and told him to be on the lookout for Pastor Hann and his four charges. Paul heard a timid yet urgent knock at his front door. As he opened the door, he saw the small group looking around furtively to see if anyone had followed them.

Dickerson quickly scanned the tree-lined brick street as he ushered them into his home. "Come with me, quickly. I have cots and food waiting for you in the basement."

Hann spoke for the group, "Thank you. Your brother was in a very tough spot when he led us out of the camp. I don't know what happened after we left."

"It's okay, Pastor. Josh and I are both ready to lay down our lives to assure the safety of our brothers and sisters." Dickerson led them to the basement door. It was an old facility with shelves built into the walls, remarkably like the pictures of the ancient Catacombs underneath Rome. There were ten cots lined up near the wall.

Dickerson invited them to sit down and relax, "I'll come for you as soon as I get the van loaded with supplies. I need to take to the Light in the Forest."

Hann responded, "Wasn't that a Disney movie?"

"Yes, based on the novel by Conrad Richter."

Hann smiled, "So what is 'The Light in the Forest' for you?"

Dickerson explained, "To us, it means the Light of Christ. It's in the woods about five miles out of town between here and Plainfield."

"What is going on there? And what supplies do you need?" Hann asked.

He gathered heavy bags strapped to each arm, "We have bags of rice, Kidney Beans, and corn meal. In the garage, I also have already gathered more tools. I even have a pedal grinding stone wheel to sharpen the four axes already at the camp. We are building some cabins, just like our ancestors did. We started out with Wigwams and a Longhouse. The Lenape tribe really knew how to survive the winters here."

Dickerson went on to explain, "Many of the Christians who are hiding from the authorities are living in the woods. They gather for daily worship and study. Unfortunately, because of the organized war on Christianity, we have only been able to locate two Bibles."

Wallace, Olivia, Mohammed, and Ibrahim had arrived at an abandoned apartment in The Bronx. Mohammed had finished hooking up the wireless internet over Wi-Fi. He began the process of routing the signal out of New York City and into Pennsylvania north through Buffalo, New York and then into Canada before returning through Cleveland, Ohio, for distribution.

Wallace had finished setting up the camera and lighting which included two lamp soft boxes and two backdrop umbrella continuous lighting stands. To save space and for quick set-up and tear-down, Wallace always used a music stand to hold his notes along with an iPad and universal multimedia tripod mount to hold the tablet.

Mohammed gave the signal that they were online, ready to stream live and record video and audio for the upcoming Podcast.

Wallace looked intently at the camera and began, "I'm Robert Wallace and I pray that this finds you well. There are so many things happening today that it is almost impossible to believe that any good can come from the events of the past two days in Washington, D. C. The long and rich history of the United States has come to an end. Our nation no longer exists. There are those who have said for years that the United States is not mentioned in any of the End times Prophecies in the Bible. Many of the prophecies in Ezekiel 38 and 39, for example, mention the names of all the nations that will be aligned against Israel. The United States is not among the nations mentioned that will stay true to Israel. Many scholars studying end times prophecy have wondered how that would come to pass. None of the authors I have ever read mentioned the U.S. just giving up its sovereignty and joining the Anti-Christ. I'm new to this whole thing, but there are many sources I have studied that helped me understand Gog and Magog, as well as Persia, Cush and so many others."

"It has only been a couple of years since Russia and Israel's Arab neighbors attempted to invade Israel. People are still amazed at the fact that millions of invaders died in such rapid succession. Their capital cities were wiped out. And then just a few months later, millions upon millions world-wide came up missing. That is the entire phenomenon that first started this reporter down the path of seeking answers in Christianity. I don't know all the answers, but I am realizing that what I used to think of as utter superstition, just may be true."

He went on, "I assure you, dear friends, that we are seeing the final days of the world being played out before our very eyes. If you can still find a Bible, pick it up and study the book of Daniel, then the book of Revelation, the book of Ezekiel, and, read the words of Jesus in Matthew chapter 24. Daniel and Revelation are filled with many difficult images that are difficult to understand. The words of Jesus in Matthew twenty-

361

four, though, are very clear. Jesus clearly explained the signs."

"Many of those signs have been on the increase for the past one hundred years. Wars and rumors of wars, increased earthquake activity, and wickedness on a wide-spread scale have all been visible to anyone who wanted to see them. The sins that have been committed by people are nothing new. Sin is sin. Sins of the flesh, and of the heart and mind are nothing new."

Wallace became more intense as he leaned in toward the camera, "But I believe the final puzzle pieces are falling into place. Paolino Esposito is not a kind-hearted peacemaker. I believe that he is the Anti-Christ. I personally believe that there have been many 'Anti-Christs' throughout history, especially within the past one hundred years. None of them, though, turned out to be the one who would lead the world into the final conflict with God. Not until now. Esposito has fooled many people. The man he has chosen to lead his version of the church, Nunzio Assidi, is, in my opinion, a true pawn of the Devil himself. Do not be fooled by…"

At this point all the lights in the small apartment went out and there was a loud crashing sound as a battering ram destroyed the front door. The sound of the Flash-Bang Grenade was deafening, and the light was blinding.

The four people in the apartment fell prostrate on the floor as men in black uniforms filled the room. Each man held a Kalashnikov Assault Rifle. Since the end of World War Two, the infamous AK-47 had been the weapon of choice for communist militaries, Third World dictators' armies, and terrorist organizations.

The men pounced on Robert Wallace first, binding his hands with plastic zip ties. They then roughly grabbed Olivia and pulled her by the hair into an upright position. Her hands were forcefully pulled behind her and she too was cuffed with zip ties.

Mohammed and Ibrahim were quickly clubbed into submission as they were dragged by their hair to an upright position and cuffed with standard police issue handcuffs.

As the smoke cleared in the room, Andrew Benetti, the U.S. security chief for Col. Vito Lombardo entered. He struck a pose with feet apart and hands behind his back. He barked the order to take the four prisoners to the alley behind the apartment building and put them into a waiting van.

Paul Dickerson drove his van southeast on route 541 toward Plainfield. A little more than halfway there he turned south on Township 124. They drove past a couple of farm buildings and took the road to its end.

Daniel Schaffer

Dickerson put the van into park and said, "That's as far as the road goes. The rest of the way is on foot. We'll be there in about fifteen minutes. The woods are thick here, and there are a couple places where there are thick briar patches. It's a lot less luxurious than Camp Dickerson."

Pastor Hann replied, "Any idea how long we'll be here?"

"Looks like we're talking about at least a month before we can move you on to the west. I think that we'll either go toward Springfield or maybe north to Toledo." Dickerson was still deciding which community would be the safest permanent home, to these travelers.

The group had been walking for fifteen minutes. Hann's right hand and forearm had deep scratches. Very soon they were beginning to smell the aroma of wood burning. The air was a mixture of smoke and the haze of a late afternoon near the end of September. They could hear people talking but suddenly the talking stopped. Dickerson called out, "I have hidden your word in my heart that I might not sin against you."

"Aha, Psalm one nineteen eleven," Sheila Peterson said as she walked toward them. She was one of Hann's people committed to memorizing the Old Testament.

Dickerson smiled, turned to her and said, "Oh, so you've gotten that far in your memorization so far."

364

That's great. It's our password, so to speak. People here are working on the same task as you. To memorize the entire Bible is the goal of everyone here. We have a seventeen-year-old fellow who has the book of Leviticus memorized."

Hann began to laugh, "So, you have a budding Lawyer in the making?"

The thick woods ahead of them gave way to a small clearing where there were three buildings. There were two Wigwams and a Longhouse. Just as Dickerson had told them, this encampment did not appear to be extremely luxurious. As they looked around, they saw two men who were in the process of skinning four rabbits and two pheasants. One lady was cleaning a twelve-gauge pump action Remington Shotgun. She was wearing a hunting vest with shells in the pouch that hung from her side.

There was a fire at the center of the encampment. Hanging over the fire was a large kettle into which the meat was placed for stew.

why blank page?

CHAPTER 23

Wallace's bleary-eyed view of the room was slowly coming into focus. The side of his face felt like he had not jumped out of the way of a high, inside fast ball. Now it began to come back to him. He and Olivia, along with Mohammed and Ibrahim had been taken into custody by the people who had been pursuing them for the past three days.

His wrists chafed terribly from the tie bands that tightly gripped them. The last thing he remembered was doing his Vlog. He had been attempting to warn people not to be fooled by Esposito.

All four now sat in front of a table with Benetti sitting opposite them, "Mr. Wallace, you have become a real problem for us. You are holding back the progress that the world needs. Paolino Esposito has only the good of the world in his heart. You are clinging to antiquated philosophies of superstitious people who wanted to believe in a higher power. People need to believe, that is true. But this ancient system you are clinging to is not the one. You need to stop trying to undermine Lord Esposito. He is the leader of the world and people need him. Do not continue down this path. If you halt your campaign, you will be allowed to live. If you continue with this crusade, you and your friends will be put to death."

Wallace looked into the eyes of Benetti. Then he turned and gazed upon his wife and two brothers and responded, "I cannot keep quiet. As Peter told the Sanhedrin in the book of Acts, 'Which is right in God's eyes: to listen to you, or to Him? You be the judges! As for us, we cannot help speaking about what we have seen and heard.' Therefore, following the lead of Peter, I will continue to tell the story of Jesus and of the things to come."

In a fury, Benetti yelled, "Then you leave me no choice, you and your friends will all die!"

As Benetti called out for the rest of his men to come and take the four away, the air was split with a loud thunderous bang and a blinding light. In a moment of suspended animation, Benetti and his men were frozen as a portion of the outside wall fell away. The light from outside was extremely bright, and Wallace, Olivia, Mohammed and Ibrahim all ran outside."

As they ran, Mohammed cried out, "This was certainly a miracle of God!"

The four made their way down the alley behind the apartment building. There was the van they had ridden in with the keys still in the ignition. Olivia opened the door and squealed with excitement. God had indeed provided a method for them to escape the area completely.

Pastor James Hann had arrived at the encampment, and as he looked around, he heard a steady hum of voices coming from every corner. The noise came to a sudden halt as everyone looked up at the strangers being brought into their presence by Paul Dickerson, who gave an almost imperceptible smile and nod, and the buzz of voices returned.

Dickerson told Hann, "Their voices are speaking the words as they memorize the entire Bible. Even a few moments not working on this task would take away from the goal. Someday, no one will be able to find a Bible. Someday no one will be able to find writings such as those of C. S. Lewis or Billy Graham. We are committing as many of these to memory as well as the Bible. Then, their minds will be able to recreate the great writings. Our singers also play and sing the old hymns and songs of praise and worship. We are preserving as much as possible."

"That's a huge undertaking, Brother," came Hann's reply. "I know from my own studies that many of the great books I used to take for granted are now no longer readily available."

Hann and his group were taken to the Longhouse, where they were shown the small library. There were two sections of the library, labeled Learning and the side with fewer books, labeled Completed.

Dickerson gestured to the shelves, "Obviously we have a long way to go. We also have people out combing some of the abandoned homes of missing believers for their personal collections. The problem is, when they disappeared, authorities entered most of their homes and cleaned out any references to their Christian beliefs. It is becoming harder and harder to find books and Bibles. The two Bibles that we do have were in my home. I had those and a few song books, but I had hardly ever opened them for purposes of study. I was always a Christian in name only."

The new arrivals were shown to their quarters. Men and women slept in separate sections of the Longhouse. The next day they would begin building their own Wigwams in the traditional design. Husbands and wives would then be able to re-unite in what would become their own homes.

After two hours behind the wheel, Mohammed suggested that they abandon the van. It was a good idea. The authorities had issued BOLO for them. The Be on the Lookout had most likely been issued to all area law enforcement agencies. It would not be long before they were found.

After abandoning the van, Olivia and Wallace walked about three steps behind Mohammed and Ibrahim as they made their way back to one of the main streets. Olivia's eyes betrayed a worry that, despite all she had endured in the past months, Wallace had never seen before.

"What's on your mind, Sweetheart? You're somewhere else. What are you thinking?"

She did not answer. She was carrying with her a burden that she had yet to share with her husband. She shook her head and remained quiet as they walked on.

Sitting around the huge conference table in the White House Situation Room, Joint Chiefs Chairman Admiral William Blanding was shaking his head to indicate his distaste for the order he had been given. In his hand was a single sheet of paper. In bold type was the new oath that members of the United States military, all branches, would soon be ordered to take.

"Madam President, with all due respect to your office, I have to protest. This order is absurd. Our military has a long and storied history of serving the people of the United States, as we defend the Constitution and the United States against all enemies, foreign and domestic. This new oath is an afront to those brave men and women who have died in service to their country."

The President spoke clearly, "My dear Admiral. Might I remind you that the United States as you used to know it no longer exists. We are now a part of something bigger and, in my opinion, even better. You will encourage all men and women who wish to stay in the service to take this new oath. We will join our forces all over the world in a united video conference. A representative of our new leader will administer this oath one week from today. You will join with them prominently or you will no longer hold your current rank or status."

The President then turned her eyes toward each member of the Joint Chiefs and added, "That means all of you. General Avery. You have been a ground breaker, or should I say glass ceiling breaker. There has never been a woman representing any branch of the service on the Joint Chiefs. As a pioneering jet fighter pilot, you were named the Air Force Chief during my administration. I am proud to say that you won't be the last. I am about to name General Earlean Jackson to be the final Army Chief. She replaces General Walter Owens who has just announced his retirement after forty years of stellar service. I am not sure exactly how the new government plans to handle the U.S. military, but let it be known here that the United States has not been afraid to promote women to prominent posts in the Defense Department."

President Blair then asked if anyone had any objections to her choice, or to the new oath to be taken by the current military and all future members of the armed forces.

Admiral Blanding stood and once more addressed the group, "Ladies and gentlemen. I cannot, after my many years of service through three wars, condone this oath. I will not pledge allegiance to this foreign power. And as a student of military history, I feel I must point out that with only a name change, this is nearly word for word the very same oath that Germany's armed forces pledged to Adolf Hitler. The only real change is that we are being asked to pledge our lives in service to Paolino Esposito. Listen to this, 'I swear by God this holy oath, that I will render to Lord Paolino Esposito, leader of Europe and the entire free world and all its people, Supreme Commander of the Armed Forces, unconditional obedience, and that I am ready, as a brave soldier, to risk my life at any time for this oath.' The Wehrmacht, and the Waffen SS repeated that same pledge, only Germany and Hitler were to whom they made their pledge. I simply cannot do it and therefore, Madam President, I must resign from the United States Navy and from the Joint Chiefs of Staff. I do this regretfully."

With that statement, Admiral Blanding left the Situation Room. The President stood and summoned the Marine Guard from the entry, "Sergeant Ramos, could you come here a moment." She whispered something in the Marine's ear. He waited for a moment and then followed behind Blanding.

Olivia had been silent for several minutes. She broke the silence as they made their way through the streets of the city, "Bobby, I think it would be a good idea if we split up as soon as possible. They're looking for three men and a woman. I think that if they have put out a BOLO, we'd stand a better chance in two groups instead of one."

Wallace consented as Mohammed and Ibrahim nodded in agreement, "She's right. Let's get out of the city and try to make our way back to Ohio. We need to centralize our efforts with the rest of our people."

They all embraced each other, then Wallace and Olivia started walking toward the Hudson River, as Mohammed and Ibrahim turned northward.

"What's wrong, Liv? There's something troubling you. I noticed it before Esposito's men caught us."

"Bobby, I'm scared. I'm pretty sure that I'm pregnant. I'm fearful that our child will be born into a horrible world, one much worse – worse even than the world was, before our daughter was caught up in the Rapture. I am afraid of what this child will have to endure. Yet at the same time I am excited about seeing the face of our baby."

Wallace was totally surprised. He smiled broadly, "Liv, I'm not going to worry about what we can't control. Our baby will have two parents who love him or her completely, and who will be here to teach the ways of the Lord. This child will have eternal protection and will be here to populate the New Earth that Revelation promises to be here for a thousand years."

She gave a slight smile, "I suppose God has intended this child for us. He will watch over our child for us, even if we are killed by Esposito's men. I just want to be here for him."

"Him?"

"Well, our last was a girl, and I'm hoping for Robert Wallace II."

They hugged, then broke the embrace just long enough to hail a cab.

Just outside the Situation Room at the White House, the former Chairman of the Joint Chiefs of Staff, Admiral William Blanding, was detained by the Marine Sergeant who had been summoned into room by the President, "Sir, the President has ordered me to hold you here and turn you over to an armed detail. I'm not sure where they will take you, but the President was very steadfast in her order that I hold you here. I'm sorry, Sir. I have always respected your leadership with the Joint Chiefs. As a Marine, I respectfully follow the orders of my President, but I do this with much regret."

"That's alright, Sergeant. You are duty bound to follow the orders of your Commander in Chief. I am, or I was, only an Admiral. She outranks even me. I hold no ill will toward you for doing your duty as a United States Marine."

"Thank you, Sir. I'm an American, not a European. My grandfather was a Marine, and his father before him came here from Mexico, and fought alongside Chesty Puller on Guadalcanal, to take and keep Henderson Field. I'm a sixth generation Devil Dog. I can't swear allegiance to some guy in Europe. I'm a United States Marine, Admiral. They may say they have ended the United States of America, but I ain't buyin' it," the Sergeant snapped to attention and saluted sharply. "I am truly sorry, Admiral, I have to take you into custody.

Andrew Benetti was looking dazed and confused as he and his men looked at the gaping hole in the wall of the first-floor apartment where once he had held four prisoners who were enemies of the state. He quickly barked an order to his men, "Get out there and find them. We cannot let them get away again. I'm afraid that Lord Esposito will not look kindly upon us. Our positions will be eliminated and so will we if we don't catch them and kill them. Your orders are to take them dead or alive, but I must have proof to show Rome."

His men ran out the hole in the wall and into the alley, where a crowd of homeless men and women had gathered to stare at the opening.

Danny Lloyd pulled his Beretta 92S, fired it into the air and screamed, "Move away from here. There is nothing here that should interest you. Just move on and don't look back!"

Lloyd fired once more into the air and the hapless men and women fell all over themselves trying to get away, with a trail of shopping carts and aluminum cans falling all over the alleyway. They rounded the corner and scattered into the street.

Lloyd and two others ran down the alley until they came to the street. They stood there flabbergasted as they scanned both directions. He called out to his charges, "You go that way and I'll search here. Call me if you see any sign of them. Go into the apartments on the street side and see if anyone saw any sign of those four. We can't go back to Benetti without finding them."

Mickey Fitzgerald sprinted to the end of the next block. There he charged into a Bodega and, waving his Beretta 92S called out to the owners, "Did you see three men and a woman run by here?"

The man behind the counter was obviously scared, "You a cop? What'd they do?"

Fitzgerald angrily replied, "Yeah, they robbed a Bodega just like this. And they killed the owner and his wife. Did you see them or not?"

The Bodega owner was now seething at the thought of killers getting away with murdering two of his own, "Yeah, they weren't on foot though, they were in a van. They had the strangest light around them, though. Their faces were glowing. It was the strangest thing I've ever seen. Who lights up a van that way? The light was so bright. How can you drive in the daylight with that much light inside your car? Weird. Anyway, they turned left at the end of the block."

Fitzgerald quickly called Lloyd, "Yeah... some store clerk saw them. Come back this way, I'll meet you where we separated. Yeah, I know it's missing. They took off with it. We're gonna have more trouble finding them now."

As Fitzgerald stood on the corner with his phone still to his ear, a black BMW pulled up next to him. and

Benetti called out to him, "Get in! Don't ask! I found it sitting alone with unlocked doors. They're all easy to take when you find the keys under the visor. What'd you find out?"

As Fitzgerald got into the car, he was already on the phone with Lloyd to tell him they had a lead on Wallace and the group. "Yeah, we'll see you there."

Fitzgerald then quickly shared with Benetti, "He went two blocks down, but didn't see them. I found out from the bodega owner that they got away in our van."

Not to be outdone, Benetti responded, "I... figured that one out. I have put out the word. We have people all over the city looking for the van. We even have a lady who has hacked into the city's security cameras. We're using the new Le Roux Enigma Search Software. If anything can home in on where they've taken the van, that will."

The Enigma Search Software had been originally developed by Le Roux to track the microchips that people would have imbedded in their heads. It would also be easily interfaced with facial recognition software and could be programmed to find license plates or auto model nameplates. It could even be used with the video downloaded from high power spy satellites. It seems that George Orwell was not imaginative enough when he wrote 1984. It has become apparent that there is literally no place on earth where you can hide from "Big

Brother". He had the general idea, but the technology was nowhere close to being ready at that time.

Benetti had a prideful smirk on his face as he described the current and future applications of the Enigma Search Software, "It still needs to be perfected when it comes to tracing motor vehicles, but the day is coming when no one will be able to get away with anything."

The car swiftly rounded a corner and found Danny Lloyd waiting there. He jumped into the cavernous back seat of the BMW 850. The newest model from Bavaria had the roomiest interior of any. Lloyd sat quietly as he was following the instant updates from the CCTV cameras all over the city. It was not long before he got the message from headquarters that the van had been discovered a mere three blocks from their current location. Suddenly the big car in which they were comfortably riding came to a screeching halt.

Benetti gave a subdued curse as he took a hankie from his pocket and wiped his fingerprints from the steering wheel and the key fob. "Apparently they noticed their car missing. Let's get to our van before we lose Wallace and his associates."

They left the big car behind at a fast pace. Benetti led the pack, and there it was just ahead, the van they had commandeered the night before. They swarmed around it and found that the keys were no longer inside.

Benetti began to curse as he saw there was no key in sight.

Lloyd smiled, "Don't worry, Boss. This is a classic. Goes way back to the 1970s. They have kept it in exceptionally good condition. The plush carpet on the walls was a popular thing to do with this model back in those days. I used to collect magazines with lots of pictures of these things. The downside was that they were extremely easy to hotwire and steal."

It took Lloyd only about ten seconds to cut and strip two wires near the steering wheel and the engine surged to life. Their next problem was finding what had happen to their prisoners. Benetti grabbed his phone and called headquarters, "Let me talk to Anthony in the Enigma Lab." After a brief pause Benetti pleaded his case for finding the escaped prisoners, "Anthony, listen, I know that finding people isn't as easy as finding a 1970s Van Conversion, but please tell me you have video of those four people leaving the van. Good, that's a start. Did you see which way they went from there?"

Anthony was incredibly good at his job. He told Benetti that all four got out of the van, but within two blocks they split up and went different directions.

Benetti conveyed the information to his two associates, "Apparently, Wallace and the girl went west while the two Arabs went north. There's no sign of them since they split, but it appears that the Hudson is the destination for Wallace and his wife. There aren't that many ways across, so we should be able to catch up to them soon."

CHAPTER 24

Marine Sergeant Jorge Ramos had just escorted the former Chairman of the Joint Chiefs of Staff to a small room on the main floor of the White House. Admiral William Blanding was facing an uncertain future. Less than thirty minutes ago he was the top U.S. military officer, and suddenly he was on the verge of being suspected of treason.

The room was sparce with green linoleum on the floor. Linoleum in a room in the White House would not be something one would expect to see, but this room was meant for a very short stay before someone was transferred to another location. The door opened slowly, and Sergeant Ramos put his head in, "Admiral, the detail to transfer you is scheduled to be here in forty-five minutes. I can have coffee sent in for you if you'd like."

Within five minutes Ramos returned and glanced up and down the hallway before entering the room, "Begging your pardon, Sir. I agree with what you had to say about the new oath. And even more I am an American. I refuse to take an oath to a foreign leader. I took an oath to defend the United States against all enemies foreign and domestic. Right now, you and I are the only ones I know who see that a foreign enemy exists, and we are gaining many domestic enemies. I am going to transfer you from this room as though I have authority to do so before your prison detail arrives."

"We are not alone, Sergeant. There are many wearing the uniform who agree with us. It is time, perhaps, to exercise our duty. Let's get out of here."

They both departed the White House with no questions asked by anyone at the door. Sergeant Ramos walked just behind the Admiral whose shackled hands were behind him. The Admiral played his part looking slightly defiant, while the Sergeant held his rifle at the ready as he escorted his prisoner.

The Marine Corporal at the door snapped to attention as the pair made their way to a sedan with the U.S. Navy label on the doors. Sergeant Ramos told the Corporal, "President Blair wants the Admiral taken into custody. I'm taking him to the brig at the Navy Yard."

The Corporal saluted smartly, "Yes, Sergeant. Please sign the release order here."

After signing, Sergeant Ramos opened the back door and the Admiral sat down in the back seat of the car. After that, he got behind the wheel and drove off the White House grounds. At the Secret Service checkpoint, they waved the car through the gate without incident.

After driving for a little more than fifteen minutes, they arrived at the Navy Yard in Washington. Sergeant Ramos had explained to the Admiral that he had a friend who was deployed as an Agent Afloat with Naval Criminal Investigative Service. They could use his friend's car and leave the Navy vehicle with less chance of being charged with auto theft. They were already in enough trouble by planning what would be considered Treason against the new government of Paolino Esposito.

Sergeant Ramos uncuffed the Admiral and they got into his friend's car and left the Navy Yard.

In the eastern Ohio town of Plainfield, the season was deep into the Autumn change and the leaves were a beautiful palate of colors. The encampment of more than thirty-five Christian residents just southwest of town was a busy place. Paul Dickerson was conducting a meeting with the village council. The group had been planning the expansion of the facility. They wanted to build a second Longhouse to serve as a barracks, as well as a meeting place. Pastor James Hann and the others from Camp Dickerson were fitting right in with the group. They had each been assigned jobs, including their memorization duties.

Everyone froze for a moment as they heard an all-terrain vehicle coming down the path toward the facility. The apprehension quickly gave way to calm, as they saw the driver was one of their own. Willie Fischer returned from the market with news that had been on the television at the coffee shop.

"Paul, your son's in the army. Have you heard the latest news? The military is going to have to take a pledge of allegiance to Paolino Esposito. They no longer are considered members of the United States Army or other branches of the military. What do you think of that?"

Paul Dickerson's son Gerald was a helicopter pilot with the First Air Cavalry. He had been home from deployment for about six months updating his training in the latest upgrade of the Apache helicopter gunships. The last thing Dickerson had heard from Gerald was that he had been transferred to California, for desert warfare training with armored forces.

"He hasn't said anything about a new oath. I do believe, though, that he is not happy to be serving in the army of Rome. They have joked about being Centurions. I think that it's a form of denial." Dickerson was not happy that the United States was about to become a thing of the past. One of his ancestors, John Dickerson, was at Valley Forge with George Washington. There was a long family history of service and love of country by his family.

Known by the world as the Ambassador from the Andromeda Galaxy, Baalazaar, stood before his protégé, Paolino Esposito. He had appeared as always, unannounced. Esposito was now the ruler of more than eighty-five percent of the world. Not since the time of the Caesars has one man ruled so much of the known world.

After being silent for more than a full minute, Baalazaar spoke, "My son, I need you to concentrate the full measure of your military might to quell potential enemies to our goals. There are people in America who have openly tried to stop what we seek to accomplish. They are telling false stories that what we have accomplished up to this point in time, is a false narrative."

Esposito answered angrily, "Robert Wallace has been a thorn in my side for too long. My men in America once again, had Wallace, his wife and two others in custody, but a mysterious event shook them free from custody."

no cap

"I know, my son. This has happened to my plans in the Past. It must stop, and this time, we have more power behind us. I know where they are going. The plan is to return to their encampment in Dresden, Ohio. We have closed it down and taken into custody most of those who are intent upon rebelling against our plans. You will be given a location where your newly acquired American military forces are to be sent. Their mission is to eliminate a group that is intent on spreading the centuries old scourge known as Christianity. Someday I will defeat it. And with your help I will see this small pocket eliminated soon."

As was usually the case whenever Baalazaar entered the room, the air had a slight smell of sulfur. It was evident that Baalazaar was not who the world thought he was. *duh!*

Colonel Vito Lombardo was standing next to one of the giant projectors that was aimed toward the sky. There were six such projectors. For the past fifteen minutes they had put on a light show above Rome that had the population watching the sky and pointing. Here again they were seeing for themselves the proof of life from other worlds. There had been six UFOs darting about above the Roman Colosseum, the Vatican, and the rest of the ancient city on seven hills. The lights in the sky had appeared first in the eastern sky and then in a series of rather erratic moves traversing the sky. This light show lasted for fifteen minutes, then the lights shot further into the sky and disappeared. No one knew the source of these 3D Holographic projections. Even airplane pilots flying in the area saw the objects in their shared airspace.

Speaking to his crew, Lombardo said, "That's enough for now, gentlemen. Occasionally, we need to let the people know that we are protecting them from potential enemies. During this same time, our projectors in Washington, New York, London, Paris, St. Petersburg, and Moscow have projected the same objects into the sky. The whole world can see for themselves that we have visitors from other worlds living among us."

As a Warrant Officer 2, Gerald Dickerson had his own room in the barracks. It was sparse, containing his bunk, a locker that served as a closet for his uniforms, a small area rug and a door that would lock.

He was contemplating the events of the past twenty-four hours. He, along with his entire squadron had just completed taking the oath of allegiance to Paolino Esposito. It was weighing heavily on his mind. He had always prided himself as an officer who was willing to follow all legal orders of his superiors, but there was something about this order to take the new oath that did not sit well with him. His air group was just given new orders to go to Ohio for a special operation. They were to leave the next morning. They had no current details, the rumors were that it was to be a big domestic operation for the security of the new government.

At 0400 Pacific Time in the pre-dawn light the following day, his unit set out on a cross country flight to Ohio. According to the orders, something there was amiss. They were to help quell a revolutionary action by an extremist militia group of religious kooks.

Chief Warrant Officer 2 Gerald Dickerson had been in mental turmoil since taking the new oath to Paolino Esposito. His family history with the army went back to before the American Revolution. He somehow felt as though he was betraying the memory of ancestors who had fought so honorably for the United States.

The countryside slid by them quickly. Flying at only two thousand feet above the terrain, Dickerson could see small mountain villages slip by below his squadron. They were told to fly full speed, with refueling stops along the way. They should make it to Columbus, Ohio before lunch the next day.

Robert Wallace and his wife Olivia managed to make their way to Zanesville, Ohio in a day and a half.

Neither of them had ever ridden on a Greyhound Bus. They had only flown Business Class and when traveling through Europe, they enjoyed staterooms on trains.

"That was a little rough, wasn't it?" Robert smiled as he stretched his legs feigning stiff hips and knees. They both relaxed a bit and laughed.

Starting at the Zanesville bus depot, they were only four or five blocks from the Muskingum County Sheriff's office, near the courthouse. They began the short fifteen-minute hike. Robert needed to find Deputy Tom Baker. He was hoping to catch a ride with Baker to Dresden, and Camp Dickerson.

The lobby of the office looked a lot different than it did the last time Wallace was here, as a prisoner about to be kidnaped by Paolino Esposito's henchmen. In place of the glass enclosed counter, there was an added layer of protection for the Desk Sergeant. To access the offices and holding areas, one would now have to pass through a maze of security glass, intended to prevent a repeat of the incident of late last year. Never before, nor since, has there been an attempted escape, or a plan to steal a prisoner from the Muskingum County Sheriff's Department.

Wallace wove his way through each check-in station and at the final checkpoint he asked, "Is there a block of cheese at the end of this maze?"

The Sheriff's Volunteer looked up from her desk but did not smile. Perhaps she had never taken a Psychology class in school and learned about the science experiments to measure a rodent's ability to remember and to learn. Probably nothing has changed in centuries of government employees and a sense of humor with the public.

"I'd like to get in touch with Tom Baker. I need to get a new phone, so I don't have a number to leave for you now. My wife and I are staying at the Zanesvillian Inn on Sixth Street. Just tell him it's about Camp Dickerson in Dresden."

The volunteer eyed him and said, "You haven't' heard? That place was wiped out recently by our new 'Fearless Leader.'" She then quickly glanced around as though making sure there was no one to report her remark. "I'm sorry, I shouldn't have said that."

"Wiped out? What do you mean?"

The look of deep apprehension on Wallace's face caused the volunteer to glance side to side and lower her voice as she responded, "Mr. Wallace, right?" He nodded and she continued, "Mr. Wallace, Deputy Baker has expressed rather loudly here at times that he isn't happy with the way things have been going with outside influences from the new European government on our American law enforcement community."

"Is he coming in soon? I'd like to be able to talk with him about that very issue. Deputy Baker helped both my wife and me out in the past when we were having some problems with the European authorities long before they began to 'interfere with American law enforcement.'"

The previously cold acting volunteer stood up and came around her desk, "My name is Lashonda, Mr. Wallace. Let me give Deputy Baker a call right now. He has been placed on administrative leave for the next week because he has questioned several new policy moves regarding our local laws and how they need to be changed to adhere to what that Mr. Esposito wants to happen here in America, now that we are a part of... the Roman Empire – boy, that is hard to say. Anyways, let me call him for you."

As she pulled her cell phone out of her purse behind the desk and turned her back on Wallace, he was relieved that Lashonda was apparently a like-minded individual and he also was happy that Baker was being somewhat a rebel when it came to the new alliance of the United States. He could hear snippets of her conversation, and he could hear that she was on the phone with Baker.

CHAPTER 25

Rickenbacker Air National Guard Base was home to an Air Force refueling wing, as well as a base for U.S. Army helicopters. Gerald Dickerson awoke after a short night's sleep in the Bachelor Officer Quarters. He surveyed the site as he made his way to the Officers' Mess. The early morning was crisp, and his All-Season Duty Jacket helped stem the tide of the early morning chill.

Dickerson's mind was still churning with doubt regarding his recent swearing of allegiance to Paolino Esposito. He could not imagine any of his ancestors ever doing such a thing.

However, the President of the United States, his commander in chief, had passed down the orders that all U.S. Military personnel were to become members of a much larger world-wide military. As the thought of only following orders crossed his mind, he thought what a lame excuse that had been for Nazi officials in 1945, when confronted with the horrors of what they had done in subduing Europe and inflicting so much pain and sorrow upon the world. They thought they were only following orders and therefore, they were to be exonerated for their crimes.

As of yet, Dickerson had not committed any crimes against humanity, but he was not totally sure what his next orders would be, under a man who was known by many as Lord Esposito. Dickerson was wary that his next set of orders could in fact, be something more heinous than anything he had yet faced. He was on American soil. He knew that his father and uncle had become involved in the new re-emergence of the Christian faith here in Ohio. He knew that many of his fellow soldiers had expressed a strong dislike for those "holy rollers."

Dickerson was awaiting word about why he had been transferred here on emergency orders. He knew that his Co-Pilot/Gunner felt the same way he did about the new oath of allegiance. Fearful of being overheard, they had spent many hours discussing their distrust of a government centered in another country ruling their United States. Dickerson also had had many discussions with his father and uncle on his last two furloughs about Christianity and a newly learned theory that his aunt and mother had each been taken from Earth, not by some space force from Andromeda Galaxy, but by something called the Rapture. He also knew that many of these new Christians were being arrested for various violations related to not being loyal supporters of the government.

Warrant Officer Raheem Jefferson joined Dickerson on their walk toward the Officers' Mess. He was a tall Black man with the true bearing of an officer in the U.S. Army. His uniform was always impeccably ordered. He was proud to be a man of great skills. He was in line for a promotion within the next six weeks and had been recommended to become a command pilot in one of the Army's newest helicopter gunships. He and Dickerson had been working together for the past two years. They had discussed at length their thoughts on the resurgence of the Christian faith in America. Jefferson's father had been in prison at the time of the birth of his son. He had insisted on naming his new son Raheem in honor of one of his fellow inmates who had taken him under his wing to protect him from the Skinheads and Mexicans in prison.

Jefferson's mother was a devout Christian lady who had raised him to be a gentleman. He studied hard in school and received top grades. He entered the army upon graduation from high school and went to flight school at Fort Rucker, Alabama. His mother had seen him graduate and prayed diligently for him as he made his way up the ranks. She was one of the people who had disappeared. Jefferson remembered that she had told him constantly about Jesus, but he couldn't find the time to embrace the faith, as she had done. Then when she became one of the millions of missing persons, he knew in his heart where she was. He didn't believe for one minute the stories about spacemen taking her to some far-off planet in another galaxy.

Dickerson looked at his Co-Pilot and said, "Welcome to the team of doubters. I haven't heard anything about our mission yet, have you?"

Checking around and then moving away from any of the near-by structures, Jefferson said, "No, Brother. I haven't heard yet, either."

They both entered the large Officers' Mess. It was typical of most they had seen in all parts of the world, outside of a battle zone, where the walls were shiny tile, and the tables were neatly spaced. There were four seats to a table and there were servers who brought the food.

The mealtime was spent with small talk between Dickerson and Jefferson. They finished and their dinnerware was taken to the Scullery. They rose in unison and made their way to the exit. Outside activity was beginning to pick up. Mechanics and ground crew members were busy preparing for an upcoming mission.

Four gunships were being loaded with ordinance. Air to ground missiles were loaded into their pods, and the Gatling Guns were loaded and ready to go.

Late morning saw the time had arrived to find out what their orders were. The ready room doors were opened by a Staff Sergeant. The air crews climbed the three steps pouring into the room. Each man took his seat, and a Colonel stood before a map of Northeastern Ohio. Not much has changed since the Eighth Air Force prepared for raids over Nazi Germany. The only difference is that instead of hundreds of bomber crewmembers, there were only eight men sitting in the room ready to hear what the Colonel had to say about their upcoming mission.

The Colonel stepped front and center, "Gentlemen, we are about to undertake the first mission under the overall command of the military forces of Lord Paolino Esposito. Please take out your navigation computers and enter the co-ordinates for your evening mission. Download them now and save them. It will be approximately a one-hour flight. The element of surprise should keep our time over the target to a bare minimum."

"We have been given the assigned task of removing one pocket of the subversive religious fanatics groups. They are responsible for much of the unrest taking place in our country lately. They are trying to stop people from following Lord Esposito. Our orders are firm. I know that this will be a difficult mission tonight. You have never had to attack people on American soil. However, this is a necessary mission. They are attempting to subvert the progress that is being made currently in Europe. Now that America has joined with Europe, that will be the kind of limitless progress our country sees as well."

"There are some reports that they have a large cache of weapons and ammunition stored at their base. It looks from our satellite surveillance that this is a small contingent. It is disguised as an innocent looking village among the woods. On the photos you see the two larger buildings, where we believe the ammunition is stored. We will attack shortly after sunset at eighteen-thirty hours."

Dickerson and Jefferson walked out with the rest of the crews. In unison, they peeled off from the group and walked toward their gunship.

Jefferson broke the silence when he began to pour out his heart, "I'm tellin' you, man, I don't like this at all. My mother used to try and warn me about the Last Days, she called it. She always said that someday a man would fool the whole world into pledging their allegiance to him. And that he would wage war against all who believed in Jesus. I wish I would have paid attention to her then. I miss her so much."

Dickerson agreed, "We need to go for a ride. We need an excuse to take the ship up and go warn those people."

"Don't you need to take me on a quick ride to share your great knowledge about being an aircraft commander before this mission?"

They both smiled and Dickerson agreed, "That's a capitol idea my friend. You're almost ready to take command, but there are still a few things I need to share with you."

They returned to their room, hurriedly put on their flight suits, and went to the flight line.

Approaching the crew chief, Dickerson explained that he needed to take Jefferson up to prepare him for his next duty station before he takes command of his own ship.

There was, surprisingly, only slight resistance to the copter being taken up before that evening's mission. As a compromise, Dickerson talked the crew chief into allowing him to take up one of the Apaches belonging to the Ohio National Guard. He signed out the ship and the two men climbed aboard and began the pre-flight. All the while, Dickerson went through the motions of teaching Jefferson what the commander would do during the pre-flight. They checked and found that the ship was fully fueled. They took their seats and began the takeoff procedure. Once airborne, they circled the field once and then headed north. After only one minute they turned in a more easterly direction. They set their navigation computer to the coordinates they had been given during the briefing.

It was shortly after lunchtime when Paul Dickerson heard the approaching helicopter. It made a close-in pass, circled the encampment, and then set down in a nearby field.

With Dickerson in the lead, everyone sprinted to the clearing to see why an army helicopter had landed so close to their little village. As he got closer, he saw that the pilot was his own son, Gerald. With Gerald, was his best friend Raheem Jefferson.

Gerald leapt from his seat in the copter and ran to his father, stealing a quick embrace before shouting with urgency, "Dad, Raheem and I are going to be in a lot of trouble for this, but we stole this National Guard 'copter to warn the people here. There is an attack planned for just after sunset to wipe out what the army is calling a "nest of subversives". Even though we shut off our transponder, they still tracked us on Radar to this location. I believe that they are going to move up the attack. You need to get everyone out of here as soon as possible!"

Those who were near enough to hear the conversation, turned and began to run back to the village. As they shouted warnings and tried to gather their belongings, the sound of approaching attack helicopters over-powered their cries.

The first missile hit its target, the Longhouse at the northern edge of the encampment. The concussion of the explosion knocked five people to the ground as they were struck by splinters from the logs.

Paul Dickerson screamed above the din, "Why? Why are they doing this? We have done nothing to bring about this kind of attack."

Raheem was shouting as he and the group were running toward the shelter of the trees, "Mr. Dickerson, in their minds they don't need a reason. They are following orders that have been issued from Rome."

The Gatling Guns whirred a terrible buzzing sound as they sprayed lead into the wooded area where people were vainly trying to seek sanctuary from the chaos.

Gerald Dickerson was shouting, "Their goggles help them see our heat signatures under the canopy of trees. Don't group up. There is no safety in numbers. Scatter and try to find a low-lying area. Hit the ground and hold still, as still as you've ever been before.

The cries of the wounded and injured were beginning to rise and mingle with the sounds of exploding missiles and fifty caliber projectiles, tearing through the trees, and churning up the ground. People were lying where they had fallen. Some were not badly hurt, and then just as suddenly as the attack had begun, the remaining helicopters broke off the attack and turned west to leave the area.

Paul Dickerson shouted to his son with terror in his voice, "Will they be back?"

"I don't know Dad. They weren't supposed to come until this evening. I guess they figured out that Raheem and I were coming here to warn you."

The two stood still side by side for only a few seconds, before they began efforts to tend to the wounded and dying.

Just outside Washington, D. C., Admiral William Blanding, former Chairman of the Joint Chiefs of Staff, and Marine Sergeant Jorge Ramos arrived at a house in the suburb of Arlington, Virginia. The late Autumn evening air was crisp, and a light rain had begun to fall.

Pulling into the driveway next to the front porch, Ramos told the Admiral to sit still, and he would be right back. Sergeant Ramos, a decorated infantryman, used his experience and as though his head was on a swivel, he made his way to the front porch. He saw no one watching from any of the nearby houses or yards.

If the plans he and a few of his friends had in place were working, there should be a few of them inside the house, and it would be safe to bring the Admiral inside.

He, knocked twice, and rang the doorbell once before knocking two more knocks. The door opened and was face to face with a Marine Captain. No words were exchanged, but they nodded to each other, and Ramos turned and walked briskly back to the car. He held the door as the Admiral climbed out, then he led the Admiral through the door and into the living room.

"Attention on Deck!" The Marine Captain barked as the Admiral entered the room. Five men jumped to attention at the sight of the Admiral.

Blanding nodded acknowledgement and said, "As you were, men. As you were."

Captain Bernard Lowery followed the Admiral's command and everyone resumed their positions of guarded relaxation. Some were peering out from the curtains while others just sat still and carried on quiet conversations with each other.

Still standing in the entryway to the living room, Admiral Blanding spoke, "I must admit, we at the Joint Chiefs had heard that there were a number of personnel who were not happy. What has been happening within the ranks of the military has concerned a great many. However, this is the first time that I have met anyone who is, just as I am, more than a little disappointed that our country would acquiesce to the desires of a foreign leader. I'm glad to see so many, fellow true compatriots standing with me."

Sergeant Ramos smiled and replied, "Admiral Blanding, Sir, there are many more. However, for security reasons, none of us knows exactly how many, or where they all are."

News reports were beginning to go out over the air. The official party-line coming from Rome was that the Army had carried out an attack on a base camp of rebels who were plotting to overthrow the newly formed government. They were reported to be religious dissidents of a far-right militia who claimed to be Christians, but obviously were simply anti-government revolutionaries.

It was being reported that rewards were being offered to anyone who could lead to the elimination of other such pockets of resistance to the enlightened government of Lord Paolino Esposito. Americans were now members of a growing world-wide movement of people who knew that world peace was truly on the horizon. The American economy was now linked with that of most of the western world. Only Israel seemed to be resisting the leadership of Rome.

However, with the plans that were falling into place for Israel, Lord Esposito expected to start hearing a different response from Israel very soon. He was laying the groundwork for erecting a new temple in Jerusalem. The Orthodox Jews would want to follow him once the temple was rebuilt on the Temple Mount.

CHAPTER 26

It was a well-known fact that the debt incurred by the United States over a period of decades could not be maintained indefinitely. Maintaining a strong military and taking care of her citizens from cradle to grave was more than could ever be preserved. Paolino Esposito promised that if the U.S. joined his coalition, her debts would be completely forgiven. No foreign bank based in any nation that was a part of the alliance would try to collect from America.

Many in the country believed this to be fact. President Blair pushed extremely hard for this pact for many years, first in the Congress, Senate and then as the President. It was the culmination of her political goal for the country.

Robert Wallace had been streaming his editorial comments online for almost a full year warning the country that this was all part of a massive plan to halt America's support of Israel. The Bible said that God will bless all who bless Israel and will curse all who curse her.

Since the U.S. had stopped supporting Israel, the signs were there. Disease and devastating economic calamity brought on by severe weather and earthquakes were among the many problems that plagued the once proud nation. The people of the United States had forgotten to serve God first. Instead, they were first going after their own selfish ambitions.

Food supplies had dwindled radically as more and more farmland was turned over for commercial development. The rich were getting richer, and the poor were only getting poorer. The stresses of everyday life brought about more and more stress related illnesses from high blood pressure to psychiatric troubles. Divorce and crimes were at an all-time high. It did not matter which political party was in control of the country, the results were still the same. People were grabbing for all they could get.

Even in times of trouble when some people began reaching out to help others, most people were still more worried about their own welfare. The stories of someone's heartwarming attitude to help others may bring about a sigh of acknowledgement from some people, but most people usually had their personal guilt assuaged because, "someone is doing something for those people, so I don't have to worry about it. That's why I pay taxes."

Paul Dickerson was glad to see his son for the first time in more than a year. The circumstances under which Gerald Dickerson returned were a pure fluke, however.

Gerald spoke to his father, "Dad, I had no idea you were even here. Raheem and I were given the assignment to attack this camp, and our consciences would not let us. I thought you were still at home."

As the two men walked back toward what was left of the two Longhouses, they were surveying the ruin. Where once had stood two beautifully constructed Longhouses and a few Wigwams, there were piles of shattered logs and splintered sticks. Where they had just been, in the surrounding woods, there was human devastation. Among the thirty people who had lived there, ten of them were dead. Some of the wounds were so severe that death would probably take five more souls.

"Why? Why, Son? Why would our own soldiers try to kill us?"

The younger man looked at his father and replied, "I don't know, Dad. The orders made no sense to Raheem and me. That's why we had to go against them. I keep thinking that if more German soldiers in World War II had done the same, perhaps the carnage of the 1940s might not have been so fierce. Of course, the downside of this whole matter now means that we are wanted men. We disobeyed direct orders and aided and abetted what our new leadership considers the enemy. I guess my army is over."

The statement hit his father like a sucker punch from the schoolyard bully. Paul Dickerson knew that his son's desire since childhood was to be a flight officer in the army. As they arrived at what was left of the village, Gerald winced as he looked at the scene of the massacre. The ground looked furrowed like a freshly plowed field. The rapid firing of the Gatling Guns left neat rows of ruts. Here and there along the lines, there were deep marks where some unfortunate person was unable to avoid the bullets that felled them where they stood.

Gerald and Raheem came together at the remains of the Longhouse. As they both stood on the stoop and surveyed what had happened, Raheem spoke, "Brother, we need to get away from these people. They need to get to another location without being pursued by the Army looking for us. Now we are all being targeted by the government."

Paolino Esposito was pacing angrily in his office, "I can no longer have this kind of incompetency. How hard is it to find and kill one of our highest profile enemies?"

Baalazaar the Ambassador from the Andromeda Galaxy was also in the office. "Perhaps we need to put my legions of security people in charge of this. I have been trying to use influence on your people. They just don't seem to have the natural instincts to do this."

Esposito turned to face the man who had become his mentor and chief advisor. He slowly walked toward him and placed his hand on the Baalazaar's sleeve, "My Lord, I do not want to fail you. You have given me so much. I am on the verge of ruling the entire world. I shall be the first man ever to do what so many men in the past have failed to do."

Baalazaar placed his free hand on top of Esposito's and in a voice dripping with sheer malevolence said, "You will, my son. I only need you to obey me completely. Do not rely on your own sense of what is going on around you. My legions are poised and ready to take over. Very seldom do they fail. Human nature is easily under my control. I have given people so many flaws that they nearly always succumb to my wishes."

Esposito wanted to know more, "What about those small bands of Christians that seem to be increasing in size?"

"I can certainly get to them. They have desires for money and power. Their lust for sexual pleasure has always been one of the easiest ways to break down the walls of protection against me. I will put a few well-placed temptations in their way, and they will begin to falter as though nothing was ever keeping them from my power. You only need to make sure that your people follow the orders of the new leaders I will send to them."

The meaning was clear to Esposito. He made the decision to turn over to Baalazaar all the security forces that had been loyal to Esposito from the beginning.

The aroma of sulfur was suddenly fading, and then Baalazaar was gone. Esposito had grown used to Baalazaar's entrances and exits. He picked up his phone and called Colonel Lombardo, the head of his security forces. He gave the order that there would soon be a change in the chain of command. Lombardo was to become the liaison between Esposito and the newly arriving officers.

For much of the twentieth and early twenty-first centuries, the United States military was a leading force in the Western World, projecting a presence on the seven seas, on the continent of Europe and the South Pacific and much of Asia from Japan to Formosa. There were U.S. Army or Air Force bases in many of her allied nations. The U.S. Navy had a few bases in allied nations or made any free nation's seaports one of America's many ports of call.

Now, what was at one time the largest U.S. Naval base in the world, Norfolk, Virginia, was filling up with aircraft carriers and submarines from Europe. There were also fighter planes and bombers making Andrews Air Force Base their new bases of operations. After only a few weeks at those locations, those squadrons and wings began to fan out to military outposts across the nation, making them their new homes. Never in history had so many military personnel from other foreign powers occupied American bases.

From his new outpost in Zanesville, Ohio, Robert Wallace was beginning once again to stream his video podcasts. After he and Mohammed Zacharius were reunited, he was able to go back online passing from network to network and through countless servers across North America, to resume his clandestine news commentaries and reports.

Wallace's wife, Olivia, was getting closer to her due date to deliver their child. She was feeling uncomfortable, yet at the same time, filled with excitement about the prospect of giving birth to their second child. Their first-born, a girl, came before they were married, and was taken up in the Rapture. Robert had never met his daughter. He hadn't known of Olivia's pregnancy. He had traveled to the other side of the world to cover a big news story, leaving his fiancé behind. It wasn't until a few years later when he began to investigate the missing people phenomenon, they were reunited.

Now, here they were, a married couple, having to keep traveling to avoid capture and possible execution by forces loyal to the new world leader, Paolino Esposito.

Wallace took his place in the big easy chair next to a fireplace. It was from this location in the home of Muskingum County Deputy Sheriff Tom Baker that he planned to make his first address in nearly a month.

"Good evening, Friends. It has been too long since we have been able to share information with you. America, as we have always known her, no longer exists. People from another country have managed to take over our law enforcement agencies, and now our military has bowed its knee to Paolino Esposito. The man behind the rise of Esposito is believed to be an extraterrestrial ambassador from the Andromedin Galaxy. He calls himself Baalazaar. Any of you who have ever even glanced at the Old Testament in the Bible, can clearly see the similarity to his name, and that of the ancient Canaanite god of fertility, Baal."

"Baalazaar has misled so many people around the world into thinking that the millions of people who disappeared from our lives recently had been taken aboard spaceships and transported to another galaxy.

This is one way to try to make sense of it if you are not a believer in the God of the Bible. Even those of us who were totally unfamiliar with the Bible stories, after thinking it through, could see the emptiness in his story."

Wallace began to lay out the short history of Paolino Esposito's rise to power. He explained that under the guidance and leadership of one of the world's richest and most powerful men, Albert Le Roux, Paolino Esposito rose through the political ranks of Italian government until he was elected the leader of the European Union. Albert Le Roux had been a leading electronics manufacturer. His companies were constantly on the cutting edge of communications and computing equipment.

Wallace continued explaining that he believed that Le Roux was given much of his knowledge by Baalazaar, or even by the Devil himself. Le Roux had been a leader in the development of implantable microchips. His technology was used in the early twenty-first century in the manufacture of implantable medical devices that had been able to reanimate the human brain and spine to restore mobility to victims of spinal injuries. Then the company began to make microchips that could be loaded with a person's medical history, financial records and even be used with satellite tracking to locate people.

Wallace spoke more emphatically, "Anyone who has tried to go against Esposito here in the United

States has become a target of massive defamation campaigns or eliminated completely. The most recent case in point was the small colony of believers in Jesus Christ at the camp in Dresden, Ohio, known as New Zion or Camp Dickerson. The small group came under scrutiny and, according to local law enforcement, many were slaughtered by forces loyal to Esposito. My wife and I have been captured on at least two occasions and tortured to get us to turn away from following Jesus as our Lord. Each time, with God's help, we miraculously escaped and kept bringing you the truth as best we could. As soon as I finish this message, we will be on the move again."

"We just found out this morning, that former units of the United States Army, now sworn to follow the leadership of Esposito, have attacked and murdered an encampment of Christian believers near Plainfield, Ohio. If it had not been for the heroic action of one helicopter crew who warned those in the encampment, perhaps everyone there would have been killed. Jesus said in Matthew 10:28, "Do not be afraid of those who kill the body but cannot kill the soul. Rather, be afraid of the One who can destroy both soul and body in hell. So, I say to you, do not fear what men may do to you. God can and will restore your soul."

Wallace closed out the report, and within five minutes, he, Olivia, Mohammed, and Ibrahim were once again driving away from Zanesville. They began a long trek westward. Not knowing where they were going next, they knew they had to get as far away from any previous locations as possible. It was becoming increasingly dangerous to use telephones or personally contact anyone they knew.

The security staff office in Rome reeked of stale cigar smoke. Gathered around a large conference table were Colonel Vito Lombardo and five of his security officers.

Security Chief Lombardo was railing against the fact that Robert Wallace had once again been able to elude capture and was giving reports that were deemed treasonous by the Esposito government, "We cannot allow this to ever happen again. There must be a way to halt the use of the internet. Stopping Wallace is the number one priority for our forces. We have an extraordinarily strong military and law enforcement presence in America. If we use those forces and investigative powers, there should be no place for him to hide. We have positioned our forces."

As Lombardo seethed, his adjutant entered the room and handed him an urgent communique, "Sir, this just arrived from the Vatican. Pope Cephas has asked that I wait for your reply."

Lombardo tore open the envelope. There, in the impeccably neat handwriting of Pope Cephas, were explicit orders. From this point forward, Lombardo was to report directly to him. The directive given to Lombardo also said that he was to follow the orders of a contingent of troops from Ambassador Baalazaar. It was plain that the Esposito government was not satisfied with the way Lombardo's forces had failed to eliminate the problem being presented by Robert Wallace. Lombardo was to meet with Baalazaar's men within thirty minutes at the Presidential Office in the new Parliament Building in Rome.

The Parliament Building in Rome had just been completed. Even though Colonel Lombardo had seen much of the building during construction, this was to be the first time he would meet with Esposito since its completion.

Lombardo climbed the steps of the gleaming edifice. Thirteen steps and then six columns all made of the finest marble from many of the same quarries that had provided marble for the many statues and monuments that had beautifully graced the streets and squares of Rome for centuries.

The massive, gilded doors were flanked by soldiers in full dress uniform, with two rows of ribbons on their crimson dress blouses, showing their military accomplishments. Each were each Sergeants-Major, who rigidly stood facing forward, showing no emotion. Lombardo opened one of the doors and entered the building's long entrance hall. The floor gleamed with a mirror-like sheen. His footsteps echoed off the cold, opulent walls. Hanging from the ceiling in the long hallway were five massive chandeliers dripping with diamond-like crystal.

The Presidential office was at the far end of the lengthy hall. Two more rigid guards, each one more than six feet tall, flanked the door. Lombardo thought they appeared to be Andromedins.

Lombardo saluted them as he opened the door and entered. Waiting near the large fireplace, adorned with artwork from ancient Rome, were Paolino Esposito, Pope Cephas, and Baalazaar. Lombardo could read the disappointment on their faces. He knew they felt his efforts to stop Robert Wallace had completely failed.

Breaking the tense silence, Baalazaar was the first to speak, "Your position in this government has become tenuous at best, my dear Colonel. Your leadership of the security forces in America has been seriously lacking. You have allowed a rabble-rouser to inflict damage on our cause. He has been able to give too many streamed reports calling this government evil, as he encouraged people to follow the ancient son of a carpenter from Galilee."

Assidi joined the condemnation, "Colonel, it has been up to you to secure our flanks, but with this Wallace fiasco, you have left our flanks exposed."

Esposito gave the final assessment of the situation, "Colonel, you gained your position mainly because of your many years of service to Albert Le Roux and Le Roux enterprises. I am beginning to think that perhaps you are not in your proper element. I have been speaking with Ambassador Baalazaar, and my conclusion is that I need to have a change of command in my security forces. From this point forward, you will answer to the Ambassador's security chief, General Penzone. The Andromedins don't age the way we humans do. His expertise in matters such as this goes back centuries. In fact, he worked closely with Emperor Trajan based here in Rome. You will follow his guidance and adhere to his orders in a strict adjustment in the chain of command."

Though Lombardo was disturbed by this loss of confidence in his abilities, he could not say that it was totally unexpected. For some reason, Robert Wallace had avoided capture and execution by the Esposito government.

Baalazaar waved his hand over a badge that was pinned just an inch above his left hip. General Penzone suddenly appeared in the far corner opposite the fireplace. He was a strikingly handsome man with sharp features. He stood nearly six feet five inches tall.

His uniform was like the fatigues worn by most nations' soldiers. The uniform had a nametag, along with the emblem of his military. On his collars were clusters of five stars signifying his high rank. His imposing figure sent shudders down Lombardo's spine. Lombardo had faced many foes in his lifetime, but he couldn't help thinking that he would not have wanted to ever cross paths with this man in combat.

Wallace, Olivia, and their companions had been on the road for more than five hours. They were west of Indianapolis, Indiana on Interstate 70. Mohammed and Ibrahim alternated driving duties, Olivia sat cuddled up next to her husband. Wallace had been searching online for information about current news events.

News was becoming harder and harder to find. Wallace was becoming exasperated over not being able to find out what he needed to know. He knew there were many small enclaves of Christians. He needed to know how they were being targeted by foreign military members within the borders of the United States.

"I don't know what to do. Our brothers and sisters have been murdered systematically and I can't find out much information. Mohammed, do you have any contacts who are believers in Indiana or Illinois? We need to find people who can access information."

As they drove into Illinois, Mohammed spoke in confidence to Ibrahim who was in the front passenger seat, "My brother, I am totally unfamiliar with any of the Christian groups west of Ohio. Have you received anything from our Lord to indicate where a place of safety could be found?"

Ibrahim had been praying silently as Mohammed drove. His answer surprised not only Mohammed, but also he was personally astonished as the words flowed from his mouth, "Mohammed, the Lord says that we are to take the first exit. When we get off the Interstate, we are to continue westbound on the old Route 40. The Lord is telling me we are to seek the name Maxwell. We will then turn north on that road until we come to a small farm. It is there that we will find an encampment of believers." He sat back in awe; his eyes wide in wonder.

As they quickly came to the freeway exit, Mohammed followed the directions the Lord had given his friend. They drove another two miles. There on the side of the highway, they noticed a row of mailboxes. One was painted white, but the paint motif looked like a cow hide. Prominently painted was the name "Maxwell". About twenty yards beyond the mailboxes was a gravel road winding north. Mohammed turned the car onto the gravel road, and they continued for close to five minutes. Both sides of the narrow road were thick with trees, many still covered with colorful late Fall leaves.

From the back seat, Wallace commented, "It looks as though we are headed into a potential wilderness. Was God speaking to you, Ibrahim, or was it just the voice of Moses in the wilderness?"

"I'm exceptionally gifted at hearing the voice of God. He has spoken to me many times. He has never led me astray, and I don't expect Him to. The Bible tells us that in the last days we will prophesy, and I have even seen visions. It was because of a vision given by God that Mohammed and I came to know Christ as savior. I will not doubt Him now. This is the right way to go."

They rounded a curve and there was a large, old farmhouse that looked as though it had been built in the early nineteen-hundreds. The screened-in porch went around all sides, offering a cool place to sleep on hot and humid summer nights. No doubt, generations of family had lived here.

Standing at the foot of the porch stood Thomas Maxwell. He was a man in his mid to late fifties. He stood a little less than six feet tall, with a slight protruding tummy over his belt. He wore a pair of Wrangler Jeans and on his feet was a pair of western work boots.

He waved and walked toward the car, "I've been expecting you folks. Isn't it amazing that our Lord would guide us to each other? Interesting times we live in."

General Andriolli Penzone was proudly showing Lord Paolino Esposito and Colonel Vito Lombardo around his command center. The walls were lined with large screen television monitors. There were webpage news feeds from every major news organization in the world.

Esposito and Lombardo had managed to gain control of every European based news network. The lead story on many of the North American news networks was the escape of Robert Wallace and his group of friends. Being journalists from America, they had dubbed them The Followers.

The headlines shouted the escapades of the quartet as they had once again eluded capture by authorities. Time and again the military and police had tried and failed to capture them. It was said that people in North America were becoming close followers of Robert Wallace's video blogs.

At the urging of Lombardo, Lord Esposito had put the equivalent of a one-million-dollar bounty for information leading to the location and arrest of the group.

Lombardo was seething. It was clear that he was fighting for his job, and perhaps even his life, as General Andriolli Penzone was now fully in command of the situation. The General knew what was on Lombardo's mind, and there was slight sneering smile on his lips as he showed his guests around the center.

Penzone told his guests that his officers had just received word that Wallace and his cohorts had been seen whisking their way along Interstate seventy west of Indianapolis. Penzone had his men checking every stationary CCTV camera on I-70 West as they searched for a car containing three men and one woman. Using their driver's license photos, facial recognition software was finely tuned to find any one of the four escapees, it was surmised that if one of their faces popped on the software, it was understood that the other three would be in the same vehicle.

Penzone studied Lombardo's face. To add to the discomfort, Penzone's face was smirking as he caught Lombard's eye, "There is a stationary CCTV camera just one mile east of the Indiana/Illinois border. We just received word that Mohammed Zacharius had been seen driving the car, and there appeared to be three others in the vehicle with him. It won't be long now until we have them again in custody. I assure you gentlemen that my forces will not let them out of our control."

The recent sighting in western Indiana was not followed by another sighting beyond the first CCTV camera in Illinois. Penzone gave the order to begin studying satellite video footage. If they left the interstate, the satellite should be able to find them. There were about two miles between the CCTV camera that had last seen the car, and the first camera that missed sighting the fugitives.

CHAPTER 27

There was a large red barn on the Maxwell farm. Even though it was more than one hundred years old, it showed a century of care in its quality workmanship. Any restorations over the years kept faith with the original construction. There were even places where wooden pegs held the siding to the framework.

When Thomas Maxwell led Wallace and the group into the barn, it was obvious that the same quality workmanship existed throughout the entire barn.

Guiding his guests to a back room that was obviously set up as a bunk room for workers, Maxwell spoke, "I know it's not the Ritz, but it is warm and comfortable, and I can see the lady could use some rest. Is she close to her time?"

Olivia answered him with a slight gulp in her voice, "I was ready weeks ago. This baby is more difficult than my first one."

Maxwell continued, "So, the first one was taken up in the great Rapture? My Missus and I lost our little one, a boy, the same way. We searched and searched for him for weeks before I began to hear people talking about something I'd never heard of before. I didn't know what a 'Rapture' was. It was a term I'd never heard of. But the more and more I began to study an old family Bible which was my Great grandfather's, the more I became convinced that my son was missing for another reason. I realized the Lord God Almighty had removed him to save him from what was to come in this world. I am eternally grateful that my boy is still alive in His presence, and safe from all the folly that exists on this earth."

Wallace was checking the entire room, looking for electrical hook-ups for a makeshift broadcast booth. He noticed there was plenty of power, and the lighting wasn't bad in this room. He returned to Maxwell, "Mr. Maxwell, I'd like to make a quick video recording here. The background of a blank wood wall should not give away our location. And I plan to hold off sending it to the world until we're ready to leave. That should keep you safe. We thank you for your hospitality."

Olivia gasped quickly and then groaned loudly. Suddenly she was sitting in a pool of liquid.

"I believe it's time for you, my dear," Maxwell said, "I'll get some clean sheets and towels. I can help you, playin' mid-wife to a human mother is not much different than helping my livestock. No offense, Ma'am."

Olivia smiled through gritted teeth, "None taken, Mr. Maxwell. I trust your skills at bringing life into this world."

Wallace was trying hard to keep his nervousness in check as his wife went into labor. It was difficult for him, but Olivia was proud of his efforts.

Wallace scanned the room for the right bunk on which to lay his wife.

Olivia managed a smile as she reached up to his face and stroked it lovingly. "It's okay, any bunk will do."

Maxwell returned to the room with clean sheets and towels and some water. He quickly put down the sheets and large beach towel on the bunk.

Olivia stretched out on the bunk and moaned. This baby was not about to wait much longer. It was as though little Junior Wallace was going to have a job to do soon. He had to get to work. He didn't want to be late. This was his time.

The room where General Penzone and Colonel Vito Lombardo watched various computer monitors was abuzz with activity. A very tall Andromedin who was observing, raised a hand.

Penzone called out, "What is it?"

"Sir, I believe I have found them. There is a farm just about a mile or so off the old Route 40. Look, this road goes back into the woods there. At the end of the woods, we see cleared land, where there is a small farm. The barn is large, and two silos are there for storage of fodder. This is the only area where they could have gone. We have no video of them beyond this area. If we send the drones there for a closer look, I'm sure we'll find their vehicle parked in the trees just beyond that barn."

Lombardo looked jealously disappointed as Penzone proudly patted his observer on the back, "Good work. We'll get a contingent of troops to the area quickly. We don't want to make too much noise, so keep the helicopters far away from that area. Put them down about a mile west of there and send the men in on foot. Tell them to be as quiet as possible. I do not want them to hear us coming and escape again."

With those orders, the message crossed the Atlantic and was at Scott Air Force Base near St. Clair, Illinois. A small troop of forty soldiers from the newly formed Army of the United World boarded two helicopters ready to be carried to their destination.

Olivia was now giving birth to her son. Wallace sat next to her bed, holding her hand. He had tears in his eyes as he thought about how the first time this happened for Olivia and him, he was in some other part of the world, fully unaware that this woman he had come to love so deeply was alone and giving birth to their first child. That little girl was now among the millions whom God had removed from this world. But now he was here to watch his son enter the world. He didn't want to miss a single moment of this child's life.

Wallace found himself wondering what kind of life his son would have as the world was falling apart around them. It wasn't the first time this had happened. Children had entered a tumultuous world ever since Adam and Eve were banished from Eden. Wallace wanted his son to have a better and safer life.

As Olivia cried out, she pushed, and the baby's head began to appear. Maxwell looked at them both and nodded, "It's almost time. I believe this little one will be with us in only a few moments."

Olivia pushed again as she tightly squeezed Wallace's hand. They both cried out as the baby slipped into Maxwell's waiting hands.

"No matter how often I see new life happen, I am always amazed," Maxwell exclaimed, "God is so good. He makes a way for his people to survive, no matter what is happening around them."

As the baby boy screamed, Wallace's tears now flowed freely. He smiled, and gave out with a slight giggle, "He's beautiful. He's perfect. Look at those tiny fingers. Look at that tiny mouth. He's really loud, but oh, so beautiful. Darlin, you did a magnificent job. Thank you for this wonderful gift. This child will be fully dedicated to Christ as he grows."

The baby turned his head toward his mother and father.

The baby's focus seemed to change as his head turned toward the west. His eyes almost seemed to begin to focus, as his little flailing arms jerked toward the west.

Heavy military boots sunk slightly into the soft soil of a large field about a mile west of the Maxwell farm as forty members of the Army of the United World stepped from their helicopters. Quickly they formed up, weapons at the ready.

Their orders were clear. They were searching for a group of people who were undermining the harmony of the United World, by spreading lies that Lord Esposito was a dictator who was going to bring destruction to the world.

Orders were shouted out, "Move into the woods directly ahead and make your way east!" They were looking for a large red barn where their prey was probably hiding. As they darted through the field, the helicopters lifted off to return to their base.

As baby Wallace continued looking west and crying, Maxwell's cell phone rang. He stepped outside the bunk room into the barn, "Hello? No, I don't know what is going on. What do you mean? Oh? Really. I'll see if I can find out what it is. Thanks."

With great urgency, Maxwell returned to the bunk room and spoke above the shrieks of the child, "I know this is going to be difficult, but we're going to need to move out of here in a hurry. For some reason, army troops just landed in my neighbor's field west of us. They have gone into the woods and are headed in our direction."

Wallace and Mohammed each helped a very tired Olivia to her feet. She was in pain, but she knew she must fight through it. The baby's crying quieted a bit and Ibrahim picked him up. They followed Maxwell to the main door of the barn, and there, just inside the entrance was a stack of hay bales. Maxwell reached out about waist high on the left edge of the center bale. He pulled it toward himself, and the entire stack opened as if it were a door opening. On the floor was a stairway that led into a dark hallway.

"Follow me quickly. My great-great grandfather kept the farm profitable by selling corn to friends of Al Capone. They had a still in the basement of this barn. This tunnel led to a large room where they would store their hootch. The Feds never found them, no matter how many times they raided this bar. Try to make yourselves comfortable down there. I'll see if I can send them away."

Olivia struggled to make it down the stairs as Wallace and Mohammed aided her. Ibrahim and the baby had just made into the opening as Maxwell began to close the secret door.

Maxwell then began to scan the floor of the barn looking for any signs of the travelers having been there. He ran into the bunk room and snatched up the sheets and towels. He stuffed them into a large laundry hamper in the far corner. He once again searched for any blood drops or other indications that a woman had just given birth in this room. Seeing none, he left the room and returned to the barn to feign tinkering on his tractor, parked at the center. He had just removed the valve cover when the barn door opened, and a loud bang accompanied a bright light. Shouting soldiers then rushed into the room and knocked Maxwell to the ground.

"Where are they?" Came the brutal voice of a Sergeant shouting directly into Maxwell's ear.

"Who? Who are… they?"

"Listen, Buddy, you don't ask me anything. All I want outta you is answers to my questions." The Sergeant punched Maxwell in the face and blood spurted out of his nose. "Where are Wallace and his crew? I know you know. We have satellite video of their car entering the woods at the end of your driveway. Where are they?"

Maxwell's head was still smarting from the punch he had received, "I haven't seen anyone. Perhaps they went deeper into the woods. There's a crick down there that will take them to some other farmhouse or barn. Did you look there?"

Another blow landed hard against the side of Maxwell's head. Two of the soldiers grabbed him and turned him onto his back. A sawhorse was used to raise one end of a large plank. They moved Maxwell onto the plank with his feet raised high above his head. They began to pour water from a bucket slowly onto his face. Maxwell was spitting and snorting, trying to grasp some air. The water continued to gush against his face, but he was determined that he was not going to share any information.

Maxwell gurgled as the water ran up his nose and down his throat. He felt like his lungs and his brain were on fire. Gasping for air became the main priority in Maxwell's mind. He felt as though he was drowning. The searing became very intense in only a few moments.

As he choked and gasped for air, he tried flailing his arms and legs, but being greatly outnumbered, there were enough men to totally disable him. The more he gasped for air, the more he choked.

The leader of the soldiers shouted, "Tell us where they have gone!"

Maxwell's voice was hoarse and raspy as he tried to respond, "I... I don't know where..." again there was violent strangling that sounded like his entire convulsing body was about to explode. His choking brought up blood and stomach fluid along with mucus, sending it all running down the sides of his face, into his ears and down onto the floor, where it pooled before running down through the spaces between the floorboards.

He suddenly gave out a guttural hacking sound and the convulsions stopped. He lay there inverted on the plank motionless. One of the soldiers shouted, "Stop pouring the water. I think he's having a major crisis here! Stop! Stop now!"

The man began slapping Maxwell's cheeks and calling out to him, "Hey, man. Wake up! Wake up, Mister. Wake up!"

There was silence as the man felt for a pulse on Maxwell's neck. There was none. He was beginning to turn blue around the lips. "I think he's had a heart attack."

The men all backed away from the now limp body of Thomas Maxwell. The men spread out around the barn and searched once again for Robert Wallace and his three accomplices. They knocked on walls and stomped on the floor in various places. They found a basement stairway just inside the bunk room. A quick search around the small basement didn't reveal anyone hiding there either. The haylofts were all empty. The troops moved back outside the barn and made their way into the house where they searched for another hour, to no avail.

CHAPTER 28

In Rome, General Andriolli Penzone slammed down the telephone receiver. He stood briefly, just long enough to sweep papers off the desk next to his. He then sat down and cursed the soldiers who had just reported to him that once again, there was no sign of Robert Wallace or any of his friends.

Everyone in the room was visibly shaken at the outburst by the General. Colonel Vito Lombardo suppressed a slight smile and feigned a concerned look. This was good for his political status, as the general who could do no wrong in the eyes of Lord Esposito, had failed in his first major attempt to capture the wily Robert Wallace. Lombardo had fallen short on numerous occasions, but this debacle proved to be every bit as inept as anything Lombardo's men had attempted over the past ten months. Inside he was thrilled, though on the outside, he showed the same concern as everyone else in the room.

General Penzone called out to his charges, "Listen to me, everyone. We were on target in locating where Wallace and his cohorts were. Our only problem was that the weak old man we chose to interrogate died before giving up the location of the criminals. We will find them. We will capture them, and we will execute them before there is any more chance of escape. I want to meet now with my executive officer corps and the Colonel as we lay out a further plan to successfully complete our mission in North America."

It had been nearly twelve hours since the birth of Wallace's son. Robert Wallace sat next to Olivia with his arm around her. Hunger, coupled with the draining event of giving birth just a few hours ago, was causing much strain on her. The small twin bed where she lay had a lumpy mattress, and her back was very tired. Thankfully, they had managed to stop the bleeding.

"Do you want some more water, Sweetheart?" Wallace's concern was hard to suppress. He tried to be calm despite the trouble in which they now found themselves.

"Water would be wonderful, but I'm beginning to feel very weak. I'm so hungry."

"It must be getting dark outside by now," said Wallace. "I'm going to go up and see if I can get to the house and find some food for us. Mohammed, come with me while Ibrahim stays with Olivia."

Ibrahim nodded, and Wallace and Mohammed started up the stairs to the doorway above them. Slowly, they slid the haybale doorway open enough to not draw attention to themselves, but a big enough opening to slide up to the floor of the barn. It was dark outside, except for the light shining above the partially open barn door.

Slowly both men crawled along the edge to get clear of the haybales before sliding that door in the floor closed. Mohammed pointed to a shadow in the middle of the barn floor. It appeared to be a man lying on his back with his arms outstretched. Looking around, Wallace and Mohammed searched for anyone else in the room. Seeing no one, they made their way toward the shadow on the floor. Wallace gave out a hoarse whisper, "Maxwell." Feeling for a pulse, Wallace's eyes showed concern and he lowered his head in prayer.

Without speaking, they both rose and backed against the wall, moving away from the large barn door with the security light above it. They were seeking another door without a light. About twenty-five feet from the tunnel beneath, near one of the four horse stalls they found a Dutch door. They opened it only an inch or two at a time until it was finally fully open. The farmhouse was about fifty feet away. There were five trees in their path that they could use for cover, as they negotiated the distance to the house.

Once on the porch, it was pitch black. Both men were hoping that the men who had come earlier in the day were gone. Momentarily tripping on a short table next to the porch swing, Wallace regained his balance and found the door. He prayed it was unlocked.

Wallace's prayer was answered as he entered the farm kitchen. There was just enough light coming from the security light that hung on a tall wooden pole in the side yard, and that was enough to allow the pair to find the pantry. Inside there were at least two dozen Mason Jars of vegetables and fruit. Carefully, they carried half of them to the kitchen table.

Mohammed went to a cabinet next to the sink and found a box containing grocery bags. He grabbed a half dozen bags and held them open while Wallace carefully placed the jars into them. He had found a few towels in a drawer next to the large farm sink and wrapped them around each jar for protection and noise suppression.

Returning to the pantry, the men found a loaf of bread and a box of Ritz Crackers. They opted not to open the refrigerator, worried that the light might give them away if anyone was watching.

With grocery bags over their arms, each man returned to the barn along the same path they had used to get into the house. The thirty minutes they had been gone from the tunnel seemed an eternity, but as they came down the stairs into the tunnel, Olivia smiled and let out a slight squeal of excitement. She needed nourishment so she could feed her baby.

They now had at least four days' worth of food. They needed to stay here and allow Olivia to build up her strength for travel. The baby was a good boy and hardly cried out, except when he got truly hungry.

The sun was beginning to set in the western sky. The view from Lord Paolino Esposito's desk was magnificent. The sky had its usual shades of pink, orange, and light gray. A streak of jet contrails, seemed to disappear into the Sun, broke the tranquil look of the beautiful sky.

Lord Esposito sat at his desk munching on traditional Bruschetta with tiny cubes of tomato, shaved garlic, sliced Mozzarella, and thin strings of onion. It was still another two hours before he was scheduled to have dinner with Pope Cephas – the former Cardinal Nunzio Assidi. Bruschetta was one of Lord Esposito's weaknesses.

As Esposito savored his snack, he was reading the latest dispatches from Israel and Palestine. There had been much success bringing about peace and tranquility among most of the western powers. They willingly came into the sphere of power he had created with the new United World government. People in most of the world were happy to look to his strong leadership, as he brought people together all over the world.

One of the main points of contention in the Middle East was the holy city of Jerusalem. Jews and Muslims both laid claim to that tiny piece of geography. Armies had fought, bled, and died for centuries in that land. Israel had claimed Jerusalem as their capital in the early 1980s. The United States officially moved its Embassy from Tel Aviv to Jerusalem during the administration of President Donald Trump. Though that move was celebrated by American Evangelical Christians and Jews alike, Muslims were angry with the U.S. as they saw the move as a slap in the face of the Palestinians.

Esposito was beginning to formulate an idea that he thought would put a stop to the turmoil in the Middle East. Many Jews wanted to rebuild the Temple, and they believed the logical place was on the Temple Mount that was currently occupied by the Dome of the Rock. However, tensions were already too high between the Jews and Muslims. He knew that it was up to him to find a compromise that would not cause more friction. Secretly he had been working on a campaign to name the City of David as the site of the previous two Temples. His representatives had been committed to convincing the Chief Rabbi of Jerusalem to support efforts to name the City of David as the official site of the Third Temple.

Many in Rome, including Pope Cephas (Assidi) and the Church believed that the Temple Mount had been the site of the Roman Tenth Legion garrison at the time of the destruction of the Second Temple. There is rubble in the City of David area that many believed are stones from the fallen Temple.

The Dome of the Rock was built on the site from which the Roman Governor oversaw the Roman Rule of all of Palestine. The Rock was believed to be the place of judgement. It was believed when Christ stood before Pilate, this is where he stood.

If, indeed, this was the case, all it would take is for Jerusalem's Chief Rabbi to agree. At that time, Esposito could negotiate a compromise between Muslims and Jews. This would allow the new Jewish Temple to be built somewhere other than the place Muslims, for centuries, have considered one of their most holy sites.

447

CHAPTER 29

People were filing out of the office of Israeli Prime Minister David Weisenstein after what was considered one of the most important meetings since the foundation of the modern state in 1948. Over the past twenty years, Israeli Prime Ministers had overseen triumph and tragedy. This day might be looked upon as the finest day in modern history.

After the last Cabinet Minister left the room, only the Prime Minister and Chief Rabbi Solomon Davidje remained. Weisenstein opened a cabinet and took out two wine glasses and a bottle of Merlot. He poured from the bottle and the two men smiled broadly as they toasted their accomplishment.

Finally, Jerusalem was going to get the Third Temple. After all the research and negotiating, the site had been found that many agreed was almost certainly the holy site of the two former houses of worship.

Rabbi Davidje spoke, "Having the House of the Most High rebuilt, and re-establishing the animal sacrifices cannot come soon enough."

"As soon as we can get the Palestinian Authority to understand that our plans do not interfere with their control of The Temple Mount, we can begin all the work we need to do to get the new Temple built. So many people have been praying for this for so long, and now it will happen," Prime Minister Weisenstein sipped the last drops of his wine. As he set the glass on his desk, his telephone rang.

"Prime Minister Weisenstein. Yes... yes, Mr. Esposito. As soon as our people can complete the planning, I would welcome having you and the Pope visit our nation. It will be a great event with Jews, Muslims and Christians coming together to oversee a long-awaited peace solution here in the Holy Land. I will have my Foreign Minister contact you and your negotiators to help set up the meetings with the Palestinians. I would like to see this begin as soon as possible. Yes sir. I will personally meet the Ambassador when she arrives. Shalom."

Underneath the floor of the barn on the Maxwell Farm in Eastern Illinois, four adults and one infant had been hiding for nearly three days. Mother Olivia Wallace cradled her newborn baby boy lovingly. Her mind raced with thoughts of what had taken place over the past year. During that time, she had lost a child, reestablished a relationship with her child's father, and married him, despite his being a wanted man.

Robert Wallace had made the mistake of questioning the ongoing story being told to the world. He didn't believe people had come from a distant galaxy and removed massive numbers of human beings. Those humans were supposed to have been taken to the Andromeda Galaxy as part of an interplanetary cultural exchange. Wallace had concluded that all things happening now had been predicted in the Bible. He had become an outspoken critic of the current government that was based in Rome and had spent much time pointing this out to people who followed his video blogs online. The authorities wanted Wallace arrested and executed.

The barn above suddenly came alive with voices. People were walking above and discovering the tragedy that had taken place here in the past twelve hours. They were heard to say that Mr. Maxwell was helping someone evade capture by the government.

Wallace turned to Olivia and whispered, "Maybe these people knew Maxwell better than we did. I don't feel comfortable going up to talk with them, though."

There was a sudden scraping noise coming from above them as the doorway in the ceiling of the tunnel opened, allowing daylight to enter the space.

A lady's voice called out, "Anybody down there?"

The tunnel dwellers remained silent until the baby cried out. As he made his way up the steps, Wallace broke the silence from below, "Yes. Four adults and one infant."

Watching the people come up the steps, the lady answered him, "We have two adults, my husband here and I. We came to check on Mr. Maxwell because we haven't heard from him since yesterday morning. We all keep a close eye on each other when we can." As she looked at Wallace, she continued, "We also try to keep below the radar when it comes to avoiding government contact. Thomas was our teacher as we came to Christ. Since you are hiding here under the barn, I take it that you are also believers."

Ibrahim was the first to speak as their eyes adjusted to the light, "This is true. I am Ibrahim, these are my brothers, Mohammed, and Robert. And this is Robert's wife Olivia, and their newborn. Mr. Maxwell assisted with the birth the day before yesterday."

"I'm Marian Judson and this is my husband, Bill. Mr. Wallace was a good man. He was our spiritual mentor. He led us, and most of the farmers in this part of the county, come to know Jesus as savior, despite the difficulties of finding Bibles and teaching material."

As they visited, it came to light that Maxwell's farm had become the center of activity for Christians in this part of Illinois and Indiana. It was estimated that nearly one hundred people had come to Christ through this simple farmer, Thomas Maxwell.

The private plane carrying Paolino Esposito, as well as ambassadors from other parts of his world-wide kingdom, touched down at Ben Gurion Airport just north of Lod. They were close to Jerusalem. It was ten o'clock on Monday morning, March seventeenth. This summit had been six months in the planning.

Ten minutes after Lord Esposito's plane landed, the jumbo jet carrying Pope Cephas and his entourage landed. At the podium stood Israel's Chief Rabbi, Solomon Davidje. He was flanked by Israel's new Prime Minister David Bar Jonah and President Abdullah Bashir of the Palestinian Authority.

Ambassadors began disembarking Esposito's plane, led by the former President of the United States, Elizabeth Blair, who now represented North America. There was a total of sixty-six Ambassadors to Rome. Most of them were former leaders of now defunct independent nations.

With much pomp, Paolino Esposito stood in the doorway of the airplane, as he surveyed the surrounding land. He knew that in a few moments the welcoming activities would finish and allow him to continue to Jerusalem. There he planned to attend the ceremony to lay the cornerstone to the third Jewish Temple. The Second Temple had been destroyed by Roman Legion posted in Israel. The future Emperor, Titus, led the attack on Jerusalem and the destruction of Herod's Temple. For centuries it was believed to have been located on the Temple Mount where the Al Aqsa Mosque and the Dome of the Rock currently stands.

Researchers had concluded that the true location of the Temple was just to the southwest of Temple Mount. A source of water was discovered at the alternate site which did not feed water to the Temple Mount. The Jews of AD 70 used a water source for the Temple under siege. This was a big clue that this was, indeed, the Temple's true location.

As all the dignitaries from the Pope to the new Caesar listened to the welcoming speeches from Israel and Palestine, they entered a motorcade and were quickly whisked away to Jerusalem for tomorrow's dedication of the Third Temple.

On the ride to Jerusalem, Esposito could hardly contain his excitement. Using the former Cardinal Assidi's first name, speaking to Pope Cephas, he said,

"Finally Nunzio, the world will see peace in this area for the first time since Moses and Joshua led God's people into the land of Canaan. I will go down in history as the greatest leader the world has ever known."

Nodding in agreement, the Pope said, "That is true, Lord Esposito. People from now until the end of time will know you as the greatest Roman Emperor who ever lived."

All along the route leading into Jerusalem, people lined both sides of the road for nearly the entire trip. They were waving signs and shouting with glee. Esposito was the man who had finally brought an end to the almost daily violence in this pair of nations. Since 1948, these two groups of people had wished to occupy the same real estate. Esposito had negotiated a deal with Israel to finally give land to the Palestinians in exchange for Temple rebuilding that would be unhindered by protests. For the first time since the nineteen thirties and nineteen forties Jews and Arabs were able to co-exist peacefully.

Pope Cephas reminded Lord Esposito that the day the new temple was to be dedicated would mark the second anniversary of his rise to power, "Lord Esposito, if you remember, it was two years ago tomorrow that you died of a serious head wound. I was able to lay hands on you and bring you back from the dead. That shows us that you are truly blessed. Economically, we are eliminating poverty. You have done so well. It is amazing."

A proud smile crossed Esposito's face. He was certain that his invincibility would convince the world that he was to be revered.

CHAPTER 30

Robert Wallace had just finished writing his next video presentation. He wanted the world to know that Lord Esposito, the man whom some were beginning to call Caesar Paolino, was falling right in line with what the Bible described as the Lawless one. He was beginning to fit the profile of the man who for more than a century had been known by many Christians as the Anti-Christ.

Wallace read aloud the middle portion of his upcoming video report. "Ladies and gentlemen do not be fooled. This man who has captured the hearts of millions of people worldwide, is indeed, in league with the devil. Lord Esposito seemingly has done what no leader has been able to do for centuries. Peace in the Middle East is upon us. This is a hollow peace. Look for him to start believing that he can do no wrong. Human nature will take control of him, making him believe that he is becoming like God, if not a god himself. This cloak of righteousness with which he has wrapped himself is completely meaningless. If you look closely, you can see through his outer layer of 'honesty' to see there is nothing there."

Olivia entered the room, carrying their son, "That news is not good news, is it?"

He responded, "I guess it depends on what you would consider to be good news. It will soon, in the next couple of years, reveal him showing his true colors. This wonderful peace that we are beginning to experience will disintegrate, and many millions of people will die as lost souls. If there's any good news in this whole thing, it would be that we are getting so remarkably close to the return of Jesus."

Clutching little Oliver closely to her chest, she patted the baby's head and kissed him. So many thoughts were overwhelming her, "I know that I am not to be fearful, but I do fear that our little boy will face so many difficulties in the next few years. I don't want him to become a victim of violence. I want him to be able to grow up living in the world that Jesus will usher in."

Wallace reached out a hand to his wife, "What is one of the most common phrases in the Bible? Fear Not... don't be afraid... be confident. God told Joshua to be brave, be strong, for the Lord your God is with you. I passionately believe that the Lord, our God is with us in this battle. The battle belongs to Him."

"I know this in my heart, but my head is struggling with it, Bobby. I just don't want him to ever face any pain or struggle. I don't want him to ever know fear, the way you and I have."

Wallace thought back over the past few years. It was only a little less than three years ago that so many human beings were taken out of this world. Powerful forces had attempted to convince the masses that beings from another world had taken them back to a planet in the Andromeda Galaxy, as a part of a cultural and educational exchange. People were led to believe that someday, those people would come back here to impart the great knowledge they were gaining in that far away world.

Since becoming a follower of Christ, Wallace had made it his mission to tell the world that there was a reason they were all still here on Earth, but that there was still hope for them. He had shared videos with the world from various locations as he and Olivia tried to stay ahead of the authorities, making it his goal to tell the whole world that Paolino Esposito was not a righteous man. He was a man who was leading many to their eternal doom.

Wallace and his friends had become adept at recording, these video warnings, and posting them online for the world to hear and share with others. His works were becoming viral messages that had helped to bring many people to Christ.

Wallace, Olivia, Mohammed, and Ibrahim had managed to stay away from authorities that wanted to harm them.

Wallace spoke words of comfort to his wife, "Don't worry, Liv, our little boy will someday be able to live without fear in a world ruled by the King of Kings. There will be no more fear.

Vito Lombardo entered the Jerusalem hotel suite of Lord Esposito, carrying an expandable folder. It contained the latest reports of security issues involving the Christian movement in Ohio.

"My Lord, the small enclaves in Plainfield, and Dresden, Ohio have been eliminated. Nearly all the surviving members of those pockets of resistance have been imprisoned. They have been given the opportunity to recognize you as Lord. Thus far, none of them have chosen to accept our offer of life. They were quickly beheaded when they refused."

Esposito had been listening intently as he slowly carved slices of cheese and apple. He eyed Lombardo without emotion he asked, "And what about Wallace? Have you seen what he has just posted on that ridiculous video log he uses to discredit us? He is saying that I am not a righteous man. He said that I have wrapped myself in a cloak of righteousness that was completely meaningless. He said that I am fooling even myself as to my sense of justice. He has been trying to undermine my leadership for too long. What has happened to him and his cohorts? I need to have him captured and executed. We cannot allow this to continue. I need for you to convey to General Penzone that this must be a top priority. I put him in charge of North American security specifically so he would capture and stop Wallace." With each utterance, Esposito's voice became louder, until he was shrieking at Lombardo.

Lombardo tried to sound confident, "My Lord, I have already increased the reward for information leading to the arrest and conviction of Robert Wallace, Mohammed Zacharius, Ibrahim Soliman, and Olivia Wallace. I am convinced that someone will come forward for the joy of gaining great wealth."

Robert and Olivia Wallace stood over the crib of their new son. They had decided to name him Joshua Paul Wallace. They had heard news reports of the fall of the Christian camps in Dresden and Plainfield, Ohio. The media reported that the sites were encampments of rebellious enemies of the state.

One of the leaders there was the namesake for their son. J.P. Dickerson had given his life for others, that they might be saved through Christ. He had worked tirelessly keeping the faith alive and had also made sure that Robert and Olivia could escape from those who would do them harm. J.P. had remained strong in the faith even in the face of overwhelming odds.

Wallace looked into the eyes of his son, "God bless you, sweet boy. You have been named for a great man and dedicated to God and His service."

He wiped a tear from his eye, turned to his wife and kissed her hands. He left the room to continue preparing his latest report to the people. Wallace was not sure if his messages were being heard by anyone. They had kept moving for so long and been unable to hear any feedback on listenership. There was no Nielson or Arbitron ratings system for what he was doing, though now and then he was able to see how many people had decided to "Like" his page. He assumed that the message of Christ was getting through despite attempts by the forces of Rome trying to stop him. He could only believe that people were coming to Christ because of the truth he was sharing. He also presumed that he was still a highly sought "enemy of the state" and was still being hunted.

Mohammed Zacharius and Ibrahim Soliman were preparing their small room for the next recording.

They would record their message, upload it to the internet, pack up everything and move on, trying to avoid leaving any traces of their world behind. They had traveled from Ohio, with stops in southern Indiana and eastern Illinois, before moving to their current location in Abilene, Kansas. Abilene was the childhood home of President Dwight Eisenhower. It was under Eisenhower's administration that the U.S. officially adopted "In God We Trust" as the national motto. Times and presidents had certainly changed since those days of the mid nineteen fifties. Presidents had come and gone, and there was a slow erosion of the dedication to God that America had claimed for so much of her history.

Slowly the United States drifted far from God. Even those who claimed to be believers gave in to beliefs that allowed for people to be pulled away from God. The message of the ancient teachings was watered down, and those who tried to stay close to the true teachings were made to feel as though they were not important. Their beliefs were explained away as being unenlightened in the modern world. Being marginalized into the category of unenlightened kept many people from even exploring the possibility that Christ was the Son of God or that he had been more than just a good teacher.

Within the church, many scholars decided that about ninety percent of what had been believed to be quotes of Jesus were merely misquotes, at best. So many of the traditional teachings of Jesus were being questioned. It was said most of those teachings were not really things that he had said. Scholars were claiming most of the sayings of Jesus had been added to the Bible long after Jesus and the Disciples had passed from this life.

Many people even went so far as to say that Jesus didn't really die on the cross and therefore, had not risen from the dead. Beliefs such as this had drastically cut back on church attendance in much of the world. However, church leaders in Africa remained strong and fought hard against what was being taught in the United States. It was ironic that European nations and the United States had sent most of the Christian missionaries into what had been considered the heathen world. Now, all those "civilized" nations had become heathen in their beliefs. The Church in Africa remained strong, and for quite a few years was able to keep American churches from straying completely away from the teachings of the Bible.

Inside a command trailer in Jerusalem, General Andriolli Penzone watched over the shoulder of one of his drone operators. The woman deftly guided the camera which picked up a small amount of activity outside a farm building in Kansas, USA. This temporary command post had been set up by the Israeli government at the request of Lord Esposito.

A Kansas farmer had called the tip line saying that he thinks he had seen the fugitives being sought by the government of Lord Esposito. The farm next to his had been abandoned. The owner and family had been taken to the Andromeda Galaxy as a part of the exchange two years before. The excitement in his voice at the prospect of having all his debts cancelled by the empire was intense. "General, my drone cannot pick up heat signatures from inside the farmhouse. We have a hunter-killer drone one hundred and fifty miles away equipped with a camera which can not only see inside a building, but it also has the capability to tap into any internet or local networks within that house. If, indeed, the target is in that building or any building nearby, we will know within the next thirty minutes."

She picked up her phone and called the operator in the next trailer. After confirming the location and giving the command to investigate her target, she turned to the general, "Sir, Bravo-21 will be able to confirm in a short time. When we confirm, you can give the command and we will totally neutralize the target."

Penzone had been searching for Wallace and his co-conspirators for weeks. He had always been a few hours behind them. "Finally, like the others, this small group of Christians will be transported to Hell. I want to make sure this time that we have them. Call Colonel Lombardo and tell him to join us. I want him to witness me doing what he should have accomplished more than a year and a half ago."

They watched as two people came out of the house and moved toward a barn approximately thirty yards away from the house. After only a moment or so, one more person exited the house and made its way to the barn also.

The drone operator told the general that the hunter-killer drone was now within ten minutes of the target.

With a devious smile on his face, Penzone quietly said, "Finally, Wallace, you are mine. In a few short minutes you will only be a memory in the minds of a few misguided people."

Colonel Lombardo entered the command trailer. He stopped and looked around the cramped quarters. There was a single chair next to the general. Penzone turned to Lombardo and beckoned him to sit next to him, "My dear Colonel Lombardo, in less than ten minutes you are about to see how we eliminate our enemies. There will be no one alive when we are finished."

Robert Wallace entered the barn where Ibrahim and Mohammed had set up their traveling studio. Just below the floor of the barn was a dairy cellar where the milk was gathered before shipping would take place. There was the desk with the white, blue, and red Christian flag to the left of the desk. The lights were set to go, the camera was on its tripod. Soon the one more message to the believers would be available. It was Wallace's hope that their labors would continue to inspire believers. He also hoped even more hearts could be encouraged to become followers of Christ.

Wallace spoke to his brothers, "I believe that the message we deliver today will be one of the most important. We will point out the folly of believing that Esposito is the savior of the world. The new temple they are about to build will quickly be defiled by Esposito. The Bible tells us that he will seek to be worshiped there by the multitudes of Jews. Worshipers will be thronging to see their new holy site rising. This miracle is something that Jews had awaited since being scattered the world over less than eighty years into the Common Era."

Needing to retrieve the final draft of his script from his bed-side table he departed the barn. Ibrahim and Mohammed knelt next to the desk, joined hands, and began to pray. Without completing their prayer time, Mohammed interrupted the reverie, "My brother, I am sensing that we must quickly leave this barn to a storm shelter. I feel there is an attack coming and we must move quickly."

They both stood and quickly crossed to the stairs that led back up to the main floor of the barn. Ibrahim went ahead of Mohammed as a loud explosion shattered the peace of the day.

Inside the house, Wallace jumped on top of his wife and child pushing them to the floor next to the bed. He reached to pull the mattress on top of them. A flash of hot, intense light accompanied an explosion so loud that all other sounds were drowned out immediately. The house and the barn both collapsed around their inhabitants.

In Jerusalem, the image on the screens showed the violence of a pair of massive explosions. No one in those structures could have survived. Lombardo was elated at what he was seeing, until Penzone began to berate his prior work, "If you were really good at your job, what you see happening here would have happened two years ago."

Lombardo had trouble disguising his disdain for this other-worldly man. Never had anything like this ever happened to him. Lombardo began to question his purpose in life. He had been a soldier, a policeman, a security expert and more. Now he felt completely lost.

Lombardo's mind went back to when he first joined the police force in Napoli. He was an idealistic rookie. He was a new rising star in the department. In his first year he quickly advanced from a rookie who could outrun any perp to being touted as a future leader on the force. He was so proud of his dedication to duty, and as the years went by, he progressed through the ranks to Chief Commissioner.

He was then recruited by French businessman Albert Le Roux, who paid him more money than Lombardo dreamed possible during his days as an Agent in the Napoli Police Department. Now he was still Chief of Security, not only for Le Roux Enterprises, but also a respected leader for Lord Paolino Esposito. He had fallen out of favor because of the American, Robert Wallace who had continuously been able to evade capture.

The crying baby sounded as though it was trapped in a heavily insulated padded room. Wallace's ears were ringing, and the aroma of burnt wood and explosive material filled his nostrils. Struggling to regain some control over his body, he was trying to rise from the rubble that covered him and his wife and child. The sound of little J.P.'s screams sounded distant, yet Wallace knew that his son and wife had been with him under the mattress, which had formed a sheltered lean-to beside the bed. Several boards from the rafters as well as bricks from the near-by fireplace were on top of the mattress.

He was just beginning to regain control of his arms and legs, and he pushed upward with his back, moving the debris on top of him. He carefully knelt back down and cradled his son in his arms. "It's okay Buddy. Daddy's got you. Daddy's got you. Oh… Jesus, help us, please help us."

Olivia began to cough, and she spoke with a raspy rattle. Her eyes were open wide, staring in fear at the horror scattered around the room.

Wallace managed to stand. Brushing splinters out of his hair he spoke, unaware that he was actually shouting, "Liv, are you alright? I don't know what happened, but I think we survived an attack from the air. They know where we are."

Unencumbered by walls that were no longer in the way, he scanned across the barnyard to where his friends had been preparing to record a last message to his followers on social media. The barn that was to be their studio was all but gone. Only a few upright boards where there had been walls stood testimony to the desolation that had taken place. The smoldering wreckage showed just how dreadful the attack had been.

Wallace wondered if Ibrahim and Mohammed were still alive, and if the attackers were still flying overhead.

He had to try to make it to the now destroyed barn. He noticed that the three Weeping Willow Trees suffered extraordinarily little damage. He knew that it was probably futile trying to locate the drones overhead, but looking skyward, he dashed quickly from tree to tree, staying mainly under the rich, full branches.

The smoldering ruins smelled of gun powder and Wallace's hope of finding his friends alive began to fade away. He could hear moaning coming from the stairway to the Milk Room below the barn floor. He was quickly dodging around the debris.

Even though he had steeled himself for the possibility of being shocked at the aftermath of battle, he was not prepared for what he saw as he investigated the stairway. There at the foot of the stairs lay the body of Ibrahim. He had a long two by four sticking straight up from his chest. Mohammed was lying nearby moaning in pain with his right arm severed at the shoulder. If he hadn't been lying on his right side, he might have bled to death.

Wallace rushed to Mohammed. Offering comfort might be the only thing he could do at this point. Mohammed smiled, and reached his still good arm toward Wallace. "My brother, I see Jesus reaching to me. He has Ibrahim next to him. I am not in pain, but I will soon be completely free."

Wallace was in denial, "No. I won't let you die. I need you to help me get the important message out to the world."

"It's alright. You can't compete with Jesus. Are Olivia and J.P. alright?"

Wallace reached to touch Mohammed's forehead, "Yes. Minor injuries. Mainly inhaled dust and debris making it hard to breathe, but okay, otherwise."

"Jesus is now reaching both hands to me. I'm going to take his hand now. Take care of your family. Stay strong in your faith. I will see you again when we return behind our Savior. But I must go now." Coughing violently, and with his voice rattling, Mohammed finally said, "I will see you in heaven. Be blessed…"

As Mohammed's voice trailed off Wallace took hold of his hand, "Oh, Jesus… bless Mohammed and Ibrahim. Jesus, please help me to protect my family."

CHAPTER 31

A smug General Andriolli Penzone leaned back in his chair. He had left the command center and had returned to his hotel suite. Finally, the problem of Robert Wallace had been eliminated. The images downloaded from the killer drone reassured him that no one could have survived the attack.

He summoned his attaché, "Bring me Colonel Lombardo. And while you're at it, bring me the surveillance photos of the attack in Kansas."

Penzone lit a cigar and laughed out loud as the thick gray smoke wafted around his head. The attaché returned to the suite and reported, "The Colonel is not in his suite, General. His assistant was unsure of his location."

"How can that be? I have made it clear that I want to know where the Colonel is at all times. He is fully aware of that. Give the order to locate him and bring him to me. I will have no insubordination among these humans. They are to be fully controlled."

The attaché departed, leaving Penzone to contemplate the possibility of a mutiny among the ranks. He must not let that happen.

As Paolino Esposito had been sharing his plans for the third Jewish Temple in Jerusalem, word came to him that there were some leaders among the Arab countries that were not going to agree with a peace plan in exchange for the new Temple. One of the roadblocks was the Israeli technology for fully autonomous electric modes of transportation. For the past three decades, Israeli scientists had been developing rechargeable batteries and small solar cells that could fully re-charge the massive batteries.

They had overcome the problems of plugging electric vehicles into wall outlets, utilizing fossil fuels to produce the electricity for recharging the batteries. They had now produced fully electric cars, trucks, trains, and they were now on the verge of perfecting an electric jet powered airliner that never need an outside power source. Batteries in all these were recharged using the wind from airflow, and additional solar electric.

Israel was now the wealthiest and most powerful nation on earth. Her Arab neighbors and many other nations of the world had become jealous of Israel's success. Demands were being made that Israel must give up the technology, make massive financial remuneration to the rest of the world, and peacefully begin construction on the long awaited Third Temple.

Esposito had summoned his old friend, Pope Cephas to join him to discuss this snag in their near perfect plan.

Using the Pope's given first name, Esposito addressed him in a familiar way, "Nunzio, we have much to discuss this day. Please sit down."

"You truly are a great leader, Paolino, but as we continue on from this point, I must demand that you address me as 'Your Holiness'. I am the leader of the church which is the underpinning to your great power and wealth. I may use your first name, but I must insist that my position and power be recognized for what it is."

Somewhat taken aback by this challenge to his position, Esposito acquiesced to the request, "Yes… Your Holiness, please forgive my informality. You are correct, though. We must continue to show the world who we really are. You are the leader of my church, and you are also the one who was able to channel the power that healed me a few years ago of a terrible wound."

The two men sat down on opposite sides of a coffee table that contained not only a tea service, but also stacks of official papers that Esposito had been studying. He looked at his notations on the papers and continued, "Your Holiness, I have found within the Israeli government one leader who is willing to agree to our demands of payments to the Arab nations. This would assure a seamless transition to clearing the property needed to erect a new temple building in Jerusalem. The City of David, as it had been known for centuries, must be seen as the true location for the new temple. This man, Shlomo bar Davidje is willing to see to it that Israel allows up to fifty percent of the income from the battery technology will go to the leaders of all the surrounding Arab-speaking nations."

As the two men were speaking, a courier entered the room with a message for Esposito. Esposito read the message and smiled slightly as he delivered the news to the Pope.

"Your Holiness, it appears that Robert Wallace, his wife and the two Muslim converts to Christianity have fallen victim to one of our Grim Reaper Unmanned Arial Vehicles. It appeared that they were hiding on a farm in rural Abilene, Kansas. General Andriolli Penzone personally carried out my orders to end the life of Wallace and anyone near him."

Pope Cephas laughed out loud, "Finally! How were you able to locate them?"

Esposito lit a cigar. He gave a long celebratory pull on it dragging the smoke deep into his lungs. As the smoke swirled around his head he said, "Now that Wallace is gone, our future is unencumbered."

Robert Wallace and his wife and child traveled for two weeks using back roads and staying off the grid until they reached the tiny town of Cambria, California. As they reached California, they found that the information they had been given in the previous years, was now outdated. Finding fellow believers for shelter and supplies was becoming a more difficult task.

Many of the western enclaves of believers had been discovered and eradicated by the government of Rome. The United States had finally finished its long descent into the throes of death. At one time America had sent out missionaries and secular relief organizations to the world, with the common goal of improving the lives of individuals everywhere. America had gone from being a beacon of hope to the world, to a stagnate pool of corruption in business, politics and even in religion.

The Christian Church has fallen on hard times just as it had in Europe at the end of World War II. It took longer for America to fall because many people tried to stop the long slide. But just as in ancient Rome, America finally fell silent as a force for good, and then slipped away. When Paolino Esposito came to power, The United States of America was on life support.

Before the phenomenon of "The Missing" happened, Christian believers boldly spoke up against the evil that was becoming so prevalent in America. They were finally silenced by government edicts and legislation that became the law of the land. Too many Christians didn't know enough about their faith to speak up, and therefore, were too shy to speak out because of fear of embarrassment.

It was near Cambria, California that the Wallace family found an encampment near San Simeon. It was in the shadow of William Randolph Hearst's castle, that a group of believers were able to stay hidden away. It was ironic that the vast tract of land once owned by a man whose life had been lived seeking his own pleasure and luxury, would become a center for sharing and memorizing the words of the Holy Bible.

It was true in the mid Twentieth Century that the newspapers owned by Hearst had played a large role in promoting the early ministry of evangelist Billy Graham. They promoted news stories about the popularity of Graham's crusades and tent revivals. It was not totally clear whether those who were currently in charge of the property were in favor of Christianity or were just living with a "live and let live" attitude to the one hundred or so people who resided there.

Wallace and Olivia arrived near sunset on a Sunday at the vast hillside tourist destination overlooking the Pacific Ocean. As they exited the borrowed car, Wallace looked out at the beautiful view of the sun setting into the glassy sea. It was beautiful. His first thought was the description in Revelation 4:6 of the awesome sight seen by John as he described it; "Also in front of the throne there was what looked like a sea of glass, clear as crystal. In the center, around the throne, were four living creatures, and they were covered with eyes, in front and in back."

There laid out before him was one of the grandest sights he had ever seen, "How beautiful that is. I see the Bible's sea of glass in front of the throne of God."

Olivia drew in a large breath of the fresh air and agreed with her husband. As she carried the baby around the back of the car, the dried grass at the edge of the parking lot crunched under her feet. She stood next to her husband as he instinctively reached around her shoulders to pull her and the baby closer to him. She spoke, "Truly, God has blessed us with this sign that we'll be alright soon."

They both became aware that a security Jeep was approaching their location in the nearly empty parking lot. The lone uniformed man stopped a good thirty feet from the Wallace vehicle. He slowly climbed out of the vehicle carrying a clipboard, and with his hand on a night stick slung on belt, he walked cautiously toward them.

"Sorry folks, the Castle is closed for the evening. I don't know how you missed reading the sign's listing of the park's hours. I'm gonna have to have you get back into your car, head back into town and try to find a room."

Wallace nodded, and held up his right hand in a passive wave. "Hi, we just finished a long day on the road and were told by friends that there was a place here that we could stay. A man named Silas is supposed to take in travelers at the end of the day."

The guard's head slowly swiveled as he looked around the parking lot. He then looked at Wallace and Olivia. He perceived no threat and then removed his hand from the handle of his night stick. "You folks come here by way of Damascus?"

They had heard that there was now a series of codes when seeking fellow believers, that working "Damascus" into a conversation was one of the ways to let people know that you were a follower of Christ. Response words were then listened for closely.

Olivia quickly spoke as she cautiously glanced from the guard to Wallace and then back to the guard, "Yes sir, we were told by Ananias that there would be people here who could help us as we traveled. Our baby needs food and we are very tired after a long day's travel."

Once again, the guard nervously looked around. It could very well be a trap, but he stepped out in faith and responded to her, "Sister, it has been a long time since anyone has been sent to us by Ananias. We are happy to take you in. Just turn around and go back down the road. On the other side of the highway, you'll see a little cluster of old buildings near the pier. Look for a sign outside one that says, 'Life Road'. It is there you'll meet a lady named Miriam. Tell her that the man from Tarsus sent you. She'll help you."

Robert and Olivia returned to their car and slowly began to leave the parking lot going back down the long driveway to Highway 1. It was interesting that the code words that had become so prevalent in their travels were all names and places from the book of Acts. They felt assured that the people they were meeting with truly were believers, as these names and places were not as likely to be well known by members of Esposito's security forces. However, they remained tentatively cautious.

On the west side of Highway 1, there was a cluster of buildings that had seen better days. They were used mainly for storage these days. There was a small café called "Life Way" that advertised its specialty of fresh fish sandwiches and fries. There was a marking next to the description of the sandwich where at one time, many years ago, a price was listed. It had been scratched out and the number "10" was neatly written, along with the sign of the Roman monetary value that was to be charged to the customer's account.

Wallace pulled into one of the few parking spaces that lined the narrow-paved road. As he parked the car, he took Olivia's hand and said a quick prayer that they had found friends among strangers.

As he exited the car, a pleasant looking middle-aged lady was eyeing them through the curtains in the front window. Wallace climbed the four steps to the wooden porch and entered. Inside it looked like it must have looked in the 1930s when these buildings were built. The floors were hardwood, and at the long counter were tall swivel stools. There were small tables with antique chairs lined along the windows, with a view of the other old buildings, and a partial view of the Pacific Ocean.

The lady in the window moved from behind the counter and spoke in the friendly manner one would expect from the waitress in a small friendly café, "You folks been traveling long?"

Wallace answered just as he had so many times when meeting strangers. He needed to know if he was speaking to friendly people, or to people who were on the lookout for those poor misguided people who had become Christians in the past few years.

"Good evening. Is Miriam here?"

"That'd be me. What can I do for you?"

"The man from… Tarsus said we could find some assistance from you."

An even warmer smile crossed Miriam's face. She invited him to usher his wife into the café and seated them at the table near the door.

Olivia had already taken little Joshua Paul out of his car seat and was making her way to the steps when her husband opened the door and stepped onto the porch. His smile let her know that they had come to the right place.

Wallace ushered his wife and son into the café and motioned toward the table by the front window. Miriam was quickly carrying a sturdy wooden highchair to the table. "How ya doin', Hon? I gather you folks have been on the road for quite a while. Let me fix you some good food, and then we can see what else we can do for you here at San Simeon."

In a short while the three of them were sharing their experiences navigating this new world. A world that was making it incredibly difficult to publicly be a Christian. For the past twenty years Christianity had been looked upon as a collection of superstitions that the truly enlightened no longer needed for everyday life.

"We here in San Simeon have been able to find shelter and relative safety from government intrusion on the castle property. It's been a haven for the past couple of years. We have been able to worship together. Most of us were not really Christians, but many of us were seeing what was being done to believers, and felt it was not right. We believed that people have a right to believe what they want to believe. There are several former "nature worshipers" in our group who now worship the Creator instead of the creation."

Olivia nodded as she answered, "I used to be a Criminal Prosecutor in New York City. Bobby, here, was a journalist with the Central News Agency based in New York. Neither of us had spent much time in churches, but we too began to question the legality of preventing people from believing what they honestly believe. We soon found ourselves running from the law because of our beliefs."

Miriam had been watching Robert closely as Olivia shared about their lives, "Wait a minute. You look familiar. Are you Robert Wallace?"

"Yes, he said, "I'm now a wanted man."

"No, you're not. Not anymore. We have been heartbroken for the past few weeks. There were reports that you had been killed in a drone attack somewhere in Kansas."

"What?" Olivia's eyes were wide with surprise.

"Yes, it's true. The news reported that the religious rebel Robert Wallace was killed along with his wife and son. Two former Muslim terrorists were said to have died with you in the attack."

Wallace looked down at his hands, then glanced out the window, "Mohammed and Ibrahim were our brothers in Christ. They each came to know Him through dreams. They both were invaluable helpers to me as I made my internet Video Blogs. I couldn't have done it without them. They both were able to step into heaven as true martyrs for the faith in that drone attack. I miss them terribly."

"I'm sorry for your loss. We have not lost anyone here since the heavy persecution began. We have one hundred fellow believers with us. We grow our own food and hunt for meat in the surrounding hills. We have even been allowed to kill one Bison per year for meat and its hide. Just like the natives that once inhabited this land, we make use of the entire animal for food and shelter. And as you can see out there, we have an abundance of fish available to us. We are able to avoid being marked with the microchip that the rest of the world has had to take under the Roman government."

Wallace stood and walked to the front door. Looking out across the street he could see all the way to the end of the long pier, "That's a rather long pier. It looks like you could moor fishing boats there."

"Perhaps we could, but that might draw unwanted attention. I'm the highest profile member of our fellowship. My position here at the café allows me to talk with travelers and find out what's going on without hearing it on the news. Your Video Blog reports were prized by us because we knew we were getting news reported by a fellow believer. I can't wait to share with the rest that you are alive." It was obvious that Miriam was sincere when she said that.

"For obvious reasons, I don't let it be known to those passing through that we have people staying in those hills up there."

Wallace turned back to her and asked, "Have you heard anything interesting in the news lately? The last thing I heard was that Esposito had talked the Jews and the Muslims in Jerusalem into believing that Solomon's Temple was not on the same property that is now occupied by the Muslim shrines on the Temple Mount."

Miriam nodded in agreement, "Yes, I've heard the same story. Esposito and his people are being hailed as miracle workers in bringing about peace for the first time in history. The fight over that piece of real estate has lasted for so many centuries. If what they are now saying is true, what a sad situation that so many have died for what they believed at the time was worthy of a fight."

The Kremlin building in Moscow was now peaceful. Only eight hours earlier, Vladimir Lenin Korsakov, the grandson of a former KGB commander had led a coup toppling the teetering government that had been in power for nearly two decades.

The Russian people were not happy that Moscow had agreed to follow Paolino Esposito's Roman government.

Korsakov had grown up listening to his grandfather's stories about the glory days of Mother Russia under Soviet rule. His grandfather had always said it was because Russia had become weak and needed to regain her prominence as a world leader. The trouble, Korsakov had learned, started when the Soviet leadership had allowed the United States and other democracies to dictate what would become of the Communist nation. The long Cold War had ended because no one had the strength to stand up to the power of America and such European nations as Great Britain.

Young Korsakov felt that only strong leadership from someone like himself could bring Russia back to the glory days of the Great Patriotic War of the 1940s. Korsakov had been taught that Russia had stood alone against the Axis Powers during World War II. Russian school children had learned that only after Josef Stalin coerced the United States and Britain into attacking Germany's western positions in France, that Germany began to weaken and then fall to the mighty Soviet military. It was time for a strong leader such as himself to take control.

Korsakov stood before the Security Council. The din of voices grew quiet as he raised his hands in a victorious gesture, 'Comrades. Tonight, begins a new life for Mother Russia. Tonight, we return to the glory of a powerful nation, feared by the world. The traitorous former leaders have been executed for their treasonous acts of selling away our birthright to follow the leadership of a man who has only visited Moscow once in his life. Paolino Esposito knows nothing of living through the Russian winter. That winter that has saved us from conquering armies many times in the past. The Russian winter stopped Napoleon and led to his downfall. The Russian winter stopped Hitler and led to his downfall. The Russian winter and its power also kept the United States from ever contemplating a land invasion into our beloved country."

The audience erupted into thunderous applause as he continued, "Now it is time for us to reestablish our place in the world. This man, Esposito, must learn that true power comes from a nation with the willingness to take what it needs by force."

CHAPTER 32

This day was six months in the making. Dignitaries lined the dais as rabbis and citizens of Jerusalem mingled together near the giant altar. The gleaming Third Jewish Temple towered over the courtyard, surrounding the altar.

Twelve Cardinals representing the Vatican waited outside the courtyard to show respect for the truly Jewish ceremony that was to take place. However, even though he was a Gentile, Paolino Esposito had received special permission to stand on the dais along with the High Priest and other priests and rabbis. He took great pride in the fact that he had brought together opposing sides allowing the building project to be expedited and finished in record time. Giant stones were transported from quarries all around Israel and Palestine. With the help of modern cranes and tools, the walls went up within two- and one-half months. The rest of the time was spent putting the finishing touches on the Sanctuary.

The Red Heifer was then taken outside the Temple gates and slaughtered. The first sacrifice to be made in the new House of God. The people were dancing about and playing traditional ancient instruments that would have been used in worship at least two millennia ago. Television coverage was world-wide with large audiences in Europe and North America, even though most Jews of the world had long since emigrated to Israel. It was the news story of the century.

Paolino Esposito very proudly surveyed the scene. He had displayed god-like skills in bringing about the agreement that ended all the fighting between the Arabs and the Jews. He had the backing of every person of influence in the world.

Esposito leaned toward Pope Cephas and whispered, "It is so wonderful to have my dreams come true. I have brought about something that no man in history has been able to accomplish. Truly God has installed me to be His representative here on Earth."

The Pope looked over the entire scene as well. He nodded in agreement, "Lord Paolino, I have been able to bring so many people into your realm of influence. It is true that the people are beginning to see you as the true Messiah. I believe that even the Jews will soon see that you are to be praised."

The din reached a fever pitch as the High Priest stepped to the blazing altar. He dipped his right index finger into the chalice of blood that he gripped tightly with his left hand. He sprinkled the blood of the Heifer seven times on the steps of the Temple. He turned and motioned toward the main gate as the leader of the attendants began throwing the dead animal upon the altar. Just as directed in the book of Numbers 9:1-10, harkening back to the days of the Tabernacle in the Wilderness. God had given specific instructions for the Heifer sacrifice. As the animal burned, the High Priest continued following the specific instructions, throwing some Cedar wood, hyssop, and scarlet wool onto the burning calf.

When the ceremony ended, the High Priest went to his quarters. He washed his clothes and ceremonially bathed, though he would remain "unclean" until evening. The man who had thrown the Heifer on the altar also followed the instructions and washed his clothes and bathed. One of the attendants who was still ceremonially clean gathered all the ashes. He carried them in a large jar to the edge of the city and placed them in a prepared area. The ashes would be used later in purifying washing and cleansing from sin.

Esposito thought of how wonderful this entire ceremony was. He took it as a personal gift from the Jewish people to him and the accomplishments that allowed this amazing day to happen. National leaders have spent centuries trying to bring peace to this volatile region. Even when the people were able to share the land, there were national and religious leaders who stirred the pot of trouble for their own gain.

The growing enclave of Christ followers in San Simeon, California now numbered nearly five hundred. Robert and Olivia Wallace had moved into a small two room cabin. They excitedly watched their son Joshua Paul walking around both rooms of the little house. His confidence was growing as he avoided hitting his head on the edge of the bookshelf.

The cool morning air was flowing in off the beautiful Pacific. As was always the case, the Marine Layer of air brought a thick fog across Highway 1. The fog usually cleared by mid-day, but it's always a pleasant start to a beautiful early summer day.

Olivia came out of the bedroom, ready to face another day of chores around the encampment. Hearst Castle was on an opposite hill from the cabins. Olivia had begun working as a Docent at the Castle along with others from the camp. Robert worked in the library researching the history of the journalism of William Randolph Hearst's news empire. He also was keeping up with the daily news coming in from around the world.

As Robert watched the television coverage of the dedication of the Third Temple in Jerusalem, he pondered with some excitement that this was one of the signs that the days were growing short until the day of Christ's return. He had long noted that Paolino Esposito was showing more and more self-pride in his accomplishment of bringing about peace. Many people were beginning to conjecture that Esposito's accomplishments in uniting the world in peace and prosperity, he surely must be like a god.

Rumors abounded that Esposito's long-time friend, Pope Cephas was hinting that because of his leadership, Lord Esposito truly had god-like powers. There was also speculation that Esposito had been able to perform healing miracles on a scale reminiscent of his own return from the dead.

Wallace was anxious to return to the world of journalism. He had discussed with Olivia many times that the end was drawing near. He wanted to be there to report the news in a way that would help more people come to know Christ as Savior. His studies had shown him that there was more to the everyday news stories than was being reported. The signs were pointing to the imminent return of Christ. The world's media was beginning to anoint Esposito with the mantel of Messiah. Wallace wanted the world to know that Esposito was certainly not the Messiah.

With J.P. in her arms, Olivia entered the media room and found her husband had returned to his files. The television was still on in the background, but the volume had been lowered. She put the toddler down and he walked to his daddy with open arms. His beaming daddy leaned forward to lift his son to his lap.

"What's going on, little guy? Is Mommy going to take you to work with her today?"

Olivia smiled, "No, I have the day off. There's some activity at the main gate of the Castle today. Miriam has come up the hill from the diner with what looks like a possible new member to our community."

"Somebody from Cambria, or Morro Bay?"

"No. I don't know where he came from. But she told someone that he has been on the run for almost a year now. She said the man is very attuned to what is happening today."

Wallace was interested. Finding out what has been going on has been a goal of his. Learning from someone who has been out in the real world while he and his family had been in hiding could prove to be valuable.

The new arrival to the camp checked in with the security team at the main dining hall. "My name's Vincent Lonelli. I have been trying to find a place like this. I think I'll be able to relax and not worry about the people in Rome finding me here."

He was greeted by Jo Anne Collins. She welcomed him with a pleasant smile, "Mr. Lonelli, you're just in time for lunch. Our morning Bible Study group should be taking a break at any time now. You'll be able to meet some of the folks who call San Simeon home."

People were beginning to enter the dining hall for lunch. The aroma of roast beef wafted through the room. Light-hearted laughter filled the dining hall.

Vincent Lonelli looked at the faces of the residents. They did not seem to have any cares. These people mingled together in a close-knit group. In the past year he had met more Christians than he had in the previous forty years of his life. He had always held them in low esteem for their seemingly twisted view of the rest of the world. They had always been people who, in his opinion, had a low opinion of everyone else. Lonelli had always thought of Christians as people who were always ready to pass judgment on everyone around them, but not noticing their own shortcomings. Human nature being what it has always been, even those who had claimed to follow Christ were still prone to the same shortcomings as the rest of humanity.

This new community at the Central Coast of California seemed different than many he had met in the past. But no matter how enthralled he was becoming with this group of people; he knew that he had a task that must be completed. His eyes continued to scan the room, looking for someone. He had been following leads for nearly a year, and those leads had brought him here. If he did not find what he was seeking here in San Simeon, he knew that he must continue his journey.

Robert and Olivia had arrived at the same time as the morning Bible Study group. Olivia held little J.P. close as she walked across the room. Finding one of the highchairs, she proceeded to a table near the kitchen entrance. Lonelli found Olivia in the tightly packed crowd and immediately scanned the rest of the crowd with a new urgency. If this was not Olivia Wallace, she could pass for her twin sister. Only a few seconds after spotting Olivia, there he was - Robert Wallace - the man who was one of the most wanted men in the world for the past three years. It was Wallace who, it was said, had personally blown up an airliner over the North Atlantic and forced a crash landing in Iceland killing so many people. It was Wallace who had led authorities on a long chase across the country while sharing a message of the love of God in Christ. Many people who had begun to find hope in Lord Paolino Esposito, had turned away from him, thanks to the urgings of Robert Wallace. A villain to those in power, Wallace was a liberator to so many others. It was because of the Webcasts of Robert Wallace that Lonelli had begun to question his own loyalty to the New World Order.

He crossed the room to where the Wallaces were seated, as Jo Anne Collins made the introductions.

"Mr. Lonelli, this is Robert Wallace, his wife Olivia and their son, J.P."

"Pleased to meet you Mr. Wallace. Robert Wallace. That name is familiar. Have we ever met before this? You're awfully familiar to me."

Jo Anne made the quick explanation for Lonelli, 'You probably have seen Mr. Wallace on his Web reports. He explains how current events were predicted more than two thousand years ago in the Bible."

"Yes, maybe that's it. Maybe that's what is so familiar about you, Mr. Wallace. At any rate, it's a pleasure to meet you."

Wallace stood and shook hands with Lonelli. As their eyes met, Wallace also had that feeling of familiarity with Lonelli. Where had they met before? Over the length of his career in journalism, Wallace had met so many people, from heads of state to journalism interns just making their way into the business.

After the introductions were complete, Jo Anne led Lonelli to another table near the entrance to the dining hall and made more introductions. All the while, Lonelli continued to steal looks toward the Wallace table. This was it. He was sure of it. This was the man he had been seeking for all this time.

Daniel Schaffer

Sundown Friday in Jerusalem saw the end of the first full week of ceremonial activities at the newly dedicated temple. The priests and rabbis were all growing weary from the activity. Many perfect, first-born male animals had shed their blood for the sins of the people of Jerusalem. The aroma of char-broiled beef and lamb filled the air. It was a reminder of what it must have been like when the practice of animal sacrifice had begun in the wilderness. It was a reminder of the verses in Leviticus that spoke to the people telling them that the aroma was pleasing to the nostrils of God. The meat from the sacrifice was to be used by the priests for their food. One could only imagine what that first temple and this temple were to the people. Jews the world over were ecstatic over the possibility that the prophesies of Scripture would usher in the long-awaited Messiah.

Most of the foreign dignitaries had long since returned to their homes. Paolino Esposito and his long-time friend Pope Cephas were still in Jerusalem. They basked in the adulation of the people who were so very pleased. Esposito had finally brought about peace in their country at the same time Esposito had knocked down all the walls that had been preventing the Third Temple from being built. There was no more opposition from the leaders of the world's many Muslims. The loudest voices of protest against the temple had been placated by the deal which had enriched their leaders.

Israeli technology was on the verge of creating fully self-charging transportation batteries for cars, trucks, trains, and airplanes.

For the past five years, Israel had become the number one world economy. They owned the expertise for batteries that needed absolutely no fossil fuels to charge them. There were solar cells so small that they were hardly noticeable on a vehicle. They were also practically indestructible. Wash after wash would not harm the protective finish on the photocells. The batteries could quickly charge with enough power to drive a car from one end of Asia to another without needing to stop for re-charging the batteries.

Newer equipment was being developed that would charge the batteries using the motion of the wheels, coupled with small wind-powered generators in the grill of the cars. Experimental aircraft had already made flights halfway around the world without having to stop and re-fuel. It was an exciting time for the transportation industry and for the environment. Fossil fuels were no longer needed to power any means of transportation. Older vehicles were being refitted with the new batteries and electric motors. The air quality in major cities around the world was beginning to clear after decades of choking pollution.

The jealousy felt by Israel's neighbors was subsiding because of the treaty of tribute payments that were to be made by Israel. As was the case in so many years past, the leaders of these countries were becoming wealthier, while their subjects continued to live in squalor.

In the meetings in the hotel suites of Esposito and of the Pope, plans were being laid out for the near future. Esposito had told Cephas that he wanted the church to begin pointing out his own accomplishments to the worshipers. It was to be known that he, Paolino Esposito, had a divine appointment to save the world. He was proud of all he had achieved in the past few years.

As the meeting continued, Pope Cephas was seated in a large wing-back chair sipping a glass of Sherry, "My Lord, I will make sure that the newest prayer books will have your name prominently displayed as the reason for this newly peaceful world. You have done what you set out to do. The world economy is stronger than it has ever been. There is no longer any need for more than one form of financial currency, and the people are cared for from cradle to grave, no matter where they live. There is no longer any reason for anyone to be poor."

Esposito was more than a little smug in his reply, "My dear friend. I have accomplished so much of what we set out to do. We would sit in your study and plan how we would make the church a much better entity by taking better control over the people's understanding of the Bible. There is too much in those old Bibles that can lead people into thinking that God fits their own interpretation of who God is. There should be no more need for the people to look anywhere but to me for their daily living. Counseling sessions by the priests, should be cleared by me. I want you to write a new book of guidelines for the priests to follow. I will then, personally, edit the book. It will be used when needed to replace any scripture readings in worship services. We will see to it that the people will fully understand that I am here to take care of them. I am the anointed one. No one will be able to enter heaven without following my leadership. I will provide for all the people's needs. Please have this book completed and in the pulpit of every church around the world within six months. See to it."

"Yes, My Lord. It is a formidable task, but with your leadership, I shall accomplish it in less time than you have requested. The people will know that you are truly the Lord Esposito."

The two men each poured another sherry and toasted their new assignment. Truly their world was about to become the world they had always envisioned.

Vincent Lonelli stood on the hillside overlooking the Pacific Ocean. The morning fog had long since dissipated. He watched the birds swoop down low over the water and scoop up the smaller fish that had the unfortunate lack of judgement to stay deeper below the surface. Unfortunately for them they quickly became the next meal for the Gulls and Brown Pelicans that call this area home. Lonelli couldn't help but think of how the survival play he was watching was so much like his life had been. For so many years, he was a leader of men who had to follow his orders or succumb to punishment.

He had been on the road for more than a year, having fallen out of favor with his superiors. Perhaps he had been wrong to put his trust in other men, when truly he should be the only leader needed in his world.

He turned and stepped back into the tiny bungalow that had been assigned to him. These people didn't seem to be the horrible people he had been told they were.

"No, I have to stay strong and on course to regain my place in this world."

Stepping into his room, he looked in the mirror. His face showed more craggy lines than he had seen only a year ago. His fears of being arrested for desertion or dereliction of duty loomed over him. He now had a new hope. He would be hailed as a hero if he chose to return home. If he chose to stay here, he could become a leader among these people, simply because of his skills. They were all so gentle, it would not be long before he would become the leader of this little town.

Lonelli realized that Robert Wallace was the person who needed his full attention.

Levi Stoker, Jerusalem's High Priest, stood before the desk of Paolino Esposito in his hotel suite. He had been summoned to talk about future plans for the temple, and Esposito's wish to have access to the holy site. Even though he was truly a Gentile, he believed that because of all he had done for the Jewish people, he deserved to be allowed into the Sanctuary. Even though he had not yet expressed this wish to Stoker, he also wanted to be granted access to the Holy of Holies.

"Mr. Esposito. My people truly thank you for all you have done for us, but there are unwavering rules regarding who is allowed into our holy place of worship. You must be a Jew. You may worship with us in the Courtyard of the Gentiles. You may even witness the sacrifice of the animals, but I am afraid that I cannot permit you access to our holy sections of the temple. The Most High, bless His holy name, will not continue to bless Israel if I allow non-Jews into the Sanctuary."

Esposito did not try to mask his feelings, "My Dear Mr. Stoker. It is only because of my blessings that you and your people find yourselves worshiping in such a beautiful place. One day, you will change your mind. You will also see who does and who does not bless your worship services. I have given you so very much in the way of great blessings. I wish only to come in and speak to your men gathered to worship."

Stoker had tears streaming down his cheeks. It was obvious that he was trying so very hard to not displease God. At the same time, he knew that Esposito did indeed have the power to take away what he had given. Perhaps this man was special, and even though he was a Gentile, a special permission could be granted that would allow him access to the places heretofore granted only to devout Jews.

"Mr. Esposito, please allow me time to pray about this. I will also need to take it before the Sanhedrin. I am the seventy-ninth High Priest. I am a true Levite and I take my calling with great pride and am serious about properly carrying out my duties."

Esposito gave a slight smile, "Of course, I fully understand. I sometimes feel that after all the work I did to ensure the safety of Israel, and to get this temple built, I deserve to be allowed anywhere I please."

Both men stood silently for a moment before Esposito gave a slight wave of his hand and turned away from Stoker. The High Priest title was the most honored in all of Judaism, but at this moment, as Stoker left the room he felt as though he was only a bug being shooed away by the leader of the world.

The sun was setting over the Pacific. Olivia strolled back to her bungalow. She was the leader of one of the women's Bible Studies. There were three women's Bible Studies, and two men's groups, as well as a couple's study. Many of the members of the community had memorized the entire Bible. Many groups of believers had committed to memorizing the Bible because of the scarcity of Bibles around the country. Olivia had committed the entire New Testament to memory. They can take away the Bibles, but they can't erase God's Word in the memory.

Robert could recite the entire books of Daniel, Ezekiel, and Revelation. He had spent so much time studying the prophecy that it had become easy for him. This afternoon the men had been discussing the visions of Daniel, coupled with the visions of John in Revelation. There were so many parallels in the Scriptures. Even though the visions of Daniel and John on Patmos were them more than six hundred years apart when the men saw they were so very similar. God had spoken to each man and revealed his plan. That Prophecy told of a man who would come to rule the entire world, bringing

505

peace and prosperity for the first time in history. People would follow him and someday believe him to be God.

Jesus had warned in Matthew 24, that in the last days, someone would come on the scene and proclaim himself to be the Messiah.

Lonelli walked beside Wallace as they made their way back to their respective bungalows. He was still processing in his mind what was being taught in the Bible study, "So, what you're saying is this Paolino Esposito is the man that Daniel spoke about six hundred years before Christ?"

"All the signs point to that fact, yes. For the first time in history, we have a one world government, and a single monetary system. Also, the Church of Rome has shifted from centuries of being a Church of Christ, to a church that is teetering on the edge of proclaiming Esposito as lord of all."

Wallace stopped in front of Lonelli's bungalow, saying a quick prayer of blessing before going on his own way home.

This was almost too much for Lonelli to process. He had never heard of this before, outside of listening to the periodic podcasts in the past year. Even though he had been fighting it, he was seeing for himself that it could be true. That would mean leaving behind his entire life-long set of beliefs. He had attended church on Christmas and Easter, but was never a regular at

Sunday services. He occasionally attended Sunday blessings in Vatican Square since childhood. He had believed that all he did for his job in the military and law enforcement was his God-given duty to his country and church. He couldn't have been wrong. It just wasn't possible.

Lonelli was also concerned that Wallace had figured out his identity. He was going to have to decide on his next move.

Without going inside, he turned back to Robert Wallace. Calling out to him, "Mr. Wallace. Mr. Wallace, I need to tell you something important."

Wallace turned to Lonelli when he was a good twenty-five feet away, "It looks like we are thinking the same thing, aren't we?"

In a flat voice Lonelli responded, "Mr. Wallace, I need to speak with you."

"Your name isn't Lonelli, is it?"

Lonelli slowed his pace for a second or two before responding, "I believe that you and I are in similar positions. We need to have a few questions answered."

"I am sorry, Mr. Wallace. I have been pursuing you for more than a year. I have done much soul searching in that time. I am not happy with my life anymore.

Wallace thought it was good to know that the man who had pursued him for so long was seeking truth from the gospel.

Wallace had stopped at his front door. He paused with his hand on the knob. So much was going through his mind. After a few seconds he opened the door and called out, "Liv, I've got to take care of something. I'll be home in a little while."

"What's going on?"

"Someone from our past has caught up with us. I need to iron out a few things."

He stepped back outside, and the two men strolled down the hill a bit. The cool night air was very refreshing. As Wallace thought back on the past two days, he realized there were many signs that he had been discovered by Esposito's men.

As the two men approached the front of the dining hall, the full moon brightened the path.

Wallace gestured toward a bench in the courtyard, and he sat down ahead of Lonelli. They sat next to each other, looking out at Hearst Castle, glowing on the hilltop in the light of the full moon.

"Mr. Lonelli, for some strange reason, I'm thinking that Lonelli is not your name. I can't be sure, but I've been wondering about you since your arrival."

There was an uncomfortable silence before Lonelli quietly answered. "No Mr. Wallace. My name is Colonel Vito Lombardo. About a year ago, I was replaced as the chief law enforcement officer by one of the Andromedins, a man named General Andriolli Penzone. This was very humiliating. I was replaced because every attempt made under my command to capture you had ended in failure. Lord Esposito turned to the Andromedin Penzone, who guaranteed that he'd make sure you did not survive much longer. I was called before Lord Esposito and General Penzone a few times, and further humiliated for not doing my job properly. It was then that I went into hiding rather than feel the wrath of those two again."

"So, you've been trying to find me on your own for the past year?"

"That is true. I began following your video blogs to gather evidence. You left a very faint trail, but it was a trail I could follow."

"Did you learn anything else from my videos other than where to find me?"

There was a wry smile on Lombardo's face. He didn't really want to admit it, but many of the videos started him thinking about his position in this world.

Both men sat silently for a while before a security guard came to them, "Are you two alright?"

Wallace answered right away, "I believe so. We have been discussing current events. Things that make you sit up and take notice in this world."

The security guard gave a slight salute of acknowledgement and moved on to finish his patrol of the grounds.

"Mr. Lonelli, er Lombardo, what's your next move?"

"I have been thinking," Lombardo answered, "I'd like to know more about your research. What led you to believe that Lord Esposito is an evil man? I mean, look at what he has accomplished. We have a thriving economy, there are no current wars anywhere in the world. There are only a few outlaws that must be rounded up and imprisoned. Otherwise, we live in a world of relative peace and quiet."

Wallace questioned, "I am wondering who those 'outlaws' are, according to Esposito and those who are in control? They are mainly people who are choosing not to follow the leadership in Rome. Believers in Christ."

"There are people like you, Mr. Wallace, who have committed a major crime in the killing of all those people on that airliner. We have been looking for you to bring you to justice."

From the beach they could hear the Gulls. Wallace nodded and said, "You know as well as I do, Mr.

Lombardo, I did not plant the bomb that killed all those people."

"There are many conspiracy theories, Mr. Wallace. Some are real, and some are just there to detract from reality. Throughout history, people have had to die for the greater good. People in power will do what is necessary to stay in power. Sometimes people have to die for that to happen."

Wallace brought up the ruse that Lombardo had perpetrated in order to gain access into the group of Christians at San Simeon, "You must have studied in order to convince people that you were seeking more knowledge about Christ. You have heard the words of Christ Followers, and were able to speak them back to us. I believe that you are on the verge of genuinely seeking truth."

Lombardo thought back to his childhood when he had attended church most Sundays. Into his adult years, his military and law enforcement profession began to pull him away, as he was always too busy. Even though as a child, he followed the church's teaching, he began to drift away from the church.

"It's true, I have drifted far from the teachings that my mother wanted me to follow. She saw to it that I attended Mass every weekend. As I began chasing criminals and enemies of the state, my life didn't involve going to church. Then I met Paolino Esposito. When

Pope Cephas was Cardinal Nunzio Assidi, I began to believe that controlling people was the true mission of the church."

Wallace recalled, "You were there with Le Roux when he fooled so many people into believing that people had been taken from Earth by a race of people from the Andromeda Galaxy. Didn't that make you question the legality of a government leading so many people astray?"

Lombardo stood up and paced in front of the bench, "Mr. Wallace, I was only able to see that this world was truly going to Hell because of drugs, greed and criminal enterprises. Mr. Le Roux had gained supernatural intelligence and was bringing technology into this world that could help law enforcement apprehend criminals. His microchip technology could store so much information. We had a way to keep all medical records on a single microchip, as well as all a person's banking information. This allowed for a world without cash. No more would criminals be able to steal money from people who earned it. Once the security of that kind of a system had been guaranteed, business could grow without interruption by criminals. Albert Le Roux was a genius beyond any this world had ever seen."

Wallace countered, "Did you ever read the Bible, or any books about Bible prophecy that told of a day when a single world leader would come to lead the world away from the one true God, and require that people bow down and worship him? People would be required to take what they called the 'mark of the beast', to do business? And if you read any Bible prophecy, couldn't you see that you were at ground zero of that movement?"

Lombardo admitted, "There have been times that I have questioned what I've done for the past thirty years of my life. I had thought that when I met Lord Esposito, I was seeing God in action. I had learned very little in church about those things of which you speak."

Lombardo stood still with his back to Wallace, staring out at the reflection of the full moon over the Pacific. The hillside was basking in a soft, bright glow. He was very introspective as he continued, "I have actually begun thinking again about the God that my mother believed in. I had rejected that teaching for so long. Recently, as I listened to your video blogs, I have been thinking more and more about what you've had to say. But I fear that I have gone too far away from the God of my youth. I have pledged allegiance to Paolino Esposito's leadership and government. I have drifted too far from God. I am a lost soul. I have done things to advance Esposito's leadership. When I couldn't bring you to the justice of the Roman Government, my position of power and prestige in this world was taken away from me."

He turned to Wallace, "Mr. Wallace, I deserted my post in Rome to hunt for you so that I could be restored to my role next to Lord Esposito, and Pope Cephas. I have kept in touch with my most trusted lieutenant, giving him reports on my progress. Yesterday, I told him that I had finally found you, and that my suspicions were confirmed. General Penzone's claims of having killed you and your family were false. I was still the greatest detective in the world. My diligence had paid off. I would soon be bringing you home. Now, I'm not so sure that's what I really want to do. I am afraid Rome will send destruction upon this compound of believers, that they'll send an overwhelming force of troops to arrest you and take you away. Mr. Wallace, I am warning you now, so you can escape."

The world peace that Rome had instituted was in danger of unraveling. Members of the Arab nations were seeking more from Israel, than had already been given to them by Esposito. The peace that he had negotiated was merely a house of cards ready to collapse.

Russia, and several Asian nations were also threatening to come into Israel and take what they all thought should be theirs. The technologies that had enriched Israel over the past few years was greatly coveted by the rest of the world.

Esposito was still able to hold off the impending war, even though threats were being made. He was still in charge and had the most powerful weapons at his beck and call. He also had the forces of the Andromedins in his corner. It had been they who had brought him to power and had guided Cephas hand, bringing him back from death. He had put himself in their hands.

Wallace had returned to his bungalow, and he began gathering a few items together. He picked up the Bible that he had been using since he had left Dresden, Ohio. It was the well-worn bible given to him by J.P. Dickerson when they left Camp Dickerson.

Olivia picked up her tablet. Its files contained so many of her writings on grace. She also had already taken little J.P.'s toys to the car. At the foot of the hill, she could see a line of vehicles coming through the Hearst Castle gate.

Lombardo was running toward the center of the encampment, shouting to anyone who could hear him that they were all in danger. He knew that he too was in danger of being arrested, but he resisted the urge to flee into the hills around the small village.

As the first vehicles arrived, troops jumped out and surrounded Lombardo and the Wallace bungalow. With weapons drawn, it was obvious that resistance was futile.

Calling out to Wallace, he shouted, "Mr. Wallace, I am truly sorry. Please forgive me." He quickly overpowered a trooper, took his weapon, and began running back down the hill, firing at the troops. As he ran, many of the troops gave chase. After a short exchange of gunfire, Lombardo lay dying, surrounded by the men he used to lead.

The Wallace family was roughly shoved into the back of an armored van, the troops re-entered their vehicles and drove back down the hill.

The rage in Esposito's voice could be heard from his office suite in Jerusalem to the souks at the foot of the Temple Mount. General Andriolli Penzone had just informed him that one of their lieutenants had been in contact with the deserter, Vito Lombardo.

Screaming at Penzone, Esposito gave a new set of orders, "I do not want any more excuses. Robert Wallace is to be arrested and brought before me. I will look him in the eye and show him that I am the only god in this world. He will die here in Jerusalem. In fact, I will have him crucified! I will see to it that he first watches those he loves die."

Penzone nodded, "Yes, my Lord. I have already given the command to arrest Wallace and his family. We will then bring in Lombardo to face justice for deserting. Might I suggest that he too be crucified? These crucifixions will serve as an example to anyone who would defy our commands."

Esposito's rage continued, "Yes. Yes, you make sure that they are all brought here to face the justice of Rome. Tomorrow, I will see to it that these Jews here in Jerusalem will understand who I really am. I will go to the Temple at noon tomorrow and they will see the miracles I have done in bringing peace to them. I will make a sacrifice and eat the meat from the sacrifice in the chamber where they keep the most holy relics. Those relics are mine. Make sure that the High Priest and all the Sanhedrin attends. They will be inspired to bring the people into line. Then and only then will we return to Rome.

A messenger entered the room and handed a message to General Penzone. He read it and smiled an evil smile, "My Lord, the traitor Lombardo is dead, and the Wallace family is being taken to Santa Barbara. Our transports are waiting there. They will be brought here before you go to the Temple tomorrow.

Esposito was delighted, "That is excellent news. After my trip to the Temple, we will put them on trial and soon have them executed."

Penzone nodded and left the room. As Esposito walked to the window, the stale smell of sulfur filled the room and an entity walked toward him. Without notice, Ambassador Baalazaar moved toward Esposito, "Paolino, our plans are nearly complete. Tomorrow all will know that you are truly the Messiah."

After their arrival in Lompoc, and the former U.S. Air Force Base at Vandenberg, the vehicles and their passengers were placed in one of two military transport planes.

The muffled sound of a toddler crying awakened Olivia Wallace. She and her husband and son had been roughly placed inside a military transport plane. The seats were folding seats, secured along with cargo netting to the sides of the fuselage. The fifty troops who were charged with capturing and returning Robert Wallace and his family to Jerusalem, showed great indifference to the plight of their captives.

Olivia looked around and saw that Robert was lashed to the bulkhead between her and their son. As she scanned the rest of the cabin, she noticed that most of the troopers were young men and women in their early twenties. A grizzled man sported sergeant's stripes on his sleeves. He was the last man to take a seat. As Olivia struggled to focus her eyes on him, his scowl gave her pause. The hatred he had for her family was obvious. She thought he looked as though he would execute them for no reason other than their very existence.

The propellers began to turn as the sound of the whirring turbo jet grew stronger. First one engine, followed quickly by the other three. The sound had begun to bring Robert Wallace back to consciousness, albeit very slowly. The sore spot he felt on the back of his neck must be where he was injected with a low dose of Ketamine. It had knocked him out. He began a frantic search of his surroundings, looking for his family. Just to his right was Olivia. On his left, little JP was squirming in his restraints. Wallace struggled to reach his left hand down a few inches to stroke the forehead of his son.

As the plane began to taxi, Olivia mumbled, "Bobby… what happened? Where are we going?"

Continuing to touch JP, Wallace struggled to answer, "Ah… I think that these guys… um… I'm not totally…"

He had to continue clearing his throat. The dryness was painful as he tried speaking.

Olivia saw that the floor of the cabin had brackets to secure more vehicles than the three trucks that were anchored. She turned to look out the small window and watched the hangars as they passed them. One of the signs she read said "Vandenberg AFB." Remembering what they had heard at various times during their stay at Hearst Castle, they must have been on the road in the trucks for about two hours.

The plane turned onto the threshold of the runway and began its runup. After a slight shudder, all the occupants began to slide slightly in their seats toward the rear of the plane. It lifted easily off the runway and moved westward over the Pacific. The view of the California coast in the early morning was only slightly foggy. In a few short minutes, the plane turned toward the north-northeast.

As the plane flew along the coast before going further inland, the coastline began to fade in the distance. The view of Morro Rock was silhouetted against the western horizon. Within a few minutes Olivia let out a loud gasp.

Robert saw the sight that had taken her breath away. The former majesty of Hearst Castle and its surrounding hillside were a smoldering ruin. Not one stone remained on top of the other. The grass and trees around the castle were blackened, and a ring of fire advanced away from what only a few hours what had been ground zero of an attack by killer drone aircraft.

Wallace couldn't control his emotional reaction, "Oh, my dear Lord, Jesus! What have they done?"

The battle-hardened sergeant spoke, "That's what happens to people who preach revolution against following Lord Esposito. There is no place in the world for them. You and your family will be facing justice in Jerusalem in only a few more hours. Perhaps you should have given more thought to your actions before you decided to go against our lord."

Wallace continued to stare in disbelief as the smoke from the devastation faded behind them. As the plane continued to climb, the Sierra Nevada Mountain range was beginning to pass beneath the transport plane. The second transport could be seen off to the left rear of their plane. The ride was loud and bumpy. Little JP Wallace was not at all happy about being strapped in his uncomfortable seat.

The sergeant told one of his men to release Olivia's restraints. He then told her, "There's no place for you to go from here, so I guess it's alright for you to quiet your brat."

Wallace studied the man's face. It was obvious that he had seen so much death and destruction in his lifetime that his calloused exterior was not just an act. This man was truly a hard-hearted man.

The second her hands were free Olivia quickly moved toward her precious child. She cradled him close to her heart as she leaned against her husband, "This is not going to be an easy time for us. But Jesus told us to take heart because he had overcome this world. We need to realize that we belong to Him and that we, too, will overcome this world as long as we hold tightly to Him."

CHAPTER 33

Paolino Esposito rose early on Saturday morning. He could see the throngs of Jews making their way to the Temple. The phone in his room rang. It was answered by his Administrative Assistant. Within a few seconds the message was delivered that Pope Cephas was on his way to Esposito's suite.

There were big plans in the offing for this day. For it was on this day that the Jews would finally have their Messiah revealed to them. Esposito stood before the full-length mirror in his room. Staring back at him was a very sophisticated gentleman. His stately tuxedo was perfectly tailored. The sash that crossed his heart contained pins and medals from each of the nation states that had pledged their allegiance to him only a few years before. Recently, though, many of the subjects of those states had begun to defy his leadership. Today, he would re-assert his authority.

There was a knock at the door, "Enter."

His Administrative Assistant informed him that Pope Cephas was waiting in the Office of his suite. Esposito took a final tug on the bow tie and left the comfort of his room to greet the man who had been so very loyal to him since his ascension to power.

"My Dear Holy Father. Welcome. I have been waiting for you, as today will be the culmination of our plans. Today, the world will see who I really am."

Pope Cephas smiled and responded, "Yes, My Lord. Today is indeed, an incredibly special day for us all."

Esposito picked up his cape and threw it over his shoulders, tying it in front of him. As he secured the cape, he spoke, "I received a visit last evening from Ambassador Baalazaar. He told me that today, I must show all present at the Temple that I am their Messiah. And that they must bow down and worship me."

The Pope nodded, "Yes, my Lord. I too received the same visitor in my suite last night. Today we will both be recognized as the leaders that we are. I am to lead the procession of security people, and that we are to not allow any resistance. I have been given power to silence any challenge to your authority. A simple wave of my hand will paralyze the vocal cords of anyone wishing to defy you."

Both men nodded toward each other and left the suite. A security detail marched with them down the hallway to the elevators. Awaiting them outside was a motorcade of four limousines and a troop truck with twelve soldiers in full dress uniforms, armed with rifles.

The cacophony of voices and animal shrieks at the Temple could be heard all over this portion of Jerusalem. The priests were slaughtering sheep, bulls and doves that had been brought to them by the people seeking absolution from their sins. The smoke rose from the altar into the sky. The aroma was very strong.

The motorcade arrived at the Temple, and Pope Cephas made sure that all his security troops were surrounding Lord Esposito. Their sharply pressed uniforms were perfect in a deep blue, almost black, against their stiffly starched shirts and white gloves. They each wore Shiny silver helmets. It was an overwhelming sight to see. The men quickly fell into line behind Pope Cephas. As they began advancing toward the Temple steps. Waiting for them at the foot of the steps, Levi Stoker stood shoulder to shoulder with the entire Sanhedrin.

Stoker spoke before Esposito could advance up the steps, "My Dear Lord Esposito, may I ask if you are planning to enter the Temple?"

Esposito marched up to the line of holy men, "Mr. Stoker, as I told you yesterday, I need to have access to my Temple. I built it for you and your people, and therefore, is mine. I am the leader of this world and have come to Jerusalem from my seat of government in Rome, to be recognized as your Messiah."

Stoker stood firm, "Lord Esposito, the Jews of Jerusalem and the few left in the rest of the world are truly grateful to you for bringing about this miracle for our faith. However, we cannot let you, a non-Jew who has not been consecrated, to enter the Temple. You are a Gentile and therefore must remain outside…"

His voice trailed off into a raspy sound. He struggled for air. There, beside Esposito stood Cephas with his hands held high, palms facing Stoker and the entire Sanhedrin. Each one of them tried to speak, as they all were straining to breathe. They were unable to speak.

Cephas nodded to the security detail and as one, they marched forward up the steps surrounding Esposito and ascended.

At the Altar in the courtyard of the Temple, praying Jews rocked back and forth before moving out of the way of the security detail.

Pope Cephas climbed the stairs at the altar and raised his hands in blessing, "People of Jerusalem and the world. Today, I present to you, your long-awaited

Messiah. For millennia you have been waiting to be delivered from your enemies. For the past few years, you have seen Lord Esposito bring peace and safety to Israel for the first time in history. This proves that Rome is here for Israel. Paolino Esposito has brought true peace to all of Jerusalem and Israel."

The violent sounds at the altar had subsided, as there were no more animals being killed. The spilling of blood had stopped. Esposito with the boldness of a man who was sure that he, indeed, belonged in the Temple, followed the lead of Pope Cephas and his security detail. They walked past the priests who had ceased their sacrifices, as they silently watched Esposito enter the massive, ornately appointed doors to the Temple. Jew or not, he deserved to make his presence known. Inside, he stood still taking in all the fine linen and gold braid. Incense burned near the front of the sanctuary. The colossal curtains covered an area that he knew was reserved only for the High Priest. It was the area where the Jews believed God visited His magnificence on His people. It was there in the Most Holy Place where He gave absolution for the sins of the repentant. Esposito passionately believed that it was he who was God on earth.

After a mid-air refueling over northern Canada, the two military transports continued their journey. Entering

European airspace, it would be at least another four and a half to five hours before they would be landing in Israel.

Robert Wallace, his wife Olivia, and their son JP were becoming very restless. The stress of the long flight was evident on the faces of everyone on the airplane. The flight did not have any of the amenities of business class or even coach, on a regularly scheduled airliner. Every two hours their captors had allowed them to get up from their seats and go to the crude restroom near the giant loading ramp at the rear of the plane. There was a fold down seat, hidden by a large gray privacy curtain. On this flight, Olivia was the only female on board. It merely added to her humiliation.

The meals consisted of canned meat and a hard biscuit that had weevils in it. Wallace began to long for the mercy of a plane crash. He was not looking forward to seeing his family go through this disgrace. They had seen the sun rise in California, and watched it set as they crossed into European airspace. The sergeant had been talking with the pilot who confirmed that they were about four and half hours away from Jerusalem. A fighter escort joined their formation.

The sergeant pointed out the window, "Take a look out there. Some of our finest fighters are here to see that we get you safely to your destination. A big trial awaits you, Mr. Wallace. Your stubborn refusal to accept the leadership of Lord Esposito has cost so many lives. Soon this will cost you your life and that of your family."

"So, why all the firepower for us? Are they afraid that I'll overpower you all and take control of the airplane for our dramatic escape?"

A boisterous laugh emanated from the sergeant, "Don't be a fool. Apparently there has been some activity near the northern border of Israel. Russia has joined with a few of Israel's neighbors and made some threats. Lord Esposito will bring everyone back under control very soon. I wouldn't worry much about it."

Wallace made eye contact with Olivia and they both smiled slightly. Were they about to see the return of Jesus soon? Israel was being surrounded by enemies. If they made it all the way to Jerusalem, perhaps the Wallaces would be there for the return of Jesus.

Levi Stoker stood at the foot of the steps in the Temple courtyard. He sat in the ashes that he had taken from the altar where only a few hours earlier, Paolino Esposito and Pope Cephas had defiled the holiness of the Temple. Yes, it was true that Esposito had made sure that the spectacular House of God was built in record time. Only the finest gems and linens were used. What had at one time been a celebration had taken a nasty turn.

Stoker had ripped his fine robes as he threw ashes into the air, letting them fall upon his head. The high position that he had enjoyed for only a short time was now over. It would take a long time to reconsecrate the Temple. Not since the time of Judah Maccabee had such a project been needed. When the Roman Legions destroyed Herod's Temple, they left no stone on top of another. Perhaps he could be forgiven for allowing the desolation caused by Esposito to happen. He would need to wait for the Day of Atonement. Until that time he would live in shame for not stopping what had taken place earlier this day.

Esposito was enjoying a drink of fine brandy in his Jerusalem office. His long-time friend Pope Cephas was also sharing in his reverie, "My Lord, your performance today was magnificent. The people there to witness your entry into the Holy of Holies will never forget the day they saw their Messiah come into their presence."

"You are correct, Your Holiness, but now, many people have begun protesting in the streets near the Temple. They say that I have defiled their holy place. They forget that if it were not for me, they would not have this holy place. Now they need to learn to worship me as their savior."

In the background, a television on the wall was flashing news clips from around Israel. Not only were they covering the story of the civil unrest, but they were also showing arial footage of the gathering of armies on all sides of Israel. East of the Jordan, troops of the Arab nations gathered. There was also a story reporting that the Euphrates River was at record low levels. The once deep river could be crossed on foot in many locations near Baghdad. Millions of soldiers had been making their way from Asia. They too wanted to take their share of Israel's bounty.

The door to the suite opened, and Esposito's Administrative Assistant entered with a large manila envelope.

"My Lord, a message for you from the first transport squadron. The fighter escorts were on time and there has been no threat of any activity from any other nation. They have crossed over the midway point of the Mediterranean. They should be in Jerusalem within an hour and a half."

Esposito smiled at Cephas, "How should we show the justice of Rome to the world. The man who has caused more resistance to my government than any other in this world will soon be here. I hope he sees how futile his plans have been. I cannot be stopped by a mere man. I am Lord of All in this world. When the people see what I will do with this enemy of the state, they will surely drop all resistance and follow me. We will then be able to defeat the enemies that surround Israel and threaten my rule."

"How should we show the Justice of Rome?" interjected Pope Cephas, "I think that the bigger question is how much longer should we wait to show the justice of Rome? I have already spoken with news organizations all over the world. They will be available to bear witness to our Justice on noticeably short notice. People the world over will be able to witness the death of a traitor and his family, my dear Lord Esposito."

Esposito was pondering his plan. Should they perhaps not show the execution of Olivia Wallace? Their son will be taken to one of the Roman children's boarding schools where he will be instructed in all things relating to the rule of Paolino Esposito.

CHAPTER 34

Thousands of people had followed the news reports of problems at the Temple. The High Priest, Levi Stoker, along with the Sanhedrin, were banned from stopping Paolino Esposito's entrance into the Holy places of the Temple. The High Priest has always commanded the respect of all the people whenever he spoke. He had been mortified yesterday when Esposito and his men marched right past the holy entourage and shamed themselves by entering the House of the Most High.

Of course, they did not understand that they had shamed themselves. Someday, perhaps, Esposito will know for sure that there is One who truly is higher than he.

Levi Stoker still bore the signs of yesterday's display of shame - his torn robes and the showering of ashes upon himself were very evident. His face was filthy from the ash, dirt, and tear stains on his cheeks. One of the rabbis approached him with news of what had happened overnight.

Stoker opened the large manila envelope and pulled out a half dozen eight by ten satellite photos from Israel's northern border. There were also news dispatches from Russia. A coup had taken place in Moscow. A group of dissidents who wanted to return to a Soviet Union style of government had taken control of the Kremlin. There had been bloodshed and a strong leader had emerged. The former heads of government had been arrested and executed for treason.

Stoker called out to his assistant, "Benjamin, come here. What are we to make of this development in Russia?"

"Sir, it is believed that the new leadership of Russia wants the technology that we hold. They want the plans and the manufacturing rights to our electric recharging systems. They say that because the scientists here were children and grandchildren who had been born in Russia, and that by rights, their inventions also belonged to Russia."

"What does the 'great and powerful' wizard Esposito have to say about all this?"

"He is scheduled to hold a news conference at noon today on the steps of the Temple."

"Not there. Please, the Temple is a holy place and only The Most High can say what Israel's position in a situation like this may be. Paolino Esposito is an interloper here. He is a Gentile who has no right to speak on behalf of Israel from the Temple."

Stoker and his assistant quickly began to prepare for the trip to the Temple. They wanted to let the media know that they were against Esposito speaking from the steps of the Temple. Only the all powerful Most High, was their leader.

Stoker hurriedly changed into clean robes and was ceremonially washed clean of yesterday's ritual of sitting in ashes. It was eleven thirty when both men left their rooms to take their place at the foot of the Temple steps.

The media had already begun to gather when the pair took their place in front of the podium.

A reporter asked, "What is happening here today? Why is Esposito calling us all together? Does it have anything to do with what is happening at the borders?"

Stoker raised his hands, "Ladies and Gentlemen, please, please be patient. We cannot speak for Lord Esposito, but it is our position that what took place here yesterday was an afront to our true Lord. Mr. Esposito, being a Gentile, had no business in the holy places of our Temple…"

Suddenly soldiers surrounded the two men and whisked them away from the podium.

Cameras were flashing, as the reporters shouted questions. This scene was something never seen at the foot of the Temple. Perhaps in ancient days, High Priests had been taken away as they tried to speak against the leadership of the nation. This, however, was truly unprecedented.

The twin military transports carrying Robert and Olivia Wallace, and their son JP, were about to touch down at Ben Gurion Airport, just north of Lod. They would be in Jerusalem in a short while. The pilot had informed them of the precarious situation to the north at the Syrian border. Armies from many nations were gathering. It looked as though within a few hours, or a few days at the most, an invasion was about to take place.

In spite of the seriousness of their situation, Robert and Olivia smiled at each other as they were lifted from their seats and forced to walk down the rear ramp to the waiting military vehicles. A matronly looking woman had taken JP in her arms and was carrying him in the opposite direction.

Olivia screamed, "JP... JP... where are you taking him? JP, Mama's right here!"

The Sergeant put his hand on her shoulder in a vain attempt to calm her, "Don't worry, he'll be taken care of. He will get the best schooling and grow up in the care of Lord Esposito himself."

Olivia was screaming, "Bobby! No! They can't do that! How do we stop them?"

Wallace spoke in a wavering voice, "Don't stop praying, Liv. Jesus has JP in His care. No matter what plans Esposito has for him, our little boy will be alright. If my understanding of Bible Prophecy is correct, we are all about to see the power of Almighty God right before our very eyes, Jesus will be here in a very short while."

With great harshness, Robert and Olivia were shoved into a waiting vehicle. The soldiers piled into the troop trucks that had had been brought from the second transport plane. They were heavily armed and showed the determination of an invading army.

The entourage of Lord Esposito surrounded the dais as he was introduced by his Press Secretary.

Esposito raised his hands in a display of confidence, as though he had just been introduced following a political victory.

He began to speak with the same confidence, "Ladies and Gentlemen of the world press. I have come here today to address a serious situation unfolding just to our north. The armies of at least a half dozen nations are gathering north of Israel's borders with Syria and Lebanon. It appears that an ultimatum has been issued by the new leader of the former Russian Federation. Russia is desiring to pull out of our alliance. They are wishing to return to the days of the powerful Soviet Union. In fact, their new leader, Vladimir Lenin Korsakov, is the grandson of a former head of the KGB. Demands have been made. The scientists living in Israel at this time, the men and women who invented the current automatic charging batteries, were born in the old Russian Federation. They came to Israel as small children when their Jewish parents desired to return to the land of their ancestors. Russia feels that those people and their invention should belong to Russia."

The members of the media were jostling for position as they were waiting to shout out their questions.

Esposito raised his hands in a calming gesture. "Ladies and Gentlemen, I have been in contact with the new leader of Russia by phone this morning. I have also been on the phone with the leaders of the other nations that are gathering around Israel currently. I am holding the Arab nations to their earlier firm commitment of peace with Israel. Although, I have not yet secured that recommitment from them, I am confident that they will do the honorable thing and keep their word.

I have also been in contact with the Ambassador from Andromeda Galaxy, Mr. Baalazaar, and he assures me that his federation will stand with us in Rome."

One of the journalists called out, "Lord Esposito, what if the surrounding coalition will not back down? What will you do to protect us all from attack?"

"That is a very good question. Mr. Korsakov assures me that he oversees all the forces around us, and that despite how dangerous our current situation may seem, he will hold them back. At the current time, I have sent a negotiating team from Rome to Moscow to reach an agreement that will be advantageous to all."

"There is, amid all this, some very good news. The American criminal Robert Wallace and his wife have been arrested. You will recall that he was the man who placed a bomb on an airliner that crash landed in Iceland a few years ago. Many people were killed on the flight, and Mr. Wallace has spent a great deal of time spreading messages of treason against our peaceful government. He claims to be a follower of Jesus Christ. That antiquated religion that no longer holds any power over people who have been enlightened. Many of the former members of that church have joined with us and Pope Cephas in Rome. Wallace, with his hateful lies, has led many people away from our way of life. Many of those people have been led to their death because of the lies he fed them."

The reporters continued calling out. They wanted to know how Wallace had been captured. They wondered if he put up a struggle with the authorities.

General Andriolli Penzone stood in front of the military jail that had been set up in Jerusalem. After the trip from the airport, the vehicles containing the Wallaces and their guards came to a stop.

Penzone smiled wryly at Wallace as he was pulled from the car, "Mr. Wallace. Where is your Jesus now? You are about to see the justice of Rome. After you are found guilty of treason and inciting division among the citizens, you will truly find out what crucifixion is. We have already started erecting the place of execution just outside the gates of the city. You and your wife will both be dead within twenty-four hours."

Wallace stole a look at Olivia. He smiled at her and mouthed words of love and encouragement. She lowered her eyes and nodded.

Robert and Olivia were escorted to jail cells opposite each other in the passageway. They could see each other. Wallace stood, looking through the grating in the steel door. He could make out the face of his wife. He prayed that she would be protected, and that Jesus would return soon. He was not afraid to die, but the process of dying, and the thought of seeing his beloved wife suffer, was almost too much to bear.

From the far end of the hallway, Wallace could hear his name being called out, "Mr. Robert Wallace? I heard that you were being brought here from America. Is it true that you killed people on an airliner flying to America?"

Wallace called out, "No, that is not true. I saw another man place a package in the luggage compartment of that airliner. I don't know if he was the one who did it, but he was watching me and then pursued me as I got away from that airport. Who are you?

"I'm Levi Stoker, High Priest at the Temple in Jerusalem. I am now a prisoner of the man who only yesterday defiled our holy place of worship. That man is a monster."

Wallace replied, "That's why we call him 'The Anti-Christ'. He is the epitome of evil. He was prophesied by Daniel, and by John of Patmos."

"Anti-Christ. We Jews do not follow your belief about Jesus being the Son of The Most High. We believe it is an abomination to believe that he is. Too many men throughout time have claimed to be sent as our Messiah. We had strayed away from God so many times, and as a result we were scattered away from out rightful homeland promised to Abraham. Throughout the centuries men have used Jesus as a weapon against us. We children of Abraham have suffered greatly for our sins at the hands of you followers of Christ."

Wallace continued this awkward hallway conversation, "I know that many people over the centuries have hurt your people thinking that they were following what Jesus would want. They didn't read their Bibles, though. Jesus was never against the Jews."

Stoker interrupted, "Too many of you Christians forget that Jesus was a Jew."

Wallace replied, "That is true. We do know that Jesus was a Jew. He did not come to condemn the Jews. He came to fulfill the Law. Jesus was Emmanuel, God among us. He came to teach why God gave the Law. All the Laws were given to show God's love. As he said, we are to love the Lord our God with all our heart, mind, and strength. He also told us that we are to love our neighbors as ourselves. Jesus was not and is not your enemy. He was the perfect sin offering when he shed his blood on the cross. He died once for all. Anyone who believes will be saved and live eternally with God, the Father."

Stoker sat silently as he listened to Wallace speak from his heart. He had heard of other believers who were raised as Jews and then became followers of Christ. These Christians always let it be known that they did not abandon their belief as Jews but had simply taken their beliefs even deeper. The things they had told him years ago had always haunted him. He had a desire to know more, but his position as the High Priest had prevented him from becoming a follower of the God of the Gentiles. He would have preferred to be speaking with Wallace face to face.

Vladimir Korsakov looked out over the newly re-built Red Square. Not that long ago, this entire city lay in utter desolation. The buildings had been restored to their former glory The history of this place had brought great pride to him. He knew that his family had been honored members of the Soviet government since the beginning. His own name was given him in honor of Vladimir Lenin, whose tomb has overlooked Red Square for more than a century.

Dimitry Murashko stood at his side. It was Murashko who had always encouraged Korsakov to pursue his dreams of restoring the Soviet Union to her glory days. The opposition had been removed, and the people of Russia had been primed for this takeover. The leadership had convinced the people over the past few years that Russia needed to be the world leader. Following the rest of the world under the leadership of Rome was not in their best interest.

Korsakov spoke, "Dimitry, tomorrow I will make a speech extolling the virtues of our nation as a leader of this coalition of armies surrounding Israel. I shall tell how that tiny nation has defied her neighbors for too many years. It is only the right thing to do. That fool, Esposito, thinks that he can continue to keep peace there. Even though he is currently in Jerusalem, he cannot halt the pending storm. Within a few days we will take Jerusalem, and we will begin exterminating those people who stand between us and what should be rightfully ours. I will give gold to the leaders of Israel's neighbors. They will think that Russia is on their side. When we have taken Israel, we will keep other nations under our rule. We have supplied arms to those nations for so many years. The Jews in Israel have been feeling the effects of Russian genius in weaponry, and soon they will feel our boots on their necks."

Murashko pointed toward the brightly lit Red Square. Both men had seen films of parades of strength displayed by the mighty Red Army and Air Forces. It was stirring to know that soon they too would be able to flex the mighty muscles of a great force. "Look out there, Vladimir. Your family used to be on the reviewing stands as our forces and weapons paraded past them. They must have felt such pride."

The two men had each served in the military when they were young. Each had been an infantryman.

Murashko's father had served in Afghanistan in the late twentieth century. They each felt a great pride that they were, at heart, warriors. They believed that the strength and power of a nation was best measured by its military.

By sweeping into Israel, Vladimir Korsakov had great plans to show the strength of his nation. Though he had begun planning this in his mind months ago, the movement of troops had been hurriedly put together in the past forty-eight hours.

The low rumble of thunder could be heard coming into Jerusalem from the northwest. A light breeze from the south brought warm air from the southeast. Otherwise, it was peaceful, giving no indication of the political situation at the borders of Israel, Lebanon, Syria, and Jordan. Armies were facing off, and the diplomats consulted as they shuttled proposals back and forth between capitals. There was an uneasy truce holding things together, despite the possibility of an accidental spark setting off a conflagration.

Paolino Esposito had just spent the last hour on the telephone with Vladimir Korsakov, who was not willing to bend. He wanted to make sure that Russia received all proceeds from the battery technology that has been exclusively held by Israel for the past four years. Because of the world-wide proliferation of the fully autonomous batteries, the use of fossil fuels has been on the decline. As a result, many of the cities with the worst air pollution were beginning to see an improvement in air quality. Because of the expansion of electric modes of transportation not requiring fossil fuels for recharging, Israel had become the richest nation in the world. The average citizens of Israel also benefitted from that wealth. The overall cost of living was among the most equitable in the world. Jews and Palestinians alike enjoyed a better lifestyle.

The former oil producing giants of the Persian Gulf region had been feeling the pinch of a product that was no longer in great demand. Therefore, they too were seeking compensation for the loss of their vast income. The royal families of those nations were also seeing a major loss of income. Their subjects were becoming more unhappy with their leadership. For those nations, painting Israel as the reason for their troubles alleviated some of the potential unrest within their own borders. When Russia called upon those nations for their help in threatening Israel, there was no shortage of willing participants.

Esposito put the finishing touches on an address that he was going to present to the Knesset. He wanted it to be known that he was standing in the gap to continue protecting the national integrity of Israel. However, if Israel did not want to cooperate with his demands of sharing their wealth with the rest of the world, he wanted it known that his threats were real.

The first incursion into Israeli air space came from Russian built MIGs flying low across the Golan Heights. The air attack by the latest stealth MIG fighter bombers swept in across the border with Syria, followed quickly by ground forces in staggering numbers. They were Syrian, Lebanese, Jordanian and thousands of elite fighters from the Far East.

Paolino Esposito felt his leadership had been insulted. He was angry that no one waited for his guidance to delay an attack from Israel's enemies. Russia had stoked the fires of hatred and jealousy. Esposito was throwing items from his desk around the room. Crashing against the wall were antique vases and pottery. "This is the most insulting thing that has ever happened to me! Who do those people think they are dealing with? I am GOD!"

He picked up the direct line telephone to the office of General Andriolli Penzone, "General, I need your advice. I have been personally insulted by Russia and the nations that surround Israel. I need you to put together a large security force to fly into Jerusalem and bring some troops to get me out of Jerusalem and back to Rome."

Within thirty minutes, General Penzone had summoned two thousand elite Special Forces troops from the Esercito Italiano.

The troops entered Israeli air space within a few hours of take-off. As they proceeded toward Jerusalem, a Russian made MIG made a threatening advance toward one of the planes in the squadron. One of the Andromedin officers raised his hand toward the MIG, time seemed to stand still, and then suddenly, the MIG appeared to hit an invisible wall. It disintegrated and the pieces of it fell from the sky.

The entire flight of Roman planes continued on its way to Jerusalem. Their task was to rescue Paolino Esposito. They would let nothing interfere with that assignment.

In the deep underground jail cell in Jerusalem, Robert Wallace, his wife, and the Temple High Priest Levi Stoker were being held so Paolino Esposito could personally deal with them. Stoker had defied the man claiming to be the savior of Israel and the world. The Wallaces had been resisting Esposito for more than six years.

A small patrol of eight men marched down the hallway to the cells of Robert and Olivia Wallace. They were taken forcefully into the hallway and marched outside through the courtyard. Esposito was sitting on the balcony, waiting to pass judgement upon them.

Pope Cephas took his place alongside Esposito with a smug expression on his face. He was the most powerful man in the church. He was proud to be serving the most powerful man on earth. Cephas was leading people in the belief that Esposito was, indeed, God here on Earth.

The Wallaces looked up toward the throne where Esposito sat in judgement. A bright sky behind him caused him to appear in silhouette that stood stark against the sky. With an arrogant wave of his hand, he summoned the two forward. He studied Robert Wallace and thought of how for just a little more than six years, Wallace had managed to elude capture as all the while he was preaching defiance of the Roman authorities.

Shaking his head side to side, Esposito spoke in a taunting voice, "Robert Wallace. Robert Wallace, the man who has been a thorn in my side for too long. Today will be the last day of your life. I will condemn you to an eternity of damnation and torture, never to know my mercy."

As Wallace listened to this sentence being pronounced, he was fascinated by what was happening on top of Esposito's head. There was a high amount of static electricity in the air and his hair was beginning to have a few strands rise wildly. It was very slight, but not so drastic that it was noticed by many people.

outside through the courtyard. Esposito was sitting on the balcony, waiting to pass judgement upon them.

Pope Cephas took his place alongside Esposito with a smug expression on his face. He was the most powerful man in the church. He was proud to be serving the most powerful man on earth. Cephas was leading people in the belief that Esposito was, indeed, God here on Earth.

The Wallaces looked up toward the throne where Esposito sat in judgement. A bright sky behind him caused him to appear in silhouette that stood stark against the sky. With an arrogant wave of his hand, he summoned the two forward. He studied Robert Wallace and thought of how for just a little more than six years, Wallace had managed to elude capture as all the while he was preaching defiance of the Roman authorities.

Shaking his head side to side, Esposito spoke in a taunting voice, "Robert Wallace. Robert Wallace, the man who has been a thorn in my side for too long. Today will be the last day of your life. I will condemn you to an eternity of damnation and torture, never to know my mercy."

As Wallace listened to this sentence being pronounced, he was fascinated by what was happening on top of Esposito's head. There was a high amount of static electricity in the air and his hair was beginning to have a few strands rise wildly. It was very slight, but not so drastic that it was noticed by many people.

The plains of the Jezreel Valley surround the area. The main trade route from Mesopotamia and Babylon go through the area, and it has been one of the most contested pieces of real estate in history. Major battles from a thousand years before Christ and into the twentieth Century have been fought there.

Ground forces had entered Israel from Lebanon and Syria, and quickly crushed all Israeli resistance. Amphibious troops had landed north of Haifa, and quickly swept into the valley. The Israeli Defense Forces were standing to the south side of the Jezreel valley. Their backs were toward Jerusalem. They must not allow anyone past them. Long range artillery forces had taken their place on the ridges of the southeast side of the valley. They were vastly outnumbered. They did not fear though, because throughout the history of God's people, He had intervened whenever His people faced annihilation at the hands of vastly superior forces. God had swept away the armies of the Pharoah when Moses led them into the wilderness. God had stepped in to help His people in the time of the Judges, helping people such as Samson and Gideon. The Lord was also there when the small shepherd boy David defeated the Philistine giant Goliath. The Israelis had faith that God would not fail His people this time either.

The armies each set their positions. Tactical nuclear weapons were carried on the ordinance laden trucks. Each of the artillery shells carried enough destructive power to wipe out an entire company of soldiers. That power would be needed to prevent a breakthrough allowing the enemy to travel down the highway southward toward Jerusalem.

Israeli fighters were doing battle against MIG fighters from Russia and Syria. The Israelis were holding their own, not allowing the MIGs to attack their troops, nor to fly south of Megiddo and make their way to Jerusalem.

Just to the East lay the small town of Nazareth. Some of the Israeli troops were new Christians. They knew the significance of this land. They also knew that the boyhood home of Jesus was only a few miles away, lying between their position and the Sea of Galilee.

It seemed that every soldier on earth was gathering in this place. Israel's generals were making plans for what some have compared to Samson bringing down the Philistine temple down upon himself. His sacrifice wiped out the leadership of Israel's enemy. The generals had plans to launch nuclear weapons against all these soldiers, including their own, if that's what it took, to stop them from invading the heart of their nation in Jerusalem.

Israel must survive. They knew God would be with them.

General Penzone's force was rapidly advancing on the location where Lord Esposito was waiting to be spirited away. Esposito did not want to fall into the hands of invading armies from all around Israel.

As the convoy arrived at the location where Esposito was holding court, the elite forces disembarked their vehicles and quickly surrounded the building. In a protective show of force, they placed themselves between Esposito and any real or perceived enemy who would wish to do him harm.

Esposito waved his hand in a grand gesture to show that he had no fear of what was taking place to the north.

"Let it be known that this man, Robert Wallace and this woman Olivia Wallace are guilty of stirring up hatred and resistance to the peaceful world that I have created. They have turned many people away from me, the one true god of this world. I must not allow that to happen. I pronounce both of you guilty as charged, and sentence you to death. You will die as the man you have chosen to follow died. So many centuries ago, Jesus of Nazareth died on a cross just a few yards from where you now stand. I have erected, in this courtyard, a cross for each of you. I am also ordering that Levi Stoker will be placed on a third cross in this courtyard. Each of you will die according to the ancient justice of Rome. People watched and knew that Rome was not to be trifled with. I have spoken this into being. People must know that

I am a vengeful god. No one may defy my authority. Robert and Olivia Wallace, you will now be shown the Justice of Rome. Prepare to die."

Inside an Israeli bunker, commanders were in constant contact with the field generals near Megiddo. The situation was growing untenable. Though the enemy troops had not yet begun their move toward Jerusalem, the field commanders had been made aware that their men and women would soon be dead along with the invaders.

It was agreed that there seemed to be no other way. Soldiers in the bunker and at Megiddo reached out for each other. They knew that they were about to be sacrificed to save Israel. They knew when they took their oath to protect their homeland, that this day could come to pass. They would die fighting if need be. Unless God could intervene, they would all be gone in a flash.

The weapons were armed, and the command was about to be given.

Robert had tears in his eyes as he looked at his beloved wife, "Be strong. Jesus is close. He will be here. I know in my heart; we will see him soon."

Olivia pursed her lips and nodded, "I know, Bobby. JP will be with us soon, too. Jesus is with him right now protecting him."

They were roughly taken to where three crosses were lying flat on the ground. Robert and Olivia were laid on their backs, arms spread apart. Ropes were looped around the crossbars and then large nails were pounded into their wrists causing each to cry out in pain. Through the tears they watched the roiling clouds continue to thicken. Flashes of lighting crisscrossed the sky. It would be over soon.

The sky was growing dark as Pitch, as Levi Stoker was led into the courtyard. He nervously looked around, not fully understanding what was happening. Only yesterday he had attempted to keep Paolino Esposito from defiling the holy Temple of God. If he was to die for that, he felt that he would proudly lay down his life for God. He looked at the Wallaces as he was roughly laid on his back and arms stretched out to be fastened to the cross. Why were they doing this? His heart felt as though it would jump out of his chest. Why was such an ancient form of torture being used on modern people? It cannot be that this man was so cruel as to kill people this way.

Esposito looked down upon the courtyard and directed his statement to Stoker, "Mr. Stoker, you may avoid this horrible death by simply admitting that because of all the miraculous things I have done for your nation I am God. I brought peace to Israel a few years ago, and your people prospered beyond measure. I personally built the new temple for your worship. But you forgot who I am. I AM YOUR GOD. There is no other god before me. I am your messiah. I died and was brought back to life just so I could do all these wonderful things for this world. It is MY WORLD. It is MY TEMPLE. If you will only admit before all these witnesses who I am, I will not allow you to suffer any pain. The others must die because they led so many people away from me. But you, you can be spared simply by pointing the way to me. Let your people know who I am. I am your Messiah. I am your god. Worship me and you will live."

Stoker's face appeared to glow, "Lord Esposito, I have been truly grateful for the peace you brought to my homeland for these past few years. I have been truly grateful to you for presenting my people with a holy place of worship. I know that only The Most High could ever bring true peace to us. I know that only The Most High can give us unity with our neighbors. You sir… are NOT The Most High. You are not our Messiah. Our messiah will be here soon. Mr. and Mrs. Wallace have inspired me to look deeper into my own heart as I studied deeper into your heart. You have been created in the bowels of Hell. You will die and return there."

"Then YOU WILL DIE, STOKER! I WILL SEE TO IT THAT YOU NEVER see the inside of my temple again."

As Stoker was prepared for crucifixion, the ground began to shake. Pieces of the building where Esposito stood began to crumble around him. A large fissure began to open across Jerusalem. It ran directly through the building where Esposito had created his Jerusalem headquarters only a few weeks before. The giant opening in the earth saw the total collapse of that building as it crumbled into the hole. The earth began to come back together, and separated again, as though it was chewing up the building and all those who remained inside.

As all this happened, bright lights flashed across the sky and to the east, the clouds parted and there, standing against the bright backdrop was a man. Robert, Olivia, and Stoker knew immediately it was Jesus. He was being followed by millions of people as he returned to the Mount of Olives. The nails in the wrists of Robert, Olivia and Levi Stoker fell away and their wounds were immediately healed. They were able to sit upright. They were seeing the long-promised return of Jesus.

Two men in bright white robes stood on either side of Jesus and addressed the crowd, "Men and women of Galilee, do not be surprised. Just as we told you so long ago would happen, Jesus has returned. The clouds that had obscured him for so long have parted, and He stands before you. Now, true peace will reign in this and in all lands of the Earth. Just as He promised, our Lord has returned."

Made in the USA
Columbia, SC
30 July 2021

42459587R00311